LITTLE
WHISPERS

BOOKS BY K.L. SLATER

Safe with Me
Blink
Liar
The Mistake
The Visitor
The Secret
Closer
Finding Grace
The Silent Ones
Single

LITTLE WHISPERS

K.L. SLATER

bookouture

Published by Bookouture in 2020

An imprint of Storyfire Ltd.
Carmelite House
50 Victoria Embankment
London EC4Y 0DZ

www.bookouture.com

ISBN: 978-1-83888-660-8
eBook ISBN: 978-1-83888-659-2

This book is a work of fiction. Names, characters, businesses,
organizations, places and events other than those clearly in the
public domain, are either the product of the author's imagination
or are used fictitiously. Any resemblance to actual persons, living or
dead, events or locales is entirely coincidental.

For my daughter, Francesca Kim x

PROLOGUE

Four months earlier

Irene places the last items in the box, kisses her own fingers and presses them on top of the contents before closing the lid one last time.

Soon, she will leave this world and its pain and miseries behind and for her, that time can't come fast enough.

Since she found out about her illness, Irene has done little but debate whether to tell her daughter the truth. She has lurched between feeling sure the past should stay buried to convincing herself that Janey needs to know and she needs to hear it from her own mother, her flesh and blood.

Irene glances down at the box, her breathing ragged, her bony hands shaking and pale. All the answers are here for Janey when she feels ready for them. All Irene needs do now, is to set the ball rolling and tell her everything.

She hears Janey's footsteps down the hallway and her daughter appears with two mugs of tea.

'Ready for a cuppa, Mum?' she says, her voice bright but her face is grey and drawn and tells a different story.

'Come and sit down beside me, Janey,' Irene says, her voice like scratchy parchment paper. 'There's something you need to know. Something that will change everything.'

1

When I'm stressed, worried or upset, I clean. Needless to say, with everything that's been happening over the last few months, my house looks more immaculate than usual. Even though it feels like our lives are falling apart in other ways.

I've been cleaning the kitchen for the last hour. Not just a cursory wiping-down of the worktops and mopping the floor; I mean proper grafting. Bottoming out the cupboards, disinfecting the shelves, sorting through the out-of-date jars and throwing half of them away before putting stuff back.

I look at the clock again. Eleven thirty, four minutes later than when I last looked. Rowan will be in his last lesson before lunch, and my husband, Isaac, will probably just have taken his seat in the interview room at the smart glass-fronted offices he texted me a snap of earlier: the regional headquarters of Abacus, an innovative technology firm that reached the *Sunday Times* Hot New Company Top 100 list last year. A company that has very recently headhunted Isaac and wooed him for interview with a stunning remuneration package.

I scrub harder at a stubborn rusty stain in the cupboard under the sink. I don't know whether to hope Isaac gets the job or not, and it feels like being stuck between a rock and a hard place.

On the one hand, I want life to get back on an even keel after dealing with Mum's death just four months ago. The thought of

Isaac getting a dynamic new job and us moving to a new house in another area, with everything that entails… Well, my heart sinks just thinking about it.

Mum's death changed me in ways I can't even put into words. I've only told my husband the bare bones of it so far, although I've promised to tell him everything in time, when I feel ready to go through the stuff she left. He's offered to sit with me, look through it together, but although I've tried, I can't bring myself to do it. I just… *can't*. The mere thought of watching the horror settle over his face is all too much, even though he's reassured me it will change nothing about his feelings for me.

And that's why another part of me longs for the fresh start Isaac says this new job might offer.

'Relocation expenses fully paid, double my current salary, and even a mortgage subsidy for the first twelve months,' he read from the emailed information pack.

Plus on top of all that, it could gift us with a relationship boost we're in desperate need of.

It's not that we're constantly arguing or particularly want different things in life. In some ways that would be easier to bear, because at least it would indicate that there's still some energy, some passion there. But the emotional rot is way more pervasive than that.

Over the past year, we've seemed to slowly fade away from each other. Nothing dramatic and measurable; it feels more like we're drifting off in separate hot air balloons. As if we're mere acquaintances now instead of the best friends and passionate lovers we used to be.

At first, when we sensed things were going wrong, we made countless efforts to reconnect. We scheduled date nights when Rowan would stay over at Mum's and spent quality time together without television or phones. Sometimes we'd just talk, making a conscious effort to look at each other rather than Isaac keeping one eye on his emails.

Nowadays, we don't bother with any of that. Without even discussing it, we seem to have somehow both decided it's hopeless to even try any more. We've come to a dull acceptance that this is how it is between us.

After maxing out three credit cards to the limit eighteen months ago, we took out a ten-year loan and paid them off. The bank would only sanction the deal if we agreed to secure the debt on the house. So we did.

The day we used the loan to pay off the cards, it felt so liberating to cut them into little pieces. Three little bits of plastic that had held so much power over us. Isaac gathered them up and threw them in the air. We laughed as the tiny, sharp chips showered down on us in the kitchen like celebratory confetti.

But within months, the toll of the loan payment swiftly dampened down our optimism. When the head gasket blew on Isaac's car, essential to him doing his job, he was forced to ask the bank for a replacement credit card to enable us to carry out the necessary repairs.

I stopped suggesting modest improvements to our three-bed semi a long time ago. Ideas like refreshing the kitchen cupboards or finally getting rid of the peach bathroom suite in favour of a modern white one. The family holiday abroad we'd hoped to take soon became just a pipe dream.

A year ago, I gave up my job as a teaching assistant at Rowan's primary school to become Mum's carer and we've just about scraped by each month with barely a penny to spare. She lived in a little council flat just around the corner from us and, apart from some meagre savings she'd put by, Mum lived on her state pension. Cobbling together her funeral costs using her own little bit of money made me feel hollow inside.

In our early years together, that flush of new love, a scarcity of available funds never seemed to matter. But ten years down the road, it's pretty hard to get fired up about a rosy future when there are no holidays, no social life and hardly a week passing without another bill landing on the mat.

It's just life, I suppose. One that plenty of people will recognise. The shiny newness of each other is bound to wear off over time, isn't it? It's the same for most married couples, I think. I read about it often enough online and in magazines.

The only trouble is, we haven't been married for twenty-plus years. We wed in Cyprus ten years ago and enjoyed a couple of years of early married life just the two of us, before having our much-wanted son, Rowan, who is now eight.

Finally triumphing over the rusty mark, I stand up with slightly stiff knees and mop my brow with the back of my hand as I look around at the sparkling surfaces and smear-free cupboard doors. Yes, this effort would meet even Mum's high standards, I think, and that's saying something. While I was growing up, she always seemed to be scrubbing or ironing or cleaning the windows… it was as if she couldn't keep still or rest at all.

Now I realise she was probably terrified of giving herself any time to think.

I throw the cloth in the sink, wash my hands and make a coffee. I'm sitting on a stool at the breakfast bar when my phone rings, making me jump.

Isaac's name flashes up on the screen and I snatch it up. 'Hello?'

'Janey, I got it,' he blurts out excitedly. 'Bob, the CEO, offered me the job on the spot!'

2

Later, when Rowan is in bed, Isaac shuffles closer to me on the sofa so I can see his laptop screen. 'Look at this house. Bob put me on to it; he reckons it'll attract a buyer almost immediately.'

The warmth of his body, so close to mine, should be the most natural thing in the world, but it feels a bit strange. We usually sit separately at night, going for the comfort of stretching out on our own sofas rather than snuggling up together like we used to do.

'I thought the properties in a place like that were way out of our league,' I remark, glancing at my husband's bright, animated face. It's been a long time since I've seen him like this, upbeat and full of hope. My heart lightens a touch.

He clicks on the main picture of the house, and I admit I'm surprised at the low asking price, even though it's still way up on the steep side for us.

It's a modern four-bedroom detached with a square bay window on the ground floor and a smart red-brick front. It's set back from the road with a generous front garden and enough block paved area to park a car. The imposing glossy green door with a big shiny chrome knocker is fitting of the estate agent's description of 'this ultra-smart executive property'. He clicks on other photographs that show a substantial rear garden bordered with mature trees and shrubs.

Rowan could actually play in a garden like that, rather than the postage stamp of mossy grass we have here in our shabby Victorian semi, overlooked by several of our neighbours. I have a flash-forward of me sitting on the neatly flagged patio at Buckingham Crescent, reading a book with a cool drink to hand, while Rowan practises his football skills on the grass with one of his new friends.

Buckingham Crescent is one of the poshest streets in the whole of West Bridgford. The town sits on the River Trent, south of Nottingham, and is about a fifty-minute drive from our current house in Mansfield. I remember reading about the street's status in our local newspaper and wondering how it must feel to live there.

'I wonder why it's so cheap,' I murmur.

'Well it's not exactly *cheap*,' Isaac laughs. 'It's what they call "keenly priced". Bob says it was only added to Rightmove yesterday.'

He points out a shortlist on the right-hand side of the screen that gives details of similar houses sold in the area over the last twelve months. There are only two in Buckingham Crescent – people seem to stay put there – but one of them is the house we're looking at right now.

'The owners have only been there a year,' he remarks. 'They've put it on at nearly ten grand less than they bought it for, so maybe it's a marriage break-up or something and they need a quick sale.'

He clicks lazily through the remaining photographs in the property's gallery, and I take in the glossy black-and-white kitchen, the pristine family bathroom with its free-standing tub and separate rainforest shower, and the master bedroom complete with en suite and small dressing area.

I can't imagine living somewhere like that, even if we had money to spare from Isaac's new salary. The thought of asking new friends around for drinks and nibbles at the weekend is part of a lifestyle I daren't even dream about.

Don't get me wrong, we're friendly with our neighbours here. We'll stop to pass the time of day on the school run and often bump into them at after-school football matches, but that's about it. Once the front doors on our street close at the end of the day, people keep themselves to themselves. Folks around here don't hold dinner parties or invite each other around for Pimm's on the patio. It's enough just trying to put a decent meal on the table for our kids each night without feeding everyone else.

Yet I can't help dreaming a little, either.

Rowan's such a bright, friendly boy, he'd easily make friends if we moved to a different town. The new postcode would mean we could enrol him at one of the small, OFSTED-ranked 'outstanding' schools, instead of the sprawling academy on the outskirts of Mansfield he currently attends. With its oversized classes and profusion of supply teachers due to a high rate of staff absence, Isaac and I both worry that Rowan isn't getting the attention he deserves.

I'm a qualified teaching assistant, so maybe I could even get a part-time position at one of the primary schools, now that my responsibility for looking after Mum is over. I've not really considered going back to work yet, but a highly rated school in a middle-class catchment area would be so much less stressful than my last job, which was at a failing primary school in an ex-mining village, a government targeted 'area of deprivation'. Despite the challenges, it's a job I used to really love doing. It was more than just my work with the kids in class; I felt useful in other ways, too.

If they had a problem, parents often felt they could approach me more easily than the class teacher because they saw me as one of their own. I miss the feeling that I'm helping to make a difference to people's lives and helping shape their children's future.

There would also be a lot less physical strain than I had caring for Mum and it would help to take my mind off the obvious.

Confusion twists and turns inside my body. I make a tremendous effort to push the thought of my mum's pale, wasted face away. She'd looked blotchy with nerves before she died. Then her face cleared like a weight had been lifted at the exact moment I felt the burden of her secret passing to me. It felt as real as if she'd handed me a baton in a relay race. I swear I felt the weight of the responsibility leaving Mum and becoming my own.

That was her final legacy to me, imprisoning me for the rest of my life. I could never do that to my boy. Never.

I swallow down the festering ball of fury in my throat, battling as ever the raw burn in my chest that feels just like a brand new hatred for a woman I've loved all my life. Since Mum died I've alternated between this fury and an aching grief so deep and bottomless, I feel as if I am drowning with each and every breath I take. In the days following her death, it felt as if I was slowly dying too.

'I could ring the estate agent before they close to arrange a viewing for tomorrow, if you like?' Isaac fixes me with a look that snaps me out of my stupor.

This all feels like it's moving a bit too fast. This morning, life was dragging along as normal; now, suddenly, Isaac has his fancy new job and everything is about to change. I don't know where the resistance I feel is coming from. I want to change our lives just as much as he does; in fact, I've hoped for little else recently.

'OK, if you can get the time off.' I don't want to spoil his upbeat mood. 'It's only a viewing, isn't it? We don't have to make any decisions right away.'

'Of course, but with our moving expenses paid and a house like this going for a song, we don't want to look a gift horse in the mouth either.'

'No,' I murmur, taking a breath to ease the sudden tightness in my chest. 'I suppose we don't.'

3

Six weeks later

When I arrive at the new house with Rowan, I'm forced to park a little way down Buckingham Crescent from the halfway point where our house is located. Two wheels of the removal lorry are on the kerb, but the vehicle is still blocking the road, and judging by the amount of furniture still stacked in the back, they're only about halfway through unloading.

'Come on.' I chivvy Rowan out of the car. 'Let's go and see our new home.'

I take his hand-held gaming device from him and slip it in my handbag, and for once, he doesn't complain. Instead, he grabs his football from the back seat and stares with bright eyes at the house we're parked directly outside.

'Wow, it's big!' he exclaims, his eyes travelling from the front door up three storeys to the roof.

He hasn't been inside the new place yet, but we've driven past a couple of times to show him the exterior.

'It's not this one, silly billy. Come on, let's go.'

Rowan bounces the ball as he walks. 'What number is our house?' he asks, checking out the shining numbers on the doors.

'It's number—'

'Excuse me!' a sharp female voice interrupts me. 'You can't leave your car there.'

I turn to see a wiry middle-aged woman with no-nonsense short grey hair standing halfway down the path of the house we're parked outside. She pulls the edges of an oversized mauve cardigan together across her front and folds her arms.

'I'm sorry,' I say. 'I won't be long. I'm just waiting for the lorry to move so I can park outside my own house.' I glance left and right. There are no double yellow lines outside her property, no 'Permit Holder Only' signs. 'I didn't realise there were designated parking spots on the road.'

She stalks to the gate and looks up the road at the lorry, and her frown disappears.

'Oh, are you… are you moving in?'

'That's right.' I nod. 'Number fifty-four.'

Her eyes widen slightly, and I wonder if it's because the house has only just gone up for sale, and here we are, the new people, already moving in.

'It's the one with the green door,' Rowan adds helpfully.

'I know the exact one you mean,' she says. 'In that case, don't worry about your car, if we're to be neighbours. I'm Polly Finch.' She holds out a small, pale hand.

'Thank you.' I shake her hand. 'I'm Janey Markham, and this is my son, Rowan.'

Polly leans forward at the gate to look up the road at the lorry again.

'Your husband's at the house already, is he?'

'Yes, he picked up the keys first thing and came over with the removals men to get things started.'

'I get to choose which bedroom I want out of the three that are left,' Rowan says.

'How exciting.' Polly watches as he bounces his ball up to the next gate.

The move happened so fast, there was no time to bring Rowan over to see the house before we moved in. We sold our house to a young couple, first-time buyers, in record time, due to its proximity to a main bus route into the city. We viewed the new house twice while Rowan was at school, and as it was vacant possession, it seemed to take no time at all to complete.

'Lovely to meet you, Janey.' Polly's voice breaks into my thoughts and her eyes flick from my feet to my face in the blink of an eye, but I notice all the same. 'When you're settled in, pop down and have a cup of tea. There'll be a piece of home-made lemon drizzle cake here with your name on it.'

'Thank you.' I smile, touched by her friendly gesture. 'I'll take you up on that.'

We wave goodbye to Polly and carry on walking up the road, squeezing past the removals lorry.

'This one's ours!' Rowan declares when he sees the wide-open green front door. He presses his finger to the polished wooden plaque on the gatepost. 'Number fifty-four.'

'This is it,' I agree. 'What do you think?'

'Cool!' Rowan bounds up the path and into the house. 'Dad?'

'In here.' Isaac's faint voice echoes beyond the hallway.

Heading for the living room, I pass two harassed-looking removals men.

I walk in to find that Isaac has already recruited Rowan to help him gather up a scattering of small black screws from the plain biscuit-coloured carpet.

'You look busy already,' I say, taking in Isaac's scowl, the scattered IKEA boxes and the numerous pieces of wood that are propped up against the sofa and the wall.

'"Easy assembly", it said on the box. I've been trying to figure out how the thing fits together, and I've just realised there's a key piece missing, so it'll have to go back. Can you believe it? No hall table today, I'm afraid.' Isaac's cheeks look hot and flushed.

'Have they brought the kitchen box in yet?' I say, digging the carton of milk I stopped off to buy earlier out of my bag. 'If I can find the kettle and a couple of mugs, I'll make us a cuppa.'

'Music to my ears, love,' one of the removals men says cheekily from the doorway, holding out in front of him the box I'm referring to. 'Milk and two sugars for my mate, and just milk for me. I'm sweet enough, see.' The other man pops his head round and winks at me before disappearing outside again.

Isaac laughs at my irked expression. 'Don't worry, they'll be gone soon – *love*.' He laughs and dodges my pretend slap.

I give him a thin smile. 'Tell you what, *you* can make the cavemen's tea. Looks like you need a break anyway, before you start throwing the flat-pack furniture around.'

Isaac pulls a face, but to give him his due, he gets to his feet and heads for the kitchen.

4

Once all the furniture and boxes are inside and the removals men have left, the day flies by. I make us countless cups of tea and unpack more boxes, while Isaac assembles the beds. Rowan helps by fetching and carrying bits and bobs in between his frequent kickabouts in the lovely big back garden.

It feels so weird, pottering around together in our new house. In the end, I couldn't wait to leave our old place behind, but now that we're actually here, I'm surprised to feel the uncertainty sloshing around in the pit of my stomach.

It's not as if I've left a lot of friends behind. I let that side of things slip as caring for Mum took priority. Still, I might miss my Saturday morning aerobics class at the local leisure centre. Sometimes I'd stay afterwards for a coffee and chat with the women there, although Mum always hated the fact that I was gone for longer than I'd told her. I suppose I could carry on going there, but part of me thinks the time would be better spent putting my efforts into making new friends here.

Rowan, on the other hand, has been quiet about leaving his friends at the academy behind. I've tried to talk to him about his feelings, but he won't be pinned down. I know he must be gutted about having to leave the football team he worked so hard to win a place in, and Isaac has promised to take him back soon for a friendly training session at the weekend.

At six o'clock, Isaac pops out to the chippy a few streets away that I spotted driving over here. We eat straight from the paper, savouring the gloriously crisp batter and proper hand-cut chips drenched in vinegar.

With our lower backs griping from the physical work, Isaac and I agree that we've done enough in the house for one day. But when Rowan begs his dad to connect up the television, to my amazement, Isaac obliges without complaining. Rowan settles on an ancient episode of *Family Guy*, and we've all just got comfy together on the sofa – a big improvement already on sitting in different rooms at our old house – when the doorbell rings.

I sit bolt upright, startled.

'Typical!' Isaac grumbles, getting to his feet. 'Seems as if we're not meant to get any rest at all today.'

'Who is it, Mum?' Rowan asks, looking worried and muting the television.

'I don't know, I haven't unpacked my crystal ball yet!' I joke, tickling his belly. As he gets older, he seems to be developing into a bit of a nervous child. He spent a lot of time with Mum before she became really poorly, and she hated unplanned visitors, so maybe that's the reason.

When Isaac doesn't return right away, Rowan picks up his Nintendo Switch to fill the space, and I flick idly through the television channels, keeping the sound off. I heard the front door open, but I didn't hear Isaac say anything. Then the door closed again and now his footsteps thump up the stairs.

He's up there for about five minutes, and I'm just about to go up and find him when he returns. His face looks pale and he quickly masks a strange expression with a smile that's just a little too bright and breezy.

'Sorry. Just popped upstairs for my slippers.'

'Who was it?' I ask.

He looks at me, puzzled.

'At the door?' I add.

'Oh, no one. I mean, there was nobody there. Must've been kids messing about.'

I frown, but Isaac claps his hands. 'Right then. Back to *Family Guy*?'

He takes the remote control from me and changes channels again. I hope this sort of thing isn't going to happen a lot. Bored kids playing knock-a-door-run. Maybe that's one of the reasons the last people here got fed up; it's the sort of thing that can wear you down after a while.

Rowan and I both fall asleep watching television, and an hour later, Isaac wakes us so we can all troop up to bed. When he picks up his phone, face down on the coffee table, I see the screen is full of text notifications.

'It's just the football scores,' he explains, noticing me looking. He slides the phone into his pocket without opening the messages.

Finally in bed, and under the covers, his arm snakes around me and I relax into the warmth of him. He traces his finger down from my shoulder and slides his hand round my waist. Goosebumps prickle the tops of my arms, sending looping shivers down my spine. I can't remember the last time we held each other this close, skin to skin.

I close my eyes as he shifts closer until I feel the weight of his leg on mine. 'It's been a lovely first day in our new home.'

'Let's make sure it's the first lovely day of many,' he murmurs, nuzzling into my neck. 'Once I get settled into the job, I'll have the option to work from home a bit more. I'm aiming to organise my work around our family life. Not the other way around like before.'

The thought of Isaac being around more so we can prioritise our family time is music to my ears. In this moment, I feel so safe and secure in my husband's arms. I'm relieved and excited that our life together has finally turned a corner. Right now, it feels like it's truly in my power to leave the past behind.

I allow my heavy eyelids to close, and wonder what Mum would make of our fresh start. Would she find it in her heart to be pleased for us? Would she think I deserved it? I'm not sure about that. She'd no doubt disapprove of something, perhaps how quickly we made the decision to move. That was just the way she was, looking for signs, exaggerating in her head the slightest indication that something was wrong. She passed the curse of it on to me and it resulted in the feeling I've always had, of never quite fitting in. It has followed me all through school, and even work.

I think it was selfish of her and I often wonder now if she'd planned that final blow to ensure I end up a sad, bitter old woman like her.

But it's Isaac's wise words, spoken on the day Mum died, that echo in my ears: *You've got to learn to let go of stuff that doesn't matter. Whatever happened, it's all in the past. It has no bearing on your own happiness today.*

That's where my focus has to lie. That's what I have to remind myself of every day to negate Mum's final bid to destroy any chance I have of living peacefully.

Tomorrow, the three of us will wake up to our new life on Buckingham Crescent, and nobody can take that away from us. Not even her.

5

The entire weekend is filled with all the usual house-moving tasks, and there hardly seems to be a minute to spare.

I'm immersed in unpacking boxes and allocating the contents to various cupboards, in between washing crockery and glasses. Isaac keeps himself busy putting up curtain rails and fitting blinds upstairs and down.

Rowan is an absolute star, unpacking his boxes of toys without being asked and organising his bedroom. He chose the one overlooking the crescent. 'So I can see my new friends when they walk by,' he says.

His 'new friends' include a boy around his age he's seen zooming up and down the street on what Rowan informs me is 'a top-of-the-range stunt scooter', and a girl who apparently walked by with her mum and waved at him when she spotted him at the window, he said.

'You could walk down to the front gate and say hello next time you spot them,' I suggest, but he doesn't seem too keen. I'm sure he'll come out of his shell a bit once he starts his new school.

If I let him, Rowan would spend most of his time on his computer or watching television. But the one exception is that he does love his football: following his beloved Manchester United matches on television or playing in his school team. I've done everything I can to encourage his participation in the game and intend to double my efforts now that we've moved.

Rowan's face is sour right now; he's not at all impressed when Isaac informs him our Sky subscription won't be up and running for another week yet. We're busying about so much I barely notice he's playing non-stop arcade games on his Nintendo Switch.

On Sunday morning, in the interests of limiting his screen time, I spread newspaper over the kitchen table and set up his paints. Rowan is a talented artist and used to love drawing and painting. About a year ago, though, he seemed to lose his interest in creativity and become fixated on playing computer games. This change in routine might just be the opportunity he needs to rekindle his interest.

As the weekend draws inexorably to a close, there's still so much to do. But on Sunday afternoon, Isaac begins to open yet another large box and then stops, stands up and arches his back, stretching his arms above his head.

'That's it. Everyone stop what you're doing,' he says in a playfully authoritative tone. 'I'm calling time. We're going for a walk.'

'A *walk*?' Rowan looks up from his screen in horror.

'A walk?' I repeat, my face lighting up at the possibility of escaping unpacking hell for an hour.

'It's the ideal time to get out into our new neighbourhood, have a scout around. With no work or school, we might even *meet* a few people… how's that for a radical thought?'

We shrug on our light jackets and training shoes and head out into the fresh air and weak sunshine.

Buckingham Crescent is a fifteen-minute walk from the centre of West Bridgford. Isaac opens up Google Maps on his phone and finds a pleasant shortcut down a quiet, tree-lined road, which reduces the walk by around five minutes.

The main drag of the town, Central Avenue, is lined with shops, restaurants and artisan bakeries and delis. Lots of independent shops are still open, despite it being a Sunday, and we're drawn to a kitsch little deli, Ergon, with stools and a sandwich bar in the window. Isaac happens to mention to the owner, a rotund Greek man with a wide, friendly smile who introduces himself as Barak, that we've just moved to the town, and he sits us down with complimentary coffees, a glass of juice for Rowan and a giant slice of baklava cut into three neat pieces. Ergon is already a firm favourite. When we leave, we're loaded up with fresh bread, meats, cheeses and olives for a snacky tea in our smart new kitchen.

The sunshine has brought the locals out of their houses, and the outdoor seating areas of the cafés and bars are full. As we walk along the sun-dappled pavements, strangers smile and nod hello in the friendliest way, quite the opposite of what we're used to. Entering shops, people stand courteously aside to let each other go first, and a man who bumps into Rowan is mortified, issuing a string of apologies to both him and us.

Isaac and I glance at each other without comment. His face shines and I can feel my own doing the same. We're beaming, upbeat and glad to be here. Rowan's eyes are bright as he points out stuff in shop windows, bouncing ahead of us. This feels a good place to be part of.

6

At the top end of Central Avenue, we stumble upon a small food market, which we saunter around, sampling unusual cheeses and fruit teas. Rowan persuades me to buy a home-baked almond tart and a tub of clotted cream for dessert from one of the stalls.

'It'll take us a bit longer, but let's walk the full length of Buckingham Crescent on our way home,' I suggest. 'We might see one of our neighbours.'

'Great idea,' Isaac agrees.

'If I see the boy with the cool scooter, he might let me have a go on it,' Rowan says hopefully.

As we turn into the road, a big white Range Rover passes us, booming bass beats invading the peace, even though the windows are closed. I peer closer, but the tinted glass prevents me seeing inside.

'The houses up this end are *massive*,' Rowan exclaims. 'How come our house is so titchy?'

Isaac laughs. 'It's a lot bigger than our last one,' he points out. 'But it's not a competition, son.'

I follow Rowan's eyes, taking in the properties, some of which have been built on double plots. Lots have been extended to three storeys high, too, and most of them have electric gates and security keypads. The tall gates are open at the entrance to the property we're passing and we gawk up the driveway.

'I wonder who lives in these massive houses, Dad,' Rowan muses.

'Looks like we're about to find out,' Isaac says from the side of his mouth, as a girl around Rowan's age with a brown bob and large brown eyes hares to the front gate, followed by a smiling woman with the same hairstyle and eyes.

'Are you the new people at number fifty-four?' the little girl asks. She looks at Rowan without waiting for an answer. 'I saw you looking out of your bedroom window. My name's Aisha, what's yours?'

Instead of replying, Rowan looks up at me.

I smile at the girl, impressed by her confidence. 'Hi, Aisha. I'm Janey and this is my husband, Isaac.' I nudge Rowan from behind. 'Introduce yourself to Aisha, Rowan.'

'I'm Rowan,' he says shyly, and shoves his hands into the pockets of his jeans.

'I'm eight, how old are you?' Aisha says in her clear, slightly demanding voice.

'I'm eight too,' Rowan mumbles, suddenly engrossed in the pavement.

'Welcome to Buckingham Crescent. I'm Edie.' The woman holds out a hand when she reaches the gate, and I introduce myself and Rowan again.

Edie looks at Isaac expectantly and he reaches for her outstretched hand. 'Isaac.'

I give Edie what I hope is a welcoming smile. Fortunately, she doesn't seem to notice my husband has forgotten his manners.

'I see you've already met Aisha.' Edie ruffles her daughter's hair. 'Will Rowan be going to Lady Bridge school?'

'Yes, he starts there tomorrow,' I say. 'Miss Packton's class.'

'That's my class too!' Aisha bounces up and down. 'I'm a class buddy, so I can tell you everyone's name.'

'Thanks,' Rowan says, wilting a little in the glare of her confidence.

'That's really kind of you, Aisha,' I say.

'You found your way into town then?' Edie points to the brown paper bags nestling in Isaac's overloaded arms. 'It's a great little food market, isn't it? There's a farmers' market too, on the second Saturday of each month, and lots of other pop-up events happen on a regular basis. I have a list somewhere; I'll dig it out for you and bring it to school tomorrow.'

'Thank you!' I say. 'When we get settled in, you'll have to pop round for a coffee, Edie. You too, Aisha.'

Edie looks delighted. 'I can't wait,' she says warmly.

I glance at Isaac, who has barely said a word yet. He's too busy staring at Edie's house in what seems like utter awe and disbelief. I give him a pointed look and he coughs and jiggles the bags.

Edie says, 'I'll let you all get off then; you must have so much to do. Come on, Aisha, back to clearing out the shed.'

Aisha groans loudly, and the three of us set off again.

'You were rude!' I admonish Isaac.

'Huh?'

'You weren't very friendly and staring at her house like that… it was embarrassing.'

'Did you see the size of the place, though? It was ridiculous,' he says peevishly. 'They're not our kind of people. They're greedy.'

I stop walking and glare at him.

'And who exactly are our kind of people? Our old neighbours who lived hand to mouth like we've done for the past eighteen months? People who have to rely on credit cards to pay the bills?'

He snorts. 'Guess I'd better watch my Ps and Qs then, eh? Don't want the neighbours looking down their cosmetically enhanced noses at me.'

'*You* were the one who pushed to buy this house, Isaac. *You* were the one who couldn't wait to get away from our old life,' I snap. 'And unless I'm mistaken, you're the one who insisted we come out for a walk today and meet our neighbours. You'd do well to remember that.'

I clamp my mouth shut and set off walking again before I say something I might regret. I want people around here to get the right impression of us. It's important to me they accept us from the off and today, I really feel, for the first time, that I don't want to live my life in the shadows any more.

Rowan skips ahead, over his initial shyness and buoyant from his friendly exchange with Aisha. Another fifty yards, and a bright voice rings out.

'Hello again!'

It's Polly Finch, the woman whose house I parked outside on Saturday morning.

'Hello, Polly!' I stop at her gate to say a few words. 'This is my husband, Isaac.' I turn to him and explain that Polly and I have already met.

'Pleased to meet you.' Isaac smiles and shakes her hand.

'Lovely to meet you, Isaac,' she says. 'Hello again, Rowan.'

My son stares at the floor and I jiggle his hand. 'Say hello to Polly, Rowan.'

'Hello,' he mumbles dutifully.

'Rowan starts his new school tomorrow,' I tell her as she leans on the gate, a small trowel in her hand. I pull a nervous face that he can't see. 'His first morning.'

'Which one is he going to? All Saints is a lovely school. Unpretentious and very much focused in the community.'

All Saints is a C of E school that's pretty close to our house, but its OFSTED rating isn't as high as Lady Bridge.

'I've enrolled Rowan at Lady Bridge,' I say tentatively.

'I see. Well, there are lots of children living on Buckingham Crescent who attend Lady Bridge.' Polly's smile falters slightly. 'I must be getting on, so I'll let you go on your way.' She looks at the patch of soil she's been weeding before glancing up at me again. 'We must get together for a cup of tea and a natter next week, Janey.'

'Sounds lovely,' I say as Polly gets back to work.

'Everybody seems friendly enough,' Isaac says as we approach our own front gate. 'You're gathering quite a collection of invites. I just think it's best we don't get too involved with people too soon.'

I pull the door key out of my handbag and roll my eyes. I don't know what's eating him but his comment doesn't warrant a reply.

Later, I arrange our spoils from the deli on the table and we sit down in the kitchen together to eat.

'This bread is delicious,' Isaac raves, dunking a thick wedge into a shallow saucer of olive oil and balsamic vinegar.

'Tastes even better 'cos we're eating it in our posh new house,' Rowan says in all seriousness, popping an olive into his mouth.

'You know, I think you might be right, son,' Isaac agrees. 'I reckon *everything* will be so much better here. Footie in the garden, movie nights with pizza, and best of all, you'll get an earlier bedtime.'

'Hey... no way!' Rowan scowls and we all laugh, even him.

'You wait, you'll be so tired from making friends at your new school, you'll be begging to go to bed at six o'clock.' Isaac nudges him. 'Looking forward to it?'

'Yes,' Rowan says apprehensively. He prods at his food and goes quiet.

I give Isaac a look. I wish he hadn't brought the subject of the new school up so late in the day. I don't want Rowan lying awake and worrying about what the morning might bring when he should be getting a good night's rest for his big day.

'It's OK, sweetie, Dad's only teasing.' I touch his arm.

Isaac winks, and Rowan's frown disappears. He breaks off more bread, and chews, his mouth full.

We're acting like a proper family again. Sitting at the table together, enjoying our food and chatting... it seems so long since we've done it. In his other job, Isaac hardly ever got back from work before seven at night, and Rowan was always starving the minute he came in from school. Isaac would grab something to eat on the road, and so rather than wait for him, I'd eat my meal about an hour after Rowan. It was virtually impossible for us all to sit down together.

I think about Isaac's potentially more relaxed working schedule. Although he'll obviously have to show commitment and prove himself at the new company, he seems to think that working from home will be a definite possibility. My heart swells at the thought of the three of us spending more time together.

Today feels like just a taste of what's to come.

7

Monday morning doesn't quite start in the way I'd hoped.

Isaac's phone rings at seven-thirty as the three of us are about to sit down to an early breakfast of poached eggs on toast. It's part of my effort to encourage us to eat our meals together as often as possible. He disappears out into the hallway to answer it, and I linger at the kitchen door and listen to the one-way conversation.

'Oh, hi, Bob! Yes, good, thank you… OK… I see, yes. No problem at all. I'll leave right now.'

Before he ends the call, I'm back at the table. He stands in the doorway and looks guiltily at his breakfast plate.

'That was Bob, my new boss.'

'He needs you to go in?' *Here we go again.* I take a breath and swallow down the unhelpful comment.

'I'm so sorry, Janey.' I soften a bit when I see his wretched expression. 'I know I said we could both take Rowan to school this morning, but apparently there are some bigwigs travelling up from London a day earlier than they expected and Bob needs me to…'

Rowan stops eating and looks up at his father.

'But if you go to work now, you won't get to meet my new teacher, Dad.'

'I know, son. It's a stinker, it really is.' Isaac runs a hand through his hair. 'It's just this first morning, though. I'll definitely be able to meet her tomorrow.' He hesitates. 'Or the next day.'

Rowan dips his spoon into his cereal and stirs it round and round. I take his dish and replace it with a plate of toast and eggs.

I look at Isaac and he mouths the word *sorry*.

'It can't be helped, these things happen.' I shrug, disappointed but trying to be practical. 'You go up and get ready. It's important you make the right impression with your new boss. Just leave your breakfast; I'll clear it away.' Before he can leave, he's got to shower and shave and then get dressed. Eating breakfast with us will only slow him down.

'Thanks for understanding, Janey.' He kisses me on the cheek and musses Rowan's hair as he leans over. 'Have a great day at your new school, champ.'

It occurs to me I haven't really got much choice but to understand. In his first few weeks at the company there's bound to be a pull on his time. He has a responsible new role and it's his chance to prove himself. I'd be naïve to think he'll be home more from day one.

He snatches a piece of toast from his plate and disappears upstairs. Two minutes later, I hear the low, continuous drone of the shower pump above our heads.

'Come on, Rowan, you're making hard work of that.' He's pushing triangles of toast around his plate and chopping into his egg without actually eating any of it. 'Do you feel OK about going in this morning?'

'I liked my old school,' he mumbles as the poached egg receives another meaningless stab from his fork. 'We had that cool new adventure play area, and Mrs Anderson had just given me the job of collecting up the bean bags after our games sessions.'

I've always thought it amazing how, up to about nine or ten years of age, kids see chores and responsibilities as proof of a kind of grown-up status. But once they get any older than that, it's like pulling teeth to get them to do anything to help.

'I know Mrs Anderson thought a lot of you, sweetie. And it's always hard to leave a nice teacher and your friends behind.' I put down my cutlery and reach for his hand. 'But I honestly think you'll like Lady Bridge even more. There's a full-sized climbing wall there, remember? Much better than a poky adventure play area.'

His fork clatters onto his plate and he puts his elbow on the table and balances his chin on his clenched fist.

'I know, but… I won't know anyone there, Mum.'

'Bet you'll have made a friend or two by lunchtime. You know Aisha is in your class now, and maybe the boy with the scooter is too,' I say brightly, trying to reassure him. Starting a new class just a month before the end of the summer term is a very big deal at any age, but particularly so when you're only eight years old. 'And Miss Packton seems lovely, doesn't she? I know she's really looking forward to having you in her class.'

We managed to squeeze in a short visit to Lady Bridge school last week, prior to the move. Although the head teacher was away at a conference that day, we were able to complete the necessary admission forms and meet Miss Packton, who is a sweet-natured, gentle young woman in her mid twenties.

The move coincided nicely with May half-term, so all the children will be back this morning after the break.

'Don't worry,' Miss Packton confided when Rowan ran ahead on our way back to reception, 'I'll appoint a class buddy to show Rowan the ropes. I'm sure he'll feel quite at home here in no time.'

After breakfast, Rowan reluctantly starts to get ready. When I go to find him ten minutes later, he's standing at the lounge window looking out onto Buckingham Crescent.

'The other children are all in their school uniforms,' he calls to me when I step back out into the hall to check I've put my purse and phone in my handbag. 'My blazer and trousers haven't even come yet.'

'No, but all your uniform is ordered and you'll have it by the end of the week. Miss Packton knows that, so don't worry, you won't get into trouble.'

'But everyone will know I'm *new*.' He turns away from the window. 'I wish I was back at my old school and I wish we still lived in our old house.'

I smile and take his hand, pouring all my energy into appearing enthusiastic about his first day.

'You're going to love it at Lady Bridge, trust me. When we get your bedroom exactly as you want it and your dad's put the goalposts up in the garden, you'll feel more at home here and you'll be able to have friends over.'

I pull the door closed behind me and we head down the path and out of the front gate onto the crescent. There are several children of varying ages walking along the road, some with mums, some with their dads.

The school is just three streets away, and although there's a busy road at the bottom, there's a pedestrian crossing with a school crossing officer present. I've already promised Rowan that when he's older, he can walk to school alone. I didn't mention that that wouldn't be happening until he's at least ten, though.

I smile and nod at a smart lady walking parallel with us on the other side of the road. She's holding the hands of a girl and a boy who look like twins. They appear to be about the same age as Rowan, maybe slightly younger, and they're dressed in green and white, the colours of Lady Bridge. The woman nods back, and her glossy ponytail swings elegantly at the back of her head.

'They look like nice children,' I say to Rowan. 'Maybe they'll be in your class like your new friend, Aisha.'

'I don't want to be friends with a *girl*.' He scowls. 'I want to play football with the boys on the school field.'

'Aisha might be a future Lioness, though, thought of that?' I shake his hand playfully. 'They're World Cup qualifiers, don't forget.'

But it seems there's no chance at all of raising a smile from him this morning.

8

On our initial visit to Lady Bridge, Miss Packton asked me to check Rowan in at the school office on his first morning. So rather than follow the stream of children and parents who are heading left around the side of the building towards the classrooms, we veer off to the right and walk directly to reception.

It's a lovely old school with lots of preserved original features, like a bell on the roof and a quaint porch with an information sign saying that years ago, children used to queue here for their free milk. The building has been kept in good repair, and all the original windows, including the glass double doors of the classrooms, have been replaced with new UPVC units. It's nice to see a school that's had some money spent on it. Some of the schools near to our old house are in dire need of upgrading.

I draw Rowan's attention to a striking engraved stone that's set into the wall high above the modern reception doors.

'Look at that. Your new school was built in the year 1910... that's a hundred and ten years ago. Imagine that!'

Rowan seems less than impressed, and I notice he's chewing the inside of his cheek, which he tends to do when he's nervous. I think he's probably still a bit upset that Isaac couldn't come with us today.

The receptionist takes down Rowan's details and hands me some general permission forms that will need filling in and dropping back here tomorrow morning.

'Welcome to Lady Bridge, Rowan.' She smiles at him. 'If you'd like to have a seat with your mum, Miss Packton will be here shortly to take you through to your classroom.'

I approve of how she speaks to Rowan as a person in his own right, treating him like a grown-up.

We perch on the comfy seats that run along the wall opposite the glass hatch. There's a short queue of people waiting, mainly other students. Some children clutch signed pieces of paper – probably trip forms – and money.

I look down at the low coffee table between the seats and pick up a flyer detailing current vacancies at the school. The first position is for a midday supervisor to work an hour a day, but the second one gets my heart racing.

> Part-time qualified teaching assistant required – Key Stage 1 experience preferred.
>
> We require a part-time (three days a week) teaching assistant in our Year 2 class to work with individual children to offer support and raise attainment levels. This role also requires involvement in whole-class work when necessary.
>
> Starting date: as soon as possible. Please apply online at…

Feeling a rush of possibility, I quickly fold up the flyer and push it into my handbag. Three days would be perfect once Rowan gets settled into his new class. Not only am I fully qualified, but I also have experience working in Key Stage 1. That has to give me a decent chance of getting an interview, surely?

Rowan is quiet, engrossed in tangling and untangling his fingers. His cheeks look rather ruddy and hot. Every so often, his eyes dart to the queue and back to his hands again, and I realise the kids waiting to see the office assistant are staring. Two boys of around nine or ten are nudging each other mischievously as they look in his direction. Both are dressed in smart black trousers, white shirts and green and red striped ties. Their olive-green blazers, with the richly embroidered school badge on the breast pocket, complete the distinctive Lady Bridge uniform. It's the only state primary school in the area where uniform is mandatory.

The new kid is the unwelcome phrase that comes to mind. Just as Rowan feared, he stands out like a sore thumb in his non-uniform clothing.

'Morning, Rowan, morning, Mrs Markham!' Miss Packton's voice sings out as she flings the interior security door open. She looks fresh and bright in her long floral dress and cardigan and sensible flat brown leather sandals.

'Good morning,' I say, and smile, but Rowan doesn't acknowledge her, and I poke him discreetly with my elbow.

The young teacher seems undaunted. She indicates for him to go through the door before her. 'Welcome to your first morning at Lady Bridge, Rowan. We'll get you settled in your seat before the rest of the class come in. Say goodbye to your mum.'

'Bye, Mum,' Rowan says in a small voice. He looks so young and apprehensive, I want to scoop him up in my arms, shower him with kisses and tell him it's going to be fine, but of course, I don't. He'd never forgive me, not in front of his new teacher and the other pupils.

I stand for a moment in the reception area once he's gone through. The receptionist who checked him in catches my eye and silently mouths, *He'll be fine.*

I give her a grateful smile, but it's all I can do to stop myself bursting into floods of tears as I scurry past the office hatch and the queue of people waiting there.

Back outside, I take in a few deep breaths. I can't believe that leaving Rowan there this morning has affected me like this. On a logical level I know he'll be absolutely fine, but from an emotional point of view it's a different story altogether.

Rowan was very close to my mum, and he took her death hard. He seemed to lose interest in all the things he'd once loved: his artwork and, for a while, even playing and watching football. He began complaining of tummy aches and feeling sick to avoid going to school. Isaac and I both tried talking to him about it, but nothing seemed to help, and he refused to open up at all.

I spoke to Mrs Anderson, his old teacher, and she arranged for him to have a few sessions with the school counsellor. Within a few weeks, I noticed a big difference in him. Of his own accord, he asked for a framed photograph of his nan, which he placed on his bedside table, and very slowly, as the weeks went on, he began picking up again on the activities he'd let slip.

'Sometimes it's easier for a child to talk to someone who's completely independent, rather than a family member or even a teacher,' Mrs Anderson explained when I told her the good news. 'The main thing is he's contributing to class conversations again and his attention span seems to be back on track.'

But just now, when I left him, I saw that same vulnerable look on his face as on the cold mornings after Mum died, when he'd say anything not to go to school. I confess the thought of him slipping back into that mindset rattles me.

Still, I have every confidence in Miss Packton's ability to get him settled in. I take a deep breath and purposely inject a bit of a spring into my step. I need to stop worrying and get back to the house to tackle the mountain of packing boxes in the spare room.

Although it's still early, it's already pleasantly mild out, and I've needlessly worn a padded denim jacket. Flushed from the stress of Rowan's first morning and my brisk pace, I slip it off and feel cool relief around my neck and under my arms. I hang the jacket over the crook of my arm and realise I've managed to put a black bra on under a thin pale pink top. Oh well, it looks a bit unsightly, but it's only a short walk home and I feel far more comfortable like this.

Behind me, the shrill screech of an electronic bell signals nine a.m., the official start of the school day. Rowan will already be in his seat as the other children pour into the classroom. I hope everyone is friendly and that Aisha sticks to her promise to introduce him to his new classmates.

I walk towards the gates, thinking how much quieter it is now the children are inside. Save for the odd late student rushing past me, most people have now dispersed. I can even hear a blackbird singing way above me in an impressive majestic oak tree in the tidy grounds. What a difference to Rowan's old academy. That was a vast new-build that sat on the edge of the busy ring road one side and a noisy industrial estate the other.

As I draw closer to the school gates, I hear female voices and hoots of laughter. I step out into the street and see a cluster of seven or eight women in their early thirties standing behind the wall next to the gates. A white Range Rover with a private number plate is parked on double yellows, half on, half off the pavement, and I recognise it as the one we saw yesterday turning out of Buckingham Crescent. A gleaming silver soft-top Mercedes sports car is parked just behind it.

I don't stare long enough to make out individual faces among the small crowd, but the impression is of expensive clothing and groomed appearances. A sea of immaculate hair and glossy lips. Distinctive Gucci handbags with red and green shoulder straps, and diamond-bejewelled fingers, necks and ears.

They fall quiet as I walk past. I hear a whisper and stifled laughter, and I'm suddenly conscious of my transparent top.

I look up and spot Edie. She looks stunning; no trace now of the dressed-down cropped jeans and T-shirt she wore in the garden. She's done up to the nines in tailored trousers and heels, and her sleek brown bob looks newly coiffured. Just as I open my mouth to speak, she turns and says something to the tall blonde woman standing beside her. There is none of the casual friendliness she displayed yesterday.

Next to them is the woman I saw this morning with the silky ponytail and the uniformed twins. She looks at me sympathetically and smiles.

'Hello,' I whisper as I walk past the group, but the silence is deafening. Rowan must have felt just like this when the other kids in reception stared at him.

As I lower my eyes and walk on, the conversation behind me starts up again.

'*She's* just moved to Buckingham Crescent?' I hear someone say loudly in disbelief. 'Looks like the place is going downhill fast.'

9

When I get back home after the school run, I make a cup of coffee and take it straight up to the spare room to begin unpacking boxes. The last thing I need to do is waste time sitting staring out of the window, wondering if we've done the right thing in moving here.

We had such a good start here yesterday, but now I'm smarting from the afterburn of the school gate animosity. Enduring the unfriendly silence from the group that included Aisha's mum, Edie and also the woman with the twins who smiled at me earlier was bad enough. But overhearing that bitchy comment about the crescent going down fast just completed my humiliation. The positive impression I got of the area yesterday feels completely undone.

I stick the radio on, and in an hour or so, I've unpacked a good stack of boxes and the burning sensation in my chest has abated a little. What was I thinking, believing I could be friends with a set like that? Turns out Isaac was right after all; we're like chalk and cheese.

I grew up in a small mining village with my mum and her younger sister, Aunt Pat. Their parents had both died young and Mum, who was six years older, had essentially raised Aunt Pat. When Mum got married, she'd taken her in as one of the family. Aunt Pat worked as a travelling cosmetics sales rep and spent long periods away from home on the road. Dad was killed in an accident at the coal face, crushed by a faulty conveyer belt, before my first birthday. So most of the time it was just me and Mum.

We weren't too badly off financially. Mum had received a modest payout from the National Coal Board. There was always enough food, and, unlike some of my classmates, I always had new clothes and shoes when I grew out of them. But Mum was a naturally frugal woman and her budget never stretched to an annual holiday or little luxuries.

The only bit of excitement came when Aunt Pat returned home from a trip, glamorous and looking so vibrant and young. She'd always bring me a gift, a 'meaningless trinket' as Mum called jewellery or anything remotely pretty that didn't have a practical use.

'Loosen up, Irene,' Aunt Pat would taunt her disapproving sister. 'Learn to live a bit. You've got enough put by that you could treat yourself and our Janey now and again. Maybe a little break by the seaside, or a meal and a night out at the theatre. Janey would love that, wouldn't you, princess?'

'You leave her out of it,' Mum would snap. 'We don't want her getting ideas above her station, like you.'

'Charming!' Aunt Pat would huff, but then she'd wink at me and we'd have a little grin at Mum's expense behind her back. Mum's insults were like water off a duck's back to Aunt Pat, but I internalised every last one of her criticisms.

I remember my aunt giving me a dazzling gold and ruby necklace when I was ten and encouraging me to wear it to school under my blouse so that Mum wouldn't know. Then, just before she died, there was a white-gold bangle studded all the way round with tiny diamonds. They were the most beautiful things I'd ever seen. I have no idea if they were real precious metals and gems, but Mum snatched the bracelet out of my hands and she and Aunt Pat had a blazing row in the kitchen about the 'inappropriate gifts'. I never saw the bracelet or the necklace again.

Aunt Pat and I mostly kept her gifts a secret between the two of us. She'd slip me the odd tenner, and once, when I was just thirteen, she loaned me an expensive designer handbag for the school disco that she said was made from real snakeskin. She just seemed so cool compared to the local people and the humdrum village life I led. When she was home, my life seemed full of colour and excitement and when she went away, everything turned grey again.

When I became an adult, as a result of Mum's disapproval of Aunt Pat's gifts, I learned to harbour a great deal of guilt when it came to buying myself anything nice. This extended to splashing out on an outfit for a special night out, make-up, accessories… anything that couldn't be labelled as 'useful'. Mum's words echo in my head still, but these days our tight budget stops any impulse purchases, so it's not really a problem.

Even though we're worlds apart, I do feel I know the sort of women I encountered at the school gates this morning. Like Aunt Pat, their self-value comes from the very possessions Mum frowned upon. Their razor-sharp tongues might wind me up on one level, but at least I can hold my head high in the knowledge that I don't judge myself by the size and clarity of the diamonds on my fingers. I suppose I have Mum to thank for that.

Still, the parents back at Rowan's old school seemed so much more normal. The mums with their hair hurriedly stuck up in a ponytail, the dads in sweatpants and sliders in the summer months. Just ordinary people, doing their best under often difficult circumstances.

I looked smarter before I became Mum's carer because I had to dress for work before the school run. Once I stopped having a good reason to make an effort, I quickly lost interest in what garments I pulled on before leaving the house.

At Lady Bridge, the women who gathered outside the gate looked as if they were meeting up for a night out. Hair all done, full face of make-up, and ostentatious designer labels that screeched silently from casually cut clothing that was clearly not casual at all. I didn't dress up to take Rowan in this morning, but perhaps I ought to have done. Edie had certainly pulled out all the stops, looking far more groomed than yesterday, so maybe it was the done thing around here.

I want our new life to be perfect in every way. I don't want Rowan feeling different to the other kids and being excluded because their mums turn their pert little noses up at me.

'You must do something to irritate them,' I remember Mum saying when I got older and a couple of the other teenage girls in my year started to bully me at school. 'You've got to learn how to fit in, Janey.'

Rightly or wrongly, I tried to change to make the popular girls like me. I copied their hairstyles, persuaded Mum to buy me some second-hand shoes that were more modern than the flat lace-ups she favoured for me. I even applied a little mascara and eyeliner before I left the house to look older, but it never worked. I was consistently bullied from the age of thirteen until I left school at sixteen and finally escaped to college to train as a classroom assistant, initially caring for kids under four and then studying at night school and graduating to working as a qualified teaching assistant for older children.

I sigh and shake myself out of this maudlin mood, troubled that these deep feelings of inadequacy still run through me like a core of ice.

Moving here represents the start of our new family life. Plus, it's early days, and who knows, maybe given time, I can start to make conversation with the other parents and fit in a little more. One thoughtless comment doesn't add up to complete exoneration.

I stand up with my hands on my hips and arch my back to ease the dull ache in my coccyx brought on by hours spent sitting on the floor. My eyes alight on the box in the corner of the room. It's secured with brown packing tape like the others but written across the top in thick black marker is the single word *MUM*. Inside, under a ton of screwed-up brown packing paper, is a small wooden chest that, for as long as I can remember, was kept under

Mum's bed, stuffed with old photographs and various papers. It's a box I've never taken more than a cursory glance inside. All I know is that Mum pulled important documents out of there as and when they were needed: birth certificates, passports, insurance certificates and that sort of thing. *Mum's box*, I've always called it.

It's definitely not mine, even though she's gone now. I don't want any of it to be mine, and so I haven't opened it since she died.

'The complete picture is in there, Janey,' she told me in her final days. 'And when you feel strong enough, it will answer all your questions.'

But I haven't got any questions, because I've no wish to hear the answers.

When we moved, Isaac offered to take the chest off my hands. 'If keeping that stuff upsets you, why not just get rid of it?'

He's so logical, so pragmatic. He can't possibly know how I feel about it all. But I did consider the idea, imagining the freedom it might bring. Would leaving the box behind also lock its secrets firmly in the past? If only. Deep down inside, I know I can't run away from it indefinitely and yet nothing I do will ever make what happened right. Nothing.

10

I'm shaken out of my ruminating by the doorbell. It's far louder than the one we had at the old house, and it instantly sets my teeth on edge. Recalling Saturday night's mystery caller, I stand at the top of the stairs and look down towards the narrow opaque glass panels either side of the door. Although I can't identify who the visitor is from up here, if I walk downstairs they'll easily spot my movement and know someone is home.

When Aunt Pat was away, Mum and I rarely had visitors to the house. On the odd occasion a caller came to the door, perhaps a salesman touting double-glazing or a Jehovah's Witness, spreading the Word, we'd dash into the back kitchen and actually hide until the caller had gone. At the time I thought everyone did it and when I got older, it took several trips to friends' houses before I realised it wasn't normal behaviour at all.

As I reach the hall, I dust down my jeans and curse myself for managing to look even more slovenly than when I took Rowan to school this morning. The bell rings again and I spring forward to open the door.

'Janey, hello!' The lady from down the road, Polly, stands there clutching a bunch of colourful sweet peas with a wodge of newspaper wrapped around the bottom. 'I saw you get back from the school run this morning and I know you haven't been out again, so I thought I'd pop over and give you these.' She holds out the flowers, beaming.

I know you haven't been out again… How creepy. Has she been watching the house?

'Thank you.' I take the blooms and sniff them. 'They're lovely; they'll brighten up the kitchen no end. Did you grow them yourself?'

She nods.

There's an awkward moment of silence, which I force myself to snap out of. I've got a thousand things to do, but I'll look rude if I don't invite her in.

'Would you like a cup of tea? I'm afraid we're still in a dreadful mess, though,' I add when her face lights up.

'I won't stay long, just for a quick cuppa and a chat,' she says happily.

An hour and a half and two cups of tea later, I'm getting restless. I've dropped a couple of hints about having things to get on with, but Polly likes talking about herself and her family. I know all about her late husband, Jerry, who apparently spent more time on the golf course than at home with her, their three grown-up daughters, her two grandchildren and last but not least, I know every last detail about her eldest daughter's pet pug, Marlon, who is currently recovering from a recent operation on his anal glands.

'He's like a third grandchild, he really is,' she chuckles. 'He has his own personality and very firm likes and dislikes when it comes to food and his favourite spot for napping. But oh, the stench when he… well, you know, when he had his wind problem. It smelt just like—'

'Marlon sounds adorable, Polly, he really does,' I say, standing up. 'Perhaps I'll get to meet him when he's feeling better. But for now, I'm afraid I really need to get cracking on my list of jobs.'

If I offer Polly a third drink, I genuinely fear she'll sit here chatting for the entire afternoon. Yet I feel a bit rotten making it this obvious I want her to leave because, despite her obviously having a big, close family, I have this hunch that Polly is quite lonely underneath.

Isaac is going to wonder what I've been doing all day if I don't make a bit more progress. I'm sure he's had a busy first day with his unexpected early start, and I want to get downstairs tidied and straightened so we can relax over a nice meal later. Plus, I'm itching to get online and have a proper look at the job vacancy at the school.

'Enough about me and my family.' Polly ignores the fact I've stood up and tips her head to one side, folding her hands in her lap. 'Tell me about yourself, Janey.'

'Actually, I think that's going to have to be a conversation for another day, Polly.' Her face falls, but I don't weaken. 'It's just that I still have so much to get done. I'm sure you understand.'

'Of course, how thoughtless of me.'

My shoulders relax as she shuffles to the edge of her seat, ready to stand up.

Then she says, 'You know, I have very little on this afternoon. I could be at your complete disposal if you just tell me where you want me to start.' She's sitting bolt upright now, wanting to please.

'That's really kind of you, and thanks so much for offering.' I make a point of checking my watch. 'But I'm expecting Isaac home soon and we have various tasks planned that we'll need to do together, like moving some of the heavier bits of furniture around.'

Isaac already texted mid morning to say the bigwigs were staying later than expected so he might struggle to get home until after six. But Polly's reluctance to move calls for drastic measures.

'I could help you with the furniture. The two of us can manage, can't we? It will save Isaac the trouble when he gets in from work.'

'Thank you, but no,' I say firmly. 'I won't hear of you humping furniture around for our benefit.'

I stifle a sigh of relief when, finally, Polly gets to her feet to leave.

11

It's nearly eight p.m. when Isaac finally arrives home. I peer though the living room door into the hallway, and the instant he walks in, I can tell he's distracted. Glancing at his watch, putting down his briefcase then picking it up again like he can't decide what to do for the best.

'Sorry I'm late,' he calls out, his voice strained and tired.

He texted again to say he'd be back even later than he'd first thought, but I didn't expect it would be a full two hours later.

When he hears the front door open, Rowan jumps up from the floor, snatching up the artwork he did in class, and runs through to the hallway to see his father. As it was his first day at school, I've allowed him to stay up a little later than usual so he can see Isaac.

'I did a painting of our fossil hunt on the beach last year, Dad, and Miss Packton gave me a sticker because it was so good!' he bellows out in one long breath, clearly anxious to impress Isaac.

He was far more reserved about his day when I picked him up at the end of school. I stood for a good five minutes amongst the other parents in the playground waiting for the classroom doors to open. Nobody spoke to me, but I didn't feel particularly shunned or left out. It was just that people were standing around in small groups with other parents they knew, immersed in their chats.

After a minute or two, I spotted the group of mothers I'd seen at the gates that morning. Edie was amongst them again, and she raised her eyebrows and nodded discreetly, as if she didn't want to blank me but didn't want to greet me openly in front of the others. Mischievously, I toyed with the idea of walking over and asking if she had the list of events in town, as she'd promised when we chatted at her gate.

The women stood apart from the other parents, who, I'd already noticed with relief, were far more like me, dressed in casual clothes that hadn't been carefully selected and accessorised. They looked as if they'd glanced at the clock and then rushed out to pick up the kids – just regular people.

I wondered if it was my imagination that the other parents appeared to give the school gate women a wide berth as they bragged in loud voices about their children's recent test results and made scathing comments about a private maths tutor who wasn't meeting their expectations and who they were all planning to dismiss en masse in the next couple of days. I noticed that the ordinary parents shot surreptitious glances their way indicating a mixture of curiosity and distrust.

I'd changed my transparent top for a soft cotton tunic that looked good with my bootcut jeans and I made an effort to hold my head high as I waited alone outside Rowan's class, reasoning that even if I still felt inadequate inside, I needn't let everyone see it.

When Miss Packton flung open the doors, dead on 3.15, she gestured to me to approach the classroom. Only when she'd ensured that the other children had all been delivered safely to their designated pickups did she steer Rowan out last, beaming at me.

'He's been an absolute star,' she said brightly. 'I think he's thoroughly enjoyed his first day, right, Rowan?'

'Yes, miss,' Rowan said bashfully, his cheeks turning pink.

'And this' – she brandished a large sheet of paper, turning it so I could see the carefully applied strokes of colour – 'is the masterpiece he produced when I asked the children to draw or paint their favourite outing.'

It was a painting of two figures on a beach. Even I could see it was impressive for an eight-year-old. The tall figure I instantly recognised as Isaac and the short one was obviously Rowan himself. The sea was behind them as the figures stooped to gather tiny pieces of rock. I recalled the outing immediately. Isaac and Rowan had searched for fossils at Saltburn-by-the-Sea while I relaxed with my Kindle and a flask of tea in a fold-up deckchair on the stony beach. I felt a pinch of regret when I realised this had been last summer. Since then, we hadn't had any full days out as a family at all.

Rowan shakes the painting at his father now, eager to get his full attention after waiting hours to show him. Isaac glances at the artwork but he doesn't take it from Rowan's hands to inspect it further.

'It's fabulous, buddy. We had a great time that day, didn't we?' He opens his briefcase and looks inside distractedly.

Rowan nods, but I notice the effect that Isaac's lack of enthusiasm has on his mood. He puts the paper down on the hall table and returns to the living room, the spring in his step gone. I glare at Isaac.

This is exactly what we had to put up with in his old job, with its unsociable hours and emails streaming in twenty-four-seven. It took every drop of energy and attention from him, leaving us, his family, with nothing. There were times when it felt like we just got to see his exhausted husk at the end of the day before it all started again early the next morning.

He catches my pointed look and tries to rescue the situation by injecting some false enthusiasm into his voice. 'Well done, champ. Did you have a good first day?'

Of course, Rowan, like most kids, is wise to the tricks of busy adults, and Isaac's ploy to sound interested doesn't work.

'It was OK,' he mumbles.

'I can't tell you what a bitch of a first day it's been for me, Janey,' Isaac says in a low voice. He closes his eyes briefly and allows the weight of his head to hang a moment. 'Hot shower, meal and bed, I think. In that order.'

'Fine.' I don't bother to remark on anything about my own day. I'm certainly not going to tell him how I'm excited about the school job that's up for grabs, and I'm shelving my plans to cook the two rib-eye steaks I have in the fridge. It might sound petty, but I feel like he doesn't deserve my efforts. Maybe if I treat him in the same offhand manner he uses with me, he might twig that he needs to up his game a bit.

'Is there anything to eat?' he asks. 'I'm starving.'

'I suppose I could rustle up an omelette,' I say.

'An omelette?' His voice is laced with disappointment.

'Yes, Isaac, an omelette. I didn't plan on cooking a meal this late, and I'm tired, too.'

'OK. Thanks,' he says, and heads upstairs still in his shoes and coat. Still clutching that bloody briefcase like his life depends on it.

12

As Susan Marsh boarded the number 342 bus, she realised that at that moment, for the first time in her life, she felt truly happy. Turning eighteen had made all the difference to her being told what to do and when to do it by her parents. She knew they meant well, but they were… well, just being parents.

Best of all, she'd learned on her birthday last week that she had been successful in winning a place at nursing college. She was really excited about that. Way back in primary school, when all her friends had seemed to enjoy dressing up as Disney princesses and pirates, Susan had felt happiest in her play nurse's uniform. Not a doctor, mind, it had to be a nurse, because nurses had more time to be with patients and spread their kindness. Susan had developed the opinion, through childhood visits to the hospital to battle severe asthma that she had thankfully grown out of, that doctors always seemed to be racing against the clock, with little time to chat.

Achieving her dream of earning a place at the nursing college in the city, with vocational training in the Queen's Medical Centre, had just blown her mind.

Even better, when her mother raised an eyebrow at a brief glimpse of midriff, or her father remarked on the fact that she hadn't got home until half past eleven when she'd always been expected to return from a night out no later than eleven, Susan was able to say in a smug voice, 'Remember, I'm an adult now.'

They had no need to worry really. She had always been quite a conservative dresser, and because of her nursing ambitions, she had no problem in turning down all-night parties in favour of an early night with a cup of Horlicks so she could be at her best for lessons the next day.

She brushed off a couple of flecks on her new tailored beige trousers and ran admiring fingers over the silky-smooth blouse her mum had grudgingly bought for her birthday.

'Isn't it a bit see-through?' Erin Marsh had murmured, narrowing her eyes and tilting her head this way and that.

Susan had laughed. 'I think you can just about glimpse the fact that I have a lacy bra on, Mum, but it's not as if I'm baring my cleavage.'

Her parents didn't realise how lucky they were. Susan knew girls at college who wore dresses so tight that they had to leave their knickers off!

Susan and her friend Melissa Deakin had been looking forward to tonight's event for ages. First had been Susan's eighteenth last week, which she'd thoroughly enjoyed. There had been a slap-up birthday lunch with her parents during the day, and then Melissa had arranged surprise tickets to see a favourite rock band, who were appearing at the Royal Concert Hall. Afterwards they had gone to Ye Olde Trip to Jerusalem, reputedly the oldest pub in England, where a group of college friends had gathered to help her celebrate.

The countdown had then started in earnest for Melissa's own eighteenth, which, thanks to her barrister parents being rather well off and living in a mansion in Wollaton, was going to be a fancy affair with a proper band, catering and even a magician performing in a hired marquee in the grounds.

Susan was arriving a good hour before anyone else, and was one of the select few staying overnight in one of the Deakins' spare bedrooms.

'I've got a bottle of fizz stashed away in my wardrobe,' Melissa had whispered to her behind her mother's back when she'd gone over there yesterday to see the marquee. 'We can put some music on and get into the party spirit so we hit the ground running when everyone arrives.'

And now here she was, done up to the nines and sitting on a double-decker bus that was trundling slowly towards the city centre, Susan felt like shouting down to the driver to get a move on. Still, Melissa had insisted on paying for her to get a cab out to the house instead of waiting around for another bus.

When Susan alighted from the bus at 4.30, it was already dark. She stepped off into the brightly illuminated bus station, then, pulling her woollen edge-to-edge jacket closer, walked briskly across the road and cut down a side street that she knew would lead her to the taxi rank up near the university buildings.

She'd just emerged back onto a quiet stretch of the main road when the girl approached her. She was young, with blonde hair pulled back into a low-slung ponytail. She wore tight jeans, and Susan caught a glimpse of a sparkly top under her black jacket.

'Excuse me, can you help?' the girl said nervously. 'I'm not from around here and we're late for a tea party for my great-gran. I'm looking for Riverdene Care Home. It's close to the city centre.'

'I don't live in the city myself, but I might recognise the street name if you have it,' Susan said.

The girl nodded. 'My boyfriend's waiting in the car; he's got the invitation. He's parked just around the corner, hang on.' She set off and then paused a moment. 'Probably quicker if you come with me, if you don't mind.'

Susan hesitated. The bus journey had taken longer than she'd thought it would. If she delayed getting in the cab, Melissa would start wondering where she'd got to.

'My great-gran is ninety today, you see,' the girl added, her tone increasingly panicky. 'It's a really special party and we're her surprise guests, as she thinks I'm on holiday. But if we don't get there soon, we're in danger of missing the whole thing.'

Susan relented. 'OK, but I've only got a minute or two. I'm on my way to a birthday party myself.'

'Thanks so much!' The girl turned, and Susan followed. After twenty or thirty yards, she turned sharply right. This narrow side road was a dead end, so there was no through traffic or people using it as a shortcuts. It seemed eerily quiet compared to the main drag they'd just left. There was just one dark-coloured car parked halfway down, its headlights off.

'There he is,' the girl said, sounding relieved. 'That's my boyfriend's car.'

They approached the passenger side, closest to the pavement, and the girl opened the door, but no light came on and the interior of the car remained dark.

'I've found someone to help us,' she said, and Susan noticed that her voice sounded strained and high-pitched. 'Can you show her the invitation?'

The girl stood back, and Susan stepped forward and dipped her head. As she squinted inside the dim car, the hooded figure in the driver's seat produced a piece of paper and held it towards her, but not close enough for her to take it.

Her heart rate suddenly doubled as a warning sparked in her head. Something about the situation suddenly didn't ring true. Inside of leaning further in, she stepped back, ready to duck her head out again.

An almighty shove sent her sprawling down into the passenger seat. Something damp and acrid covered her mouth, and she gagged and coughed, clawing at her face.

'Keep her down,' a man's voice hissed, and the hand pressed harder until she felt sure she would be smothered right there.

The male voice barked out again, and Susan heard the girl say something in return, but their voices seemed to fade further and further away... until suddenly Susan wasn't in the car any more, but at Melissa's house, and then, a second later, outside the nursing college. Finally, as a blanket of darkness descended, cloaking her entire head, closing in until there was just the tiniest speck of light, she was home again, lying in the warmth and safety of her mother's arms.

13

Isaac is up super-early for the next few mornings, and today, Thursday, is no exception.

'It's just for the first week or so,' he explains yet again before heading for the shower while I'm still fighting the grogginess of being woken by the evil 5.45 alarm he insists on setting each night before turning his bedside lamp off. 'Bob says it won't always be like this, and the earlier I get in, the earlier I can leave.'

Except his logic is skewed, because it doesn't seem to work like that at all. He leaves early and gets back home later and later.

I'd actually begun to believe in the dream he sold me so enthusiastically – his being able to work half the week from home so we can spend more time together as a family in our lovely new home – but it feels like it's already fading fast. So I'm trying to think about other benefits of the job, other ways it will bring us all closer.

The secured loan was settled when we sold the house although paying it off took all the available equity we had in the property. But thanks to Isaac's signing-on bonus at Abacus, he was also able to settle the credit card balance that had started to slowly creep up again. We'll also be in a position to take a holiday abroad for the first time in five years.

This is all great news and yet I can't seem to get through to Isaac that more family time and a renewed intimacy between the two of us are the really important things.

Half asleep, I hear Isaac get out of the shower. He dresses quickly and kisses me on the cheek before leaving for work.

Instead of drifting between waking and sleeping like I usually do when Isaac has left, I get out of bed to make coffee. Then I take a bit more time getting myself showered and ready before I wake Rowan. He's not settling into life at Lady Bridge nearly as smoothly as I'd hoped, so leaving less time for him to worry before we leave the house each morning seems like a sensible plan.

On Tuesday, he complained of a tummy ache, which promptly disappeared when I said he still had to go into school. Yesterday, he locked himself in the bathroom claiming he was about to be sick.

Each day at school pickup, he trudges out of the classroom, glum and listless. Always the last child and always on his own. Miss Packton gives me a sympathetic look and nods in encouragement to silently convey her conviction that, given time, he'll be fine.

On principle, I don't get dressed up to take Rowan into school. I certainly don't look nearly as polished as the yummy Buckingham Crescent mummies who gather at the gates, but my clothes do match, and thankfully there's been no underwear on show since my little faux pas on Monday morning.

The weather has been a bit damp and dull these past few days, but today is turning out fine, and I begin to feel a little brighter, managing to stop myself from worrying about Isaac's punishing new hours and Rowan's slow settling-in period. Plus, on Tuesday afternoon, I took the plunge and applied for the part-time teaching assistant position at the school. Isaac has been so distracted with his new job, I decided not to raise the subject in case I don't get an interview. The school may have rules I'm as yet unaware of about current parents not being allowed to be employees.

But I'm really hoping I have a chance.

I've always loved working with children but I had no choice but to shelve my career.

We found out Mum was ill by mistake eighteenth months ago when she was invited to an old school-friend's wedding. She'd felt so miffed because she had no choice but to buy a new outfit for Doreen's big day and yet, unusually for her, she really did seem to want to go.

I'd helped her sift through her wardrobe, including the stuff she hadn't worn in years and even I had to admit she had nothing in there that was remotely suitable.

So we went shopping. We selected a couple of dresses and matching jackets from the rails and Mum disappeared into the changing room. Within a couple of minutes, she called me in.

'I'm getting all tangled up while you stand out there looking at your phone,' she snapped, twisting and turning as she tried in vain to adjust the mint green dress. 'It's so hot in here. Why is the heating turned up so high?'

It was warm but not excessively so, I felt, but I didn't comment. It was the safest way when she was in one of her moods.

'You've got yourself all flustered. Let's start again,' I said, helping her slip the dress back over her head. 'This colour looks lovely on you, Mum.'

'It's a bit insipid if you ask me. I don't want to look all washed out next to Doreen's Benidorm tan.' She scowled. 'I shouldn't have taken your advice on the shade.'

It was when she lifted up her arms so I could pull the dress back over her head that I saw it. A bumpy red, inflamed patch of skin under her arm.

'That looks sore,' I said, shaking the dress out before we tried again. 'Is it a boil?'

Mum followed my eyes and, looking in the mirror, she gingerly ran her fingers over the visible lump.

'It's bigger than it looks.' She pressed two fingertips on to the small lump. 'It feels hard here, under my skin.'

I felt the colour drain from my face.

Two days later we were in the doctor's surgery and he told Mum she'd have to undergo a biopsy. Within a week she'd been diagnosed with Stage 4 Hodgkin lymphoma with a life expectancy between one and two years. It was that brutal.

Outside the consultant's office, in the carpeted corridor that blunted the sound of our footsteps, I threw my arms around her and told her I loved her and that I would give up work and look after her.

But she pushed me away. 'I deserve to die alone,' she whispered.

14

Outside, the sky is already a picture-perfect blue without any cloud although there's still a slight chill in the air.

I dress warmly but leave my fine light brown hair down and use a bit of mascara and lipstick and a sweep of bronzer to lift my sallow complexion.

Rowan sits at the breakfast bar, swirling his spoon around in his cereal but not eating anything.

'I know it's hard when you're the newbie, sweetie. But it will get better, honestly.'

He scowls. 'But nobody even wants talk to me.'

'What about your class buddy, Aisha? She's nice to you, isn't she?'

He shrugs but says nothing.

'I could have a word with Miss Packton if you like, about getting you a trial for the football team, and then you'd meet the other—'

'No!' He puts his spoon down with a clatter. 'I don't want to play football… not at that stupid school.'

My stomach cramps at his words. Back at the old house, he'd spend all his free time watching it on television, poring over his sticker books, or kicking a ball around the garden with his mates. But of course, he left his mates behind when we moved, and with them, it seems, his passion for the beautiful game.

Despite his protests, I make my mind up to try and get a quick word with Miss Packton without him knowing. Playing football would be such a brilliant way for him to make some new friends. I feel cheered at my little plan and wonder why I haven't thought of it before.

Then, five minutes before we're due to leave the house, Rowan manages to tip half a bowl of cornflakes and milk into his lap. He's obviously still terribly nervous about the new school, so I swallow my irritation.

'Don't worry, let's pop back upstairs and get you changed,' I say, glancing at the clock and wondering what Miss Packton will make of him being late just a few days into his time at Lady Bridge. But if we get a move on, we might still make it.

I strip off his milk-soaked school trousers, which arrived with the rest of his uniform yesterday, and manage to get him changed in record time. We half walk, half run all the way down Buckingham Crescent. As we pass Polly's gate, I see she's in the front garden. I wave but I can see she looks upset.

'You OK Polly?' I call, slowing down to stop despite Rowan impatiently pulling at my hand to get a move on.

'Not really.' She indicates the ground around her. Canes snapped and tossed aside and sweet peas, just like the ones she brought for me, scattered strewn across the front lawn.

'Mum, come *on*!' Rowan urges me.

'Sorry, Polly, we're late. I'm coming straight home so I'll stop by on my way back.'

She nods, her mouth slack with dismay as she looks over the garden damage.

We've got seven minutes to make the bell – a journey that's usually a ten- to twelve-minute walk. It's not impossible, but it's definitely tight.

When the school gates finally come into sight, we only have two minutes to go.

'We can do it, Rowan, keep running!' I urge him.

He's exaggerating his panting and gasping for air, but his face is ruddy and bright and I can see he's treating our mad dash as quite the little adventure. It's nice to see a bit of his old energy back again.

As we approach the gate, the burly uniformed figure of a traffic warden appears. She makes a beeline for the oversized white Range Rover that's parked on double yellows in the same place it has been every day this week. As we whizz past, she looks up from her handheld device with a smug expression.

The bell sounds as we dash around the back of the building. I kiss Rowan on the top of his head and he skips past Miss Packton just before she closes the classroom doors.

I jut out my bottom lip and puff cool air up into my face, blowing wisps of hair from my sticky forehead. We made it! I turn around to withering looks of disapproval from some of the designer mothers, no doubt appalled that anyone who lives on Buckingham Crescent could be so terribly disorganised. I smile, but get flared nostrils and sweeping lashes in return. If looks could kill!

As I walk past them, I pause.

'Does the big white Range Rover at the gates belong to one of you?'

'Why, who wants to know?' A willowy blonde woman with cheekbones you could sharpen a knife on looks down on me snootily like I've just crawled out from under a rock. It's the same woman I saw Edie standing next to on Rowan's first day, the one who always seems to be holding court amongst the other women.

'There's a traffic warden out there about to issue it with a ticket. Thought you might like to know.' I turn to walk away.

'Jeez!' The woman flies past me, wailing, heading around the building towards the main gate. No sign now of her ice-cool demeanour. 'That'll be the third fine in two weeks... Tristan will *kill* me!'

The other women flutter manicured fingers up to their pantomime faces, as if it's the worst disaster imaginable, and I smile to myself as I walk on.

As I walk past the office, the receptionist who welcomed us on Rowan's first morning calls from the entrance doors.

'Mrs Markham? I've been looking out for you.' She waves an envelope in the air. 'Can I give you this to take with you? It'll save us a stamp.'

I walk over and she hands me the letter. 'It's an invitation to come in for an interview.' She drops her voice confidentially. 'For the teaching assistant post.'

'Oh, thank you!' I look at the letter, my heart rate picking up. 'That was quick.'

'They need someone as soon as possible. Bear that in mind when they ask when you can start.' She gives me a wink and a grin and disappears back inside.

My mood instantly soars. An interview! What a great start to the day.

A couple of minutes later, when I reach the road, I come across the frustrated traffic warden standing with her hands on her hips, watching as the Range Rover zooms away in the distance at breakneck speed.

'Thirty seconds more and I would've had her,' she hisses between bared teeth as she plunges the device back into her pocket in disgust.

Obviously the blonde woman managed to get back to her car before the warden had the chance to finish taking photographs and printing the legally binding fine. And all thanks to my tip-off.

I walk home at a pleasantly leisurely pace, smiling as I think about Rowan loving the drama of our rush to beat the bell. I think he'd be pleased if I worked at the school; I hope so, anyway. I know I have to tell Isaac about my work plans, although I'm reluctant because I've seen him quash Rowan's excitement with his lack of attention. I really don't need to be brushed off right now, and I know his thoughts on me taking time to get my head properly together after Mum's death and everything associated with that.

I cross the busy road and turn onto Buckingham Crescent. As I walk past the first few houses on the right-hand side, I can't help but marvel at the size of them. When we saw our house up for such a good price, we felt as if we'd zoomed up the social ladder living here. But now I take a closer look, I can see that ours is positively small and ordinary compared to most of these properties. Exactly as Rowan pointed out at the weekend.

The house next to Polly's is particularly grand. A white stucco palace with enormous Greek-style pillars framing the outsize front door. It's too big for its plot; some might even say a little vulgar.

I'm shaken out of my thoughts by a purring presence on the roadside. I stop walking in case a vehicle needs to turn and see it's the blonde woman from school in the white Range Rover.

The car pulls to a halt and the passenger-side window rolls smoothly down.

My eyes are drawn to the pristine cream leather of the gleaming interior. A fresh smell of lemony polish emanates from within. I think about my own tatty Ford Fiesta, due its MOT in a couple of months. The back seat is currently littered with coats and Rowan's old school football kit. If I were to give anyone a lift, my passenger would have to kick rubbish out from under their feet to make room in the footwell. My cheeks flush with heat at the shame of the comparison.

'I'm Tanya,' the blonde woman says in her plummy accent, leaning across from the driver's seat. 'Thanks for the tip-off. My husband would've probably divorced me if I'd suffered yet another ticket, so your thoughtfulness was gold dust.'

'That's OK.' I smile. 'Glad you got back to the car in time.'

'Thanks to you, I did.' She sits back in her seat again.

'I'm Janey, by the way. We've just moved into the crescent.'

'Oh yes, in one of the smaller houses in the middle, aren't you? Have a nice day… and thanks again!' The window rolls back up before I can respond and the car turns into the driveway of the big white mansion next to Polly's house.

Polly isn't in her front garden so I step inside the gate and stand looking at the mess. She's tied the broken canes into a bundle and gathered the butchered plants into a droopy, pastel-coloured mound.

She appears from the side of the house carrying a black bin bag. A car door opens and closes next door.

'Polly, what happened?' I ask her.

I thought she might be upset but her expression is steely as she crouches down to stuff the flowers into the bin bag.

'Wilful vandalism. That's what's happened yet again.'

'Someone's done this before?' I'm shocked in an area like this. But then I think about the phantom caller on our moving in day. 'Do you think it's bored kids?'

'No, definitely not,' Polly says shortly. She stands up and juts her chin forward, raising her voice. 'I know exactly who's responsible for this and they won't get away with it. Mark my words.'

She stares pointedly at the tall hedge that acts as a border between her house and Tanya's.

'Did you want me to help you tidy it up?' I say, feeling a bit awkward after a couple of seconds of Polly's staring silence.

'No, thank you, Janey, I've nearly finished now.' She bends to pick up the bundle of garden canes. 'All I'll say is be careful who you upset around here. Choose your company wisely, that's my advice.'

I nod and continue on my way, eager to escape Polly's strange comments and behaviour.

Tanya's thoughtless remarks about our small house have really got to me. I don't know why. In my heart of hearts I know we have as much right to live here as anyone else regardless of their bank balance. It's incredible how, when I first saw the property on Rightmove, it seemed so big and spacious. Now that I've seen the palaces that surround us, and with comments like the one Tanya just made flying around, I almost feel like the poor relations around here.

Still, I have an interview for the school job, and that could be a way back into the career I had to walk away from. The move here would be worth that if nothing else.

15

I tear open the letter excitedly and read it. It's an invitation for an interview on Monday morning at 9.30, which works quite well for me. I'll drive to school that day, drop Rowan off and then wait in the car until the interview time. It will stop me getting too hot and bothered walking there in the navy trouser suit and heels I plan on wearing.

I confirm my attendance via the email address provided, then grab my handbag and, with a spring in my step, walk into town to get a few things we need. Staples like milk and fruit, until I get round to sorting out our online grocery delivery.

My first stop, when I reach Central Avenue, is to call into Ergon for more of the delicious sourdough bread we polished off so quickly on Sunday.

I step inside the small shop and inhale the aromas of fresh coffee and spices. Within seconds, I sense a slight drop in the volume of customer chatter, and when I turn towards the tables near the window, it becomes apparent why. The familiar cluster of Lady Bridge mothers are looking my way.

Something pinches hard at my throat and I fight the urge to walk back out again. Running away has always been my standard response to feeling uncomfortable. But I remind myself that I can be whoever I want to be here. There's nothing to be afraid of, and I'm as good as any one of them.

Before I know it, I'm heading straight for the gathering. The conversation dips further as several pairs of dramatic brows knit together, apparently in genteel shock at my audacity.

'Hello!' I keep my eyes on Tanya's face. 'This is a great little place, isn't it? We found it on Sunday.'

Tanya looks slightly taken aback, but she recovers within seconds and turns to the others.

'This is Janey, everyone, she's my little lifesaver!' She grasps my hand and pulls me gently into their tight seated circle. 'Come and have a coffee with us. What would you like?'

'Thanks. I… I'll have a latte.' I stand there awkwardly, everyone looking up at me from their seats.

'Barak! Another latte please, darling,' Tanya calls, and I see the owner's arm wave in acknowledgement from behind a customer who's being served at the counter.

Tanya turns to the woman sitting next to her. It's the lady I spotted with her children across the street at the beginning of the week. Her hair was swept up in a ponytail then, but now it looks freshly blow-dried. She's dressed in a silver velvet lounge suit and has impossibly long, pointed silver nails that match her outfit perfectly. 'Ky, budge up, sweetie, so Janey can sit here, next to me. Pull that chair over for yourself.'

'But I've just got the photos of my new outfit ready to show you,' the woman says petulantly, holding up her phone.

'It's OK, we can look at them later,' Tanya says.

A scowl flits across Ky's face. Her glossy black hair falls across her face like a crow's wing as she pulls an empty chair from the next table towards her and slides over onto it, leaving the seat next to Tanya free for me to sit down.

'Everyone, this is Janey. She's new in the crescent. Her son, Rowan, is in Miss Packton's class.' I'm surprised that Tanya has remembered my name, and also knows Rowan's. 'Janey, time for you to meet everyone. This is Edie Chase.'

It's the woman with the brown bob, class buddy Aisha's mum.

'Hi, Janey, we've already met, I think?' Edie phrases it as a question, but she *knows* we've already met. We talked at her gate just a few days ago, and she even agreed to come round to the house for a coffee at some point.

'Nice to see you again, Edie,' I say.

'This gorgeous creature is Kyoko Nagasawa, but her friends call her Ky.'

'Pleased to meet you, Ky,' I say. 'Thanks for making room for me.'

Silently she presses her hands together and performs the tiniest head bow, but her dark eyes remain suspicious.

'Ky's twins, Cherry and Jun, are in Year 2 at Lady Bridge. The year below Rowan and my Dexter,' Tanya says.

It occurs to me that if I get the job on Monday, I'll be working in Year 2. Maybe I'll even be in Ky's children's class, although there are two classes in each year group, so this might not be the case.

'I saw your twins from across the crescent; they look adorable,' I say, but save for a light pressing together of her glossy lips, there is no obvious thaw in Ky's mood.

I look over her shoulder and see the other women watching me with interest. I'll never remember everyone's names, but I needn't have worried.

'Everyone else here lives close to Buckingham Crescent.' Tanya waves a limp hand around the table. 'You'll get to meet them all in time, I'm sure.'

One or two of the women smile and nod hello at me, but most go back to their conversations with rather sour faces, seemingly aware that they've been dismissed because they don't quite make the full Buckingham grade.

Barak appears, beaming in welcome before handing me a coffee in a slender glass with matching tiny saucer and a biscotti on the side.

I thank him, and Edie stands up and moves her chair next to me so the four of us, including Ky, form a tight little circle within the bigger group.

'So, Janey' – she smiles – 'tell us a bit about yourself. Where did you live before?'

'We lived in North Notts,' I say, wiping froth from my upper lip. 'Near Mansfield.'

'Coal-mining country,' Ky remarks and I'm convinced I can hear a little sneer in her tone.

'That's right,' I say, meeting her stare. 'My father was a face worker in the mine. He lost his life down there when the machine belt malfunctioned.'

'My God, how awful.' Tanya's hand flies to her mouth. 'You poor thing, it must've been so traumatic.'

'I was still a baby.' I shrug. 'Mum brought me up alone.'

I pick up my cup again and hold it close to my mouth. I can feel a pressure building in my head. I wish we could talk about something or someone else apart from me.

'Any siblings?' Tanya asks.

I shake my head. 'Just me. My mum died just over five months ago.'

'So sorry to hear that, Janey,' Edie says softly. 'That's quite some upheaval, moving house so close to the loss of your mum. I hope you're looking after yourself.'

Her kindness takes me by surprise, almost chokes me. I give her a little nod, take a sip of my coffee and keep my eyes lowered, willing myself not to cry.

'My mum died over five years ago, but I think about her every day.' Edie reaches across and squeezes my hand. 'Any time you want to chat, I'm here. I mean it. Any time.'

'Thanks so much, Edie,' I manage, and meet her eyes to convey my sincerity.

'And your husband?' Ky says in clipped tones. 'What does he do for a living?'

I tell them about Isaac's new job, glad the spotlight is off me for now.

'It's a big hike in salary and responsibility,' I say. 'He's hoping he can rise quickly in the organisation.'

'Abacus, you say?' Ky raises an eyebrow. 'Haven't heard of that one.'

'It's a fairly new company, but they made the top hundred new start-ups in *The Times* two years ago.' For some reason I feel like I'm defending Isaac's career decision. Tanya and Edie are friendly, but I'm clearly on the back foot with Kyoko.

'Sounds like he'll make a real success of it. Good for him, taking the plunge,' Edie says. 'You'll be buying one of the bigger houses on the crescent in no time at all.'

16

Later, I buy an ice lolly from the shop on the corner as a treat for Rowan to hopefully cheer him up.

Each day I've picked him up, he's been progressively more miserable, to the point where I'm beginning to wonder if it's ever going to improve, although Miss Packton continues to assure me it will happen.

The classroom doors are still shut as I turn the corner and walk across the playground. I get a little thrill when I think how I'm one step closer to being on the other side of those doors, actually working with kids in the classroom again. I glance around and see the usual clusters of waiting parents, including the Buckingham mums.

Edie sees me and gives me a little wave, and I wave back. She breaks away from the group and I meet her halfway across the playground.

'I just wanted to say, pop over to mine any time for a coffee. It'd be so nice to get to know you a bit better,' she says easily. 'I'm in all day tomorrow if you're free for an hour.'

'Oh, that's kind. Thanks, Edie. If you're sure, I could probably pop over late morning.'

'Of course I'm sure. You'd be doing me a favour, saving me from paperwork.'

The classroom doors fly open and all the parents turn towards them.

'Tomorrow, then,' Edie calls above the increasing noise level as children appear and start shouting to each other and their parents.

So far, Rowan has always been the last child out of the classroom, so today I'm shocked when he's one of the first to bounce off the classroom step in a friendly jostle with another boy – the one we saw riding up and down the crescent on his scooter. The two of them are chatting and laughing together, and Rowan barely glances up to see where I'm standing.

He says something to the other boy and slaps him jauntily on the back, then bounds up to me, full of energy, with ruddy cheeks.

'Hi, Mum!' he says. 'I've made *loads* of new friends today.'

'That's great news, sweetie.' My heart feels fit to burst, so much so that I want to run in and tell Miss Packton her reassurances were spot on after all. 'That boy you came out with… is he one of your new friends?'

Rowan nods, unable to stop the smile breaking over his face.

'We're *best* friends. His name's Dexter and everyone wants to be pals with him, but he says I'm his best friend now.'

I'm sure Dexter was a name Tanya mentioned in Ergon.

'Wow, a whole new set of pals made in one day… that was quick! And who are your other friends?'

'They're all Dexter's friends. They're my friends now too.'

I unwrap the ice lolly and hand it to him. His eyes widen in appreciation, but he looks almost too excited to eat it.

'We played footie on the field at lunch break, and Dexter says I'm the best striker he's seen. He's in the school football team and he says he's going to tell the coach I should be in it too.'

'Fantastic,' I say, awestruck by this boy Dexter. He seems to have an awful lot of influence for an eight-year-old.

I start to walk slowly away, gently steering Rowan as he finally turns his attention to the lolly.

'Can we stay here for a bit?' He looks alarmed. 'Dexter's just asking his mum if I can go over to his house for tea tomorrow after school.'

He turns and scans the playground behind us.

'There's Dexter with his mum.' He grins and starts waving.

I follow his gaze and see Tanya walking towards us with the boy. Behind them, Edie is smiling, but Kyoko stands staring in our direction, her perfectly made-up features looking more than a little piqued.

Tanya calls over to me. 'I hear from Dexter that he and Rowan are good friends now.'

'Yes, Rowan just told me.' I smile. 'That's great news.'

When they reach us, she flashes her startlingly white teeth. 'Dexter wants Rowan to come over for tea. How does tomorrow sound?'

I glance at Rowan to check, but he looks really eager. Incredibly, there's no trace of his usual apprehensive nature when it comes to socialising with new people.

'That sounds great, if you're sure,' I say, nodding. 'Thanks, Tanya.'

'Hey, why don't you come over too? After tea we can catch up with a glass of fizz while the boys play out in the garden.'

'Oh! That would be lovely, thanks,' I say easily, but underneath I'm already nervous.

Fizz at teatime? Sounds very upmarket. Trouble is, I'm such a lightweight when it comes to alcohol, I'll be asleep before Isaac gets home from work, and I'm not joking. But if this is the way things are done on Buckingham Crescent, then I might have to up my game, at least until I get to know everyone and can relax and be a bit more myself.

'That's settled then,' Tanya confirms. 'Come to school at the usual pickup time and we'll all go back to our house together.'

I'm so accustomed to squeezing every last word about his day at school out of Rowan, it's a pleasure to listen to him rattling on all the way home. *Dexter this* and *Dexter that*…

'Dexter has a cinema room in his *actual* house,' he declares in between bites of his ice lolly. 'And Dexter's uncle Dan plays for Nottingham Forest and gets him free match tickets. How cool is that?'

He barely takes a breath, but it's a joy to hear his energy and enthusiasm after four long days of dull misery.

17

Unbelievably, on Friday morning Isaac is still in bed when I wake up at 7.15. I've slept much later than I would've liked as he didn't set the alarm.

I heard him come home last night, and it was late. After midnight. I'd planned to cook and tell him my interview news, but as the hours ticked by after Rowan had gone to bed, I felt the enthusiasm drain out of me.

I listened, on edge, as Isaac clattered around in the kitchen, making himself a sandwich before padding softly upstairs and creeping into bed. I couldn't face listening to his apologies and promises about his late returns home never happening again, so I pretended to be asleep. It was simpler.

I sit up now, take a sip of water from my cooler bottle and swing my legs silently over my side of the bed.

'You stay put, I'll get up.' Springing suddenly awake, Isaac presses a hand on my shoulder from behind and hoists himself up. 'I'm going to make you a cup of tea and then sort out Rowan's breakfast. I've got a relaxed start because I have new client meetings but not until late morning, early afternoon. But I'm going to get ready for work now so I can take him to school and give you a morning off.'

I look at him in amazement. 'You know, for a weird moment, I actually thought I heard you say you're taking your son to school today.'

He rewards my sarcasm with a gentle swipe of his pillow.

'Look, I know I'm still miles off winning the Husband of the Year award, but I think you'll agree a cup of tea in bed for you while I get Rowan ready for school is a good start.'

I nod. 'Why were you so late home last night? What on earth were you doing until that time?'

Isaac pads barefooted over to the window in his pyjama bottoms to open the curtains before looking back at me.

'We had another unforeseen problem at work, I'm afraid, Janey. I think, until I get everything running the way I want it, this is going to keep happening. I'm sorry.'

He pulls open the blackout curtains and stands in the flood of daylight. I realise he's lost quite a bit of weight without me noticing. His bare back is smooth and pale and tapers into a newly neat waistline. No evidence of the slight love handles he's had for most of the years I've known him.

'You're wasting away to nothing,' I remark a little peevishly. I've been trying to lose a stubborn half a stone for ages now.

'No time for overeating. That's what it is,' he says lightly, slipping on a T-shirt. 'Or not until I've got this job licked, at least.'

'You should at least build a bit of relaxation into your schedule. Constant stress is bad for you.' I know my comment will fall on deaf ears, but I say it anyway.

Last summer, Isaac barely spent any time in the garden or in the sun at all. He was always out at work or squirreled away in his home office. Occasionally he might have sat in front of the television watching sport. He was a keen reader when I met him, but he can't seem to focus on anything now but work. I bought him the latest Lee Child hardback last Christmas, and I noticed he packed it for the move still swathed in its torn festive wrapping and clearly unread.

'But you taking Rowan to school *is* a great start.' I stretch out, luxuriating in the thought of staying in bed and listening to half an hour of my audiobook without interruption.

But Isaac hasn't finished yet.

'I'm aiming to get home around five today, so I thought the three of us could go out for tea later, somewhere like Pizza Express or TGI Fridays, maybe?'

'That's a lovely idea, but no can do tonight, I'm afraid.' I prop myself up on an elbow. 'Rowan's been invited over for tea by his new school friend, Dexter. I think the family are loaded, live in one of the biggest houses, but his mum, Tanya, seems nice enough, once you get past the snootiness.'

Isaac stops nibbling on a thumbnail. 'They seem a bit cliquey around here. I wouldn't get too involved if you can help it.'

'Cliquey?' I look at him. 'What's given you that impression?' He's never here during the day so hasn't been able to meet anyone yet, apart from briefly seeing Edie at her gate on Sunday.

'I dunno, it's an impression I get.' He shrugs. 'I know these sorts of people: moneyed, privileged, time on their hands. They all operate the same way, forming their little gangs, quibbling amongst themselves. We don't want them knowing all our business, Janey.'

I laugh, think he's joking. 'I'm only going because it's Rowan's first time at Dexter's for tea and Tanya was kind enough to invite me too.'

He stands up, laces his fingers together and stretches towards the ceiling. His T-shirt rides up, affording me a glimpse of his toned stomach and the scattering of dark downy hair I know so well that disappears under his waistband.

'Do you ever get the urge to just run away?' he says, still looking up at the ceiling. 'Not from us – I don't mean from the people you love.' He looks at me. 'I mean from all the responsibilities, all the expectations. All the stuff you said you'd do for people who don't matter and then regretted?'

'Isaac? What is it you're trying to say?' I think maybe he's going to open up to me about work at last.

He laughs. 'I'm just fantasising. You, me and Rowan on a desert island with nothing to do all day but swim, barbecue fish and drink coconut milk. Fancy it?'

I say, 'I've got a job interview on Monday.'

When Isaac gets back from the school run, his eyebrows are still knitted together.

'I just don't understand why you want to put that kind of pressure on yourself,' he says again. 'Losing your mum and all that upset then moving house… I'd have thought you'd have more than enough on your plate, and it's not as if we need the money now.'

All that upset. It's the phrase Isaac uses to neatly package up the devastating last day before Mum died. It's just how he deals with it. Some men might struggle with what I had to tell him, but not Isaac. In 'all that upset', he's found a viable solution for avoiding the unpleasant details. It's what he does in his day job: finds workable solutions for corporate IT problems. I wish I could do the same, instead of letting Mum's final words seep insidiously into every corner of my life, into every cell of my body.

'This job is something I want to do for me,' I say, my throat pinching as I try to justify myself. 'I think getting the career I loved back on track will have so many benefits in the long run. It's a way I can feel better about myself. Do some good.'

Going for this job feels proactive and positive, planning for a bright future rather than just trying to contain all the broken pieces of my life and trying to dodge the sharp edges.

'I think that's a great idea,' Isaac says, ignoring the hooks by the door and throwing his keys down on the worktop. I wait for the 'but'. 'But I just question whether now is the right time. I mean, there are still boxes unpacked in half the rooms upstairs and there are a thousand other jobs to be done before this place feels like a proper home.'

My chest sparks. 'Well, if you'd been around more, we could have made better progress,' I say, snatching up his keys and striding over to the hook with them. 'I'm doing the best I can, Isaac, I'm not the hired help.'

He moves towards me, his arms outstretched. 'I'm not criticising you, Janey, honestly I'm not. I want what's best for you, and if that's getting a little job again, then fine.'

A little job.

I jab the keys onto the hook and walk past him, ignoring his open arms.

He doesn't ask me anything else about the job, like when it starts, what the salary is or how many hours. He doesn't enquire if we'll need to make alternative arrangements for Rowan for the school run, or if he himself needs to amend his hours at all in light of the fact I'll be working again.

It's just assumed I will ensure my career fits around the needs of our son. It's taken as read that I'll make any necessary arrangements in terms of taking and picking Rowan up from school.

What it really amounts to is that Isaac's job is important and mine isn't.

'It was good to see our boy keen to get to school earlier,' he says in a new buoyed-up tone.

Rowan didn't need to be woken up this morning. I heard him bounding downstairs a good ten minutes before I usually go into his room to coerce him out of bed. When I popped down to see if they needed my help a little later, I found him already packing his rucksack with his reading book and lunch box. Apparently, he'd transformed overnight into the model pupil, organised and eager to get to school.

'Come on, Dad,' he urged as Isaac sat on the stairs to put on his shoes. 'I don't want to be late for registration.'

'I don't know what you've been going on about all week, saying he's been glum. Just look at him,' Isaac teased as I watched – not without wonder – the magical effect that making a new friend had had on my son.

Now he reports that Dexter, Kyoko's twins, Cherry and Jun, Aisha and a group of other children immediately rushed up to Rowan when he arrived in the playground and they all trooped into their respective classes together.

'Tanya came over and introduced herself just before the bell,' he adds casually.

Isaac looked handsome when he took Rowan to school in his suit this morning, a Ted Baker one he bought about five years ago but that had become a little tight in the past couple of years, until his recent weight loss. I even commented how smart he looked before he left. The thought of a perfectly groomed Tanya fawning over him makes my stomach churn.

I'm suddenly aware of my own scruffiness. Old leggings and an ancient T-shirt with a tear under the arm. Plus I forgot to remove my mascara before bed last night so I look extra rough this morning.

'That's nice,' I say thinly. 'She's very glamorous, isn't she?'

I can't stop thinking about how many hours he spends out of the house and what might be distracting him.

'I suppose she is, given how early in the day it is.' He grins, and a bitter taste swills around my tongue.

I frown. 'What did you talk about?'

He shrugs. 'She asked me about my work. Which company it is, what I do there. I suppose it's just a way of making small talk but like I've said, I don't want all the neighbours to know our business.'

'It's normal to ask other people what they do for a living when you're getting to know them,' I remark, busying myself with folding clean tea towels. 'She was probably just being friendly.'

He makes a small noise in his throat as if he's doubtful but willing to consider it.

When Isaac leaves for work, I go upstairs and sit on the floor with my legs stretched out, pressing my warm back against the cool plaster of our bedroom wall. I think about Isaac's comments about saying too much to the neighbours and my chest feels tight when I think about going to Tanya's house later.

I'm way out of practice when it comes to making new friends, and I get the feeling Isaac doesn't really approve of me hanging around with the other Buckingham mums.

Not as if I'm going to let that stop me. I'm looking forward to getting to know Tanya and the rest of the women. I think they may be just the tonic I need to get myself out of the rut I've been stuck in. I feel lucky that Tanya seems to have accepted me into her friendship circle so readily, and now that she's met Isaac, it's paved the way to us inviting her and her family round here for an early supper one weekend.

Rowan would love that, and I want to do everything I can to support his friendship with Dexter.

18

My closeness to my mother was all-consuming for as long as I can remember and there's not really been room for anyone but her and Isaac in my life in recent years.

Yes, I had friends at school and quite a few at college, but soon as I left, they fizzled out. It even happened at the school I worked at before Mum got ill and I gave up my job. I really liked the people I worked with there: colleagues I'd meet up with once a term for out-of-school drinks, the first time I'd done anything like that.

I'm not sure whether *I* distanced myself or they did, but losing touch with people is something I've just accepted happens throughout my life. It seems… safer somehow, relying on no one but yourself.

'If you can find someone to trust like you can trust me, then go ahead. Spill your guts to your so-called friends,' Mum would say if I arranged a night out with girls from college. 'But my advice is to watch what you say, because at some time in the future, people will use it against you. That you can depend on.'

'Ignore her,' Aunt Pat would whisper if she overheard. 'Have fun and reach out to like-minded people, Janey. The world is such an exciting place if you find the right ones to share it with, growing up. Don't end up miserable and alone like your mum.'

But despite Aunt Pat's advice, close female relationships remained an enigma to me.

I was so used to Mum preaching her litany of distrust from my early school days that, as I got older, I never stopped to think why she might hold such an opinion. And then, over the years that followed, I witnessed time and time again girls at school and college falling out and spreading confidences, secrets and lies about each other. Each time it happened I remember feeling lucky that, thanks to Mum's advice, I had insured myself against it happening to me.

It almost felt worth the nights sitting at home with Mum watching another replay of her favourite new show *Strictly Come Dancing* while my peers were out partying and having fun.

I bite down fury thinking about it now. All her warnings, her fears, all the things she said, were just her way of stopping me enjoying life. She was punishing me for the awful truth she'd been forced to swallow down.

The question now is, do I let her legacy continue… maybe subconsciously even pass it on to Rowan? Or is it time to break Mum's twisted logic?

Now feels the right time to let all that go and make some long-term friends. Learn to relax a little and be who I want to be.

If only it were as easy to do as to say because I've no sooner embraced the thought than I can hear Mum's warning ring out as clear as if she is standing right next me. I guess old habits die hard.

You're asking for trouble getting involved with that stuck-up shower at the school gates. Mind you watch what you say, our Janey.

I glance over at the unopened packing box that contains her things and feel my stomach flip over.

19

At 10.45, I finish cleaning the family bathroom and wash my face and apply some fresh make-up: minimal, but enough that it brightens my skin a bit. I pin up my hair, leaving a few wispy bits, and leave the house.

Edie's house is at the other end of the crescent to Tanya's grand place, which is nestled amongst more ordinary properties. Edie's, on the other hand, is surrounded by the biggest and best houses, with her mansion, which we saw when the gates were open at the weekend, being the jewel in the crown.

The houses at this end all have large front gardens and driveways, and Edie's has seven-foot-high wooden gates with keypad entry. They're closed today and from the pavement, I can only see the roof of the house.

I press the bell on the intercom and Edie's voice answers right away.

'Hi, Edie, it's Janey,' I say, already fretting that she's forgotten I was coming, or that she was expecting me a bit later in the morning.

'Come on in!' She sounds pleased, and the gates begin to swing open. I wait until there's enough room to slink through the middle before they're fully open and, like I did when we stopped to chat at the gate that day, I gape at the landscaped gardens that surround me. Every inch of the grounds is immaculate. A gravelled circular driveway snakes around a tall stone fountain and is framed by shaped and trimmed topiary bushes of all shapes and sizes.

The front door opens and Edie appears, wiping her hands on a tea towel.

'Janey… welcome!' When I reach her, she hugs me warmly and plants a solid kiss on my cheek, quite different to the other women's air-kissing. 'Come through. Ignore the mess.' She indicates some full bin bags in the hallway. 'I'm having a wardrobe clear-out ready for the new-season styles. Let's get some coffee on.'

I allow myself a little smile as I slip off my shoes and follow her through the large marbled entrance hall with a staircase each side leading to a smart mezzanine landing above. My own wardrobe has seen me through the last few summers and winters. Although I know Edie means fashion seasons. It's another world.

'Make yourself comfy on the sofa,' she says, leading me into a stunning pale grey and white lounge, the size of most people's entire ground floor. She perches on the arm of a silver curved sofa you could fit eight people on.

'Wow.' I let out a breath and sit down on another, smaller velvet couch with a crystal-buttoned back and chrome-coloured Queen Anne legs. 'This is… your house is just incredible, Edie.'

Edie glances critically around the walls, lingering on the recessed television wall that houses an outsize flat screen and a modern oblong fire inset below it.

'Yes, it is quite nice, I suppose. We gutted the place when we moved in four years ago, so it's way overdue for a spruce-up. Coffee?'

I thank her and she disappears into the kitchen where I hear the chink of crockery. I sit back in my seat and take a proper look around.

Seriously, I can't spot a sign of wear and tear anywhere. The walls are decorated in a delicate satin wallpaper embossed with a tasteful silver feather pattern and it's as immaculate as a show home. We only decorated once in the eight years we were at our old house and it will be a good while before we get each room done in the new place.

The sun breaks through the clouds outside and fractured rainbows dance over the walls as the light hits the huge crystal chandeliers hanging low on either side of the room. A black granite panther stretches out in front of the glass patio doors and draws my attention to the enormous back garden. I'd hazard a guess it's at least twice as big as Tanya's.

Velvety green lawns are framed by immaculate borders and trimmed bushes and trees. There's a pink and grey log cabin half hidden by the foliage which has got to be the most perfect hideout I can imagine for a kid. Aisha is a very lucky little girl.

I scrunch my toes into the deep pile of the pale grey carpet thinking how *House Beautiful* magazine could literally step in this room right now and take a photo fit for their cover without tweaking a single detail. If they came to our place, they'd have to clean it top to bottom first and then tidy away Rowan's discarded trainers, Isaac's scattered paperwork on the table and my dressing gown which I remember draping over the arm of the sofa and then forgetting to take upstairs with me again. And that's just for starters.

Edie appears in the doorway and carries over a tray. She lowers it onto the coffee table, then sits on the sofa opposite me.

'Well, this is nice, us having a little catch-up,' she says, passing a mug to me. 'Help yourself to milk and sugar.'

'Thanks so much for asking me over.' I add milk to my drink and Edie proffers a small plate laden with cookies.

'White chocolate and lemon,' she says without taking one herself. 'I can't take credit, the housekeeper baked them yesterday.'

I take a bite. Delicious.

'Low calorie, too,' she jokes, pushing the plate towards me and away from herself.

'Do you work from home?' I ask, remembering her comment about my visit saving her from paperwork.

'I do sometimes, yes. But I have a rule that I only work when Aisha is at school. Soon as she's home, I like to give her my full attention.'

I nod. 'What is it you do?'

I hope Edie doesn't mind me asking but a place like this is bound to make you wonder where the money comes from.

'Me and my husband have our own company. Wealth management just about covers it. We used to both work for other companies but then Alistair had this idea to start up on our own and it was the best thing we did.'

'So, wealthy clients give you their money to invest?'

'Yes, pretty much that's it. Interest rates are so dire now, and property is no longer the investment it was. So we look for companies that are doing well and buy shares that have a good chance of increasing in value for our clients. And we're good at what we do. Simple as.' She picks up her mug and cradles it between her hands.

Talk about getting rich from other people's money!

'Good for you,' I say, sipping my coffee. 'Sounds like you work hard and totally deserve your beautiful home.'

'Thank you, Janey,' she says. 'That's sweet of you to say. I know your husband is in IT, how's his new job going?'

She fixes her eyes on mine, so startlingly emerald, I wonder if she's wearing coloured contact lenses.

'It's going well, I think. It's hard to tell, you know? He's working very long hours, longer than he'd hoped, I think.'

She seems to sense my drop in mood, talking about Isaac's work.

'Well, we're always on the lookout for talented IT people, so if he gets fed up, send him our way.'

'I will, thanks, Edie.' I study her face, expecting a grin, but she looks deadly serious.

I will definitely tell Isaac what she's just said although I'll have to tread carefully. He's seems to be trying to rule out getting too friendly with the people here.

'And what about you?' Edie says, sipping her black coffee. 'Do you work?'

I tell her about my career working with children and how I gave it up to be Mum's carer. Working in school sounds so... I don't know, so *ordinary* compared with her own high-risk, high-reward work. But I am proud of what I do.

'I'm hoping to return to it soon,' I say, not yet quite prepared to tell her about my interview in case I jinx things for myself.

'It's really admirable,' she says. 'Playing such an important role in children's lives. I commend you, Janey!'

Shyly, I thank her.

'I think going back to work will really help you get over your mum's death.'

Edie talks briefly about the loss of her own mum, who died from coronary heart disease five years ago. 'People always say you should cherish every day with loved ones, but I never fully understood that until it was too late.' She looks around the room disparagingly. 'Losing Mum spurred me on to strive for a better life for my family but none of this comes close to having her here.'

Regret blights her features for a second, her bright eyes dimming, the corners of her mouth drooping. Then she seems to catch herself and the dazzling smile is back.

I think about growing up now as wasted years when, instead of doing the right thing, Mum instead poured her shame and confusion into criticising me and warning me against getting close to other people.

I was just fourteen when Aunt Pat tragically died in a car accident. She and a boyfriend had been travelling at speed and he had lost control of the vehicle on a sharp bend. They'd both been killed on impact. I felt devastated, the only light in my life snuffed out. But even then, Mum used Aunt Pat's death as an excuse to drone on, constantly criticising the way she lived her life.

'At least she had fun! At least she enjoyed her life instead of living like a hermit,' I remember screaming at Mum in a rare moment of rebellion.

She didn't speak to me for nearly a week after that and I never forgave her for making the executive decision that we would not be going to Aunt Pat's funeral. I didn't know it was happening until it was too late.

The conversation grows lighter as we discuss our kids, and I keep an eye on the clock, conscious of not overstaying my welcome like Polly did. An hour quickly passes, and I thank Edie for her hospitality.

'I'm going to throw a dinner party and get everyone together in the next couple of weeks or so,' she says, giving me another hug at the door. 'Don't forget to give Isaac my message. The door is always open here for someone like him. I always think it's a terrible thing, talent going to waste.'

20

If I was nervous about Tanya looking down her nose at me, then I have to admit I'm pleasantly surprised. She makes us feel very welcome.

'Make yourself at home, Janey,' she says, flinging open the front door and ushering me in as Rowan bolts after Dexter. 'I want you to feel comfortable here.'

The house is massive. Not quite as big as Edie's, it has to be said, but the moment I walk in and see the glossy kitchen units, the state-of-the-art cooking range and oversized island with breakfast bar, the nightmare of inviting people back to our house starts to loom. Obviously, with Tanya inviting me here today and Edie threatening to throw a full-scale dinner party, I have to show some return hospitality. The best I can hope to do is get the house cleaned up and organised to make the most of what's there; I could never compete with Edie's place or with *this*.

Everything is just so perfect, right down to the food. Tanya has organised mini pizzas and fries for the boys and prepared fresh chicken Caesar salads for us. No digging about in the freezer, or moving mounds of coats and bags tossed onto the table, the sort of thing that would be par for the course in our house after school.

'You're so organised,' I marvel when I see the kids' food is already prepared on baking trays and ready to go into the oven, with our salads just waiting for dressing.

'Benefits of having a housekeeper.' She winks at me as she shoos the boys outside, makes us a coffee and potters around sorting out the tea. 'Three days a week and we get a house that runs like a finely oiled machine. Marianne is worth every penny, trust me. I could ask if she's got any spare hours going, if you like?'

That's both Edie and Tanya who employ a housekeeper. Even with our increased household budget, I can imagine Isaac would probably have a hernia if I told him I intended buying in help. I know Edie works but it begs the question of what Tanya does all day when Dexter is at school.

'I hardly have a minute spare during the day,' she says as if she's just read my mind. 'I'm involved in so many local groups and initiatives, and that's before the endless hair, nails and beauty appointments. And the gym, of course.' She shakes her head, genuinely worn out with the thought of it.

Talk about first-world problems. I smile to myself inwardly.

'I'm always telling Tristan, all of this' – she wiggles her fingers up and down her face and body – 'takes work. Lots of *hard* work. If he wants a frumpy wife, it can be arranged.'

We share a little giggle and I offer to help serve up the boys' meals, but she waves me back to my coffee.

I feel the tension give a little in my neck and shoulders as I call them in from the garden. Tanya is witty, and I admire the way she has strong opinions and isn't afraid to voice them. Over the years I've kept my lip buttoned so many times, having learned from Mum not to draw attention to myself, never stand out from the crowd. So it's refreshing to see someone speak so freely. Tanya seems to know exactly who she is and what she believes in, and doesn't need anyone else's approval.

We all eat together in the kitchen and Tanya easily engages Dexter and Rowan into talking about what they've been up to at school. To my amazement, Rowan describes their PE lesson in great detail, naming all the exercises they've learned how to do using their own body weight: squats, lunges, burpees… the list goes on. The most I can get out of him is usually just a surly grunt or two.

Everything is going so well – until Tanya drops a bombshell as we're clearing the table.

'So, how do you fancy a glass of fizz in the hot tub?' She walks to the enormous American-style fridge and pulls out a bottle of pink Moët still in its box, holding it aloft like a trophy. I think Isaac and I have only had this once, and that was for our first wedding anniversary, years ago. Sadly, even pink champagne is not worth baring my pale, flabby body for. I haven't shaved my legs and underarms for about three days.

Hastily, I mumble an excuse. 'I haven't brought a cozzie… maybe next time.'

'Oh, that's no problem at all.' Tanya opens the box and extracts the bottle. 'I've got a ton of swimwear upstairs. You can take your pick.'

I can't help flicking my eyes over her diminutive frame. I'd say she's a size 8 – a 10 at the most. I, on the other hand, would worry about squeezing my curvy bits into a size 14 at the moment. I silently lambast myself for eating so much rubbish over the moving period and snacking in the afternoons. I finish off Rowan's leftovers at teatime most days too.

I watch helplessly as Tanya fills a cooler with ice and pushes the bottle of champagne into it.

'We'll give that ten minutes to chill nicely while we get changed. Come on, follow me.' Her voice is upbeat; she's blissfully unaware of my discomfort.

I follow her upstairs feeling like a lamb to the slaughter. Her calves are shapely, the muscles taut as she springs on to each polished wooden step.

Tanya's bedroom is a vast mirrored enclave that runs half the length of the back of the house. As she strides across the sumptuous silver-grey carpet, leaving footprints, I catch a glimpse of hanging clothes and handbags through one open door, and a sparkling run of white cupboards and double sinks through another. The word 'bedroom' is far too humble for what is essentially a master suite that practically all the bedrooms at our house could fit inside.

She slides open a floor-to-ceiling mirrored wardrobe and opens a drawer, flinging an armful of brightly coloured swimwear onto the super-king-sized bed. 'Take your pick!'

I sort gingerly through the silky fabrics, pushing aside tiny triangles that just about pass for bikini bottoms and picking up one-piece swimsuits that have so much fabric cut out, I have to turn them this way and that way before I can understand how they'd sit on the human body.

I become aware that Tanya is finally still and silent. I look up, but can't erase the forlorn look I can feel on my face quickly enough.

'What's wrong, Janey?' She looks baffled. 'Don't you like any of them?' She picks one up. 'This is Gucci. The colours would look fab on you and—'

'It's not that, Tanya,' I say, turning away slightly. 'It's just that… well, I don't think any of them will actually fit me.'

'Oh!' This time, it's Tanya who's taken aback. The smile slides from her face as the awful reality hits her: shock, horror… outside of her pink bubble, not everyone is a perfect size 10. But she's not beaten for long and springs towards the bedroom door. 'I've got just the thing. Wait here!'

She's irrepressible and it's exhausting. Why can't we just sit out in the garden and have our drink?

I hear a door opening further down the hall and I move over to the large window, which has a great view of the hills and fields in the distance. What must it feel like to live in a house as perfect as this? I'd need a week's notice to clear up if one of the other mums from school came upstairs to my bedroom. I'd be mortified at someone seeing the way we're living right now, still upside down from the move. Mismatched bedding, half-empty boxes and cheap

IKEA rails instead of wardrobes. My heart sinks afresh when I think about the task ahead of us.

Although the side of Tanya's garden that borders with Polly's land is screened by conifers, there's a section of smaller trees at the end that look as if they've been planted to lengthen the area of privacy.

When I look over there, I see a flash of mauve dart behind one of the taller trees. Polly, in her favourite cardigan.

'Here we go!' Tanya reappears in the doorway, her face a shining beacon of achievement. She holds a silky bronze swimsuit up in the air, reassuringly generous in its size, with actual fabric to cover the body.

'Oh, that looks more like it.' Relief relaxes my voice and I turn away from the window.

'I bought it when I was pregnant and couldn't fit into my usual gear. I'm glad I kept it now,' she says in a jolly tone, completely oblivious to the implication behind her words. 'You can pop it on in here.'

She pushes open the dressing room door, revealing rows and rows of heeled shoes in addition to the handbags and rails of clothes clearly organised according to colour, including at least a dozen of the distinctive velour lounge suits several of the women seem keen on wearing for the school run. Although I'm no expert, I recognise the studded creations of Valentino and the startling red soles of Christian Louboutin nestling amongst the shoes.

I feel like an imposter amid such tens of thousands of pounds' worth of gear, and I hastily shrug my clothes off and climb into the swimsuit, avoiding glancing in the full-length mirrors until I've sucked in my stomach and tugged the fabric gently to encourage it over my ample hips. But the dread in the pit of my stomach finally dissipates when I slip my arms through the straps and I'm finally wearing it. Mission accomplished. Now all I need is to whisk myself into the hot tub as quickly as possible.

'Your legs are fabulous, so shapely and toned!'

I nearly jump out of my skin as Tanya sticks her head around the dressing room door without warning.

'Thanks. I… well, I feel a bit self-conscious really. I've not been eating very well, and—'

'Hey!' Tanya holds up a hand. 'You look great, and you're here to have some fun, not put yourself down.'

I nod, momentarily speechless. I assumed Tanya would be scathing about anyone who looked less than perfect in the buff. She'd be well within her rights, standing there in her white one-piece with its cut-out sides, a fine gold anklet sparkling on her bronzed ankle.

When I met Isaac, much to his delight, I used to wear short skirts to show my legs off. I considered them my best feature back then. I hardly ever wore leggings or trousers. Now, if I could only forget about the rest of my apple shape – the rounded tummy, matronly boobs and woeful lack of waist – I suppose I might make more of them again.

21

Outside, the boys bound up to us like overstrung puppies.

'Can we go in there too?' Rowan squeals, peering in when Tanya presses a button and the jets start up as she slides the hot tub cover back. Dexter, who's clearly more accustomed to this, stands back a little, grinning.

'Why don't you see how many garden birds you can spot?' I suggest. 'Take some paper and pencils down the bottom of the garden… You can show Dexter how well you can draw.'

'It's water guns and soldier games for you two while we have some mummy time,' Tanya says firmly. 'Off you go into the bushes and be boys. Have fun. Be nice.'

I slip off the white waffle robe she provided me with and clamber quickly into the steaming froth of the hot tub. I'm so eager to get my pasty body in there, I slip and nearly go under.

Tanya hoots with laughter as she lowers herself elegantly into the water, and within seconds we're giggling like schoolgirls. It really breaks the remaining ice. The final bit of tension in my shoulders evaporates and I relax my head back against the corner cushion and sigh contentedly.

Tanya reaches down behind the tub and hands me an elegant flute filled with pink champagne, complete with a raspberry nestling in the bottom of the glass. As always, no detail has been overlooked.

'They get on so well, don't they?' I follow her approving gaze towards Rowan and Dexter, who are zooming around the enormous garden, pursuing each other aggressively with outsize water guns. 'It's as if they've been friends for ages. It's such a relief to have Dex spend time with a boy like Rowan. I love Ky's twins dearly, but they're so spoiled and not nearly as bright as she likes to think. Dexter was just as advanced at their age.'

I take a sip of fizz. I don't feel qualified to comment on other people's children just yet, but I'm pleased that Tanya looks on Rowan and Dexter's friendship favourably.

'It's great to see,' I agree, savouring the sharp dryness of bubbles popping over my tongue. The boys weave in and out of mature trees and shrubs, the perfect place for a friendly water fight. 'Rowan spends hours in front of his computer, so it's lovely that he's enjoying being outdoors.'

Tanya raises an eyebrow, and I realise that what I've just said sounds a bit negligent on my part.

'He's a bit of an IT whizz, so it's not just playing games,' I explain quickly. 'Isaac taught him a bit of simple HTML coding about a year ago, and he loved it and plagued him to show him more. Then he was selected for the G&T programme at his last school, so he's quite advanced now. According to Isaac, anyway.'

I don't want to say the title of the programme out loud – Gifted and Talented – as it sounds a bit of a brag. But Isaac and I were so proud when Rowan was picked for it last autumn. In practical terms it meant additional IT tutoring and extracurricular support activities in computer studies. Of course, Rowan enjoys gaming too, but I've always tried to keep a strict eye on how his time is spent on the computer. Just before we moved house, his teacher reported back that he's at least three years ahead of his age group in terms of various IT skills that don't mean much to me as a bit of a technophobe.

'Really? Gifted and talented in computer programming?' Tanya's eyes widen and she turns her attention away from the boys and the garden and on to me. 'That's amazing. Most of Dexter's friends are sporty, so he has a definite gap in his friendship circle for an IT genius.'

It seems an odd thing to say about a group of seven- and eight-year-olds, I think, but she smiles and I think she must be joking.

'Given that he runs an IT company himself, Tristan despairs of Dexter's lack of interest in technology. Ten years ago, Tristan designed a software package, TrendPal, to help businesses figure out which product lines to increase and which to drop at differing points in the retail year. It made him a fortune and he's never looked back. He started his own company and carried on devising business analysis tools.'

I raise my glass to my lips. Tristan's business must be doing extremely well, judging by the size of this super-modern house of theirs. It seems quite big for just the three of them.

Tanya beams and reaches for the bottle of champagne propped in the ice bucket behind her. She tops up her empty glass, but I put my hand over my own, which is still half full. 'I'm fine, thanks.'

'You'd better get a move on; there's another bottle that needs drinking in the fridge,' she says, taking another deep draught from her own glass.

I'm never quite sure whether Tanya is serious or joking, but I suppose that's why I've come round here – to get to know her better.

'It's so hard, isn't it? Ticking all the boxes, I mean.' She has already moved on. 'I was thinking of getting Dex an IT tutor on top of his maths and literacy ones, but I reckon now that Rowan's expertise and enthusiasm might just rub off on him and do a better job of it.'

'Couldn't Tristan get Dexter interested in the subject?'

There's a beat before she answers me, and when she does speak, I swear her eyes have dulled slightly.

'You must be joking. He's far too busy to spend his precious time with his son.' She sweeps a hand towards the house behind us, and I realise the drink is taking the edge off her usually carefully crafted manner. 'We all pay the price for this lifestyle, for his success. Sometimes Dexter barely sees his father for days on end, if he's working away with clients in Europe.'

I nod sympathetically. 'I know how that feels. Well, not days on end, but it often feels like we're passing ships in the night. Isaac promised that things would be different when he started at the new company, but I'm afraid there's been no evidence of that as yet.'

'We've all been fed that line.' For a moment, the mask slips and a wash of sadness moves across her face. 'Sometimes I question if it's worth it, though. A great big house and the mortgage to go with it… and just three of us rattling around in it most of the time, as there are certain times of the year when Tristan is hardly here.'

Three of them? 'I didn't realise Dexter had a sibling.'

'My daughter, Angel,' Tanya says as if I should have known. 'She's fifteen. Sixteen in a couple of months' time.'

'Wow, nearly sixteen,' I repeat, wondering why there's such a big age gap between Angel and Dexter.

'I know, I know, I don't look old enough,' Tanya jokes, flicking her hair. 'I had her when I was very young… a previous relationship. She doesn't see her biological father. Never has.' Is it my imagination, or do her cheeks colour slightly? 'Thank goodness I have her,' she continues, knocking back the last bit of fizz in her glass. 'She's my best friend. And God knows I need one at times.'

It's an odd thing to say, I think. Tanya seems to have dozens of friends. Women are drawn to her at school, gather around her while she holds court. Sometimes, though, you can feel your loneliest in the middle of a crowd. I should know.

'Do you miss your old friends?' she says. 'Moving here, I mean?'

'Not so much. I sort of let my friendships slip really. It was a casualty of becoming a full-time carer.' I explain briefly about Mum's illness. 'Looking after her took every minute of my time.

Mum was always demanding of attention, but especially so towards the end.'

'I can only imagine.' Her face creases with concern. 'Was Isaac a big support to you? Sometimes things can slip at home before you realise it, right?'

It feels like she really does understand, and I've already begun to say the words before I can even think of choking them back.

'Isaac and I, we used to be so... so close. We've talked about it and both of us agreed we need to carve out some time to do stuff together again as a family, but also as a couple.' She nods sympathetically and I feel warm and comfortable and spurred on to continue. 'But the way things are going with his new job, I doubt it's going to be any different from before. I already feel so alone in our new house instead of excited for the future, although I have to say, he did suggest we go out for tea together today. Before he realised you'd kindly invited us round here.'

I clamp my mouth shut, feeling both ashamed and alarmed at my candour to someone who is essentially a stranger. But Tanya reaches over and pats my hand, diamonds glinting on several of her manicured fingers.

'It's not just you. We're all of us the same, darling,' she says in a confidential manner, reaching down for the bottle again. 'That's why we have to make our own life, build our own social circle for support. For pure *survival*. Ready for a top-up now?'

I nod and Tanya pours.

'We Buckingham mums take the children swimming on a Saturday. It's an organised class with a coach, so there's no danger of the adults having to get wet and chlorinated or anything unpleasant like that. It's all very civilised.' She grins. 'Once the kids are in the water, we sit with coffee and cake and have a good old natter, put the world to rights. How's that sound?'

'Sounds great.' I smile, touched that she's thought to include me.

'Your lonely days are over, Janey. You're a Buckingham mum now.'

I scrunch up my shoulders shyly and give her a grateful smile, but inside I feel like a fraud. I'm not really one of them. I'm too ordinary, and frankly, a bit dull in comparison to all their gloss.

'Give us a few weeks to transform your diary and you'll be kicking and screaming for some quiet time to yourself.' She grins, topping her own glass up again.

I smile, wondering if I'll have a job to fit diary entries around soon.

'Do you do everything together? I mean, all the mums you stand with outside school?'

'Not all of those are Buckingham mums,' Tanya says with a sniff. 'They're nice enough, but there's a little tight knot of us at the centre who are *really* good friends.'

She's talking about a clique. The sort I've always been excluded from in the past, at work and at Rowan's old school. I'm astonished Isaac picked up on this so early on.

'It's really just me, Edie, Ky, and now you. The rest are acquaintances who live on surrounding streets. We hang around together because our kids know each other, that's all.'

'I feel like I've joined an exclusive private club, living here.' I laugh, enjoying the pressure of the water jets on my skin and the alcoholic warmth that's disposing of my inferiority complex with record speed.

'You'd better believe it. We look after our own here.' We both fall quiet for a moment, savouring the relaxation and the sun breaking through the light cloud. The boys dash in and out of the bushes at the bottom of the garden, and it feels… right. It suddenly feels right for me to be here. 'You remind me a little of myself, Janey. Before I had all this,' Tanya adds, indicating the house and garden. 'I haven't always been confident in my own skin; I've had some tough obstacles in my past to get through. I know how it feels to struggle.'

My head is buzzing lightly, pleasantly, but I still receive her point loud and clear. She's trying to say she understands my hang-ups and wants to help.

'Don't think I can't see you!' Tanya suddenly barks out. Her face darkens as she glares beyond my shoulder.

Alarmed, I turn around. 'Who are you shouting at?'

'Polly, next door,' she says, her mouth twisting up at one side. 'Nosy cow, skulking behind the trees as if I can't see her.'

'Oh, Polly came round to the house and brought me some flowers.' I can't just sit here and pretend I don't know who Polly is but it sets me off thinking again, about the torn blooms all over the lawn. Polly had definitely seemed to direct blame in this direction. She probably suspects Dexter of causing damage to her garden, but I'm not going to be the one to tell Tanya.

'Stay away from her, Janey.' Tanya's vitriolic tone takes me aback and I widen my eyes. 'She lures you in, nice and friendly, then when you're least expecting it, she'll stab you in the back. Another drink?'

22

Tanya suddenly sits up to attention, causing the steaming water to splash around, and I spill a little of my drink.

'Hello there, darling,' she calls, her face brightening at someone behind me. 'Are you coming in?'

I turn toward the object of Tanya's attention, dread pooling in my stomach at the thought of Tristan joining us in the hot tub. But it's a tall, slim teenage girl with a long, poker-straight blonde ponytail standing in her school uniform on the swathe of pale ceramic patio that hems the back of the house. She shields her eyes with a hand to watch the boys darting around at the bottom of the garden.

'No thanks, Mum, Bianca's invited me over. She's having a little get-together at her house. It's just girls from school.'

'This is my sweet Angel,' Tanya tells me before turning back to her daughter. 'Are Bianca's parents home? Because I'm not happy if they're out and—'

'Don't worry, they're home.'

Tanya's face relaxes. Call me cynical, but it sounds to me as if Angel is saying just what her mother wants to hear. Her voice is mechanical, bored even.

Tanya calls out, a touch too loudly, 'Come and say hi to my new friend Janey.'

'Hi, Janey.' The same dead eyes, emotionless tone.

'There she is, Janey… my Angel.' Tanya smiles, a dreamy look on her face. 'Beautiful, intelligent and my best friend.'

Angel opens her mouth as if she's about to issue a retort, and then thinks better of it and merely gives her mother a quizzical look. Am I to conclude Tanya changes her best friend quite frequently? I'm still trying to process what she said about Polly.

'Lovely to meet you, Angel,' I say pleasantly from the tub. 'I won't shake your hand as mine is all wet. That mad boy down the garden chasing your brother is my son, Rowan.'

'They've just moved into the crescent,' Tanya says, the edges of her words slightly blunt. 'With Janey's lovely husband Ivan… I mean Isaac.'

Angel screws up her pretty features. 'Mum, how much have you had to drink? It's only teatime.'

Tanya lets out a raucous laugh. 'See how she keeps me in line, Janey? She's so sensible, my girl. Darling, have you eaten?'

Angel raises an eyebrow. 'I'm going to grab a few snacks to take over to Bianca's before I go.'

'Don't be too late back,' Tanya calls, splashing more champagne into her glass.

Angel heads down the garden towards the boys. She calls them over and chats to them for a few seconds, and although we're too far away to hear, it's obvious by the way the boys are nodding and laughing that they approve of whatever it is she's saying.

'I'm trying not to make too big a deal of it,' Tanya says, 'but she's spending a lot of time at her friends' houses recently. She seems… I don't know, very secretive. It's like someone flipped a switch just before she's about to turn sixteen. I seem to have become quite the enemy.'

'You're sure it's her school friends she's with?'

'Oh yes, I know all her friends' parents. We get together periodically to cry on each other's shoulders about how our kids are all growing up far too fast. It's been a while, though, actually. Maybe

I'll get everyone together again soon. I'm keeping an eye on her but trying not to treat her like a kid because that will only inflame her. She just doesn't realise she's still the centre of my world.'

We watch as Dexter hands Angel his water gun and Rowan lays his on the grass, then Angel turns her back and the boys disappear into the bushes. After a minute or so, she whips around and starts to systematically hunt through the bushes with the gun. Yelling and squealing and finally laughter reaches our ears as she obviously finds her targets.

'She's so brilliant with kids.' Tanya grins approvingly. 'She's just got this way with them, knows exactly how to entertain them, you know?'

I nod, watching as the boys emerge from the bushes, sopping wet but happy. Angel looks like a young woman, but she's still a kid at heart, just as it should be.

'Anything she turns her hand to she makes a success of. Playing the piano, reciting poetry, styling her friends' hair… nothing seems to faze her.' Tanya swigs her drink and presses her lips together as if to rein herself in. 'Mind you, it doesn't stop her being a pain in the backside at times!'

Angel strides back up the garden, still smiling to herself at the boys' reaction. 'That looked fun!' Tanya calls. 'Bring us another bottle out, will you, sweetie?'

I hear Angel tut and mutter in disapproval and the patio door slams closed behind us. I look at Tanya sympathetically, but she simply rolls her eyes.

'Teenagers, eh?' The last dregs of the champagne disappear into her empty glass. 'More fizz coming up.'

'No, honestly, Tanya, no more for me,' I protest. Although when I look down at my glass, I've almost drained it without really noticing.

'Nonsense! We've got loads more gossiping to do yet!'

Angel comes back with another bottle and hands it to her mother. Then she produces Tanya's distinctive Mulberry purse from behind her back.

'Have you got twenty pounds for me to take, Mum? We're getting pizza.'

Tanya unzips the purse with damp hands and wordlessly hands her the money, seeming to forget that Angel said she was taking snacks over to her friend's house.

Angel checks the notes and her face brightens when she sees Tanya has given her thirty pounds.

'No more this week, princess. You're bleeding me dry.'

'Everything's just so expensive,' Angel whines. 'I need my allowance revising.'

'You need a job, is what you need.' Tanya winks at me and then lets out a little yelp. 'I've just had a fabulous idea! Angel can babysit for you so you can have a date night with Isaac – that's just what you two need right now.'

'No, no,' I stammer. 'That's OK, Angel, you don't have to do that.' I wouldn't want to leave Rowan in the care of someone he doesn't know and I've barely met, although I can't deny Rowan seems to think she's great fun.

'Nonsense. She wouldn't mind, would you, darling? And you've just seen how great she is with the boys.'

'Yes, but… Honestly, Isaac's far too busy with work to arrange anything at the moment.' I turn to Angel. 'Maybe at some point in the future, if you have time, that is.'

'Yeah, we can sort something out.' She manages a little smile and disappears back inside.

Tanya leans towards me, dropping her voice. 'I wanted to take Angel to a modelling agency in London. I think she'd do so well at that sort of thing. But you know kids these days; she'd rather sit watching Netflix all day in her bedroom than think about her future.'

The look of longing on Tanya's face is almost too painful to witness, and I find myself wondering if the modelling ambition is hers rather than Angel's own.

'Anyway, she could come over and revise or something while Rowan's in bed. Give you two lovebirds a much-needed break.'

'Thanks,' I say, 'we'll see.' I'm tired now of fending Tanya off. She's like a terrier once she's latched onto something she deems a good idea. Hopefully she'll soon forget all about it. Somehow, through my alcohol-induced blabbing, I've managed to give her the impression that Isaac and I are at breaking point, which is thankfully not the case. Yes, we have our problems like lots of couples do. But we're a long way from needing Tanya's input, and Angel didn't seem fussed about babysitting at all.

Given a bit of time and effort when his job settles down, everything will be good as new again between us. I feel certain of it.

Angel calls goodbye and goes off to her friend's house. Tanya pops the new bottle open and beckons for my glass.

'No, no. I've had quite enough, thanks,' I say. 'I'm not used to drinking a lot any more.'

'Which is precisely why you need to build up your resistance,' she says, grabbing my glass. 'You need to drink more, not less, or you'll never get used to it.'

'I've got to be sensible now,' I giggle. 'If I'm going to be a school employee.'

'What's this?' she exclaims, handing me back my refilled glass. 'Who's a school employee?'

'Oops! Not me,' I say, closing my eyes and then opening them quickly when I get a woozy feeling in my head. 'Not yet, anyway. But I have an interview on Monday for a part-time teaching assistant post in Year 2.'

Her mouth falls open. 'You little dark horse! That's Cherry and Jun's class, you know. Ky was only complaining yesterday that the teacher seems to be struggling to cope since the last TA left for another job.'

I nod. 'That figures. They've said they need someone to start as soon as possible.'

Tanya swigs her drink and gives me a mischievous grin. 'Fancy, a Buckingham mum finally on the inside… We'll get to know *everything* now!'

I smile weakly and sip my drink. I hope she's joking.

23

Isaac hands me a gin and tonic when he comes down from taking Rowan up to bed.

I wave it away. 'No more alcohol for me, thanks. A cup of tea is what I really need.' He nods and heads back to the kitchen, returning with my hot drink.

'I take it you had a good day?' He settles down in a chair.

I nod. 'I think I can call myself a fully fledged Buckingham Crescent mum, now I've drunk pink champagne in Tanya's hot tub,' I add smugly, actually feeling quite proud of the fact. 'It's a ready-made club.'

'Hmm. Let's hope it's a club you like being part of.'

Isaac is being jolly, and yet I can sense a sharpness to his remarks, as if he's quietly mocking my new friendship. It makes me wonder what's behind it.

'So, we've covered *my* new friends. How are you finding your new colleagues at Abacus?'

The smirk fades from his lips when I turn the tables. It's clear he's still feeling very tense about work. 'Oh, you know, everyone seems nice enough. Haven't had a chance to meet everyone yet. Bob's had me scooting about all over the place, introducing me to all their major clients in the Midlands area.'

'What's Bob like to work for?'

'I suppose he's like every other boss I've ever worked for. A nice enough guy, but as you get to know them more, you also get to know their irritating little foibles, you know?'

'Like what?'

Isaac considers my question for a long moment.

'Well, Bob's got this thing about time. I'm supposed to start at eight when I'm in the office, as you know, but if I turned up at my contracted time, Bob would consider it late. He's in the office on the dot at six every day and never leaves before seven at night at the earliest.'

My heart sinks. 'So this promise of working from home was just a pipe dream?'

'Not at all. I've reminded him that's one of the reasons I wanted the job and he's assured me it will settle down soon.'

'Is Bob married? Maybe we ought to ask them round here for a meal. Soon as we get sorted, I mean.'

'Good idea. Maybe I'll flag it up with him.'

'Did I mention I went for coffee at Edie's house this morning, too?'

He looks at me steadily and glugs down the last of his gin.

'We got talking about work. Her work, my work and… your work.'

'What's my work got to do with anything?'

'She was just asking how it was going,' I say, setting down my cup. 'Don't take this the wrong way but I told her about your long hours and she said they were always on the lookout for good IT people.'

His mouth tightens. 'You told her I'm unhappy at my new company?'

'No! I said I thought it was going OK but that you're working longer hours than you expected.' I sigh, feeling tired all of a sudden. 'I knew you'd take it the wrong way.'

'I'm not taking anything the wrong way. I told you not to discuss our personal business with the people who live around here, I don't know why you find that so difficult.'

My hackles rise. 'Oh, I'm so sorry. Did I speak out of turn? I didn't realise I'm supposed to run everything I say past you now.'

Isaac stands up and raises his glass. 'I fancy another.'

I sit nursing my tea, listening to my husband in the kitchen preparing himself another drink, no doubt trying to swallow his anger before we end up having a full-scale row.

About a year ago, when the pressure at the old company really started to increase, I noticed he started drinking more at night. Before this we'd had a sort of informal agreement not to drink at home during the week if we could help it, but we'd enjoy sharing a bottle of wine with our evening meal over the weekend.

I've always been a bit of a lightweight when it comes to alcohol. Any more than two glasses of wine and I have a raging thirst during the night. Any more than three and I really feel the effects the next day. I'll definitely suffer for the teatime drinking today and I don't want to make a habit of it.

As a man, Isaac can obviously drink more than I can, but each of his drinks contain two large measures of gin and only a splash of tonic. When work was worrying him, he'd knock back at least three or even four of those a night. He became very argumentative, picking up on every last thing that irritated him. Just like his behaviour is now. Back then, I tried to raise the subject with him without seeming to lecture him.

'I was reading about units of alcohol the other day and the fact that most of us drink far more than the advised quota,' I said lightly as he sat at the breakfast bar one morning reading the newspaper on his iPad.

'Right,' he murmured.

'Yes, it got me wondering how much we drink and I thought it might be a good idea to calculate it to see if we're within safe limits.'

He looked at me then as if I'd said something unfathomable. 'A few drinks a night won't do any harm, and anyway, I drink far more than you do.' He lowered his eyes to his screen again. 'The experts tell us one thing one week and another the next, you know that.'

'Agreed, it's just that… I worry sometimes, Isaac. I worry you're drinking too much.'

I expected him to scoff at my concern, but a shadow crossed his face. 'I didn't realise you were keeping track of my habits, but I'm not going to apologise for having the odd drink in my own home at the end of a stressful day,' he snapped.

We didn't discuss it again, but I did notice he modified his drinking habits following our conversation.

I really hope he doesn't start drinking more at home again.

He strides in with another large measure and I can tell by the resolved look on his face that he's used his time in the kitchen to decide exactly what he's going to say to me.

'Janey, I really don't want to fall out about this but there's something I need to stress to you. I really, really don't want you to speak about my work at all to people. OK?'

'Fine,' I say without looking at him.

'You're right, things are a bit different to how I'd envisaged the job but I'll sort it out. I've always sorted things out and this will be no different. But I don't want every Tom, Dick and Harry on Buckingham Crescent knowing about it.'

Fury spills over inside me like a boiling pan of milk.

'For God's sake, Isaac, give me some credit! All I said, to one person, was that the hours were longer than you'd—'

'That's exactly what I'm talking about.' He clenches his jaw, unwilling to give an inch. 'Saying that one thing is too much information, Janey. Just say *nothing* about my work. OK? It's important to me.'

My eyes burn with fatigue and I just can't be bothered with his ridiculous paranoia. He's never been one to talk in great depth about work. As he's said in the past, he wants to forget about the pressure at the office when he's at home, not keep it going. I know he was desperately worried about redundancy rumours at his old place though and that's why it was so wonderful when he was offered the new job.

'I'm shattered. I'm going up to bed.' I stand up and walk across the room without kissing him goodnight.

'I'm sorry,' he sighs as I stride past him. 'I'm sorry I flipped out. I'm just stressed, that's all it is, Janey.'

I don't answer him, don't look at him. As far as I'm concerned, my line with my new friends will be that Isaac refuses to speak about his work at all. It won't be far from the truth.

I know he's struggling at the moment and I'm willing to give him some space, at least for the time being. Along with him supposedly working from home more and the benefits it would bring to us as a family, I was also hopeful Isaac would curb his drinking habits.

Maybe it's time for me to admit that so far, neither of these hopes have been realised.

But something is bothering him. I know that much.

24

The room was small and without windows. A single bare bulb hanging way above her head illuminated the concrete box she'd been caged in.

When they'd first brought her here, it had felt completely airless and she'd wondered if she'd suffocate from lack of oxygen, but now she knew there was a short pipe that protruded from the ceiling in the far corner. If she stood under that, she could sometimes feel the faintest strain of cool fresh air filtering in. But not always. She supposed it depended on which way the breeze was blowing, up there in the free world.

Susan thought about her life before, of course she did. She thought about the nursing college where she felt sure she'd have made new friends, and the course she would have started by now.

Most of all, she thought about how her parents were coping with her disappearance. Her mum's anxiety would be through the roof; her dad would be trying his best to reassure her that everything was going to be OK, to try and cope for both of them.

How soon had Melissa raised the alarm when Susan hadn't turned up to her party? She knew they'd all have realised pretty early on that she wasn't the type to run away, or let people down in any way.

Had anyone seen two young women walking up the main street in town and turning down a quiet side road? Had anyone passed by and seen a disturbance around a parked car?

Someone must have seen something… surely?

But despite these endless ruminations, mostly Susan thought about how long it might be before the man and the girl came down here again. Increasingly, as time went on, virtually every waking second was spent wondering how long she had before… well, before it happened again.

The only thing she felt certain of was that it would. Happen again. And again. And again.

Without any natural light, it was impossible to track exactly how long she'd been imprisoned down here, but she knew it was a long time. She'd tried making marks on the skirting board with a nail and even counting through the minutes and hours, but none of that was sustainable or effective. There was nothing to write with and nothing to read and she knew it would only be a matter of time before the bulb blew and plunged her into what would seem like never-ending darkness.

After a few days without much to eat or drink, she had started to feel very weak, and she found she slept a lot more. Which was a blessing.

There was nothing in the room but a brand-new bare mattress and pillow and a single blanket. And the bucket over in the far corner with half a roll of toilet tissue; there was that, too.

The air felt thick and stagnant today, as if you could cut through it with a knife. She wished she had a knife, fantasised what she might do with it when… when they came down again.

Beyond the bruising, the lacerations and pain, the constant internal aching, her body felt different, as if it had adapted to the surroundings. Her senses were on high alert to the faintest sound. A distant click, a creaking pipe… any sound at all sent her spinning towards a panic attack.

They had been down to visit – as they'd called it – nearly a dozen times since she was brought here. They came down together and the young woman filmed while the man…

Susan shook her head in a vain attempt to dispel the horror. She couldn't stand to think about it. About what he did to her.

But the girl was worse; in a way, she scared Susan more. At first glance, she seemed just like any ordinary pretty young woman you might pass in the street. She looked like someone Susan might go to college with. But then you noticed those eyes. Black as night and utterly soulless.

Like windows that looked straight down into eternal hell.

25

My worries about the pressures of Isaac's new job affecting him dissipate on Saturday morning when he does a 360-degree turn and announces he's taking the weekend off completely. 'No working at all,' he announces. 'I'm not even checking emails.'

'Wow, that's… great news,' I say, taken aback. Maybe this is the turning point I've been waiting for. He's only been in the job a short time after all but I'd already convinced myself things were getting worse, not better.

'We'll go for a kickabout with your old mates this afternoon if you like, give Mum a bit of peace, and then a family movie and a Chinese takeaway at home tonight,' he tells Rowan at breakfast. 'Tomorrow I thought we'd have a drive out to Matlock, get fish and chips for lunch and pull in a couple of rounds of crazy golf. How's that sound?'

'Wow, really?' Rowan pushes away his cereal bowl and jumps off his stool, punching the air. 'Yes! That sounds great, Dad.'

My heart squeezes watching him. Anyone would think Isaac had promised him the earth, he's so conditioned to his dad working all the time. But I have to hand it to Isaac, he seems to have put a lot of thought into our weekend.

Isaac turns to me when I remain quiet. 'Do you approve, Janey?'

'Yes, of course I do, it sounds like a great plan. It's just a surprise we have you to ourselves all weekend, that's all.' I don't know why he didn't mention all this last night when we were talking about work. 'No complaints, though.'

'That's settled then.' He smiles at both of us in turn. 'I've decided to start as I mean to go on; from now on, a couple of days with my lovely family is going to be the norm rather than a rarity from now on.'

I can't complain about that, but part of me feels slightly uneasy. I wouldn't want us to have a completely free weekend if it results in more pressure for him at work next week. I wonder if he's discussed all this with Bob before making promises in front of Rowan.

Isaac walks up behind me as I'm cleaning the hob and wraps his arms around me.

'I don't want you worrying about me, Janey. I'm fine,' he murmurs in my ear. 'I intend to work to live now, not the other way around. I want you both to know how important you are to me.'

A delicious shiver traces the back of my neck and I smile. I'm so happy he feels this way, that he's taking our fresh start seriously. I really can't ask for more than that.

At about 9.30, Isaac and Rowan leave for the community sports field, where Rowan used to play footie with his mates from school. The dads joined in too sometimes, and Isaac got to know a lot of the other parents because of it.

I texted Tanya about an hour before to say I wouldn't be able to make the swimming outing after all because Isaac had unexpectedly managed to get the weekend off, but she hasn't replied yet. I know it won't be a problem. Tanya has such a large group of friends, she won't even notice I'm not there.

I've already planned how I'm going to spend the next few hours. I've been stopping and starting a new audiobook for ages now, always finding something more important to do, like cleaning, or unpacking the endless boxes. We've been in the house a week, and there are still a hundred and one jobs to get through, but today I'm taking a leaf out of Isaac's book and putting myself first.

For the next hour, at least, I'm going to lie in a hot bubble bath with my eyes closed and my wireless AirPods in, listening to my audiobook.

I set the bath running and pin up my hair before cleansing my face and smearing on the sachet of mud face mask that Tanya gave me before I left yesterday.

'It's brilliant for tightening the skin and closing open pores,' she said, squinting critically at my face.

Back home, I unearthed my magnifying make-up mirror from an as yet unpacked box and realised with horror that she was right. I had indeed acquired a cluster of the dreaded open pores on both lower cheeks. How could I not have noticed?

I put my phone on charge on my bedside table, and just as I turn to go back into the bathroom, the thing begins to ring.

Tanya's name flashes up on the screen.

'Hi, Tanya,' I answer brightly.

'Hello, Janey, I just read your text,' she says in a measured voice.

'Yes, so sorry about that.' I head to the bathroom before the bath overfills. 'It's just that Isaac wants us to spend the weekend together as he's decided not to work, and as I said, we're desperately trying to carve out more time to—'

'What's that noise?'

'I've got the bath running, hang on.' I trap the phone between my cheek and shoulder and turn off the taps. 'That's better, I can hear you now.'

'You're having a *bath*? You said in your text you were out all weekend.'

'We are... sort of, but I've got a few hours to myself this morning as Isaac has taken Rowan to play football with his old mates from Dunkirk.'

'I see.'

There's a pregnant pause and I get a troubling feeling I've done something wrong.

'Sorry I've had to pull out of swimming. I should have checked with Isaac before I agreed it with you.'

'Hmm. The thing is, Dexter's going to be terribly upset when I tell him. He's been talking non-stop about showing Rowan how to do a proper dive.' She hesitates before continuing. 'I hate disappointing him.'

I'm suddenly desperate that she doesn't take offence. I'm racking my brains to come up with a solution. 'Tell you what, why don't I call Isaac and ask him to bring Rowan home a bit earlier than planned? Then we can still make it.'

'That's perfect!' Tanya's voice brightens. 'If you're sure, that is.'

'I'm sure,' I say, pushing away my doubt. It's vital Rowan keeps hold of Dexter's friendship. He's been so miserable at his new school and it's been lovely to see him much happier. 'I'll see you there.'

26

Isaac grumbles a bit when I call him and explain about the swimming commitment.

'If you can come back a bit earlier than you planned, we can still get Rowan there in time.'

'I'm not sure you realise the strings I've had to pull to get the weekend off,' he says dully. 'Now it feels as if I might as well have gone in to work. I thought we'd planned to spend the afternoon together.'

'I know, but I'm trying to think about Rowan here, Isaac. He's finally made friends, and I'd hate to think something as paltry as not going to the swimming class might jeopardise that.'

'My thoughts exactly, and I'm asking myself what kind of a person would allow it to. Maybe you should watch how involved you're getting with this Tanya woman if she operates via emotional blackmail.'

'She doesn't!' I'm surprised at myself, leaping to Tanya's defence so quickly. 'She wasn't blackmailing me. More than anything, she was just disappointed for Dexter.'

'Well, let's hope Rowan doesn't mind dumping his old mates in favour of the new.'

And with that, he ends the call. I pull the plug on my relaxing bath and watch as the silky bubbles I was so close to enjoying disappear down the drain.

*

The swimming pool complex is located on the edge of town. When we get to the reception area, I text Tanya as she instructed me to do and explain to a lady in thick horn-rimmed glasses and the kind of permed big hair that was popular in the eighties that we're here for the Dolphins swimming class.

She taps a screen with a long red nail. 'You're in luck, there's a space left. That'll be twenty-five pounds, please.'

'Oh! I thought… I didn't realise it would be so expensive.'

There's no way I'd have been able to fork out such an exorbitant fee for an hour's swimming even a month ago, but thanks to Isaac's new job, it's now possible. Still, I only grabbed a ten-pound note to pay for a coffee before I came out, and left my purse with my cards in at home. Foolishly, I'd assumed there would be just a nominal charge.

'It's a privately run class with only ten spaces available,' the woman says without a smile. 'This is the tenth and final space and it costs twenty-five pounds.'

Rowan looks up at me, concerned.

My neck feels hot. It's so warm in here, and for some reason I decided to wear a thick sweater rather than layers I could peel off. I glance at my watch. The class starts in fifteen minutes, so I haven't got time to dash home.

The woman taps her impressive fingernails on the desk and stares through the glass at me, and I hear another customer mutter impatiently behind me.

Movement from the other end of the foyer catches my eye and Tanya rushes up in a fragrant cloud of Miss Dior. 'Put it on my card, please, Penelope.'

'No problem at all, Mrs Conrad.' Penelope's fearsome glare melts effortlessly into an admiring smile as she gives Tanya a deferential look. 'I'm so sorry, I didn't realise this lady was with your group.'

'So pleased you could make it, Janey!' Tanya air-kisses either side of my face before we walk away from reception and towards the changing rooms. 'Dex is waiting with the other kids just through the double doors, Rowan, if you want to run ahead. He'll show you where you can get changed.'

Without a backward glance, Rowan takes off, swinging his swimming bag like a lasso as he runs.

Tanya's skin is glowing and her hair shines even under the harsh fluorescent bloom of the indoor lighting. 'I really appreciate you changing your plans to get here,' she says.

'Not at all. I wanted to come, and Rowan's been talking non-stop about Dexter's diving lesson,' I say, pushing Isaac's barbed comments about emotional blackmail out of my mind.

Tanya leads me through the double doors into a private lounge filled with comfy seats and a delicious smell of coffee. A large group of women sit on a carpeted section of the space, clustered at tables beside a glass wall that also serves as an expansive viewing window over the pool on the other side.

'We hire a coach and the pool for a couple of hours every Saturday during term-time,' Tanya explains, leading me over to the tables.

Now I see why there's such a hefty charge for each parent. It must cost a fortune to exclusively hire the pool, lounge and a swim coach at the weekend.

'There's Justin, the coach. The kids love him.' She points through the glass to a bronzed Adonis in his mid twenties, who spots us and waves, flashing his perfect smile at Tanya. 'See, it's worth the trip here already.' She nudges me and grins.

I recognise most of the women from school and watch apprehensively as they chat animatedly amongst themselves, exuding an almost tangible air of confidence and entitlement.

'Guys, Janey's here!' Tanya says brightly as we reach the gathering.

The others stop talking immediately and turn their attention to us. My throat feels tight as several pairs of eyes sweep over me. I still don't know all their names.

'Hi, Edie,' I say, relieved to see her familiar face.

'Janey! Great you could join us.'

Next to Edie, I spot the back of a head that sports a familiar glossy black ponytail.

'Hello, Ky,' I say.

She turns around slowly, still looking at her phone. At the last moment she raises her eyes. 'Oh. Hi, Janey,' she says coolly.

'You'll see some new faces here. Everyone here has kids who play together at one time or another.'

'It's really nice to meet you all.' I nod at everyone and they acknowledge me, some calling out their names before returning to their conversations.

When Tanya and Edie study a schedule for the rest of this term's swim sessions, I become aware Kyoko's eyes are still fixed to my face.

'It's a great set-up here.' It's just something to say to her to ease my awkwardness. 'Do you come every week?'

'Of course,' Ky says dismissively, turning to look at the pool. 'Tanya's my best friend, so where she goes, I go.'

It's a perfectly reasonable reply but something in her tone makes me want to grab Rowan and head back home.

27

'I'd better just go and check Rowan has got changed OK.' I make my excuses and stand up.

Tanya shakes her head and indicates for me to sit down again. 'He'll be fine. Dex and the other boys know the ropes.'

She's barely uttered the words when Rowan and Dexter bob happily back from the changing rooms. They're followed out by Aisha, Cherry and Jun and a couple of the other kids in their swimwear.

Five minutes later, the children are rounded up by the coach.

'Thanks, Justin,' Tanya simpers when he walks past our table. 'You're a star.'

'Put your eyes back in, Tan,' someone says from the next table to us. It's a woman with long red hair who introduced herself earlier as Jaime. 'He's a bit young for you.'

Tanya doesn't say anything, just turns and smiles widely at the woman.

The redhead stops grinning and settles back into her chair.

Over the next ten minutes or so, I watch, fascinated, as the two women sitting at the redhead's table make their excuses and move away. Soon she's sitting there alone, periodically glancing at Tanya from under lowered brows like a dog that knows it's done wrong. I almost feel sorry for her, but not sorry enough to risk Tanya's wrath by suggesting she joins us. There's an undercurrent running through this group and I wonder if I'll ever get to decipher it.

Tanya orders coffee and cake and the four of us sit chatting. I feel totally at ease, as if I've known these women for years. In no time at all, we're laughing and joking.

'I feel at home already,' I tell them. 'Everybody seems to be really friendly.'

'Mad Polly's taken flowers around to Janey's house.' Tanya shakes her head and I shift in my seat, mindful of my alcohol-induced gossiping yesterday. Polly can be a bit of a nuisance, but I feel her heart is in the right place and I don't want to be part of her character assassination.

'She's a sweet lady,' Edie says. 'I think she means well; she just gets a bit confused sometimes.'

I don't comment. Polly has seemed anything but confused on the occasions I've spoken to her. She's sharp as a knife.

Tanya nods. 'I find it sad, to be honest. I think she really believes it's me ruining her garden, but the last plants she accused me of sabotaging were left out on the path overnight – she'd simply forgotten to plant them!'

So it's Tanya who Polly suspects, not Dexter! I'm flabbergasted.

'Another time, she blamed you for actually pulling them out of the ground,' Kyoko says before glaring over at me. 'You shouldn't encourage her, Janey.'

'Oh, I'm not! I mean, I've made it clear I'm too busy to chat, but… well, I think she's a bit lonely.'

'The lies she's told about me… it's all so upsetting.' Tanya looks at me.

'I'd never tolerate her saying such things about you,' Ky murmurs, inspecting her nails.

'But why would she make stuff up about you like that?' I say, baffled.

Tanya shakes her head sadly and lowers her eyes. 'I think she really believes it's true. She's delusional, it's sad really.'

'I'm afraid nobody on the crescent trusts her anymore,' Edie adds. 'She has this way of turning on the people who take pity on her being on her own.'

'On her own? I thought she had a big family?' I think about the grown-up kids, the grandchildren who are always visiting, the adorable but smelly pet pug.

'You must have got her mixed up with someone else,' Kyoko says shortly. 'She lives alone, no family to be seen.'

'I think her daughters live down south so they don't get to visit that often,' Edie adds diplomatically.

I think about Polly overstaying her welcome and talking non-stop about her beloved family. I'd been so irritated in the end.

Tanya runs a finger around the edge of her coffee cup. 'We're just trying to give you fair warning about Polly, that's all. You should take anything she says with a big pinch of salt. We wouldn't be good friends if we weren't looking out for you, now would we?'

'It's best you know about Polly from the get-go,' Edie says. 'You can be on your guard now.'

I nod and yet I can't deny that something doesn't sit quite right about their withering assassination of her.

Tanya seems to pick up on my confusion and lays a hand on my arm. 'You're one of the Buckingham mums now, and if anyone upsets one of us, they have us *all* to answer to. We stick together.'

'Oh no. I mean, there's no need to get annoyed with anyone on my behalf,' I say quickly. Polly may turn out to be a cantankerous old so-and-so with a vivid imagination, but I wouldn't want her upset in any way. 'I'll just be careful now I know what she's like.'

'It's admirable of you to take that line,' Kyoko says lightly. 'And sweet that you think it will be that easy.'

28

The morning of the interview, my stomach feels like a tumble dryer. I'm so out of practice at pushing myself forward in a work situation and I'm worried I'm going to make a fool of myself. I wish now I hadn't mentioned the interview to Tanya.

It's only been two years since I was last in a classroom, but teaching practices change so quickly. If there are other people being interviewed who are currently doing a similar job, they're bound to be at an advantage.

I got everything ready last night so I feel quite prepared. My smart navy suit is hanging in the wardrobe, my white silky blouse is freshly pressed, and although he still hasn't asked much about the job, to his credit, Isaac offered to buff up my navy court shoes ready for this morning. His way of showing support, I suppose.

Needless to say, he was up and off to work at 6.30. So much for ditching the unreasonable hours.

'Good luck,' he'd said, kissing my forehead before leaving. 'Knock 'em dead, Janey.'

I spend more time on my appearance than usual, opting for a soft, understated look with my make-up. Pinning my hair up into a neat French roll, I smooth it back, making sure I catch all the wispy bits for a more professional image.

I'm aware that the waistband of my trousers is perhaps a little too snug. Each time I stretch, the back of the jacket strains slightly, but it will do for the purposes of the interview. I won't be wearing it for long.

'You look nice, Mum,' Rowan says breezily when he bustles into the kitchen, stuffing his PE kit into his bag without a prompt from me.

'Thanks, sweetie,' I say, touched that he's noticed. 'I'm going for the interview this morning at your school. Remember?'

'Oh yeah,' he says. 'Have you seen my reading folder?'

I smile and point to the folder on the worktop. I'm relieved he isn't freaked out by the thought of his mum working at the school. In the unlikely event I get the job, that is.

'I wish we could go to school in the car every morning,' Rowan says, peering down at his feet nestling in the newly vacuumed footwell. 'It means I get there quicker.'

I smile, remembering the boy who, only a short time ago, had feigned illness and spilled the contents of his cereal bowl over himself to avoid going to school.

Five minutes later, I park down the road from the school gates and we walk into the playground.

'Wit woo,' calls Tanya as Rowan runs over to Dexter and I join the group. 'Look at you, all dressed up and looking like a boss.'

The other women who hang around the fringes of the Buckingham mums take their cue, all smiles as I approach. It's quite comical; they're like a living reflection of Tanya's mood. When she's happy, they're all smiles. When she disapproves of something or someone, they mirror that with their frosty glances and an audible backdrop of disapproval. I should know. On the first couple of mornings, I was on the receiving end of it.

Edie nods approvingly. 'You look really good, Janey. Good luck.'

'Thanks,' I say shyly. I actually do feel good this morning, if I ignore my churning guts, that is.

Kyoko's dark eyes sweep up from my shoes to my collar. 'Nice suit. Is it Armani? I have one similar from a few seasons ago that I keep meaning to take to the charity shop.'

I laugh, genuinely amused by her bare-faced bitchiness. 'Armani? No, Ky, sadly I've nothing hanging in my wardrobe from Armani. I bought the suit from Whistles about four years ago. In the sale, I think.'

She looks baffled, obviously unable to fathom why someone would still be wearing an outfit that's so old *and* discounted at that.

Edie rolls her eyes behind Ky's back. 'Janey's lucky,' she says pointedly. 'She looks great in anything.'

When the kids have gone inside their classrooms, I make my excuses and head back to the car. I'm starting to feel a bit sick now, wondering what they might ask me in the interview, but I'm better managing my nerves on my own rather than chatting in the group.

I keep trying to anticipate the questions the panel will throw at me. There's bound to be the classic, 'Why have you applied for this job?'

I need to find out who I am again, to finally stop hiding away in shame from everyone.

No. That sounds far too weird and dramatic and won't make sense to anyone but me.

Mum taught me to keep our business to ourselves, that much is true. Ironically, she also told me to tell the truth wherever possible. And truthfully, the reason I've applied for the job is because I'm ready to return to the career I love and to hopefully make a difference in the lives of young people.

And there's my killer answer right there.

After the interview, I come back out into the fresh air, giving the receptionist a little wave as I leave.

Opening the single button on my jacket, I waft the edges to cool myself down a little. I'm not sure whether it was warm in the conference room or whether the nerves just got to me, but by the end of the thirty minutes, I could feel my cheeks burning and sticky patches under my arms.

The interview went well. Really well. The panel consisted of the head teacher, Jennifer Harlow; Ben Sykes, the teacher whose class I'll be working in; a parent governor, and a lady from the county council's human resources department. The head also explained that the senior teaching assistant at the school, Nadine, would be sitting in to observe.

'We're interviewing three candidates today,' the HR lady told me in her introduction before the interview commenced. 'We've been careful to only select the people we feel demonstrate the specialist skills required for this position.'

Ben Sykes is one of those men who manages to look like a college student no matter how old he gets. His complexion was ruddy and healthy, as if he'd just been out for a run. He explained that the successful candidate would be working a lot of the time one-to-one with a particular child in Elder class who had learning difficulties.

I seized the opportunity to talk about the children I'd worked with in the past, and how important it was to build up a relationship of trust to bring out the best in their abilities. A look passed over Ben's face that fell somewhere between relief and approval, and I knew I'd scored a hit with him at least.

At the end of the interview, the HR woman checked my contact details again. 'We'll be letting candidates know our decision early this evening,' she said. 'We're aiming for six o'clock at the latest.'

Hope spiralled up inside me, and when I reach the car and sit quietly for a minute or two, the fresh career start I've longed for seems tantalisingly close.

I think everyone liked me, especially Ben. He's young and keen and I can tell from some of the things he said that we share the same educational ethos when it comes to getting the best out of the kids by encouraging and guiding them rather than dictating their behaviour.

29

It's Tuesday, and it's one of those days when all feels right with the world. Jennifer Harlow called last night and offered me the job, and Isaac has a relaxed start this morning. What more could I ask for?

I immediately texted Isaac when I heard and then sent the news of my new job to the Buckingham WhatsApp group. Good wishes and congratulations flooded back from my friends way before Isaac even read his message.

Still, at least we're all able to have breakfast together at the kitchen table before Rowan has to leave for school. We chat about me starting work, and Rowan is still going on about the crazy golf we played during our trip to Matlock on Sunday and which bits of the course he liked best. I'm euphoric that I got the job and I know that both Isaac and Rowan are proud of me. Yet there's something I can't put my finger on that sits between us, that seems to be invisibly stopping us getting our real family closeness back.

Isaac does his best to start up a conversation about what we might do together next weekend if he can swing the time off again.

'We'll obviously be celebrating Mum's good news, so we need to do something special,' he says to Rowan. 'Maybe Friday night?'

But Rowan is already distracted, buzzing to get to class. Confident and extrovert, he's even kicking a ball about in the garden when he gets home from school, rather than holing himself up in his bedroom.

A call comes in for Isaac and he snatches up his phone. As he speaks, his expression grows grim. I watch as fine lines etch the corners of his eyes.

'If you've got to go, I'll take Rowan in this morning,' I say when he ends the call. I actually don't mind doing the school run now that I no longer feel like Nobby No-Mates amongst the other parents.

Isaac starts to object, but I insist, and he disappears upstairs to get his stuff together.

Rowan checks his reading book is in his bag and shrugs on his school blazer, all without being asked to do so.

We set off down Buckingham Crescent and I think about stuff I have to do before I start the new job. Various cupboards and drawers need organising, the windows need cleaning… The list seems never-ending, but I feel a new urgency now to get it finished. Soon I'm going to have to return the hospitality Tanya and Edie have afforded me, so I need to get my house shipshape, ready for the play dates that seem to be organised on an informal rota system.

When we get to the playground, Rowan pulls away from me and scoots through the small groups of parents towards the double doors of his classroom. I smile to myself and slow down. It's lovely to see him running to his new friends, full of energy and anticipation of the day, instead of clinging on to me, face as long as a fiddle.

As I reach into my bag for my phone for something to do, I hear a cacophony of voices calling my name. I look up and see Tanya and the others waving and beckoning me over.

A wave of something warm rises inside me and I hurry towards them with a smile in the same manner that Rowan just did. And as I rush towards the perfectly made-up faces and designer-clad bodies, my school years flash into my mind. I was the pale, scrawny kid trying to make herself invisible in the shadowy corners of the playground, watching as the 'it' girls basked in their popularity, hugging and kissing as they greeted each other, whispering and giggling at the expense of others.

'You've done amazingly!' Tanya embraces me warmly.

'I knew you'd get the job!' Edie squeals, clapping her hands.

'Congrats,' Kyoko says in a measured voice, standing back from the others.

They'd seemed a different breed altogether to me, sharing their secrets in exactly the way Mum had warned me about. And now… well, now, despite Kyoko's reticence, for the first time in my life, it feels like I'm in with the in-crowd and I have the chance to be the person I've always wanted to be.

After the kids have gone into class, I walk to the gates with the others. Some of the women on the fringes of the group start to peel off, waving their goodbyes. That leaves the four of us: Tanya, Edie, Kyoko and me.

Instead of going home, we stand outside the gates and carry on our conversation, just like I've seen them do each morning so far. Now I'm standing with them. I'm one of them.

I glance around at the parents walking past us, some of whom take a sly look at our group. Only last week, *I* was that person! Now people are looking at me curiously, seeming to notice that I've been accepted into the inner circle. It feels weird. But I decide I'd rather be on the inside looking out. It feels, I don't know… sort of *safe*.

'Hey, does anyone need to rush off?' Kyoko says. 'Blend is launching a new coffee menu today, and I told Miu, the owner, we'd try to pop in.'

'Fine by me.' Tanya turns to me. 'The café around the corner is our official HQ when the weather is too bad to stand at the gates.'

'Sounds good to me,' Edie says. 'We can celebrate Janey's news with a latte.'

Tanya raises an eyebrow. 'Janey, are you free to come along?'

'Oh! Thanks, I'd love to.'

Ky pulls a regretful face. 'It's going to be busy, Tan, and I told Miu there'd only be three of us. Sorry, Janey.'

'No worries,' I say lightly, feeling heat channel into my face at the obvious snub. 'I'll tag along with you guys next time.'

'No you won't, you'll come with us now,' Tanya says, fixing Ky with a look. 'I'll share a chair with Janey if necessary. That'll be OK, won't it, Ky?'

It sounds more of a statement than a question.

'Yes, of course! That's settled then,' Ky blusters, as if it's what she wanted all along.

The four of us walk to Blend together and it's non-stop chatter all the way. We discuss the best series right now on Netflix, Edie talks about a lemon chicken recipe she cooked last night to big approval from her family, and they all seem interested when I tell them about our family trip to Matlock at the weekend.

'I always think of Matlock as a bit dated,' Ky remarks. 'A cheap day out. There are so many other better places closer to home, I think.'

This barbed comment seems to go over Tanya and Edie's heads, and so I pretend I haven't noticed either. Ky clams up and her face drops, which shows I did the right thing.

There was a time when I had these women down as being self-obsessed and stuck-up, and I can honestly say that two out of three of them are neither. Maybe if I can get to know Ky a little better, she'll see I'm not out to steal Tanya away from her. I'd like to have the friendship of all of them.

30

We arrive at Blend and I smell the coffee before we even walk through the door. I immediately love the interior; all reclaimed wood and brickwork with subdued lighting. Interestingly, there are lots of tables that appear to be free. I glance at Ky knowingly, but she shows no embarrassment.

Miu comes straight over when we arrive. She's in her late fifties, short and slim, with arms stacked with bangles and her hair tied up with a brightly coloured scarf.

'The coffee house looks lovely,' I tell her.

'At last! Someone who hasn't been raised in a cave and actually understands the difference between a coffee house and a plain old café.' She raises an eyebrow at Tanya, who, obviously guilty of this, pulls a face.

'I wouldn't go anywhere else for my coffee fix, you know that,' Tanya says sweetly, and Miu relents, smiling.

'You're new,' she says to me, stepping back and squinting at me.

'I'm Janey, we've just moved into the area. My son started school last week at Lady Bridge.'

Miu smiles graciously. 'Welcome, Janey. I'm glad there's someone at last with their feet on the ground to keep an eye on this glamour squad and their antics.'

More chuckles all round, but I can't help thinking her 'feet on the ground' comment translates as 'plain and sensible'. I'm just being a bit oversensitive; truthfully, I *am* sort of plain and sensible compared to the others. It wouldn't take much to make myself a bit more presentable, though. Perhaps I could get my hair coloured or a new style, and I've seen leisure wear online similar to what the others wear, although it was far from the cost of the Dolce & Gabbana range that Tanya favours.

We order coffees from the new menu and sit in the corner, where there are plentiful tables and chairs. There's a natural lull in the conversation and so I take the plunge.

'So, Mrs Harlow has confirmed that I'll be working in Elder class,' I say.

Edie's face lights up. 'Oh that's great news, isn't it, Ky?'

Ky presses her lips together. This is obviously not the news she was hoping to hear.

'I start on Friday,' I add.

'Bravo, Janey!' Tanya says. 'That's quite a quick start though, isn't it?'

'They're desperate for some help,' I say. 'And as I haven't got notice to serve in another job, there's nothing stopping me. I think that's another thing that might've gone in my favour.'

'Congratulations, Janey, it's exciting,' Edie says. 'Is your husband pleased?'

I shrug. 'I think he is. He's so distracted with his own job right now, though, he's finding it hard to focus on anything else.'

'Stuff on his mind, I expect.'

I nod. 'I think his boss is quite demanding, although I can't get much out of him. He just seems so stressed, you know?'

I realise I'm talking about Isaac's job again which he has specifically asked me not to do.

'Tell me about it. Sometimes I feel like I'm a single parent,' Tanya complains. 'I've seen Tristan for a grand total of four days out of the past ten, and frankly, it's bloody exhausting keeping Dex entertained, especially now that Angel spends more time at her friends' houses.'

'I hear you.' Edie rolls her eyes. 'Alistair's off to a three-day conference tomorrow in Bath, leaving me holding the fort. I'm dreading it, as I'm already tired. But Tanya, we have to think of the benefits we get for the sacrifices we make.'

Tanya doesn't reply but their admissions make me feel like I'm not as alone as I thought.

'Glad it's not just me,' I say, warming to the conversation. 'When we moved to Buckingham Crescent, it was supposed to be a fresh start. Isaac's new company promised him more working from home and relaxed starts, but if anything, expectations are shaping up to be even worse than the last job.'

'You can't blame the company for expecting a lot from their employees, Janey.' Kyoko frowns. 'They're hardly going to pay him for sitting at home twiddling his thumbs all morning.'

I'm a little startled at her obvious irritation, and Edie comes to the rescue.

'It sounds like a good promotion though and more funds are always welcome, right?'

I really like Edie but money seems to be her first thought in every situation.

Kyoko stacks five sugar sachets on top of each other and then knocks them down with a lethal-looking fingernail.

'Tristan simply has no off-switch at all,' Tanya remarks. 'Whether we're at home, out for dinner or doing something together as a family, he's always reading or sending emails or googling his rivals' share prices. It drives me to distraction.'

'I have to remind myself every day of the lifestyle benefit we get from the hours we work. Alistair puts in the time abroad while I stay home with Aisha,' Edie confesses. 'But increasingly it just seems to be too high a price to pay.'

'As you know, when Rupert left me for the Trollop…' Kyoko pauses meaningfully to allow Edie and Tanya a snigger. 'I found out he was bonking his brainless little secretary when we lived in

York and I threw him out,' she tells me matter-of-factly. 'And when I moved here, I had to cut my cloth a little leaner. But I can't say I'm less happy because of it.'

I say nothing, but I can't imagine that anyone who lives on Buckingham Crescent has to count the pennies.

'You do have a very generous mother, though, darling,' Tanya points out. 'You never seem to go short.'

'It's true Mum helps me out with the odd bill.' Kyoko seems a little irked at Tanya's remark. 'But the weekday eating-out and the spa treatments have largely died a death. Now I spend far more time with Cherry and Jun and we're all the better for it.'

There are a few moments of silence while the others digest this.

'I've been used to living on a shoestring budget,' I say quietly, deciding to open up, seeing as everyone else is. I take the view that it's no use trying to pretend I'm something that I'm not. 'Having more money with Isaac's new salary is a novelty; to be honest, I'm not even sure how to spend more on myself.'

'Well, that's easily sorted!' Tanya perks up, opening the calendar app on her phone. 'How are you fixed for a shopping trip tomorrow morning after we drop the rugrats off at school?'

'Oh!' Kyoko says quietly. 'Tan, we were going to pop over to the new retail park tomorrow, remember?'

'Darn it, hadn't put that in my phone.' Tanya scowls at the screen. 'No problem. We can go there in the afternoon.' Kyoko twitches her glossy nude lips and begins to stack the sugar sachets again. Tanya looks at me and says, 'So we have a date, yes?'

I shrug my shoulders and nod. 'Great, yes, if you're sure that's OK. Thanks, Tanya.'

'It's perfect,' she replies, and just at that moment, Kyoko knocks her sugar tower down so violently, the sachets fly off the table and onto the floor.

31

Tanya tells me she doesn't diet per se but does something called overnight fasting. This entails not eating anything after eight o'clock at night or before noon the following day.

'Within a couple of weeks I'd dropped a stubborn seven pounds I'd been trying to lose for ages.'

It sounds achievable and fairly painless to me, as I've never fancied breakfast first thing, so I resolve to give it a go.

Back at home, I fill the kettle, flick the switch and stare out of the window at our garden. It's about a quarter of the size of Tanya's, but twice as big as the garden we left behind. There are lots of mature bushes around the edges of the lawn, and when I've got a minute, I'm going to find out their names and get the shears out to keep them neat.

I've never been that interested in gardening before, but something about living here, surrounded by immaculate houses and gardens, makes me want to do better.

Still elated from the good news, I open my laptop and take a look at my emails. There's one from the school with my letter of appointment attached. I open it and send it to the printer to read later.

Then, flush from my commitment to get myself looking better, I log in to the ASOS site and find some leggings and a couple of tops that bear a slight resemblance to what the other Buckingham mums wear for the school run. I can't stretch to the Gucci trainers Tanya and Edie favour, so instead, I order a pair of pink and black Skechers with a bit of a sparkle, paying for next-day delivery.

Next, I google local hairdressers and find one on the high street that looks modern and trendy and whose price list falls comfortably into the mid-range bracket. I check out their Instagram page and see they're quite active, posting regular pics of attractive, modern haircuts and striking colour work.

Before I can change my mind, I give them a call and manage to get a cancellation appointment with a senior stylist for 1.30 this afternoon.

I end the call and sit back, feeling a bit breathless.

New friends, new image and a new job.

My life is on the turn for the better and it feels fantastic.

I turn up at the salon ten minutes early. My skin feels hot and clammy as I'm haunted by thoughts of what might go wrong if I choose the wrong look.

The young man behind the reception desk takes my name and points me to a seat. As I grab a copy of *Hello!* magazine and sit down on one of the comfy chairs, my eyes are drawn to someone sitting in a pink velvet tub chair to my right.

'Hi, Janey,' she says shyly.

'Angel! Hi.' My heart begins to thump as if I'm doing something underhand by being here without telling Tanya. 'Are you having your hair done too?' A stupid question, I know, but then shouldn't she be at school?

'I'm here for an interview,' she says a little coyly. 'It's for work experience week at school.'

She's acting like she's been caught out somehow, but kids who are playing truant don't usually choose to come to hair salons, or at least they didn't when I was at school. They'd hang out in the park, smoking and drinking.

'Are you having your hair done?' she asks, then play-punches herself under the chin. 'Doh! It's a hairdresser's, so I guess you totally *are*!'

I nod and grin. 'I'm here for a cut of some sort, I'm not sure what. They can't do my colour until I have a patch test. It sounds silly, but I'm a bit nervous. I want something different but I haven't got a clue what would suit me.'

She tips her head to one side and studies me for a moment. I wilt under her attention. My hair is overdue for a wash, and I've left it loose, draping lankly over my shoulders.

'I think you should crop the length a bit so it's a nice blunt bob and then get a balayage next time when you've had the patch test. That would really suit you, I think.'

I'm speechless for a moment. She seems completely different to when I first met her, so genuine and natural.

'Thanks, Angel,' I say, touched that she's taken the time to chat to me. 'You've obviously got an eye for hair. I hope your interview goes well.'

She shifts in her chair. 'Thing is… and this is a bit awks' – she presses her fingertips to her forehead – 'Mum doesn't know I'm here. For the interview, I mean.'

Ahh. I press my lips together and don't comment.

'She's trying to fix me up with work experience with Tristan for a week, which is my idea of a nightmare.'

I pull a sympathetic face. I can't think of many teenagers who'd want to spend a whole week working with their parent, to be honest.

'Mum can't accept I want to be a hairdresser, even though my goal is to have my own string of salons one day.' She sighs. 'She thinks it's below me in some way. So I thought, if I get the job lined up, she might just accept that it's what I want to do and back off a little.' She hesitates. 'Mum likes to get her own way, you see. If I'd told her about my interview, I think she'd have tried to scupper it in some way.'

I keep my expression impassive. Tanya is a determined, opinionated woman all right, but I can't imagine she'd intervene to that extent.

Angel takes a breath. 'I suppose what I'm asking is… can you not mention to her that you saw me here today? Just until I know if I got through the interview OK and have a place here?'

Just then, a tall, slim woman with bright pink hair appears in front of me.

'Janey? I'm Blaze, I'll be looking after you today.'

I stand up and wink at Angel. Her worried face softens a touch. 'See you soon. Good luck.'

'Thanks,' she says. 'Oh, and Janey?' I turn back. 'I'm very happy to babysit Rowan if you and your husband fancy a night out soon. Rowan's a great kid and… well, I could do with the cash.'

I can't help smiling inwardly at her honesty. Rowan has mentioned several times how great it was when Angel chased him and Dexter through the bushes with the water gun. She's definitely got a connection with the boys, and I've seen a different side to her just now. I think, like in lots of families, mother and daughter just rub each other up the wrong way.

'Thanks, Angel,' I say. 'I might just take you up on that.'

I follow my stylist into the minimalist white salon with its low-hanging crystal chandeliers. It feels like Angel and I just made a little pact of sorts.

32

Sleep brought the only relief from the horror of her prison; dreams about her old life. But from each sleep she had to wake, and with it came the agony of worrying about her parents and how they must be feeling. Did they know in their hearts that she'd been abducted, or did part of them now believe she'd run away from home, possibly with a boyfriend? She couldn't bear the thought that they would imagine she had abandoned them because they were too strict, but if they did, then she supposed it was better than the truth.

If she ever got out of here, she'd already sworn to God that she would take on board every piece of advice her parents gave her. Aspects of her life that had seemed so important back then – staying out late, going to parties – she now knew meant nothing at all. Going out, getting dressed up to go to the pub with Melissa… it wasn't real.

What mattered were the people you loved. What mattered was feeling safe and content.

The man was in his late thirties, maybe even forty, and his eyes were evil. If she'd seen a man like him on the street, she felt sure she'd have known there was something not right about him. Lots of men were strange; she could always sense it when she was out having a good time with Melissa. Those types could keep the pretence up for a little while, but their true nature would always break through in the end, and she'd easily spot it and make herself scarce.

This man reminded her of an ex-soldier she'd met just before her birthday, who seemed so brave and strong on the outside but got a strange gleam in his eye after they'd been talking for half an hour. He'd started talking about guns and which types could inflict the most harm to the human body. Susan had told him that she needed to make a phone call and slipped out of the pub with Melissa in tow.

But this time, she hadn't had the choice to split.

The girl who came downstairs with him each time looked young but it was hard to guess her age. Very pretty on the outside, but inside – in her heart – she had to be rotten through and through. In Susan's humble opinion, that kind of decay didn't just appear one day; it was there from the beginning. From birth. And anyway, what was someone who was close to Susan's own age doing with a man who was old enough to be her dad?

She wondered if the girl's mother knew she was seeing an older man. Had she noticed her daughter slipping out of the house at the same time that a local young woman had gone missing? Susan's own mother had eyes like a hawk when it came to her daughter. Surely someone must know what the man and the girl were up to, someone must suspect.

It was the girl who had made Susan feel safe that night. That was why she'd willingly stopped on the quiet side road and leaned into the car to help out with directions.

The man had grabbed her hair and pressed a cloth to her face. She'd tried hard to scream but had immediately felt all woozy, and then their voices had drifted far away.

Then she'd woken up in here. In this hellhole.

She was starting to think of it as the place where she might die.

33

The next morning, after dropping Rowan off at school, I call at the chemist with Isaac's prescription before heading over to Tanya's house for our shopping trip.

I wait in the small queue feeling relieved he's found the time to address his skin problem before it gets worse. I've known him be completely blindsided by work to the exclusion of everything else in the past.

I can't kick the feeling that something is a bit off with his behaviour. Something I can't quite put my finger on.

Isaac has always dealt with the finer details of our money, something I've been quite happy to take a back seat on. Eking out every penny and juggling bills is not my idea of fun and Isaac has always been happy to take the reins in that department. I've been aware of our situation at any given time, of course. We've discussed our financial problems in the past at length; Isaac hasn't had to shoulder the burden alone.

When I look at our bank account now, I can see it's so much healthier than it has been in the past. We've always lived up to our means, even in the early years before we had Rowan when we were both working full-time. In fact, if I'm honest, we've probably mostly lived *beyond* our means.

Back in those sunny days, being together and having fun were top of our list of priorities. Somehow, over time, those criteria have slipped way down the list and now, paying bills on time and somehow managing on the credit card limit the bank have consistently refused to increase, have taken top priority.

'Enjoy your shopping trip,' Isaac said before he left for work. 'I never thought I'd say it, but we're OK for money now and you deserve to treat yourself.'

He scratched at a patch of eczema that had appeared on his hand recently. His body was covered in it when we met; I remember he seemed to be forever smothering himself with steroid cream. Slowly, though, it settled down and he just sort of grew out of it as he neared his late twenties. Now it looks as if it might be making a reappearance.

'Don't worry, I'm not about to morph into Imelda Marcos and buy a stellar shoe collection in one morning,' I joked. 'But if I see anything really nice, I might splash out a bit.'

'Your prescription will be ready in about fifteen minutes,' the lady behind the chemist counter says, taking my payment. 'You can wait here or call back later if you've some shopping to do, it's up to you.'

'I'll wait in the car,' I say. 'I'm parked just outside.'

The chemist, together with other small shops including a newsagent, bakery, deli and a bistro bar are set around a large square of marked-out parking spaces. I slide back into the driver's seat and study my new haircut in the rear-view mirror. Critically, I turn my face this way and that but even I've got to admit the blunt bob suits my face shape. Isaac raved about it last night, said it made me look younger. 'Not as if you look old, of course,' he then backtracked hilariously.

I pull my Kindle out of my handbag.

After a few minutes reading the same paragraph, I realise I feel too distracted to carry on. I set my Kindle down on the passenger seat and lean back in my seat to watch the activity around the square.

It's only nine thirty but there are plenty of people milling around, no doubt getting their errands done early like me. Young mums dash around with their babies in pushchairs and pre-school children toddling alongside. Elderly people move slowly and purposefully towards their destinations.

But it's the oddly matched couple on the far side of the car park that pulls my attention away from the main square. A man and a woman stand talking, away from the fray of the shoppers.

In a split second, I take in that the young woman, standing with her back to me, looks almost young enough to be a schoolgirl, whereas the man is in his late thirties. She has her hands on her hips and her black skirt has clearly been rolled at the waist to shorten it to mid-thigh length. Knee-length black socks and flat pumps paired with a white blouse make for a provocative appearance.

My heart rate speeds up as I realise something is wrong with the tableau in front of me. The long, poker-straight blonde hair that falls almost to her waist, the slim but shapely body that looks too mature for a schoolgirl... she turns around as if she's heard someone call her name and I let out an involuntary gasp. Slink down a little in my seat.

I happen to know the young woman is, in fact, a fifteen-year-old schoolgirl. It's Angel!

This morning at the school gates after making a big fuss about my new hairstyle, Tanya entertained us all with Angel's annoyance that Tanya still insists on dropping her off at school each day.

'She thinks it ruins her street cred even though we pull up in a Range Rover Vogue with Kanye West blasting out,' Tanya laughed, rolling her eyes. 'I shouldn't complain, she's a good kid. But timekeeping isn't her strong point and that's why I take her... and make sure she's dressed properly. You should see the state of some of those girls from the council estate... skirts so short you can almost see their underwear.'

I run her words through my mind again to satisfy myself I'm not imagining things. No. She definitely said she'd dropped Angel at school this morning before bringing Dexter over to Lady Bridge.

The man, who I can only see in profile, grins and says something and Angel throws her head back and laughs. She seems completely at ease in this person's company.

Other stuff comes to me then, things that Tanya has told me recently.

'She hates me "nosing" about her friends, as she calls it,' Tanya said that first day I went over to her house and Angel had appeared when we were in the hot tub. 'But I'm lucky. I've no worries, really, she's a sensible kid unlike some of the other teenagers around here.'

Now I'm questioning if Tanya is in utter denial about Angel's sensible outlook? Is it possible there might be a reasonable explanation for Angel to be talking to a man possibly old enough to be her father in the square, when Tanya clearly thinks she is safely in school?

Just the other day, Tanya raged that a teacher had called her to discuss the fact Angel's assignment hadn't quite been up to scratch.

'I know for a fact she spent all day in her bedroom working on the damn thing, so it's ridiculous to suggest she rushed it,' Tanya fumed at the gates. 'I told him she's the hardest-working kid I know, spends hours on her laptop every night either working at a friend's house or upstairs in her room.'

Her words swirl in my head, offering a double meaning. Was Angel *really* at a friend's house doing homework or was she spending her time elsewhere?

Angel leans slightly forward and, for a moment, I think she's going to kiss him and I get ready to jump out of the car and call out to her. But she doesn't kiss him. His smile broadens, as if she's said something agreeable. Then she turns on her heel and saunters off towards the shops on the other side of the chemist, pulling her school bag up on to her shoulder.

I grab my own handbag off the passenger seat and get out of the car. I have this mad urge to run after Angel, ask if she's OK and offer her a lift home but something stops me. I don't know what, exactly… probably embarrassing her. It's not as if she's distressed or in any danger and she didn't kiss the man.

I'm obviously going to have to mention this to Tanya when I go over to her house before our shopping trip this morning. It's just a matter of how I'm going to phrase it. I don't want to get Angel into trouble or for Tanya to think I'm tittle-tattling. After all, there's every possibility something changed after Angel got to school this morning. Maybe she had an unexpected free period or something. Tanya might be fully aware she's in town.

The man she was talking to could just be a stranger and he'd struck up a friendly conversation with her although they seemed a bit too familiar for my liking.

He was a lot older than Angel and there was just something about their exchange that seemed off. It was as if the man was someone she already knew. But I have no evidence to support that view and I'm sure Tanya wouldn't appreciate me filling in the blanks.

Angel's a nice kid. I saw a softer, gentler side to her yesterday in the hairdresser's. I think there's a vulnerable girl underneath the prickly exterior she offers to her mother.

Still, when I go over there, I can casually mention to Tanya that I just saw Angel talking to someone in the square and then that's my obligation fulfilled. Problem solved.

I lock the car and look around. Angel has disappeared from view now and when I look across to where she was standing, I see the man has also moved on.

I make my way across the square and back into the chemist to pick up Isaac's medication, a weight settling on my chest.

34

When I've collected the prescription, I drive over to Tanya's house, rehearsing out loud the exact words and tone I'll use to tell her Angel isn't in school.

I thought you should know… Perhaps a bit too formal and slightly judgemental. Sounds as if I've already made my mind up Angel is being deceitful.

Ooh, guess who I just saw in the square? No. Too flippant.

In the end I stop rehearsing and just focus on driving. It will come out the way it feels right at the time. I don't know why I'm complicating it so much.

I park the car outside and approach Tanya's gate when the front door opens. She stands there, smiling and bright, obviously looking forward to our shopping trip.

'Your hair really does look amazing! How come you never said you were planning a new style?' She pushes me playfully when I reach the doorstep. 'And never even asked my advice. Charming!'

I think about seeing Angel at the hairdresser's and swallow hard. Keeping quiet about that is one thing and I really don't want to put a dampener on Tanya's mood, but I have to tell her what I just saw.

'Excited for today?' Tanya ushers me inside towards the enticing smell of fresh coffee and baked goods. 'I've popped a couple of croissants in the oven if you fancy one. I didn't have any breakfast and I'm starving. It won't delay us too long.'

I slip off my shoes at the door, following her into the kitchen where she invites me to sit at one of the plush white leather stools and perch at the island. I look out at the large corner plot and remember how Rowan and Dexter had such fun chasing each other with water guns as we lounged in the hot tub out there, not a care in the world.

'Goodness, you do look glum! We're supposed to be gearing up for some fun.' Tanya places a chunky blue Denby coffee mug in front of me, pulls on an oven glove and returns to the oven to take out the croissants. I stare down into the swirling, steaming dark liquid in the mug and say nothing. 'Let me get the jam and butter and I'll be right with you.'

She makes her way over to the outsize American-style silver fridge, hesitating over which flavour jam to select whilst I rack my brains how to begin the conversation. I could start by asking if I'm right in thinking she dropped Angel off at school this morning to sort of ease her into the subject that way.

'Here we go. Help yourself.' Tanya puts down the jam jar and butter dish and slides over a knife.

I push away the plate and take a breath but the words just won't come. I'm making such a hash of a perfectly simple task.

'I can see something is really bothering you, Janey, so just spit it out. A problem shared and all that…' She reaches for a croissant and puts it on her own plate.

A flush of heat encircles my neck.

'It's just that… well, it's hard to know where to start.' I tap a nail on the worktop. 'The last thing I want to do is—'

The front door flies open so forcefully, I hear it bang against the inside wall.

'What the—' Tanya rushes to the kitchen door and gapes out at the hallway. 'Angel! What are you doing home at this time, darling?'

'It's my stomach,' I hear Angel moan. 'I've got terrible period pains, Mum.'

'My poor baby, come and have a drink. Look who's here.'

Angel peers around the doorway. 'Hi, Janey,' she says weakly. 'Nice hair.'

Her face is pale, her eyes red-rimmed. No sign of the confident, bright girl I just saw in town.

'Hello, Angel,' I say. 'Aren't you feeling well?'

She shakes her head forlornly and steps into the kitchen. The school skirt that was hitched up to an indecent length barely an hour ago is slightly crumpled now but sits exactly on her knee. And the long black socks that added to her rather saucy look just seem a little frumpy now. Her long blonde hair is tied back into a low ponytail.

Angel looks exactly like what she is: a fifteen-year-old schoolgirl who's feeling a bit under the weather. If I hadn't seen her in the square with my own eyes…

'The PE teacher was furious with me when I insisted I needed to come home.'

'You did the right thing, darling.' Tanya frowns and pours her a small glass of orange juice which Angel ignores. 'PE teachers are always the same. They think theirs is the most important subject in the world when it's the one that least matters in building a successful business.'

'Mine used to say the exercise actually helped with stomach cramps,' I remark, thinking back.

'Exactly, and what a load of crap *that* is!' Tanya fumes. 'She's dealt with this sort of attitude all her life, Janey. The adults just as bad as the other kids at that school. Teachers who can't stand to see a beautiful girl from a good family doing well in a state school because it puts their own sad little lives into perspective.'

I rub my forehead with the heel of my hand.

'Mum! Janey doesn't want to hear one of your rants.' Angel looks at me as if she's trying to work out what's bothering me.

Tanya turns to her daughter. 'Fancy a croissant, sweetie? You've got to keep your strength up.'

The girl shakes her head. 'Not hungry,' she says. 'I think I'll just have a lie down.'

She's a good little actress, I'll give her that. There was nothing wrong with her at all in the square. She's clearly got her mother twisted around her little finger and knows it.

'You do that.' Tanya soothes her. 'Take your juice and I'll pop up and check on you when I get back from our shopping trip.'

If I don't say anything right now the moment will have passed… it probably already has. When Angel came through the door, I should have casually said I saw her in town right away.

Words bubble up in my throat and when I speak, my voice comes out high and tight like my vocal cords are about to snap.

'Did you go to town before coming home, Angel?'

'Huh?' Her eyes widen for a split second and then the acting is first-class. 'No… I just came home straight from school.'

Tanya's hands still and she puts down the butter knife. Looks at me.

'What do you mean, Janey?'

'Nothing. I mean, I thought I saw Angel in the square talking to someone, a man… when I went to the chemist.' I look at Angel. 'I must have been mistaken.'

'Angel?' Tanya puts her hands on her daughter's shoulders and looks in her eyes. 'Did you go into town before coming home?'

'No!' She puts a hand to her brow and closes her eyes. 'Mum, I feel sick and a bit faint… can I just go and lie down please?'

'Of course.' Tanya plants a kiss on her forehead and Angel disappears upstairs.

'Sorry,' I hear myself say as Tanya brightens again and goes back to her croissant. 'I could have sworn it was…'

'No worries, it's an easy mistake to make,' Tanya says. Her voice sounds bright but to me, her eyes look troubled. 'Next time you're in town maybe you should call at Specsavers, eh?'

She pulls a funny face and we both laugh.

But I know I'm not mistaken. Even if she has a doppelgänger out there, Angel's skirt is creased and the Lipsy bag she's dumped down by the kitchen island... it's identical to the one she had slung over her shoulder earlier.

She wouldn't be the first kid to play truant from school, or the last. It's not really my problem now; I've done my duty in mentioning it. It's up to Tanya to weigh up who's telling the truth.

35

In town, Tanya steers me away from my usual choice of low-end bargain shops on Long Row.

'No Primark for you today, madam,' she scolds me playfully, linking her arm through mine as we walk. 'Leave it to me to open your eyes to the wonderful world of shopping.' Her eyes flutter over to the window of an expensive-looking shoe shop we're strolling past. 'I said I'd take you to some *proper* shops, and that's exactly what I intend doing.'

My heart sinks a bit. I can't really afford designer brands yet, and I don't covet them, either. I'd rather spend serious money on getting the house smartened up, so I feel more confident about inviting people round.

'I hope Angel feels a bit better now,' I say lightly.

'Oh, she'll be fine. If you count being a teenager and rejecting every piece of sensible advice Tristan and I try to give her as progress.'

'I suppose we've all been there,' I say. 'Thinking we know everything.'

'She's set her heart on being a bloody hairdresser. Can you believe it?' Tanya huffs. 'The world's her oyster and she wants to sweep up hair for a living.'

'It wasn't too bad a choice for Vidal Sassoon.'

'He didn't work in a poxy back-street salon, though, did he?'

I shrug. 'He probably started off somewhere like that.'

'Hmm. Well, she's only gone and got herself a week's work experience at some crabby little dive called Cutz. I mean, how naff a name can you get? Tristan was so looking forward to showing her the ropes in his business.'

'That's… where I had my new haircut,' I say carefully. 'It's really nice in there.'

But Tanya isn't embarrassed at her comment and won't be placated.

'It's one thing getting a haircut there, another thing altogether when your daughter wants to *work* there.'

'It's only work experience, though, isn't it? Maybe it'll change her mind about hairdressing. She's only young. I changed my mind dozens of times at her age over what I wanted to do as a career.'

Tanya falls silent as if she's considering this. I find myself hoping I've helped Angel's cause in some way. The kid might be spoilt when it comes to material things, but yesterday her eyes lit up when she talked about her career goals in a way that had little to do with money.

'Here we are, one of my favourite shops to start off with.' Tanya takes a sharp turn off the main drag and leads me into a small alleyway that opens out into a neat little courtyard. I've never been up here, mainly because it's home to independent designer shops selling goods that are priced well out of my league.

We enter a small establishment called A Touch of Class. Its window is full of artfully arranged colourful garments, all without price tags.

Tanya introduces me to the woman behind the counter. 'This is Anita, my saviour. How are you, darling?' They air-kiss. 'This is my new friend Janey. She's starting a brand new job soon and deserves to treat herself.'

I feel heat sweeping up into my throat. There's no way I'll be buying an outfit from here. For starters, nothing seems to have a price tag attached to it, so that's a major red flag and irritating to say the least. If I was a millionaire, I'd still want to know what things cost before I bought them!

Anita's eyes sweep me from head to foot in a flash. Despite the fact that she must've noticed the shoes that need heeling and the small tear on the hem of my top where it got trapped between two pieces of furniture during the move, her professional approach remains unruffled.

'Pleased to meet you, Janey. If there's one thing I like – as you know, Tanya – it's a challenge. Sit here and Frieda will bring coffee while I put a few things together.'

I'm not sure what to make of the 'challenge' comment, but I decide to take it in the spirit of fun in which I hope it was made.

'I haven't a clue what I'm looking for,' I say to Tanya, perusing the rails of fine fabrics from my seat.

'You don't need to. Anita knows exactly what will suit you and that's what she's doing right now. She'll bring over some outfits, and if you like them, you can try them on.'

I open my mouth and close it again. Pressure is building inside my head as I try to find a way to tell Tanya this place is way out of my league.

'Anita will know your dress size just by looking at you.' Tanya grins, taking in my expression. 'She's a fully qualified image consultant too, so knows the exact shades that suit you best and which styles flatter your figure.'

A small, dark-haired woman brings through a coffee pot and two glass cups and saucers, together with a jug of cream.

'Thank you, Frieda darling,' Tanya says grandly.

'I'll say one thing, you don't get this service at Primark.' I raise an eyebrow and thank Frieda before she disappears again. 'But with so much still to do to the house, I don't think I can stretch to this sort of luxury.'

Tanya takes a sip of her coffee and shakes her head. 'Let me worry about that.'

I'm not sure what she means, but it's clear she is set on staying here, so I might as well just go with the flow, enjoy the experience as best I can. I'm not entirely comfortable with this world of personal shopping that some people seem to love – a woman I've only just met choosing the way I should look – but Tanya swears by it, so what's the harm? There's no danger of me making a purchase and giving Isaac palpitations when he scrutinises the credit card statement at the end of the month. When he told me to treat myself, he'd have been thinking of a mid-priced high street chain, I'm sure.

I unwrap one of the Elizabeth Shaw mint chocolates on the tray and pop it in my mouth while Tanya zones me out and scrolls through her Facebook feed.

Anita appears after a few minutes and calls me through, holding open a heavy velvet curtain that I can see leads to a space lined with floor-to-ceiling mirrors.

'Come and see what you think, Janey. I've selected you some really super outfits back here.'

She leads me to a chrome rail that has three groups of garments arranged on it. She takes me through them.

'First we have tailored trousers and a pure silk pussy-bow blouse by Celine. Perfect for your long legs and elegant neck. Then I've selected this body-con dress; the gathering here pulls in the waist and the shorter length shows off your shapely legs.' She moves her hands fluidly over the clothes as she describes them, as if they're an art form. 'And finally, a flared mid-length napa leather skirt and simple scoop-necked top that you can really go to town on and dress up or down with accessories.'

I thank her, and to my relief she moves towards the curtain, just as I'd convinced myself I'd be expected to try the clothes on under her eagle eye. 'Give me a shout when you've got the first outfit on,' she calls, disappearing back out into the shop.

I slip off my jacket and top, unbuttoning my jeans. I can feel a headache building between my eyes and I silently berate myself. It's so kind of Tanya to take time out of her day to bring me here, but I should never have agreed to it. These clothes, this shop… they're just not me. I could never feel comfortable wearing such expensive outfits and I haven't got the accessories or lifestyle to match. Even setting foot in a shop like this makes me feel like a fraud.

I slip on the wool-blend tailored black trousers. They fit like a glove, and to my delight, I have no trouble fastening them. The oyster-coloured silk blouse drapes over my skin, soft and fluid. The trousers are fashionably long, so I stand on tiptoes to mimic wearing heels and stare at my reflection in the full-length mirror. On the hanger the clothes looked boring, but now… well, even though I say so myself, they actually make me look almost classy. Something I considered nigh on impossible only ten minutes ago.

'How are you getting on in here?' The curtain whips back and Anita peers in. I can see Tanya hovering behind her, craning her neck to see over Anita's shoulder. I turn around to face her, holding my arms out a little from my sides.

'Oh yes, very nice,' Anita coos. 'The trousers fit you a treat.'

'I can't believe how good they feel,' I say, hooking a fingertip in the waistband to show that they fit perfectly.

'Hey, sophisticated lady!' Tanya calls. 'Where's Janey, and what have you done with her?'

I laugh, quite enjoying the fuss despite my rocky start.

Next I shimmy into the body-con dress. At first I think it's too tight, but Anita has warned me it has a sort of inbuilt scaffolding, and once I get to grips with it and give it a firm tug here and there, it soon slips into place. 'Pulls you in and plumps you out in all the right places,' she explains.

I step into the pair of size 5 heels she has provided, a near-identical shade to the dress, and gaze at my reflection, taking in the flat stomach, the pert boobs and the shapely waist that don't feel as though they belong to me at all.

'It's easy to see how celebs look so effortlessly amazing, wearing this gear all the time, isn't it?' Tanya says. 'That and a bit of airbrushing.'

Finally I try on the third outfit. The cappuccino-coloured leather skirt feels as soft as butter and clings to my body in all the right places. The top, which on the hanger looked simple and plain, is made of a fine-rib silky knitted fabric that offers invisible support and holds its shape wonderfully.

When Anita ties a pretty coloured scarf around my neck and fastens a pale gold chain-link belt round my waist, I'm forced to eat my words and admit it: I feel a million dollars.

36

I'm exhilarated when I emerge from the shop I didn't want to go into with my new leather skirt and top expertly folded in a beautifully wrapped and sticker-sealed bag.

Tanya tried to insist on buying me the outfit, but I couldn't let her do that. Anita took pity on me when she saw how much I wanted it, insisting the outfit was to be included in a forthcoming sale and knocking a huge fifty per cent off the ticket price. It was still more than I've paid for an outfit in my life, but then Isaac did tell me to treat myself, and I had what constituted a moment of madness and handed Anita my credit card.

When Tanya suggests we go back to hers for lunch and a glass of fizz to celebrate, I find myself readily agreeing. I don't feel like going home to an empty house and packing boxes, and I haven't properly celebrated my job success yet either.

We buy sandwiches from Pret to take back with us. Tanya gets Angel a salad wrap but she's gone out by the time we get back.

'She's probably feeling better and gone back to school,' Tanya says quickly, opening the fridge door and staring vacantly inside for a few moments as if she's thinking about something else.

An hour later, we've eaten the food and changed into our swimwear. Tanya lends me the same costume as before and I'm soon sitting nursing a glass of fizz with warm jets of water massaging the bottom of my back. Bliss.

'Thanks again for taking me out this morning, Tanya. It felt really special.'

'No need to keep thanking me, and it needn't be special, you know. It could be just normal. You said yourself you need a new wardrobe.'

Although I've shied away from speaking in detail about my finances, this is a really good moment to be honest with her. It will avoid embarrassing situations in the future if she knows the truth.

'The thing is, that lovely shop and Anita's services? As much as I enjoyed the experience, it's out of my league. Maybe for the odd special occasion, but Isaac and I, we've just got an ordinary budget. We have to keep a tight eye on what we spend.'

'Everyone's got a budget, even me,' she says flippantly. 'Tristan is always trying to keep me on a tighter leash, but spending limits are there to be pushed, as far as I'm concerned. You've said yourself there's a lot more money now Isaac's got this new job, so you should use today to show him that things are going to change.'

'Change how?'

'In that you demand a bit more from life, Janey. You deserve it. Looking after your mum all that time and spending next to nothing too, I bet. He's told you himself his salary has practically doubled, and you've got a job now too, so enjoy it!'

She takes a deep draught from her glass and looks at me. 'You're not in debt, are you?'

I laugh nervously, shocked at her bluntness. 'No, of course not,' I say, thinking about the secured loan we've just settled. Suddenly I feel desperate to get off the subject. 'I'm really looking forward to starting my new job. I loved working in school before but had to give it up to care for Mum.'

'I'm pleased for you, Janey, if that's what you want, but… you'll have no free time at all if you're working, doing the school runs and suchlike.' She indicates the hot tub. 'Spending the afternoon like this will be a distant memory.'

'It's only three days a week,' I say. 'And it's in Mr Sykes's class, so I'll only be a couple of rooms away from Rowan. It'll be easy to pick him up at the end of the day.'

'Maybe you'll find out the story behind Kyoko's ice cool exterior. She's a very private person.'

I'm shocked to hear Tanya's opinion of Kyoko but also a bit panicked to think she might expect me to share confidential information.

'I'll be working with a nominated child most of the time,' I say quickly. 'And as a parent *and* a member of staff, I have to sign a confidentiality agreement as well as the standard contract.'

'Of course, that's just standard. But you know I'd never breathe a word if you were to share anything juicy with me.'

Tanya reaches down again for the bottle. Only a dribble comes out and she laughs, reaching down and popping the cork on a new one.

My head feels pleasantly woozy as she pours more fizz. I've been doing a lot of talking and I haven't been keeping an eye on Tanya's surreptitious top-ups. Still, I can feel I've drunk quite a bit more than usual. I glance over to the trees where I'd spotted Polly lurking before but thankfully there are no glimpses of her mauve cardigan there today and I relax again.

'You know, life feels good,' I say. 'Like everything's coming together.'

'Coming together from what?' She frowns. 'I always think that phrase implies things have fallen apart at some point.'

'No… I didn't mean that, although it's true that Isaac and I have had our problems.'

'Marital problems, you mean? We've all had them… still have them periodically.'

I hesitate. I've always been a private person, and Mum's warnings about the duplicity of friends are ringing in my ears as is Isaac's warning to say little. But the water is deliciously hot, the drink is flowing and I feel happy. I actually feel good about myself for the first time in ages. Would it be so bad to open up a little to Tanya? She has this way of putting me at ease, and she's been so good to me.

I drain half of my fresh glass and stare at the frothing water playing around the fingers of my free hand.

'It's really hard to explain, but the closest I can get is that it feels as if I've lost my way over the last few months,' I venture cautiously.

'Since you lost your mum, you mean?' I'm vaguely aware of even more drink being poured.

'Yes, but… it wasn't the loss that got to me, you see. I was… I was…' I stumble a bit over my words and knock back more fizz, spilling some into the water in the process. 'It was what happened *before* Mum died that did it. What I found out, what she'd kept from me all those years… I just couldn't cope with it.'

'Oh, Janey.' Tanya shifts over into the seat next to me and takes my glass. She slides her arm around me, pulls me close. 'What is it, darling? We're friends and you can tell me anything. I won't say a word, you know that by now.'

And in that moment, it's like everything converges. The fear, the shame, the need to trust someone who cares with the burden of my secret. It all adds up to something enormous, something so powerful that I just can't fight it alone any more and I hear myself telling her.

I hear myself telling her everything.

37

It's the look on Tanya's face that makes me finally stop speaking. That look... I can't even adequately begin to describe it, but it's got shades of both horror and sympathy mixed into it. It's a look nobody really wants to be on the receiving end of. It tells me, even through the fog of alcoholic warmth I'm cocooned in, that I've just changed things forever between us and I can never go back. I can only hope it brings us closer.

'I... I don't know what to say,' Tanya stammers. 'I mean... are you *sure* this is true? Could your mum have been confused because of her illness?'

I shake my head. 'She gave me a box of stuff that backs up everything she told me. She said she'd kept it all for me, but I don't know because I haven't plucked up the courage to go through it all yet. I just can't get past the fact that for all those years, she *lied*. Through saying nothing, she forced herself to live a horrible lie...' The churning of the water, the pressure of the jets and the buzz of alcohol in my head is making me feel nauseous. 'I have to get out now,' I say, standing up. 'I have to pick Rowan up from school.'

'Janey, wait!' Tanya tugs at my arm but I don't sit down again. 'The school run is another two hours away yet. Let's go inside and get a coffee, yes? You need to calm down a bit before you leave.'

I nod, and we support each other getting out of the tub, both slightly wobbly on our feet. I don't like feeling like this in the early afternoon. I'm not blind drunk because I'm already regretting spilling my guts to Tanya.

Quite rightly, Isaac would go crazy if he knew I'd got myself into this state when I have to pick Rowan up. I don't know what's got into me today. The excitement of our shopping trip combined with the addictive feeling that the new me has stepped inside a brand new life. A feeling that now, I can finally leave the old me behind and telling Tanya the awful truth was part of that.

We wrap towels around us and go inside. Tanya makes a pot of coffee, all the time chattering on in an effort to normalise the situation, but I don't take in a word of it. I feel stone-cold sober and terrified of the consequences of what I've just done.

Tanya grabs my hand. 'I know you're worried I'll say something, but I won't. I give you my word, your secret is safe with me, Janey.'

I nod, shivering, even though it's warm sitting here in the kitchen with the sun flooding in though the bifold glass doors. I want to believe her, I do.

'It's a terrible burden your mum left you with, but it's not your fault, OK? You have to remember that. What happened… it's not your fault.'

It's kind of her, but so easy for someone who's safely removed from it all to say.

'I can't shake it off. I feel tainted.' It's hard to articulate with booze fogging my brain. 'I feel like my life has got so much better since we moved and I'm really excited about the school job. But I have this… this invisible black cloud hovering constantly above me. Even when I sleep, I sometimes dream about it. The worry that it somehow lives inside of me, too.'

Tanya shakes her head. 'You haven't got a bad bone in your body, Janey. I've known some pretty nasty characters over the years and you don't come close. Not a bit.'

After a few seconds of silence, Tanya says, 'I do think you need to go through your mum's stuff, though. Get a handle on the facts;

it'll help you put it behind you. I'm happy to go through it with you, to support you… if you want me to.'

I see the look on her face. The shock and the fear of being entrusted with such a hefty secret. The excitement of the possibilities contained within Mum's box.

'I think I'm going to be sick.' I dash across the smooth tiled floor to the downstairs bathroom in the utility and retch over the loo. My heart is pounding and my forehead is dappled with sweat. I feel a hand on the back of my head, and Tanya holds my hair back in a bunch while I finish being sick. When I stand up, she hands me a tissue.

'Thanks,' I whisper, taking it.

'It's what good friends do, Janey. We look after each other.' She smiles, a kind, genuine sort of smile that eases my discomfort a little. 'That and keep each other's confidences, of course.'

38

I don't start my new job until tomorrow, but Ben has asked if I'd like to pop in to Lady Bridge at lunchtime today so he and I can have a chat. There's also some new-starter paperwork the office needs signing.

I choose to wear a black skirt and blouse with a semi-fitted navy jacket. I check in at reception, and Ben appears to take me through to the staff room. He looks far more relaxed than at the interview, when he'd obviously made an effort to look smart in a shirt and tie. Today he's wearing beige canvas jeans with a white T-shirt and an unbuttoned checked flannel shirt in shades of blue.

He introduces me to the staff who are in there, most of whom I don't recognise. Everyone seems very friendly and welcoming, and I notice they're all dressed casually like Ben. I look around for Rowan's class teacher, Miss Packton, but she isn't in here.

'Right, let's get the most important job sorted then.' Ben grins, clapping his hands together. 'Coffee.'

He makes our drinks and we sit in a quiet corner away from the main gathering of staff.

'I was so relieved when you were interviewed,' he confides, immediately putting me at ease. 'You were the third and final one, and between you and me, I couldn't have imagined working with either of the first two.'

We share a little chuckle. Ben seems so laid back and easy to get on with.

I'm surprised at his casual manner, apparent so early on in our working relationship, but then I see that that's the way he interacts with all the staff. During the course of our conversation, he waves at one colleague who's leaving the room. Then he gives a thumbs-up to another who holds up a textbook Ben has obviously been waiting for. He seems a genuinely nice guy.

'When you started talking about the kids with learning difficulties you've worked with in the past, your passion came through brilliantly and I knew you were going to be such an asset to Elder class,' Ben says, sipping his coffee. 'We've got some challenging characters in our group, including Jasper Shaw, of course, who you'll be working with much of the time.' He says the name like the child's reputation precedes him.

'Jasper Shaw?'

'Yes, he's in desperate need of some quality one-to-one support. The TA who left us couldn't seem to build any trust with him and so he felt insecure and confused.' Ben hesitates before continuing. 'Before that, we've had a succession of supply support staff, so I'm really hoping you can make progress with him. He needs a bit of stability, that's all.'

He clears his throat and shuffles through the paperwork in front of him. I get the feeling there's something he isn't saying.

'That sounds… straightforward enough,' I say.

'Well, maybe not. I mean, it wouldn't be fair of me to let you come in tomorrow without you knowing that Jasper's had some problems here at Lady Bridge. He's so astute on the one hand, particularly in reading people and getting the measure of them. But on the other hand, he can get frustrated and angry really quickly.' Ben pauses and glances at his watch. 'There have been a few minor incidents already this term, and then last week, he had a bit of a meltdown in class because someone asked him the wrong sort of question. He hasn't let anyone near him since; I've had to put him on a table on his own.'

It would have been virtually impossible for Ben to keep the class on task in order for them to learn. But isolating Jasper would've felt like a punishment to him when he wasn't really being naughty, as such.

'Sounds like I'll have plenty to keep me busy,' I say in a droll voice.

'See, that's why you and I are going to get on just fine.' Ben laughs. 'We have the same sense of humour. The bell's going to go any time now, so I need to get back in there. Come on, we'll go say hi to the class and you can meet Jasper.'

Elder class is about three doors away from Rowan's classroom. I dampen down a crazy urge to peer through the glass and wave to him, and instead follow Ben into the classroom I'll be working in three days a week from tomorrow.

The children are filing in through the double doors that face on to the playground. As they enter and spot me, they stare and whisper to each other, probably speculating as to who I am.

Last in is a woman dressed in a navy tabard and sporting a lanyard, who accompanies a short, slightly overweight boy with very dark hair and sallow skin. Apart from the split second when he steps into the classroom and notices me, he averts his dark brown eyes completely and won't so much as glance in my direction.

'That's Samina, the midday supervisor who looks after Jasper at lunchtime. She's kindly agreed to stay with him in class three afternoons a week to help us out until you start,' Ben explains as the pair take their seats at an empty table.

'Settle down then, everyone.' He claps his hands above the hum of voices and the noise level quickly dies down. 'There's someone very special I want you all to meet. She's only popped in to say a quick hello, but tomorrow she'll be spending the day with us. This is Mrs Markham, our new teaching assistant, who's going to be working with us in Elder class. Can we say welcome to Mrs Markham?'

'Welcome, Mrs Markham,' the children chant in perfect unison.

I notice Jasper does not join in and is steadfastly staring at a spot on the desk in front of him without blinking.

'Thank you, everyone,' I say brightly. 'I'm so excited to be joining you here in Elder class and I can't wait to meet you all properly tomorrow.'

'OK, everyone. Project folders open and get out the piece you're currently working on.' The hum of chatter quickly resumes. '*Quietly*, please,' Ben adds sternly before turning to me. 'Sorry Jasper's not more forthcoming, I'll take you over to his table now, see if Samina can get him to say hi.'

'No, no. Let's leave it until tomorrow, give him a little space,' I say. 'There's no rush, and I've got to gradually earn his trust. I know how it works.'

Ben clasps his hands together and puffs out a relieved breath. 'You know, I'm already wondering what I ever did without you,' he says.

Later that evening, when Rowan has gone to bed, Isaac pours himself a drink and we sit together in a rare moment of companionship. It's the first chance we've had to have a proper conversation for two days as Isaac got home late again last night. Sadly, I've started reluctantly accepting his absences now, just as he's stopped offering excuses.

He rests his head back on the seat cushion and gives me a lazy smile. 'You know, your new hair really suits you.'

I feel a little pinch of pleasure inside. I like that smile and hardly see it any more. He used to look at me just like that in the early days.

He's already complimented me on my new hair style, so for him to say it again… he must really mean it.

'So,' he says. 'How did your class visit go today?'

'Really well, thanks.' I'm pleasantly surprised he's even remembered I was going into school. 'I got to meet the children and see Jasper, who I'll be working with. I think he might be a challenge at first but I'm looking forward to getting to know him. Ben Sykes, the class teacher, is really lovely. I think I'm going to be happy there.'

He reaches over and squeezes my hand. 'I'm pleased for you, Janey,' he says earnestly. 'I'm sorry I've been so crap and distracted. I've left you single-handedly stuck in the house, sorting out the mess.'

I instantly feel like a fraud. I spent yesterday afternoon half sozzled in the hot tub at Tanya's house – on the back of worrying about his drinking, too!

'I got out yesterday, enjoyed my shopping trip with Tanya.'

He takes a swig of his gin and doesn't comment. Doesn't even ask how much I spent.

'I… I did something silly yesterday,' I say in a confessional tone.

He looks steadily at me.

'Oh yes? Come on then, let's hear it. Has the credit card exploded after your shopping trip?'

'We did have a lovely morning shopping and I did buy an outfit that's way more expensive than I'd usually entertain. But that's not it.' I take a breath. 'Thing is, I went back to Tanya's and she opened a bottle of fizz, and then another one…'

'The pair of you didn't dance naked down the crescent, did you?'

'Isaac, listen!' I snap. 'This is not a joke.'

He puts down his glass.

'I told Tanya. About… Mum. You know, what she told me—'

His eyes widen. 'You told *Tanya*?'

I nod and squeeze my eyes shut, as if that will make my stupidity go away. Many times Isaac has encouraged me to find a therapist to talk to about my secret. He's also suggested I destroy the contents of Mum's box and forget she ever told me anything at all, and when I said I couldn't bring myself to do that, he offered to go through the contents with me. I pushed that offer away too.

So I'm not in the least bit surprised at the stunned look on his face right now.

'Janey... what were you thinking?'

'It was the drink, the lovely mood.' I hold my palms up. 'It was the excitement about the new job... it was *everything*. She's promised not to say a word, though.'

'And you actually believe her?' He's incredulous.

'I have to believe her!' I wail. 'I know I'm an idiot, incredibly stupid... I know all that. But I can't take it back now, so I have to believe she'll keep my confidence.'

Isaac picks up his glass and drains the last of the drink, the ice cubes rattling as they hit his mouth. 'Well, good luck with that here in gossip central,' he says shortly.

I ignore his snipe. He knows nothing about the crescent; he's never here.

'There's something else, too. I saw Angel, Tanya's daughter, talking to an older man in the square in town.' I take a breath. 'She's only fifteen and Tanya had just dropped her off at school.'

I expect Isaac to discount me like Tanya herself did but he frowns. 'Did you see what this man looked like?'

'Not really, he was side-on and across the other side of the square,' I say, encouraged by the fact he hasn't just dismissed me as paranoid. 'But he was a lot older than her and it was just the way they were talking, laughing together... *flirting*, almost.'

'And you told Tanya?'

'Yes but Angel came home just after I arrived at the house! Apparently, she'd felt ill and left school early. I asked her outright if she'd called at town first and she flat-out denied it.'

'Surely Tanya was concerned?'

'That's just it, she wasn't! She told me I should go to Specsavers!'

'Oh well, you did your duty,' Isaac says, finishing his drink. 'Forget about it now.'

And just as easily as it came, his interest disappears.

39

The next day is my first day working at Lady Bridge, and I get into school at 8.15 after dropping Rowan off at Tanya's house.

The school runs a paid breakfast club to help working parents who have to leave the house early and to ensure the children have a good, unrushed breakfast to start the day. But Tanya wouldn't hear of me enrolling Rowan.

'Drop him off at mine on the days you're working. He can have breakfast with us and go in with us. Dex will love having him there.'

I jumped at the offer and Rowan was delighted too, although this morning he did grumble about having to be up and ready much earlier than usual. Isaac had already left the house at 6.30, which has become his accepted time for leaving, and this morning I actually felt relieved, because I didn't want to face him after last night's admission of drunken foolishness with Tanya.

When I get to school, Ben is buzzing. 'Do you know, it's the first morning for ages that I've come into work actually looking forward to the day ahead. Having your help is going to transform life in Elder class, I just know it.'

I smile, feeling slightly nervous as to whether I can live up Ben's high ideal of me. But I'm really looking forward to the day too, and I try and focus on that instead.

Ben explains that the customary practice at Lady Bridge is for the teachers to stand at the classroom doors to welcome the children in each morning. 'It also gives parents an opportunity to have a quick word if they're concerned about anything,' he adds.

It's odd, having this dual viewpoint of the school as both parent and staff member. I think about all the times I've caught Miss Packton first thing in the morning, or at pickup later in the day, to voice my worries about Rowan's problems settling in. Her reassurances always made me feel better, and I hope this will help me understand the parents of the children in Elder class, too.

The bell sounds. Ben opens the doors and the children start to filter in. I'm impressed that some of them have even remembered my name from yesterday. 'Morning, Mrs Markham!'

'Morning,' I reply, asking their names and mentally pairing them with the relevant face. I've always been good at recognising faces, so I'm hoping I'll know all of their names in no time at all.

'I think someone's trying to get your attention.' Ben nods into the playground. The Buckingham mums are all waving madly, Tanya at the front, beaming proudly. Another movement catches my eye to the right as Rowan and Dexter head for their class. Rowan spots me and gives me a shy wave.

I wave back to my friends and blow Rowan a kiss.

'I don't believe it,' Ben exclaims under his breath, making me stand to attention. 'Charlie's brought him into school.'

I follow Ben's gaze and see Jasper walking towards the doors holding the hand of a diminutive young woman with the same colour hair as his. Her head is down but she keeps looking up, her eyes darting nervously this way and that.

'That's Jasper's mum?'

Ben nods, smiling as they get closer. 'Yes. We can hardly ever get Charlie in to school to talk about Jasper's learning plan, and usually a family friend brings him and picks him up. So we're honoured.' He steps out onto the playground.

'Morning, Jasper. Charlie! Lovely to see you.'

'He said he wanted me to come in and meet his new lady,' Charlie says gruffly, looking at me without smiling. 'Is it you?'

'Yes, and I'm really looking forward to working with him. Janey Markham, lovely to meet you, Charlie,' I say, holding out my hand, which she ignores.

Charlie shifts awkwardly and looks away as she holds up a canvas bag.

'He wanted to bring his Harry Potter Lego in to show you.'

'Jasper's prize for pupil with the best attendance in the spring term,' Ben adds.

'Oh brilliant. I love Lego.' I take the bag from her and step back from the doorway. 'Do you want to come and sit down now, Jasper, show me what's in the bag?'

He nods and, without meeting my eyes, steps inside the classroom and heads for his table.

I turn to his mum before I follow him inside. 'Any time you want to chat or come in and see what Jasper's been doing in class, just let me know, Charlie.'

She nods, and Ben continues to talk to her about Jasper's progress, capitalising on her presence, while I follow Jasper to his seat. He takes out about ten Lego bricks, all the same size, and sets about organising them in front of him.

We sit in companionable silence while the other children take their seats. Two girls sidle gingerly up to our table.

'Emily and Livvy are joining us at the table today, Jasper,' I say lightly. 'We thought it would be nice for you to have a little company for a change.' Yesterday, Ben and I discussed trying to integrate Jasper into the rest of the class again.

Emily slips into the chair opposite mine, on the other side of Jasper. He looks up sharply from lining up his bricks, his face dark and brooding.

'Everything OK, Jasper?' I ask.

He stands up abruptly and upends his chair. Emily squeals, and the class falls deathly quiet as the Lego bricks scatter all over the floor.

After morning break, Emily and Livvy come to Jasper's table again. This time I ask them to approach from the top of the table, rather than from the side.

Jasper tenses and the dark expression hovers over his face again.

During the break, I questioned Ben a bit about who used to sit with Jasper before, and why he suddenly wouldn't tolerate classmates.

I asked him to point out the children who had been sitting next to him the day he'd lost it at the table.

'Daniel and Parker.' He indicated two boys sitting together at another table. 'Both nice lads, never get into any trouble.'

I watched the boys, the pally way they had of nudging each other. They worked together all lesson, swapping pens and pencils and sharing a textbook.

'I have an idea,' I told Ben. 'Can we try the girls at our table once more?'

He shrugged. 'Course. But I can't see Jasper changing his mind any time soon.'

'Emily and Livvy are going to sit up the top end and we'll sit here down at the bottom, Jasper,' I tell him lightly now. 'That way we're all friends but don't get in each other's way. And nobody is going to be using your pencils or getting too close.'

After a few moments of consideration, the shadow moves from his face and his eyes brighten a little. His shoulders drop and he looks back down at his worksheet. He opens his plain black pencil case, selects a razor-sharp pencil and places it exactly perpendicular to his paper. Then he zips his pencil case up again and waits until the girls have sat down and everyone is ready to start.

Behind him, Ben gives me a thumbs-up.

40

Over the next couple of weeks Jasper seems to blossom in front of my eyes. We have an unspoken understanding: I ensure he has an environment he feels safe in and that respects his need for space and privacy, and he lets me know if there's anything that's bothering him, crucially, *before* a crisis ensues.

The days I'm not working in school, I join the Buckingham mums on a variety of outings. We enjoy girly-type films at the cinema, regular grooming appointments for hair, nails and trips to the gym where we usually take a spinning or aerobics class together and then enjoy a light lunch in the gym's bistro-style café.

Kyoko continues to keep her distance from me but my connection to Edie and Tanya deepens.

Tanya changed her joint gym membership from her husband's to my name and didn't tell me until after she'd done it. 'Tristan never uses it so you're doing me a favour,' she insisted when I tried to object.

Tanya wanted me to dye my hair a vibrant red shade. 'That cropped bob is just crying out for it,' she insisted. but Angel, who happened to be passing the lounge, stuck her head through the door and said, 'Don't listen to her, Janey. Two or three buttery shades will look sick in your hair.'

'I hope not!' I laughed at her urban-speak but Tanya's lips tightened a touch. I guess she didn't like to be criticised, even by the seemingly faultless Angel.

I'd been practising the overnight fasting idea and with the additional exercise boost, I managed to lose the final stubborn few pounds I'd been trying to shed for the last six months. Now, I feel like I've never looked, or felt, as well as I do now.

There's not much family time happening for us at home but we've all sort of settled into it now. Isaac seems completely distracted by his work, I'm spending most of my time with the other Buckingham mums and Rowan and Dexter are inseparable.

Isaac is doing well in his new position, despite the ever-present stress. There seems to be no shortage of money in the bank.

'I've hit my sales targets and I'm on track for a solid quarterly bonus,' he tells me with relief.

With the three days' salary I now earn, I'm quite forgetting to watch every penny as I had to do before and it's a very nice feeling.

I think once you've been short of cash, though, you can never completely relax and although I don't really need to check the bank balance any more before I make a purchase or join the girls for lunch, through force of habit, I nearly always do.

Yet, with or without the surplus weight and new job, the new-found friends, the extra money, there's something that continues to haunt me. The dark, yawning chasm of the secret that aches inside me, remains completely and utterly unchanged.

Mid-week at Miu's coffee house, Edie announces she's putting on a small dinner party at the weekend.

'Saturday night, nothing special. Just getting a few of our Crescent friends together and you can all bring the kids. There'll be pizza and movies in the playroom so hopefully we won't see them for hours,' she jokes.

'That sounds great, Edie,' I say. 'I assume we can bring our hubbies, too?'

Kyoko gives a little snort as she's the only one of our group not married. I never gave it a thought but she's ready to jump on me for the slightest mistake so it's nothing new and I decide to act as if I haven't realised.

'Of course! Sadly, my Alistair has been working in Europe and won't get back until Sunday.' She turns to Ky. 'So don't worry, darling, you won't be the only one on your own.'

Tristan, Tanya's husband, also works abroad a lot. Maybe Isaac's schedule isn't so bad after all.

'I know Tristan's looking forward to meeting you and Isaac,' Tanya says. 'And the kids will love it.'

All I have to do now is break the news to Isaac.

41

Saturday comes around quickly. I buy flowers and chocolates to take over to Edie's.

'You look nice.' Isaac compliments me as I pull a jacket over a safari-style midi dress I bought recently. I pair it with some leopard-print high heels and a matching neck scarf and I'm ready to go. I have so much more confidence in dressing for every occasion now and it's all thanks to Tanya.

Although it's drizzling with rain, we grab umbrellas and the three of us walk up the road to her house for six thirty that evening. Isaac uses the time to get yet another moan in.

'I'd have much rather stayed in and had a family night,' he says. 'I've also got some paperwork I need to catch up on.'

At least he sounds resigned to the fact we're going now. When I first told him about Edie's dinner party, he flat-out refused to go.

'There are other things I need to do,' he immediately countered.

'Isaac, you're never home and this is important to me,' I shot back. 'Can you think about something other than that rotten job, just this once?'

He had the grace to look ashamed but it didn't stop him complaining.

Edie's gates are open and Rowan tears up the driveway, met at the door by Aisha and Dexter. I can see Ky's twins hovering in the hallway before they all disappear inside together.

Edie appears waving at the door in one of her trademark glittery kaftans. This one is black and turquoise animal print, a little gaudy perhaps but she easily carries it off.

I wave madly back and Isaac groans.

'We won't stay too late,' I promise Isaac. 'But please, be nice. My friends are important to me.'

The longing in my voice surprises me as I feel the stirring of my old friend, the fear of rejection, and I stop talking, embarrassed. I just really want the evening to go well.

'Welcome!' Edie says grandly, holding out her arms so the glitzy fabric falls into dramatic batwings. 'We meet again, Isaac. So glad you could come.'

Grudgingly, he gives a nod.

'You look amazing! Thanks so much for inviting us,' I say quickly, worrying Isaac might give away his reluctance to attend.

Kyoko floats by us without speaking and ushers the children through the hallway into the playroom. She looks stunning dressed in a short black silk dress with a mandarin collar. Ruby lips and impossibly high heels with red soles complete her look. I see Isaac glance at her but before I can introduce them she's gone.

'Janey's told me how busy you are at work, Isaac,' Edie says. 'So it's great to have you here tonight.'

I swallow hard, hoping Isaac doesn't think I've been discussing his job again but he shows no sign of being riled.

'It's a shame Alistair isn't here,' Isaac says smoothly and I'm astonished he was actually listening when I told him Edie's husband's name. 'It would have been nice to meet him too.'

'Ahh yes and he does send his apologies.' Edie smiles. 'He asked me to tell you he'll definitely catch you next time.'

'Janey!' Tanya calls theatrically over Edie's shoulder. 'Come through, I found Edie's hidden stash of champagne!'

Edie grins and stands aside so we can walk inside.

'Is Angel here?' I ask Tanya.

'No, she's…' She glances at Edie. 'She's out tonight herself.' Tanya thrusts a cut glass flute my way. 'Say hi to my gorgeous husband, Tristan,' she simpers, cosying up to a surprisingly short, unremarkable man who looks a good few years older than her.

'I'm Janey, pleased to meet you at last, Tristan.' We shake hands and I feel a bit disconcerted by how thoroughly *bored* he looks. Furthermore, he makes no attempt whatsoever to disguise the fact.

'Tristan's been so looking forward to meeting you and Isaac, haven't you, darling?' She's blurting out words at a rate of knots and I wonder how much she's had to drink already. She's obviously trying to make up for the fact Tristan is totally disinterested in being here, so he and Isaac might have something in common after all.

I turn around to speak to Isaac and see he's still chatting to Edie in the hallway. I decide to take that as a positive sign that he's is thawing a little.

I turn back to Tristan. 'It's great everyone's managed to get together at last, isn't it?' I say inanely, struggling to find a mutually compatible subject to discuss. I'm mortified when, instead of answering, Tristan pulls his phone out of his pocket and glances at the screen.

'Hmm. Would you excuse me a moment?' He turns and walks over to a quiet corner without waiting for my reply.

I feel like crawling under the coffee table but Edie comes to the rescue and begins to encourage everyone to gravitate to the dining table. The kids are delighted to be eating pizzas in the games room but our environment is more formal; a vision of white linen and sparkling glasses.

Edie has hired a private chef so she is able to enjoy the three-course meal with us without getting up and down and dashing to the oven. I never knew there was a different way to entertain… what a life this is!

With the red and white wine now flowing, we sit down to a starter of grilled prawns and black garlic puree before moving on to a delicious main of wild mushroom risotto with tarragon. Warm madeleines and lemon curd complete our gastronomic feast.

'I'm fit to pop,' I whisper to Isaac and he laughs too loudly, boldly reaching for another bottle of Merlot and topping up his own glass.

Following the meal and after giving our compliments to the chef, who has been remarkably calm and organised throughout the evening, we retire, with coffee, to Edie's sensational lounge. If it looked amazing when I called for coffee that day, it looks nothing less than spectacular now. The entire space is illuminated with church candles ensconced in tall lanterns and elegant glass lamps. The glow of the fire as it moves through a constant loop of vivid LED colours only adds to the ambience of the room.

I sit back and enjoy the dulcet tones of Adele playing softly in the background and notice, with particular satisfaction, that Isaac is now standing over by the window, engrossed in a deep, animated conversation with Tristan.

'Look at the two of them,' Tanya says when she comes and sits down next to me on a velvet sofa. 'They get on like a house on fire, just like us.'

'I can't believe it.' I shake my head. 'I thought Isaac was going to be grumpy all night because he'd rather be cuddled up with his emails.'

'To be fair, let's not be naïve. They'll be nattering about work, not sharing tips on how to keep us, their gorgeous wives, happy.'

We lean into each other and laugh and I feel a rush of affection for my friend.

'Thanks for everything, Tanya,' I whisper. 'I mean… thanks for not judging me when I told you—'

'Hey!' She presses a finger to her lips. 'Our secret, remember? I'm here when you feel ready to look at your mum's stuff but that's totally your call. No pressure, OK?'

'OK.' I smile gratefully and rest my head momentarily on her shoulder before sitting up again and looking around the room.

Isaac has disappeared and I can't help wondering if he's gone back to the kitchen for yet another refill. He must have guzzled nearly the entire bottle of Merlot that was placed on the table between us. I drank mostly white wine and was also careful to alternate glasses of water but Isaac showed no such restraint.

He can become quite argumentative when he's had too much to drink and I'm thinking this might be a good time for us to make our excuses.

'Hold this.' I hand Tanya my glass of wine. 'I'll just be a moment.'

Out in the hallway with no music and less people, it's cool and quiet and I realise I'm quite tired now after the meal. I'd really like to get off in the next ten minutes or so. The kids are in the playroom just across the hall; I can hear them in there shouting and squealing at whatever PlayStation game they're playing, the suitability of which Edie assured me she'd checked out.

I peer around the door into the kitchen, thinking how I might dissuade Isaac from quaffing more wine without causing a scene but he isn't in there. There's just the chef and his helper still clearing up.

Back in the hall, I look up at the mezzanine floor and figure Isaac must have gone to the upstairs bathroom which is strange because there's a perfectly decent loo next to the kitchen. Still, with six adult guests plus the catering staff and all the kids, there might've been a queue downstairs.

I climb the stairs, the chrome stair rods glinting and the deep pile carpet soft on my bare feet. Nothing in this house is mediocre, nothing is less than perfect.

The door of the bathroom at the top of the stairs is open and I can see there's nobody in there. There are six bedrooms in Edie's house and I'm guessing at least half of them have en-suite bathrooms. Most of the doors that line the upper floor are closed but the one closest to me is slightly open and I hear what sounds like voices.

My heart thumping, I push open the door a little further and take one step inside the bedroom.

There, silhouetted against the window, is my husband and standing very close to him, whispering something into his ear, is Kyoko.

42

The second he hears the soft scrape of the door on the carpet, Isaac jumps away from Kyoko as if he's been hit by an electric shock. I can see it's a completely instinctive reaction but he couldn't have looked more guilty if he'd tried.

They both turn to the door and he fixes his soft grey eyes on mine. His face showcases a maelstrom of emotions that are over in a flash. Yet I recognised each one as if they'd played out in slow motion: shock, disbelief, sadness and finally… desperation.

'Janey, wait!' he calls as I turn, wordlessly, and leave the room. I stagger down the hall and pause at the top of the stairs, fighting the nausea that's threatening to overwhelm me.

I've always thought, if I ever found out my husband was being unfaithful, I'd spit and lash out like a feral cat. But sometimes we surprise ourselves and react in a completely different manner altogether.

That's how it had been for me tonight.

Kyoko just stood there, cool as a cucumber. She was *so* beautiful and haughty but maybe Isaac thought he'd sensed a hidden vulnerability in her. Little did he know she had a stone swinging in her chest instead of a human heart.

I was utterly convinced of that now.

43

'Janey… wait!'

I ignore Isaac's desperate plea that carries on the crisp night air as I thunder down the crescent towards home. It is only ten thirty but the road is quiet. Cars are stacked neatly on driveways, gates and curtains closed for the night. Families together and cosied up in their beds.

'It's not what you think,' Isaac calls, out of breath as he starts to run. I can hear his footsteps gaining ground. 'Please, Janey. Wait.'

I ignore him. If I turn around and see his lying face, I won't be able to stop screaming at him.

After rushing downstairs in a daze from the bedroom, I staggered into the lounge and blurted out that I'd caught Isaac and Kyoko together upstairs. The pleasant buzz of party chatter ground to a halt like someone just muted the volume.

Edie and Tanya rushed over to me, instinctively formed a protective little shelter around my head and shoulders with their arms.

'What's happened Janey? What did you see?' Edie looked mortified.

'I can't… I can't talk about it now,' I sob. 'I need to… I have to go home.'

I looked at her pleadingly, my cheeks wet.

'Go now,' Edie said kindly. 'Rowan can stay here tonight with Aisha and Dex. It's the best thing until you get things sorted out between the two of you.'

'I'll come with you,' Tanya said. 'You can stay over at mine tonight, sweetie.'

'Thanks but I have to just get home.' I broke away from them. 'I have to get my head around it all.'

When I left Edie's place, Isaac and Kyoko were still upstairs, adding insult to injury as far as I'm concerned.

I pick up pace and as I near the house I fish in my clutch bag for my keys, glad I had the sense to bring them out even though Isaac had been the one to lock up. As I reach the gate, Isaac catches up and I feel the weight of his hands on my shoulders.

'Janey.' He breathes heavily in my ear. 'Just listen. Please.'

I can't stand the thought of his mouth so close to my face. I don't want to breathe the same air as him, be near to the very same lips that were probably suckered to Kyoko's perfect face a couple of seconds before I walked in on them.

I wheel around and push him away as hard as I can. He staggers back a few steps, his face flushed, his pupils dilated from drinking too much wine.

He stays back as I stride up the path and open the front door, slamming it behind me. I shrug off my jacket and shoes and hear his key rattling at the lock as he tries to coordinate his clumsy fingers.

I run upstairs and lock myself in the bathroom, sitting on the closed lid of the loo, my head in my hands.

Thank goodness I watched my own alcohol intake tonight. I think, if I'd been worse the wear for drink and overly emotional, I'd probably have screamed Edie's house down when I walked into that bedroom, disgracing myself in front of my friends and all our kids.

I hear the front door open and close again and then Isaac is rushing upstairs, heading down the landing to our bedroom.

Seconds later, when he realises where I am, he taps urgently on the bathroom door. His tone less pleading, taking the no-nonsense authoritative approach now.

'Janey? Open the door, please. We have to talk about this, I want to explain.'

I bet he does. Neither he, nor Kyoko, had ventured downstairs by the time I left Edie's house. No doubt they were still busy constructing an elaborate tale that would explain why they'd been closeted away up there together.

He raps at the door again, harder this time.

'Janey. This isn't solving anything, is it now?' The resigned, tired parent approach. 'You can't stay in there forever so you might as well come out and we can talk about this like adults.'

I swallow down a string of expletives. 'Leave me alone.'

'I can't leave you alone. I live here too, remember?' He sighs, apparently realising he's not helping himself. 'Look, all I'm asking is for you listen to what I have to say. Then, if you decide never to speak to me again, so be it. Deal?'

Very cunning. He's right though, even though it kills me to admit it. I can't stay in here forever and, more to the point, why the hell should I hide away? He's the one on the back foot. I should be putting *him* on the spot.

I stand up and unlock the door. He opens it immediately and holds out his arms to embrace me.

'No thanks.' I put up my hands. 'I don't want you anywhere near me.'

Isaac sighs, a slow clarity of the dire situation breaking through his drunken fog.

I push roughly past him and walk down the hallway to our bedroom, my heart heavy as I look around in the dim sodium orange glow of the street light outside our house.

We've tried to make this room as nice as we can in a short time, buying new curtains and bedding and some fancy new mirrored bedside tables. We haven't made love much since moving here, mainly because Isaac is around so little, but the nights we have gotten close, it's been tender and loving. It made me feel like we have something to fight for and now...

'Don't cry, Janey, please.' Isaac moves in close behind me, slides his arms around me and presses his chin to the top of my head. 'I'm so sorry I've upset you but honestly, it's not what you think at all.'

I pull away and move over to the window, pulling the curtains shut and turning on my bedside lamp before sitting on the bed.

Isaac takes my place at the window, standing opposite me, leaning against the curtained windowsill.

'I'd gone upstairs to use the bathroom as there was someone in the one next to the kitchen,' he says calmly. 'When I came out, I stood at the top of the stairs to check my phone and I heard someone crying in the bedroom.'

Kyoko, *crying*? The sliver of ice that ran through her must've somehow melted, I think cynically. But I keep my face impassive and stare at a spot on the wall to the left of him.

'Of course, I went in there to see if the person was OK and that's when I saw it was Ky.'

Ky! How familiar. Tanya's voice echoes in my mind from the first time she introduced the other women.

This gorgeous creature is Kyoko Nagasawa but her friends call her Ky.

'I didn't realise you two knew each other so well,' I say witheringly.

'We don't! I mean, we didn't but... well, she was so upset, Janey. About you.'

I stare at him.

'It seems she's convinced herself you can't stand her and she asked me if I knew why that might be.'

Despite my abject misery, I actually laugh. 'You've got to be kidding me.'

'It's the truth. She was distraught, Janey. She wants to be friends with you but she feels like you've ignored her in favour of the others.'

'How dare you side with her?' I stand up, balling my fists to try and keep myself under control. 'I told you weeks ago she can't stand me, that she's been cold and bitchy because she's jealous I'm close to Tanya.'

'Yes, but—'

'But nothing! It's the most pathetic excuse I ever heard. Is that honestly the best the two of you could come up with? You were practically glued to each other when I walked in.'

'Janey, please. It's the truth.' He pinches the top of his nose and squeezes his eyes shut. 'We'd all been drinking and emotions get high, you know that. But there was nothing untoward happening, I was just trying to comfort her. I said I'd speak to you about it.'

He looks wretched. His face is pale and dark shadows circle his eyes.

Would I be a complete sap to consider the possibility Isaac might be telling the truth? That there really is nothing between the two of them?

I don't for a minute believe Kyoko is concerned about our non-existent friendship. If there's any truth at all in this unlikely tale, it's more likely she planned to bump into Isaac upstairs as another ploy to upset me and send me stomping off home, so she could take her rightful place next to Tanya again.

Isaac's usually no fool but it is possible that, with enough drink in him, he'd be comparable to a helpless, trusting little kitten in the hands of a cougar like Kyoko.

Still, I refuse to do the 'woman blaming woman' thing. He's a grown man and should've known better than to put himself in that position. The fool.

Alternatively, if the whole story is a fabrication, then I'm married to a barefaced cheating liar. Maybe Isaac has been caught red-handed and is now trying his level best to squirm his way out of a possible divorce which would see me kicking him out of the family home.

'Janey, look, I'm sorry. I should never have gone into the bedroom with her but I—'

'You can sleep in the spare room tonight,' I say shortly. 'I can't talk about this any more.'

I'm too exhausted to scream, cry or to listen to any more of Isaac's inane pleading.

'Can we talk tomorrow?' He drops his head as if he's afraid of my answer.

'You'll find spare bedding in the airing cupboard,' I say.

44

Last night I tossed and turned for what seemed like hours before finally dropping off to sleep sometime in the early hours.

I wake up just after eight feeling like I have the worst hangover, even though my thumping head and stinging eyes have nothing to do with drinking too much alcohol. When I glance at my phone I have message notifications on my phone from Edie and Tanya.

Hope everything OK. Rowan staying for lunch and then we're all going bowling until mid-afternoon… if that's fine with you.

I'm grateful to Edie. She's obviously creating some time for me and Isaac to talk and also protecting Rowan from the fallout of last night. I tap out a quick reply thanking her and saying that will be fine before clicking into the next message that Tanya sent just five minutes ago.

Croissants warming, coffee on. Fancy coming over for early breakfast? Tristan gone to golf course and Angel stayed out at friend's house.

The chance of escaping another intense chat with Isaac is too tempting. I jump out of bed and take a quick shower before dressing in one of the new velvet tracksuits and the trainers I bought online. I don't bother with make-up but brush my hair and secure the top section up in a cute little topknot that suits my new length.

Downstairs I grab my handbag and keys.

'I made us smoked salmon and eggs.' Isaac appears in the kitchen doorway. 'I've squeezed some fresh orange juice and—'

'I'm going out,' I say shortly and, grabbing my jacket from the wooden balustrade, I leave the house to his stammering objections.

I walk the short distance to Tanya's and halfway there, another message pings through on my phone. I stare at the sender's name: Kyoko.

Janey, I'm so sorry about last night. I had drunk far too much wine and become emotional. You have my word that's all it was. I'm so embarrassed.

I stuff the phone into my pocket without replying. Ky's word means nothing to me at all.

Tanya sets out breakfast and then sits and waits for me to speak.

'I've had this feeling for a while that Isaac is up to something,' I say, staring at a flake of pastry on the table that's fallen from the plate. 'So last night, when I found the two of them together upstairs, it felt like I'd found the reason.'

'When you say you think he's "up to something", can you be specific?'

'He just seems on edge all the time and you know he's been constantly saying this new job will turn out to be the start of a new way of working?' She nods. 'Well, it's just not happening. In fact, if anything, after a promising start, we're now seeing less of him than ever. When he is home, he disappears upstairs into his study for hours on end. If I try and get him to talk about his work, he changes the subject.'

Tanya nods sagely. 'And you're wondering if it *is* the job keeping him out at all hours?'

'That's about the size of it, yes.'

She sighs, her expression grave. 'Don't take this the wrong way, Janey, but I feel we know each other well enough now I can be frank with you. Do you think Isaac and Ky are having a full-blown affair?'

'I don't know. I mean, I'm shocked finding them together in the bedroom last night but they've both denied it. I can't believe he would do that to us, to me and Rowan. I just can't.'

'Men don't think about their kids when they're cheating, Janey,' Tanya says bluntly. 'In fact, their wife and kids are generally the furthest thing from their minds.'

Hearing her words makes me squirm on my stool. Of course it's occurred to me that Isaac might not be spending all this time at work but being unfaithful with Kyoko Nagasawa is something else altogether.

'I would've said that a strong, opinionated woman like Ky would terrify Isaac,' I tell Tanya, watching as she picks up the cafetière and pours the dark, viscous liquid into our cups. 'If I had to name a type he'd go for, *she'd* be at the opposite end of the scale. What do you think about it all?'

Tanya looks so genuinely concerned for me and if anything, that makes me feel worse.

'I'd value your opinion,' I add, not mentioning that I'm dreading it at the same time.

Do I want to know if my husband is having a full-blown affair with our mutual friend? Have I conveniently blamed his new job when it's been another woman who was commandeering all his time right under my very nose?

If I have, it's because I can't bear to think of my son suffering for our mistakes. I don't want him to be brought up in a single parent family like I was.

'Look, I spoke to Ky last night when she came downstairs and she was mortified. She swore to me there was nothing in it at all, that she'd had too much to drink and got herself all upset over nothing.' Tanya pushed a mug towards me. 'She said Isaac had just happened to be upstairs too, saw she was in tears and had tried to comfort her. That was all it was.'

'Fancy that, the very same story Isaac told me,' I murmur cynically, pouring milk into my coffee and watching the creamy swirl lighten up the dark liquid.

'I think she was being genuine, Janey. You know Kyoko has been there herself, when she lived in York? Me and Edie, we supported her through it after she left her husband and came to live in Nottingham.' She blows into her coffee cup and takes a sip.

'She did tell me that,' I say, although it changes nothing so far as I'm concerned.

'Ky's husband trod almost the exact path you described with Isaac: working all hours, acting out of character. Ky was immediately suspicious and got a private investigator involved. Every time he was late home, he told her he had an important "meeting". She discovered that part was true but turns out the meetings were all in a hotel room with his hot new assistant, not with the board of directors.'

I look at Tanya. What is she trying to say?

'Having been through it herself, I doubt Ky would inflict the same on one of her friends,' she remarks.

I think that's quite a naïve view. Despite Kyoko apparently claiming to Isaac she's upset because she thinks I dislike her, the real truth of it is that she's shunned me ever since Tanya brought me into the group. No way could she and I be described as friends.

'I think she'd be loyal to you and Edie,' I say, looking at the croissant in front of me and decide I can't stomach it. 'But she really doesn't care for me, Tanya. I honestly think she's jealous because you and I get on so well.'

'Oh, I don't think that's true!' Tanya laughs, adding a scrape of jam to her croissant.

I could list things like Ky's rudeness about my outfits, that day she said there was no room at the coffee shop, her surly attitude whenever I'm around. It all sounds so petty said out loud yet when you're on the receiving end, it's very real and hurtful.

'The fact remains that Isaac's behaviour hasn't been normal for some time. Then I find him in an upstairs bedroom with our mutual friend. Go figure.' I shrug, taking a sip of my coffee.

'I totally agree, what you've described sounds like classic signs. A change in routine or behaviour, an element of secrecy… it's textbook.'

'On the other hand, for the last few months, Isaac hasn't had the energy for *one* woman in his life, never mind two,' I continue. 'We've struggled to be intimate for a while, that's what I'm trying to say. Sometimes we've gone weeks without… well, you know. And we seem to have lost that closeness, even struggling to share what's happened in our day over dinner each night.'

The smile fades from my own face as I realise my marriage sounds in big trouble.

'Listen to yourself, sweetie,' Tanya says softly. It's hanging over all our heads every day, Janey, it's the downside to this lifestyle. Having a successful husband and getting older feels like there's a storm waiting to break above us in the shape of a younger woman.'

'The men are getting older too,' I point out.

Tanya shakes her head. 'It's different for men though, isn't it? Getting older isn't frowned upon in the same way. Their wrinkles and eye bags are described as "distinguished", their ageing skin and grey hair are thought of as "rugged".'

'Hmm. I've never really thought of it like that.' I frown. I've seen plenty of older men with younger partners but middle-aged women with younger men? Not so much.

'Yep. Wealthy men, they can have it all,' Tanya continues in a maudlin tone. 'I wonder all the time if Tristan is planning to trade me in for a younger model when Dex is old enough to deal with it. I feel constantly on edge because of it.'

Tanya seems to deflate in front of me, her swagger and confidence suddenly evaporating. Behind the perfect hair and immaculate make-up, I see there's a deep sadness and a vulnerability that she must work incredibly hard to keep hidden. I can imagine it must be exhausting.

'I'm sorry for raking all this up for you, Tanya,' I say, genuinely perturbed. It's obvious she has her own worries but I never expected to be talking in such great detail about my marriage concerns.

I drink the rest of my coffee and push the croissant to one side, suddenly eager to get away. 'I'll think about what you've said and keep an eye on Isaac's movements. Perhaps I have been a little naïve after all.'

'I consider myself a good judge of character and I think you're torturing yourself if you really believe they were up to something last night, Janey,' Tanya says, squeezing my hand. 'If your husband is being unfaithful, then I don't think it's with Ky. Anyway, you have your date night arranged for Wednesday, right? Angel's going to take care of Rowan and you are going to have a damn good night with your husband. It's exactly what you need.'

I'd completely forgotten about our supposed date night. Laughable now, of course. But I don't want to get into debating that with Tanya right now. Frankly, going out with Isaac on Wednesday is the *last* thing I feel like doing.

She offers me more coffee, seeming to want me to stay a little longer but I decline.

'Thanks, but I've taken up enough of your time,' I say, although I'm dreading going home.

Tanya accompanies me to the front door.

'Find his diary,' she hisses loudly from behind, making me jump.

'I'm sorry?'

'Find his work diary, that's my advice. They often have a regular desk diary they leave lying around but don't be fooled by that. It's the online version you need; he might even be sharing it with someone else… possibly some tart in his office.' Her eyes gleam with malice. 'Go through his papers in the office, look in the least obvious places. You never know what you might find.'

'I – I will.' She's sounding a bit crazy now and I push my feet hastily into my flat pumps and open the door. We air kiss. 'Thanks for breakfast and the chat.'

'I'm here any time you need to talk.' The usual public-facing smile is pasted on her face now she's standing in view of the houses opposite, but her seemingly innocent words are loaded with meaning. 'Let me know how you *get on*.'

45

Back at home, Isaac creeps around the house, servile and desperate to please.

Would I like a cup of tea? A slice of toast? Should we watch a film together? Perhaps I'd like to go out for lunch?

I respond to all his offers with a resounding 'no' and yet somehow, we seem to have reached an unspoken truce. A sort of mute agreement where we set aside, at least temporarily, what happened last night in the sense that we've stopped discussing it.

I don't see him check his emails or messages once and when he joins me in the sitting room and opens the Lee Child thriller I bought him last Christmas, I nearly fall off my chair. But we sit in companionable silence for a while. Something feels settled about the situation although I know it isn't. Not really.

Then, just before he's due to collect Rowan from Edie's house, Isaac puts down his book and walks over to the sofa where I'm reading.

'I'm truly sorry I upset you last night, Janey,' he says, just standing there, his face wrinkling with regret as he knots and unknots his fingers. 'I was foolish not to think how it might look. I just wanted to say, one last time, that nothing happened. I mean, there was nothing in it at all except I felt sorry for Kyoko.'

'Then what's wrong?' I snap in a burst of frustration. 'You're so… unsettled lately. Just not yourself.'

'Nothing's wrong,' he insists. 'Apart from the usual work pressures and it'll get better very soon. I know it will.'

He crouches down and takes my hand. Kisses it as if he's about to propose again like he did all those years ago.

My eyes settle beyond him, on the silver-framed photograph of Isaac with Rowan, arms around each other at the side of the football pitch last year. Rowan's face is muddy and joyful after scoring the winning goal. Isaac looks down at him with an undisguised 'proud dad' look that makes my heart swell every time I look at the photo. It's so important to me that Rowan remains close to his father.

When I look back at Isaac's face now, his eyes are dull and dark with anguish.

'Can you find it in your heart to believe me, Janey?'

I don't answer him but I don't pull my hand away, either.

What would Rowan do without his dad? After losing his nan and leaving all his school friends behind, he's finally happy at school and making the most of his life here on Buckingham Crescent.

I honestly don't know if my son could get through another major upheaval. If Isaac and I split up, it could surely set Rowan back so far, he might take years to recover.

I look at Isaac's face, contrite and aching for my forgiveness.

Despite his insistence to the contrary, I could swear there's something he isn't telling me… but now I don't think he's having an affair with Kyoko. I honestly don't think it's that.

When Isaac leaves to walk up to Edie's house to collect Rowan, I'm surprised to hear a knock at the door only minutes after he's gone. I rush down the hallway to open up, thinking he's forgotten something.

'Is everything alright, Janey?'

'Oh hi, Polly,' I say, trying to keep the weariness off my face. 'Yes, everything's fine thanks. Why do you ask?'

'Well, I noticed you got back quite late last night.' She pulls her cardigan tighter and folds her arms in front of her, as is her habit. 'And it looked like... it looked as if you and Isaac were quarrelling about something.'

Her uninvited intrusion burns at my throat.

'Everything's fine, Polly,' I say crisply. 'Were you watching the house all night, waiting for us to return?'

'No! Of course not,' she says, affronted. 'I happened to take out some rubbish and saw you all walking up the street about six thirty and then...'

'You happened to look out of the window at the exact moment we returned, for a guess?'

'That's about the size of it, yes.' She drops her arms to her sides for a moment and them folds them again. 'Look, Janey, I don't know where you went but I'm guessing it was up to Edie McCaid's house. Yes?'

I laugh, incredulous. 'Polly. Please don't do this, it's embarrassing. I don't have to account for where I was last night to you or to anyone else.'

But she's oblivious to my indignation. 'I know you've been going to Tanya's house a lot because I've seen you both in that spa bath contraption and you both sitting chatting in the garden.'

My chest tightens when it occurs to me that maybe Polly has been eavesdropping when we've been unaware. Has she heard me talking about my marriage problems... or other personal things? I can barely conceal a shudder.

'I'm not going to continue this conversation, Polly. You've crossed a line, you must know that.'

'The lot you're hanging around with, they're not to be trusted,' she says, as if she hasn't heard a word I've said. 'You saw what Tanya did to my beautiful flowers, didn't you? And that Edie, she's the one who—'

'Enough!' I snap and she visibly jumps a little. 'I don't want to hear any more, Polly. I know you're lonely and that your family life is quite different to how you had me believe. I'm sorry for you, I am. But I'm not interested in hearing your nasty gossip about my friends, so I'll say goodbye now.'

I make to close the door, hoping she turns and walks away before I have to close it in her face but she pushes it hard, sending me staggering back a little.

'You'll wish you listened because you're making a big mistake. I might be all the things you've said I am but I *see* things. Things you wouldn't believe.' She snarls, her face twisting up with malice. 'Don't come crying to me when you're in trouble, Janey Markham, because I won't want to know!'

And with a final thump in temper on the door, she turns and stomps back down the path.

46

Monday morning, I drop Rowan off at Tanya's house and go into work as usual. To my relief there's no sign of Polly in the front garden. I decided not to mention our altercation to Isaac yesterday and I won't be discussing it with Tanya and Edie because I don't think they'll let it go. Quite rightly, they'll be angry about the stuff Polly is saying about them. Still, I'm hoping now I've made it clear I'm not interested in her slurs, Polly will finally get the message.

Five minutes before the bell goes, I step out of the classroom doors and manage to give Rowan a peck on the cheek before he goes into his registration.

When I look up, Kyoko is standing in front of me. Alone.

'Janey, I wanted to apologise in person about what happened on Saturday night,' she says, looking at her feet. 'I've been on medication for a skin allergy and I think I had a reaction… with the alcohol, I mean. I should never have said those silly things to Isaac about you and I not getting on.'

After Ky's usual subdued attitude towards me, I'm surprised she's displaying her regret so openly. I see the group of Buckingham mums, Tanya and Edie in particular, watching our exchange anxiously.

'It's true we aren't the closest of friends,' I say frostily. 'That part didn't upset me. But finding my husband huddled together in a bedroom with you, well…'

'I know. I know how it must have looked to you, Janey, and I'm sorry,' she says again, glancing over her shoulder. 'The others, they're annoyed with me, too. I've apologised to Edie for causing a scene at her party.'

'OK. Well, part of me still doesn't know what to think but it means something that you've apologised.' I don't want to appear a pushover but I have to grudgingly admit she didn't have to do this in front of everyone.

'Thanks for understanding.' She's brighter now, as if she's ticked a box of some sort. 'Hopefully we can make more of an effort to get on after this.'

She gives me a little wave and walks back to the group, leaving me feeling a bit stung, like she's managed to get the better of me.

I still don't fully understand what happened Saturday night and truthfully, I'm not really fussed about making more of an effort with Kyoko.

She's been the one all along who's shunned *my* efforts to be friendly but she's gone to great lengths with everyone to make it sound like it was the other way around.

Ben tells me Jasper isn't in school first thing because he has an assessment out of town that his family social worker, Anna, has taken him to.

'I don't really like asking you to do this,' Ben says regretfully. 'But as you've not got to work with Jasper during PE, could you possibly stay here in the classroom and go through the kids' files and make sure they've all got an up-to-date permission letter for the Cromford Mill outing next week? The office staff will be taking over this admin task soon, but for now it falls on the class teacher who's organised the trip. I'm afraid that's me.'

'No problem,' I say, looking forward to a bit of peace and quiet for once while the rest of the class is in the school hall. I sit at Ben's desk where three tall piles of pupil folders are waiting.

Thankfully, most of the required forms seem to be at the front of the paperwork, so it doesn't take me long to whip through them.

Cherry Nagasawa has her signed form in place, but when I get to Jun's file, the form doesn't jump out at me. I flick through the first few sheets of paperwork to no avail, so to make the task quicker, I pull out everything in there and set it in front of me, ready to sort through it systematically.

It's all standard stuff: copies of teacher assessments, school reports, a hospital appointment letter. Until I get about two thirds of the way through and find an official deed poll certificate for change of name. Behind that is a photocopied driving licence, I assume, to prove identity. It features a photograph of Kyoko, but states her name is Yuno Harris and her personal details showing an address in Kent. There's also a certificate confirming Jun's surname has been changed from Harris to Nagasawa, too.

That's strange, I think. When I asked Ky how long she's lived on the crescent, she said about two years, and that before that she lived in York. She's obviously also changed the twins' surnames as well as her own. Odd. I know Tanya told me she split up with her husband but I'm surprised she changed her children's names, too.

I shrug and make a note for Ben that Jun's permission form is missing and slot the paperwork back in the file, pushing the curiosity from my mind. Despite the fact I could happily wring her neck right now, Ky's business is her own. It's not for me to poke my nose into, and I certainly won't be mentioning anything confidential to Tanya. Like Ky or loathe her, I'm perfectly aware I mustn't blur the boundaries of my work and personal life.

But seeing there's a side of Kyoko she's purposely kept hidden, the confusing paperwork trail and the events of Saturday evening, it leaves me thinking that Ms Nagasawa obviously isn't quite the person she first appears to be.

I'm just working the morning today so when I get back into the house at midday, there's nobody else home. I stand still for a few moments to relish the cool calmness of the hallway.

No Rowan shouting, singing, bounding around in his socked feet pretending to be an astronaut or a Premiership footballer who's just scored the winning goal. No television noise as an almost constant backdrop unless I personally turn it off.

Isaac, on the other hand, rarely makes any noise any more. We used to chat lots; he'd help Rowan with his homework at the kitchen table or they'd watch a footie game together, shouting their disapproval at any perceived referee unfairness against their team.

But that was then.

These days, if Isaac is home, he's nearly always upstairs, shut away in his office. If I stand outside the door, I can sometimes detect him speaking in a low, harried voice on the phone. Perhaps I'll knock and take in a cup of coffee, and he'll pause his conversation until I let myself out again, leaving him to get on with the business in hand.

I've never thought to question his behaviour before the events of Saturday evening shook me to my boots. But this morning, finding out that Kyoko is being less than honest with her friends over personal details, I'm starting to draw a line between things. When I pair my observations with Tanya's comments that Isaac's behaviour is 'textbook' unfaithful, it seems only sensible to make a few cursory checks to help put my mind at rest.

Tanya had suggested searching for his work diary but I think there's something more basic I need to do first.

I run my hand through my hair and kick off my shoes before padding along the narrow hallway into the light, airy kitchen. I plonk my handbag on the worktop and take out my phone. Then I pour a glass of water and take it into the living room.

I scroll through my phone contacts until I get to 'Isaac – Work'. I press it and wait for the call to connect. The day before he started work at Abacus, Isaac gave me his office number and the address of the new company, which is based in Long Eaton, a busy town southwest of Nottingham and about a thirty-minute drive from our house.

If I need to speak to him for any reason, I'll usually just text his mobile and leave a message for him to call me when he's free. He travels around the Midlands a lot, and when he's in the office he's constantly attending meetings. So I've never actually called the company landline before.

It's ringing now and I have a feeling, like bad indigestion in my chest. I don't mind admitting that the conversation with Tanya has really rattled me. It's got me questioning Isaac's absences and his true reasons for leaving the house early and coming home late. Even if his actions on Saturday night were innocent, I can't shake the feeling there's something else I'm not seeing.

'Good morning, Abacus, how may I help you?' a sunny female voice says on the end of the line. I feel a flood of relief, although I'm not sure what I expected.

'Could I speak to Isaac Markham, please?'

'May I ask who's calling?'

'It's Janey Markham, his wife.'

'Thank you, Mrs Markham, hold the line, please.'

I hold my breath, suddenly certain that she's going to come back and say there's no one of that name working there. That the whole headhunting thing was a big fat lie.

Then Isaac's voice comes on the line. 'Janey? Is everything OK?'

'Isaac? Yes, everything's fine.' I sound so ridiculously relieved, I'm embarrassed for myself. 'I'm ringing to check if you want me to cancel Wednesday night. Angel arranged to babysit Rowan, if you remember.'

'Janey, I'd really like us to go out. Some time together is just what we need and I've already booked that new restaurant I told you about.' He hesitates. 'Could we still go… put this crap behind us, do you think?'

He sounds so normal, just the same old Isaac but I'm not so sure. Tanya's words are still echoing in my ears. But what if he's been telling the truth and a night out could draw a line under it all? I don't want to make it easy for him.

'I don't know… after the party, it might feel awkward.'

'It won't, I promise,' he says quickly. 'Honestly, I think it'll do us the world of good.'

'I'll tell Angel she can still come over then,' I say as if I'm still not sure. I might be playing silly games but I don't want to make it too easy for him to brush aside what happened.

'That's great, and Janey?'

'Yes?'

'You won't regret this,' he says. 'I'm glad you called.'

And then he's gone and I'm left hoping I'm not making a big mistake in letting him off the hook so soon.

47

Wednesday evening, I stand in my bedroom, in front of the full-length mirror that's still propped up against the wall because Isaac hasn't got around to putting it up yet.

Thanks to Angel offering to babysit, we're going for a swish meal at a fancy new Italian restaurant in town that Isaac booked over a week ago.

It feels strange, spending time getting myself ready to go *out out*.

Tanya insisted she collect Rowan from school and give him tea. 'I'll drive Angel across with him later. She'll put him to bed, so he'll be fast asleep when you get home,' she said as I handed her the spare key.

I would never have believed it, but far from regretting drinking too much in the hot tub and spilling my guts, I'm actually grateful in a way. I feel so much closer to Tanya and it was great to be able to turn to her the morning after the party debacle. It's like we've known each other for ages and now, by some magical progress, we've fast-tracked the friendship ladder and have a new-found closeness that's been built on trust rather than judgement.

We see each other most days, not just briefly at school but during trips out as well. She's been over to my house a couple of times now which suits me because Polly saying she'd been watching us in Tanya's garden has made me feel on edge there. Rowan and Dexter had a play date at ours a couple of days ago while Tanya and I sat drinking lemon and ginger tea, looking at paint colours for the downstairs rooms.

My anxiety about Tanya judging our humble abode against her own sprawling palace has dissolved. It's as though, now she knows the worst there is to know about me, the lack of luxury and stylishness in my own home has simply paled into insignificance.

Kyoko is making an effort to be nicer. There have been no spiked comments nor shady glances since the party, which has got to be a record.

I think about how Mum brainwashed me all those years into distrusting friendships, and how that attitude deprived me of sharing my feelings or talking over worries. She had no right to do that. She might have had problems trusting people herself but a good mother would never have passed on those insecurities to her child.

Still, feeling that I have someone independent onside, someone to confide in, laugh with, even discuss paint colours with… it's been a revelation. Edie has this thing she says about good friendship that always makes us all squeal with laughter: 'It's like being in the best relationship in the world without the inconvenience of the bedroom antics.'

I stare at my image in the mirror, starting with my new balayage hair in the buttery, rich shades Angel advised me to go for in place of the harsher colours I've plumped for in the past.

My hair falls in a soft, blunt bob around my face now, my eyes seeming to appear bluer next to the flattering colours. My skin looks smooth and radiant with the make-up Tanya recommended: a new foundation and a brighter lipstick than I've previously used, even on a rare night out.

But the real difference is how my body looks in the new outfit I bought; the spoils of my shopping trip with Tanya that I've only just got chance to wear. It's money well spent. I look… curvy in all the right places, is the only way I can think to describe it. The discreet supportive built-in panel in the structured skirt nips me in, and for the first time in forever, I actually look as if I've got a waist, as the gold chain belt creates a magical line of illusion.

I touch my throat, where the delicate white-gold necklace with its tiny diamond sparkles – a gift from Isaac on the day Rowan was born that I've hardly worn because I told myself it was far too nice and valuable for everyday use. As I do so, I catch sight of my newly manicured nails in a shimmering nude shade. My eyes drop to my feet, clad in a pair of exquisite nude Christian Louboutin court shoes. Tanya insisted I borrow them when she discovered we share the same shoe size, but I live in mortal fear of scraping them as soon as I step out of the house.

I glance at my watch. Isaac is still in the shower, but the cab won't be here for half an hour, so there's plenty of time. He gets ready in a fraction of the time I need to look the part for a night out.

From the moment he walked through the door at two minutes to seven, he looked rigid with stress. I didn't need to ask what kind of a day he'd had; I knew he was probably silently rueing the fact that he'd agreed to our date night but he's putting on a good show.

'I'll dive straight in the shower,' he said, giving me a peck on the cheek, apparently without really noticing my overhauled look. Could it be that he's simply stopped looking at me and I haven't noticed until now? If so, then we need tonight even more than I thought.

I can imagine him now, standing in the shower, head down while he allows the needles of steaming water to hammer out the tension in his shoulders.

Since we came to our unspoken truce about the party, I've made sure to ask him how work is going every day, but he just gives me the briefest cursory answer, telling me precisely nothing. I'm banking on us having a good chat tonight, when he can hopefully relax enough to finally tell me what's been on his mind. There's something he isn't saying and it's acting like a sheet of glass between us, preventing any chance of us getting closer. Tonight is going to be a well-timed chance for the two of us to level with each other. It could be the turning point we so badly need.

I hear the bathroom door open and Isaac pads down the hallway into the bedroom. He stops dead in the doorway.

'Wow!'

I twirl around, my heart lifting. 'I thought you were never going to notice.'

'Janey, you look… fantastic.'

He allows his towel to drop to the floor and walks over to embrace me from behind.

I revel in the warmth and strength of his arms and tip my head back as he plants light kisses on my neck, sending a little frisson of pleasure across my shoulders and down my arms.

I think tonight is going to be a good night. I think we can put the bad stuff behind us.

I jump at the sound of the doorbell. 'That must be Rowan and Angel. They're early.' I break away from him and go out onto the landing. Downstairs, through the glass side panels of the front door, I recognise Angel's tall, slim frame and her long blonde hair, which she's wearing loose.

'Angel! Thanks so much for agreeing to babysit tonight.' I step back so she can come inside and I'm pleased to see she looks relaxed, like a normal fifteen-year-old. I really do want to believe there was nothing to worry about when she was talking to the man in the square the other day. 'I thought your mum was bringing you and Rowan over later?'

'I have some revision to do.' She indicates the large bag slung over her shoulder. 'Our house is mad at the moment, full of kids. So Mum's bringing Rowan when they've all gone.'

'I didn't realise your mum had a houseful,' I remark. I was under the impression it was just Rowan and Dexter.

'Yeah, Edie came round with Aisha and she and Mum started arguing as usual.' Angel rolls her eyes. 'I came over here to get some peace and quiet.'

Edie and Tanya have been arguing? My stomach turns a little. Could it be they have split loyalties between me and Kyoko? My skin crawls at the possibility there's stuff between them I know nothing about, a hidden closeness.

'We're not quite ready yet, so' – I turn around and beckon to her – 'make yourself comfortable here in the living room and help yourself to anything in the kitchen. There's juice in the fridge, and two sorts of crisps out on the worktop.'

'Thanks, Janey.' She edges towards the couch and puts her bag down. A smirk plays around the edges of her mouth and I realise my mistake. Angel is a young woman, not a kid. And with that trim little figure, it's clear she wouldn't touch crisps with a bargepole.

'Sorry,' I witter on. 'I'm new to this, I'm—'

'Your hair looks great, by the way!'

'Oh… thank you. I took your advice and went for the subtler shades.'

'I knew it would suit you.' She beams.

A shadow passes by the doorway as Isaac sneaks stealthily past and into the kitchen without saying hello. He hasn't met Angel yet.

'Isaac? Come and say hi to Angel.'

He backtracks to the living room door, and I'm relieved to see he's shed the small towel and dressed in his smart black trousers and his colourful Paul Smith shirt.

'Angel, this is my husband Isaac.' I turn to him and give him a look. 'Isaac, this is Angel, Tanya's daughter.'

Isaac and Angel look at each other blankly. No smiling, no speaking… they just *stare*.

I glance at Isaac, confused.

'Hi, Angel!' He springs forward and takes her hand. 'Pleased to meet you.'

'Hello, Isaac,' Angel says in a measured tone.

He looks at me, shakes his head. 'I was trying to work out where Rowan was for a moment there. Wasn't he meant to be coming back here with you?'

'I came over early to do some revision while he plays for a bit at our house with Dexter,' Angel says. 'I hope that's OK?'

'Of course it's OK,' I say, heading for the door. 'Make yourself at home, Angel. Honestly, anything you want, just help yourself. You can lock the door from inside and your mum has a key when she gets here.'

Back upstairs, I frown at Isaac. 'You were a bit stilted down there,' I say lightly. 'I thought for a moment you two knew each other.'

It might sound a bit paranoid but I'm certain I sensed an awkward moment between the two of them.

'What?' He laughs. 'Not at all. I just… I had a bit of a senior moment, that's all.' He disappears back into the en suite.

A senior moment at thirty-nine? Now that would be a thing.

48

The restaurant is busy to say it's midweek, but from the moment we walk in, I feel like we're going to have a good night. I realise how much I've missed dressing up and coming out to spend time together as a couple.

As the maître d' leads us over to a quiet table for two by the window, we're pleasantly enveloped by the subdued lighting, soft piano music and flickering candlelight.

'I love this place,' I say over my shoulder to Isaac behind me. 'How did you find out about it?'

Isaac doesn't answer, and I bite down hard on my back teeth when I see he's texting as he walks. I stop without warning, and he bumps blindly into the back of me.

'Sorry!' he mumbles, pushing his phone into his trouser pocket. 'Wasn't watching where I was going.'

The maître d' pulls out my chair and I sit down without looking at Isaac. I force myself to paste a smile on my face. I can't let my feelings ruin the night before it's even started, and yet *he* clearly hasn't considered that. I suppose that's the danger of wishing for a perfect evening.

A young waiter appears with menus and table water. He's tall and skinny with angry red patches of acne blighting both cheeks. He pours two glasses of water slowly and carefully, as if he's been warned not to spill a drop.

'The soup is tomato and red pepper,' he says, before performing an odd little bow and disappearing again.

I grin at Isaac, expecting him to have a witty comment about the waiter's behaviour, but he's distracted, staring down at his menu. His eyes dart here and there, repeatedly covering all the various courses and sides. It's glaringly obvious he isn't actually seeing anything. What the hell can be possessing his every thought like this?

'Isaac?' I fight to keep the irritation out of my voice. 'Are you going to be able to relax and enjoy it here?'

He throws me a puzzled look over the menu. 'Of course I'm going to enjoy it. I booked the place, didn't I? I've been looking forward to it for ages.'

I can't very well launch straight into my 'what are you hiding?' line of questioning just yet. I think we both need a drink or two to soften the edges first. 'I know it's hard to forget about work, but it's only for a few hours and it'll do you good.'

I turn my attention to my own menu and see that they offer an Italian cheese we tried together for the first time on a city break to Bologna six months after we met. It was a blazing weekend of strolling under cool arches, enjoying beers and live music on the Piazza Maggiore and wonderful romantic meals in hidden trattorias before scurrying back to our authentic hotel to make love until the early hours. When we returned home, Isaac produced an antique engagement ring he'd managed to buy over there while I had a lie-in one morning and proposed.

'They have burrata, your favourite,' I say, waiting for him to make the Bologna connection too and remember our amazing time there.

'What? Oh yes, I see it. I'm not that hungry, though, so I thought I might skip the starter.' He looks up and sees my expression. 'You have one though if you like. I don't want to stop you.'

He's rubbing his index finger against his thumb on the table. There's an angry red welt where his nail is catching.

I thump my menu down on the table and the couple next to us look over at the sharp slapping noise it makes. 'Isaac, I know something is wrong and it's not up for debate. You have to level with me.'

'Don't be silly, there's nothing wrong at all!' There's a suggestion of panic in his eyes for a second before he slips a jovial mask in place. 'We'll have some wine, and I'll tell you something else' – he glances at the menu – 'I'll order the burrata, too. How's that? We can pretend we're in Bologna again.'

So he does remember. I stare at him for a long moment. Is it my imagination, or is he lurching from one mood to the next in the space of a few sentences? I don't know, maybe he's a bit nervous about how tonight will go. I know I am. And although the last time we made love was far from the passion we shared in Bologna, I'm hoping we can rediscover a bit of that when we get home later.

I say, 'I want us to relax and have a lovely evening but I also need you to be truthful with me.'

He nods and smiles. 'You're right. I need to just forget about work problems for tonight.'

I push back a little. 'The stuff you're worried about, is it just the usual new job pressures or is it more than that?'

'So, have we decided what we'd like to order?' The waiter reappears, a little more confident now, his pencil poised expectantly above a small white order pad that looks brand new. Isaac's pet hate: condescending waiter-speak.

'Yes, *we* have decided. *You* can now take *our* order,' Isaac says snappily, and the waiter blanches slightly. The young man has clearly picked up this style of speaking to diners to help cover his nerves; he doesn't seem the patronising sort.

'Isaac… be nice.' I glare at him, and he has the grace to look chastened and mumbles an apology.

'Madam?' The waiter looks at me like a startled rabbit, and I smile at him.

'I'll have the tomato bruschetta to start, followed by the lasagne, please. No sides for me.'

I watch as the pencil etches marks onto the pristine white page. He turns to Isaac.

'And for you, sir?'

'I'll have the burrata, and a fillet steak cooked medium rare with a side salad, please,' he says politely. 'Oh and a bottle of the Amarone.'

The waiter nods, hurriedly scribbles down Isaac's order with his choice of rather expensive wine and then scurries off again.

'There wasn't really any need for that.' I frown. 'He's obviously nervous and he's only young.'

Isaac shrugs. 'I said I was sorry, didn't I? I love your hair.' He leans forward, elbows on the table, and rests his chin on his laced fingers. I glow a little at his compliment.

The wine arrives and we enjoy a glass, making small talk. Isaac seems interested in my work with Jasper and we talk about Rowan getting the highest mark in a recent class spelling test.

I watch Isaac drink his wine quickly and top his glass up again. I don't comment. Tonight, it suits my purpose for him to relax a little.

'I worry about you,' I say. 'I think you're keeping a lot of stuff that's bothering you bottled up.'

'Well, I'm worried about *you*, Janey,' he says. 'You seem to be acting out of character, too.'

Before I can respond to this very obvious defensive attack by Isaac, our starters arrive. He picks up his fork and uses it to break open the ball of burrata, exposing its soft, milky centre.

He says, 'Maybe I'm concerned because you've already told Tanya your deepest, darkest secret without a thought about how it might affect us.'

This from the man who is blinkered by work at the expense of our entire family life.

I stare down at my tomato bruschetta and realise I haven't an ounce of appetite left. I don't mind admitting there's a part of me that would like to spear my husband's hand to the table with my fork. Instead, I keep my expression neutral and my tone reasonable.

'I want to make some friends here, Isaac, can't you understand that?'

'I'm not sure you'll find any good friends amongst the school gate mafia,' he murmurs.

As far as I'm aware, Isaac knows next to nothing about Tanya, Edie or Kyoko. He only met them properly on Saturday night – after a brief hello when he dropped Rowan off at school on that one morning – but he was talking to Tristan for most of the evening so didn't spend much time with any of them. Apart from Kyoko, I think sourly.

'Tanya has been a big support to me and she wasn't judgemental at all when I confided in her about Mum.'

Isaac loads another forkful of food into his mouth. 'Tell you what, let's pretend I never mentioned your friendship circle.'

I pick at the bruschetta when, without warning, Isaac's fork clatters onto his plate. As I look at him, startled, his face drains of colour. He seems to be staring at something behind me.

I spin around in my seat. The restaurant is full, every available table taken. There are no disturbances and I can't see anything untoward. When I turn back, Isaac is already standing up.

'I'm sorry, Janey, all of a sudden I feel like crap.' He signals to the waiter, who hares over, instantly alarmed.

'Is everything all right, sir? Is the food—'

'The food's fine, but I'm afraid I'm feeling unwell,' Isaac replies briskly. He pulls out some twenty-pound notes and places them on the table. 'This should cover what we've had and more. Come on, Janey, let's go.'

I feel like I'm watching events from a distance. Isaac puts his arm around my shoulders and ushers me to the door, grabbing my coat from the rack on the way. The hum in the restaurant has lessened somewhat as the diners at the tables around us sense drama.

'I don't understand, what's wrong?' I feel breathless. It's clear to me that he isn't ill. Something or someone must have given him a scare. I'm certain of it.

'I've told you, I feel awful,' he hisses, urging me to the door before I've even shrugged my coat on. 'In fact, I can safely say I've never felt so sick in my life.'

He opens the door and I step outside into the cool air. Before he closes it behind him, he looks back, and I peer over his shoulder. I scan the faces I can see from the doorway but nobody looks familiar.

Then a tall man over in the corner takes a step out of the shadows, his eyes trained on the door like lasers. I hold his stare but he doesn't look away.

As the door finally closes, the faintest smile flits across his mouth and the back of my neck prickles.

49

We have to wait ten minutes in the cold for an Uber but Isaac won't go back into the restaurant and insists on waiting up the road. The air in the cab turns blue on the way home.

'For God's sake, I don't know who you're talking about,' Isaac insists for the umpteenth time. 'I didn't see any man, I just felt ill and had to leave. How many more times?'

'It'll take however many times it needs until you admit someone spooked you in there.' I'm seething and way past trying to rein my temper in. 'As soon as you got away from the restaurant, your supposed illness did one, I notice. No sign of it now whatsoever.'

He doesn't answer.

'There was a tall man watching us as we left. Over in the far corner near the waiter station. Did he have anything to do with you wanting to get away?'

'I still feel queasy and hot.' He rubs his throat as if this might convince me. 'Give it a rest, Janey, please.'

My gut feeling is screaming at me that something is seriously wrong. Yet despite our problems, I still love my husband very much. Naïve as it might be, if he's telling the truth about Saturday night, then I have faith that our family life will improve, given time. But stuff happening out of the blue like this… it's unnerving. If Isaac won't own up to anything, then maybe I need to take matters into my own hands.

Rowan adores his dad. I can't bear to think how it would affect him if… if the worst happened. It will take more than strange behaviour in a restaurant to make me willing to tear the three of us apart.

We both fall quiet. Isaac focuses on the road ahead and I stare out of the passenger-side window. Then I remember that Angel won't be expecting us home yet, and our unannounced return may startle her. She gave me her number before we left, so I text both her and Tanya.

Isaac feels ill so on our way home early.

A text pings back from Tanya.

OMG, what's wrong with him? Are you OK?

I can't bring myself to reply. Tanya will want to conduct a forensic analysis of every single detail of our very short evening, if she knows I'm doubting Isaac. I can't cope with that right now, so I push my phone back into my handbag and stare at the blurry lights of the houses as we whizz past.

We got to the restaurant at seven thirty and we'll be home before nine. Some date night it's turned out to be.

'Idiot!' The cab driver curses as a dark-coloured BMW pulls out of a parking space, narrowly missing us, and drives away up the road, way faster than the 20mph speed limit. 'Prat nearly took my front end off there.'

The cab pulls into the space the speeding car just vacated, and as soon as the vehicle stops, I jump out and head two houses up to our front door, just in time to see it closing. Angel must have been looking out for us.

The door is shut by the time I reach it and I haven't got my key, so I tap lightly with the shiny chrome knocker. There's still no reply by the time Isaac joins me on the step. He's just about to slide his key into the lock when the door flies open.

'Sorry, I was in the bathroom,' Angel says breathlessly.

Strange. I felt sure she was at the door just before we pulled up. We step inside and Isaac closes the door behind us.

'Is everything all right?' She looks at me and then studies Isaac's face as if she's looking for something.

'Yes, I started to feel unwell at the restaurant, so we thought it best to come home,' Isaac says, as if it were a joint decision.

'You don't look ill.' Angel shrugs and I feel vindicated.

Isaac glares at her but says nothing. He scratches at his wrist.

I fill the awkward space by asking if Rowan's been OK.

'Fine,' she says sulkily, leaning against the door frame. 'He's not been in bed long, he's only just gone up. I was just about to put a film on.'

'Sorry it's been a bit of a wasted trip over for you,' I say. 'But we'll pay you for the whole evening and I'll see you home.'

Rowan suddenly appears at the top of the stairs and walks down towards us.

'Hey, you should be in the Land of Nod, champ.' Isaac grins, as if the evening has gone well and we're both jolly from it.

'I heard shouting,' Rowan croaks, rubbing at his eyes. 'And banging.'

'That was just your mum and dad coming back,' Angel says.

I slide my arm around him and Rowan presses into my side. 'No. I meant before that.'

'You must have been half asleep already, silly sausage,' she says easily.

'Get back into bed.' I kiss him on the top of his head. 'I'll walk Angel home and then pop up, OK?'

'I'll be fine, it's only a five minute walk,' she says, pushing her feet into ankle boots. She reaches for her jacket, which is hooked over the banister. 'You don't need to come with me.'

'I'll walk you back,' Isaac says, to my surprise.

'I thought you were feeling ill?' Angel says tartly. In one fluid movement, she twists her long blonde hair up and secures it with a clip at the back of her head.

'I could do with the fresh air.' Isaac gives me a peck on the cheek. 'I won't be long.'

50

I take Rowan back upstairs and settle him in bed again.

When I emerge from his bedroom, leaving the door slightly ajar and the hall lamp on as he prefers, I notice a chink of light from the smallest bedroom, the one that's currently still half full of packing boxes.

Perhaps Angel was looking for the bathroom and chose the wrong door.

My scalp tightens. Rushing around, worrying about how the evening would go, I completely forgot to ask Isaac to put Mum's marked box up in the loft. How can I have been so stupid? Although surely Angel would have no reason to be poking around in here.

I reach inside and feel for the switch, clicking it off. Then I freeze.

I turn the light back on and stare into the far corner, where the box should be.

There's nothing there.

As quietly as I can, so as not to disturb Rowan, I systematically hunt through the upstairs rooms. Maybe, for some reason, Isaac had already moved the box and forgot to tell me. Maybe he'd even spotted it and taken it up to the loft out of the way.

But I know it's unlikely. As far as I know, Isaac hasn't bothered to venture into the spare room once, leaving me to unpack and organise our belongings.

Downstairs, even though there are no packing boxes, I walk through all the rooms to satisfy myself it isn't here.

I'm clamping down on my back teeth so tightly, I have pains shooting up the side of my face. I open my mouth and wiggle my jaw from side to side. If someone… Angel, went in the small bedroom, she'd think nothing of the box in the corner. It didn't stand out from the other boxes in any way apart from the fact it had 'Mum' written on it. But surely that wouldn't be of any interest.

Unless someone knew what to look for…

I trust Tanya. She wouldn't gossip to Angel what I'd told her in confidence, I'm certain of it. My skin is crawling. I don't know whether to stand up, sit down, or go and knock at Tanya's door to ask Angel if she's moved the box.

I glance at my phone. Isaac's been gone for thirty minutes now. He's probably extended his walk to clear his head of whatever freaked him out back at the restaurant. He's not ill, I'm convinced of that.

Isaac has his key so I lock up downstairs and go up to bed. I draw the curtains but not before looking up the street to see if I can see him. There's no sign. I realise I can just about see Polly's front window from here so she can probably see most of what's happening at ours, too.

A car crawls up the crescent and parks up outside a house over the road and I think about the BMW we saw speeding away on our return in the cab. If Angel was at the door and the driver of that car had been in our home… it doesn't bear thinking about on a number of fronts. But I have to ask the question even though it's really awkward.

After thinking it through a few moments, I text Angel.

Thanks again for tonight. I can't find an important box that I felt sure was in the spare room. It had 'Mum' written on it and I just wondered if you'd spotted it anywhere around the house?

It sounds a bit weird but it's the best I can come up with. She might take offense I suppose, but the question has to be asked. The worst part is, I've searched everywhere and I know it hasn't been moved anywhere in the house. Yet there's nothing I can really say if she just replies that she hasn't seen it.

My only hope is that Isaac has put it up in the attic and forgot to tell me… but my hope is fading fast.

I sit on the sofa with the television off waiting for Isaac to come home. At ten o'clock, I go to bed and try to read but I can't focus on the words in front of me. I end up lying in bed staring into the dark for another hour before Isaac comes home.

I hear the front door open and close softly, I hear him kick off his shoes at the bottom of the stairs and then creep up, padding down the landing in his sock feet to the bedroom door.

He hesitates a couple of seconds before pushing the door open and entering the room.

I sit bolt upright in bed and Isaac grasps his throat. 'Christ, you're awake.'

'Of course I'm awake.' I snap on the bedside lamp. 'Where the hell have you been?'

'I went for a walk,' he says easily, unbuttoning his shirt and hanging it in the wardrobe. 'I told you, I needed some air.'

'Two hours seems like an awful lot of air,' I remark.

'It's only eleven o'clock, Janey, not two in the morning.'

'Did Angel get home OK?'

'She did.' He slips off his trousers and folds them over a wooden hanger.

'Isaac, Mum's box is missing.'

He stands motionless for a moment, holding the coat hanger up in the air. I pinch the skin on my thigh, praying for him to say it's him who has moved the box. But he doesn't say anything. He walks over to the wardrobe and hangs up his shirt.

'I wondered if you'd moved it up into the attic?'

'I haven't touched it,' he says. 'I was told not to touch it.'

'Why do you say it like that?' I'm fighting back tears of frustration. 'I've never told you not to touch it!'

'You said you couldn't bear me to go near it. When I offered to sit with you and go through the contents. Remember?'

'Yes, but I didn't mean... well anyway, it's missing from the spare bedroom. It was in the corner, unopened, and now it's gone.'

'When did you last see it there?'

'Just the other day. It's been in the corner of the spare room since moving in day.'

He looks at me. 'What are you trying to say, Janey? What do you *think* has happened to the box?'

'Well, the only person who's been here apart from us is Angel.'

'Okay.'

'So... I'm thinking maybe she moved it or took it.'

'I walked her home and I didn't notice her carrying your mum's box.'

He's returned home leery and clever. Behind his words is this unspoken assumption I'm making all this up. I can feel it.

Then something occurs to me.

'That car... the BMW that just missed the cab. Do you think he'd been here, to our house?'

Isaac looks at me aghast, as if I've lost my mind.

51

Next morning, Isaac offers to drop Rowan off at school before carrying on into work. I jump at his offer.

When the two of them have left the house, I drive out of town to Castle Marina retail park. I need to just get out of the house for a while after spending what feels like the entire night watching the turn of each and every hour on my digital bedside clock. My plan is to sit in Costa and hunch over a latte, planning how I'm going to question Angel about the BMW we saw and the missing box, without Tanya excommunicating me.

I queue at the counter, collect my latte, then glance around looking for a free table, and that's when I see Kyoko. She's sitting alone in the corner, talking animatedly on the phone. She's facing diagonally away from me and is frowning alternately at the laptop screen in front of her and the scattering of papers to the side.

She bends closer to the screen, as if she's reading something out to the person on the other end of the line. Then she taps confidently at the keyboard, which I find interesting, seeing as she's said on a number of occasions she hates using computers and tries her best to stay away from technology.

She ends the call and immediately begins typing in earnest. So focused is she on the screen that she doesn't seem to notice me approaching her. I stand a little way off until she stops typing, reads through something on the screen and then hits a key like a concert pianist, in that triumphant way you'd shoot an email off, signalling the end of the job.

She hasn't spotted me yet so I have the chance to walk away if I want to. She'd be none the wiser and I did come here for my own bit of peace and quiet. But I think about what I saw in the school files and the feeling, in the pit of my stomach, that tells me something is just a touch off-kilter with Ms Kyoko Nagasawa.

'Hi, Kyoko!'

Her head jerks up and the look that passes over her face isn't disdain because it's me; it's an expression of genuine shock. Almost as though she's been caught doing something she shouldn't. My interest is piqued and I pull out the chair opposite. 'Mind if I join you?'

'What? Oh… yes. Please do.' In one movement she scoops up the papers and pushes them into her Louis Vuitton tote bag. 'I wasn't expecting to see anyone here this morning, given that this place is off the beaten track.'

No, I bet you weren't, I can't help thinking and I wonder what the true story of her past is. Where exactly did she live and why did she change the kids' surnames too? The question is, is it any of my business? I understand better than anyone about keeping the past private.

Ky gives me a tight smile and snaps the lid of her laptop closed, slotting it next to the paperwork in her bag.

'Sorry to disturb you when you're so busy,' I say, taking a sip of my latte. 'I didn't realise you were working until I got closer to your table.'

'Working? Oh no, not really. I was just… catching up with some stuff online.'

She's babbling, saying anything that comes to mind. I've done it myself, in various situations when I've been put on the spot in some way.

'It's nice of you to come over and say hi,' she says. 'I'd hate for the misunderstanding at the party to stand between us.'

Kyoko is smiling and acting very polite, but I know it's all an act, because on another level I can feel what amounts to an invisible electric fence around her, repelling me. I'm torn, though, because I'm never going to get a better chance than this to get some insight into the real Kyoko.

'I've wanted to say for some time, Ky, how I admire you, the way you cope so well on your own with the twins. Cherry and Jun are such great kids; they really brighten up Elder class.'

'Oh, that's sweet of you to say, Janey, thank you!' Her face lights up with a genuine smile, possibly the first one she's ever sent my way. 'That naughty boy you work with, who disrupts the class? Jun said he's been much better behaved since you've been working with him.'

'Jasper's actually a lovely kid,' I say, feeling defensive of him. 'He has to deal with a lot of challenges most of the other kids don't have. He does really well most of the time.'

She sniffs and twists her long black hair to one side.

'Cherry and Jun seem so well adjusted and grounded, which can't be easy when they've been through a painful family break-up.'

I'm using the same open, honest manner that we all use between each other. But I'm aware it's the first time I've spoken directly to Ky in this way, and without the buffer of Tanya or Edie it feels a bit full-on. I wait with bated breath to see if she's going to knock me back or open up.

'You're right, it's not been easy for them at all,' she says with a sigh. 'They've been through a terrible time and they don't see their dad. But I think I'm doing an OK job in helping make them feel safe and settled.'

I try another angle.

'I know how tough it is to relocate with kids, and we only moved a short distance in comparison to you,' I say. 'It was York where you lived before, wasn't it?' I add casually, thinking about the Kent address in the file.

'Yes. Yes, it was.' She opens her bag and looks inside it before pulling the handles closed again.

'I love York, we've been there a few times before Rowan was born; any excuse to go to Bettys tea shop for lunch!' I grin. 'Isaac has a great-aunt who lives in the city – I think it's Bermont Street, about a ten-minute walk from the minster. Do you know it?'

She purses her lips as if she's thinking. 'Sorry, not sure I do. Well, I guess I should be going, I have an appointment to get to.' She stands up and pulls the straps of her bag over her shoulder, scraping her chair back noisily in her haste to get away. 'So nice to see you, Janey. Catch you later!'

After she's gone, I sit there at the table for a while, sipping my latte and wondering exactly who this woman is, and what she's hiding.

The million dollar question is, do I keep it to myself or tell Tanya what I think?

52

When I leave the café I decide to drive into West Bridgford so I can call into the Post Office to send back one of the outfits I ordered because the colour wasn't to my liking. I've had the returns parcel in my boot for a while now.

When I get back into town, I park down a side street where there's free parking for half an hour and a shortcut leading out halfway down Central Avenue.

I'm distracted, still thinking about Kyoko and trying to piece together what I know about her. So, at first, I don't see the altercation in the small car park of what looks like a Victorian house converted into smart flats.

When I look up and see who it is, I immediately slow down and step behind a large parked Bedford van, where I have a clear view but am screened by a couple of trees at the side of the road.

Angel and a man – a younger man than I saw her with that day in the square – are standing by a black BMW with a thin silver stripe down the side, having what looks like a heated discussion. I realise with a start that this is the car that nearly hit the cab when we returned home from the restaurant. Had Angel invited this person into the house while we were out?

My blood seems to freeze in my veins as I think about the connotations of this: Rowan could have clearly been at risk from a stranger if she'd let anyone in and, because I'm an idiot, Mum's box would have been easily accessible. It was in a sealed packing box with crumpled paper on top of it but if anyone knew what to look for…

Was it possible this man had taken it because it had Mum's name scrawled on the top of it and he thought it might contain valuables or something?

Before I have time to process this troubling new theory, Angel removes one hand from her hip and prods her finger at the man, who responds in an equally aggressive manner and then begins shouting at her.

I step forward, about to call out to her, when the actual man I saw with her in the square – tall, broad-shouldered and in his late thirties – jumps out of the car and pushes the younger man so that he staggers back.

My throat tightens and I reach blindly into my handbag to pull out my phone, certain the altercation is going to develop into a full-scale fight, but then they seem to calm down and voices quieten, arms hanging down by their sides. I snap a couple of pictures before suddenly the older man grasps the younger one by the shoulders and shoves him hard again, grappling with him and forcing him into the back of the car. I can't see what's happening in there; I'm too far away. Angel glances around nervously and quickly slides into the passenger seat of the BMW.

I get ready to punch 999 into my phone just as the older man steps out of the back of the car and jumps into the driver's seat. A few seconds later, the car reverses out of its space and speeds towards the main road. I watch it until it is out of sight.

I find myself wondering if I'm overreacting before I dismiss the thought as quickly as it came. Angel is obviously spending time in the company of some very dodgy characters, men who are far too old for her. Men she shouldn't even know.

No, what I'm really fretting about is telling Tanya and her not believing me again.

This time, though, I have the photographs of Angel on my phone as evidence. This time, I have no choice but to shatter the perfect picture Tanya has of her daughter. She needs to know who Angel is spending her time with; her safety is paramount. I decide to tell Tanya first and then the police; I owe her that courtesy as my friend. Angel wasn't being attacked, wasn't being coerced into doing anything. On the contrary, she seemed to be the aggressor.

I run back to my car and leap in. Before I start the engine, I call Tanya, but it rings out and goes through to voicemail. I leave a breathless message.

'I'm coming over now, Tanya. There's something important I have to tell you about Angel.'

In my head, I have the scene on repeat of Tanya insisting that Angel spends hours in her bedroom doing her schoolwork. Is it possible that she could be doing other stuff up there? Communicating with the men I've just seen her with, perhaps. It's anyone's guess.

I call Angel on the number she gave me when she babysat for us but it goes through to voicemail.

I force myself to focus on the road, but there's a chill crawling up from the base of my spine when I think about what might be happening. As far as I can see, there's only one reason why mature men would be interested in spending time with a lovely young girl.

I curse out loud and thump the steering wheel with the heel of my hand when the traffic lights I'm approaching turn red.

The task ahead of me won't be easy, but I won't allow Tanya to dismiss me. Not this time; there's too much at stake. Of her own admission, she has self-imposed blinkers on when it comes to Angel.

'She's a young woman now, but every time I set eyes on her, I just see that vulnerable little girl without a father,' she told me one time over coffee. 'It was just me and her against the world back then and… well, sometimes I feel as if nothing has changed.'

Tanya went on to admit how she couldn't bear to hear any negative comments about her daughter. 'Honestly, I realise I'm embarrassing at parents' evening, but I know my daughter best. She struggles with her perfectionism at times and she can't accept the slightest criticism, no matter how constructive. Tristan refuses to come with me now.'

Her scowl broke and she laughed at herself then and I joined in, but now… now, what I'm about to tell her is a hundred times worse than some irritated teacher's comment about late homework at parents' evening. No matter how delicately I frame it, I'll be effectively informing Tanya that her darling daughter is lying to her when she's not at school, deceiving her about the company she's keeping and, more worryingly, may be involved in some kind of emotionally abusive or aggressive relationship with an older man.

The traffic lights change and I put my foot down so hard, I beat a Jag off the lights in my battered old Ford Fiesta.

I know I'm complicating matters by focusing on what Tanya's reaction might be. Instead I should be asking myself a couple of simple questions.

Would I want to know if Rowan was in any kind of danger?
Absolutely.

Is the moral thing to do to tell Tanya what I've seen so she can intervene before something terrible happens?

Without a shred of doubt it is.

Even if she struggles to accept the reality, Tanya will thank me for it in the end. I really value her friendship and feeling included with the other mums. I'm enjoying this new life of mine, making the best of myself and filling my time in the company of others and with Rowan instead of – and I don't mean this quite the way it sounds – spending hours alone with Mum.

I was Mum's sole carer for eighteen months, and despite everything that happened at the end, I wouldn't have had it any other way. I'd do it all again if needs be, of course I would. But that doesn't change the fact that it was rough on both of us. Mum often disgruntled and frustrated and me feeling like I could never do anything right, no matter how hard I tried to please her.

Then, in the end, it felt as if she'd slapped me in the face anyway.

I grew up treading on eggshells around Mum, weighing up everything I said or did before actually saying or doing it so I could minimise her angry reactions. The only respite was when Aunt Pat was home and brought some fun and light into my life, much to Mum's obvious disapproval. When Aunt Pat died, life just seemed to be one continuum of dull grey with no flashes of colour at all.

A childhood like that makes for a nervous adult who spends her time working out how to please others, saying yes to everything and wearing herself ragged in the process.

I pull up outside Tanya's house and run up the path. The door opens and Tanya steps towards me, her eyes filled with thinly veiled panic. 'I got your message. What is it that's so urgent? Is everything OK?'

I lay my hand on her arm. 'I think Angel might be in serious trouble, Tanya.'

53

Tanya scans the windows of the houses behind me and ushers me inside.

'You're scaring me now.' She bites her lip.

I follow her into the kitchen, where she wheels defensively, hands on hips. She doesn't offer me coffee or ask me to sit down.

'So what's happened?' she asks. 'What's all this... about Angel again?'

I take a breath and tell her exactly what I saw. I don't think I take another breath until I finish, when I drag in some air.

'Angel's at school.' Tanya smiles tightly as if she's already dismissed everything I just said. 'I took her in myself.'

But I won't let this happen again. Not this time.

'She's not in school, Tanya. She was with two men, both of them much older than she is. It looked like a violent situation to me.'

'They were hitting her?' Her voice falters.

'No. Angel seemed to be part of the aggression towards one of the men.'

Tanya shakes her head as if she doesn't believe a word of it. 'And supposedly what time was this?'

'About thirty minutes ago,' I say, a fullness in my throat. Wherever Angel is now, she could be in trouble. Aggressive situations can often escalate.

'That's impossible.' Tanya's eyebrows lower and she flicks a dismissive hand my way. 'You must be mistaken, just like you were earlier. In fact I'm starting to ask myself why you keep doing this, Janey.'

'It was her, Tanya,' I say gently. 'I'm certain of it, just like I was certain of it before but I allowed you to change my mind. Angel is involved in something very worrying and you need to wake up to that.'

'I'm telling you it couldn't be her. OK?' Her eyes flash. 'They have to sign out of school, have proof of illness or appointments. She can't just come and go as she pleases.' She snatches her phone off the worktop. 'I'll call them now and we'll sort this out once and for all.'

She presses a button and holds the phone to her ear, shooting me a withering look.

I reach into my pocket for my own phone. I silently hold up the handset and flick between the two photographs I took earlier. When I pinch the photograph and enlarge Angel's face as she's talking to the man, Tanya blanches and ends her call.

'I'm sorry,' I mumble. 'But you have to take this seriously.'

Tanya looks confused for a second and then quickly gathers herself.

'You're overstepping the mark here. I'm sure there must be a perfectly good explanation for what you think you saw.' She's putting on a commendable show, but her fingers chafe against each other and she can't keep still. 'I'll call her right now and ask her to account for her actions.'

I watch as she makes another call. After a minute or so, she presses her lips together and puts the phone down again, then looks at me with narrowed eyes. 'Her phone's turned off. She keeps it turned off during lessons.'

I pull out a stool and perch on the edge of it. I have a duty as a friend and a mother to make her see the seriousness of the situation.

'Tanya, I think you should call the police. You didn't see the altercation… I did. I saw her in the square that day too, despite her denial. Angel is spending time with men much older than herself, and that can't be right, can it?'

Tanya blows out air loudly, as if she's been winded, before looking at me, her nose wrinkling.

'There's something else, too. I think she might've had one of the men round at our house when she babysat last night.' I shudder. 'A car identical to the one I saw nearly took the front end off our cab when we turned into the crescent. And there's more… remember I told you about the box of Mum's stuff I haven't looked at yet? Well, it's missing. If she had a man round he could've—'

The expression on Tanya's face makes me stop talking.

'You'd better be very careful, going around saying things like that, Janey. Very careful. I thought we were friends, but this, what you're saying about my daughter – I won't tolerate it.'

'Tanya, you're in denial! I saw what I saw. I could hardly believe it myself and that's why I took the photos. I wanted to come and tell you in person because I respect you and I'm worried about Angel's safety, but—'

'Well, you can stop worrying now.' She waves me away. 'I'll speak to Angel and find out what this nonsense is all about. If there's anything to be done, then *I'll* deal with it, not you. Consider your burden lifted. Goodbye, Janey.'

Despite my nervousness, I bristle at her manner.

'You're making a mistake not calling the police,' I say coldly, standing up to leave. 'I can't believe you'd turn a blind eye to what I'm telling you. Angel could be in real trouble right this minute.'

I walk out of the kitchen into the large hallway and open the front door.

When I look back, I see Tanya slumped against the worktop, her head in her hands.

Then I realise that the last ten minutes have been an act for my benefit.

Tanya knows exactly what Angel is up to, but for some reason, she can't, or won't, bring herself to face it.

54

I arrive at school just ten minutes before afternoon classes are due to start. Usually Ben likes me to get in about half an hour early if I can to give us time to talk through the lesson plan.

'Sorry. I'm running late today,' I tell him, rushing into the staff room and sitting down in the vacant seat next to him. The room is already emptying rapidly, teachers and support staff heading back to their classrooms to get everything ready for the children coming back in after lunch.

'No worries.' He chews his bottom lip. 'There's something I just need to mention, a potential problem with Jasper. Samina said he's been a bit withdrawn yesterday and this morning. She managed to get out of him there are a couple of older kids bullying him in the playground.'

'Oh no! Bullying him how?' Kids can be so cruel if they perceive someone is different to them and it's really hard to police it at break and lunchtimes.

'Name-calling rather than physical I think, but still, not nice. I thought you could keep a close eye on him.'

I feel outraged on my young charge's behalf. Between us, Samina and I have worked really hard to reassure him and give him a renewed sense of routine and safety in the classroom.

'In other news…' Ben hands me the planning sheet for this afternoon's lessons. 'We're covering the Great Plague of London this afternoon and going over basic algebra again.'

I stare at the sheet, wondering if Tanya has been able to contact Angel yet.

'Are you OK, Janey?' Ben frowns, studying my face. 'You look a bit stressed.'

'I'm fine.' I force a smile to my face. 'Just been one of those mornings, you know?'

'Oh, I know all right. Most likely because of his problems in the playground, Jasper is in one of his moods today. A bad one. I'll warn you now, he's already ripped up Jun's work and kicked Jasminder. I'm so glad you're here; he's taken up enough of my time already.'

Great. As usual, I'll be working one-to-one with Jasper this afternoon and I'll need to give him my full attention. First, I'll need to take a minute before lessons start to get my head straight and leave my problems outside the classroom. Jasper will easily pick up on my stressed mood and this will no doubt affect his behaviour.

Ben stands up. 'Right then. I'll just pop to the office to photo-copy a few spare worksheets and then see you in there.'

I'm soon the only person left in the staff room. I walk over to the water cooler and pour myself a small glass, drinking it standing up and looking out of the window at the small allotment where the children are encouraged to grow plants and vegetables as part of their class projects.

I try Angel's phone again but get no joy. It's still turned off. Should I have called in at her school on the way here to tell them I'd seen Angel in town during lesson time? Tanya would never forgive me, I know. But will I forgive myself if something happens to her?

I'm doing it again: taking on other people's responsibilities. I've become worse, if anything, since Mum died, but I certainly don't need any more of it. Now that Tanya knows about Angel's association with dodgy people, I have to accept the ball is firmly in her court. She's made it clear she doesn't want my involvement.

I don't think anyone would argue it's unreasonable of me to take that view. There are only so many awful scenarios one person can fret over without losing their mind.

Jasper watches out of the corner of his eye as I enter the classroom. I approach him slowly, with a calm smile.

'Good afternoon, Jasper,' I say in a measured voice. 'How are you feeling?'

Since I started working in Elder class, we've endlessly practised greetings and how to respond to them, but Jasper looks down at the table and says nothing. I note his eyes are downcast, his fingers fidgeting against one another.

The children rotate their tables on a termly basis, but Jasper always sits in the same seat so he can benefit from interacting with different people whilst also keeping a sense of familiarity.

Because of his behaviour this morning, Ben has moved the other kids off the table, which has left Jasper sitting there alone again. He's done it for a good reason – to protect the other children and minimise class disruption – but it must feel like a form of exclusion to Jasper, who is unaware he's done anything wrong. It's also a step back after I managed to get some children onto his table by figuring out his required space parameters, one of his behaviour triggers.

I slide into the chair next to him, keeping a reasonable distance. I place my bag on the floor between us, taking out Ben's specially adapted worksheet on the Great Plague.

'The thing I like about the afternoon is that it feels like a new, fresh part of the day. We can forget all about this morning.' If only *that* were true. I push the worksheet across the table under Jasper's stony stare. 'I think this will be a very interesting lesson about the plague and I know you'll be able to draw a great picture during the art task.'

Jasper clearly isn't in the mood for talking or making a fresh start. He especially isn't interesting in studying his worksheet, it seems. He slides it back over to me and rubs at an ink mark on the table.

Ben begins talking at the front of the class and I pay attention to him, giving Jasper a bit of space and setting a good example on practising listening skills. But after a few seconds, I've already zoned out Ben's voice and am wondering if Tanya has checked up on Angel's whereabouts yet. I can't use my phone here in class but I decide I'll text her at afternoon break.

The next forty minutes is hard work, constantly trying to get Jasper on task and mostly failing. My head is thumping and it feels too warm in here. Oppressively so.

When the bell rings, signalling the afternoon break, I jump up out of my seat quicker than any of the kids.

Ben raises an eyebrow. 'You ready for a cuppa, Mrs Markham?'

'Definitely ready for a break.' I nod, wafting the neck of my top. 'I feel a bit hot; I just need some air.'

He walks over, collecting completed worksheets from each table but ignoring Jasper's untouched sheet.

'Nadine has offered to take Jasper outside, and I can lock the classroom, so go and get some fresh air,' he says.

Nadine is the very experienced senior TA who sat in on my interview and works in the classroom next door. I leave my handbag but take my phone.

'Thanks,' I tell Ben, and turn to my young charge. 'I'll see you back here after break, Jasper. Have a good run around in the playground and try to blow away the cobwebs, eh?'

Ben grins and I leave the classroom. The corridor is cool, and I rush along it, glancing through the classroom doors to see the children start funnelling out into the playground. I look out for Rowan to give him a little wave but I don't spot him.

Thankfully the staff room is still empty, so I dash through and head out towards the small allotment. Staff aren't supposed to smoke here, but they often do. I stand just around the corner in case anyone comes out and pull my phone from my pocket. I'm hoping for a text from Tanya, some sort of update – and possibly an apology. What I don't expect are twenty-two notifications from the Buckingham mums' WhatsApp group.

I click on one of the notifications and see that Tanya and Kyoko have both posted a tweet and photograph from a local man who, an hour ago, reported to police that he'd stumbled across an incident whilst walking his dog. He describes seeing a car driving away at speed before his dog alerted him to an injured man lying in a ditch.

I stop reading and squint at the grainy black-and-white photo of the man in question. I pinch the photograph larger and study his face before moving across to the car. I can just about make out a thin silver trim running along the side of the vehicle.

Prickles of sweat pop on my upper lip as, feeling slightly dazed, I realise that this is the driver and the BMW I saw this morning.

I race through Tanya, Ky and Edie's comments, only half taking them in.

Edie: *This place is literally a ten min walk from my house!*

Ky: *I'm not letting the twins out of my sight from now on. No more popping down to your house on their own to see Dex, Tanya!!*

Tanya: *This is disgusting. We have to do something to increase awareness and police activity in the area. I'll see about calling a group meeting asap.*

She's not made the link between what I told her about Angel and the assault. She barely looked at the photographs long enough to be able to recognise the men or the car again and she wouldn't be raging about the incident to the others if she thought for a minute Angel was involved. I call Tanya's number. Her phone is turned off, but I leave a message.

'Tanya? I'm at work, but I've just seen the WhatsApp messages about that assault. Have you spoken to Angel? That car and the man in the photo… that's who she was with, earlier! Can you let me know if she's OK?'

I call Angel and the answerphone kicks in. I end the call and ring Isaac, instead. It goes through to his voicemail.

'Call me… soon if you can.' I sound breathless, as if I've been running. He can't fail to hear my urgency.

I copy the link to the article and send it in a text to Isaac, together with a brief explanation of what I saw earlier.

I don't know what else to do.

There's just five minutes more before I have to go back into class. I lean against the wall and close my eyes, pulling in air before reading through the article again, more carefully this time.

Police will no doubt soon be appealing for witnesses to the incident. They'll want to speak to people in the area where the actual assault happened, but I might have crucial information leading up to that. My throat squeezes in on itself as I realise the significance of what I saw.

55

The sounds of children playing just a few yards behind me are deafening, but it's still not enough to drown out the awful thoughts.

I look through a gap in the hedging and spot Jasper standing alone near the fence but looking anxious. I thought Nadine was supposed to be monitoring his break time .

'Jasper?' I call out but my voice is lost when a boy whizzes past the hedging, his back to me, lurches forward and screams in Jasper's face.

'Nobody likes you, dummy, and that's why you have to sit on your own.'

I open my mouth to reprimand him just as another boy stomps into view and pokes Jasper hard in the chest, forcing him to stagger back.

'Everyone in our class hates you,' he screams in Jasper's face. 'We all wish you were dead!'

I gasp as the boy turns, his face full of glee. It's a face I know so well but I'd recognise him just from the voice alone. The boy is Rowan.

The boys gone, I walk in shock back towards the building, a crumbling sensation in my chest. It might seem naïve, but I honestly wouldn't have thought my son capable of such cruelty.

With a heavy heart, I think about the artwork I found on the kitchen worktop he'd done the other day for homework. It was a vibrant and carefully considered poster design for the 'Be Kind' movement.

Rowan told me the next day that his poster was one of three that Miss Packton had chosen for the 'Be Kind' display wall in class.

How has this cruel streak appeared in my boy without me noticing?

I feel like a typical blaming parent but can't help wondering if it's Dexter's influence. The two boys spend so much time together, mostly at Tanya's house. I haven't a clue what they get up to, if I'm honest.

Just as I'm reaching for the staff room door handle, my phone vibrates in my hand.

'Sorry I missed you, Janey, I was on another call.' Isaac sounds hassled. 'One of our clients has just cancelled an important—'

'Did you read the article I sent through?' I interrupt him. 'Did you look at the photograph?'

I make an instant decision not to mention the bullying incident to him. That needs to wait until we can discuss the implications calmly and decide what to do about it. In the meantime, I have a duty of care to speak to Ben about what I saw. I won't be doing Rowan any favours not mentioning it; he needs to learn he's held accountable for his actions.

'I did see the stuff you sent through.' Inexplicably, Isaac sounds relieved, as if he was expecting me to say something else. 'It didn't really make much sense. Who's that in the photo?'

'I told you in the message,' I say, flustered now. 'I saw Angel, Tanya's daughter, with that same guy earlier today. They drove away in that car with another younger man who I think might be the victim.'

'Where's the picture of the victim?'

'There isn't one!' I'm trying to stem my irritation that Isaac can't seem to grasp the crux of the matter, but I know I'm not doing a very good job of explaining myself. 'They all had some sort of disagreement and drove off together, and now... well, as the report says, someone has been assaulted and I think it might be the other man. Not the man in the photo, the man who *isn't* in the photo.'

I press the heel of my hand to my forehead. I'm confusing myself now; it all sounds like a load of mixed-up nonsense.

'And that car looks just like the one that nearly crashed into the cab when we got back from the restaurant!'

Isaac is saying something, but his voice sounds far away.

'Janey? You there?'

'I... I just...'

'Janey?' He raises his voice. 'Are you OK? Where are you?'

The bell sounds, signalling the end of afternoon break. I stand up a bit straighter and steel myself.

'I'm OK. I'm at school. But... what if Angel's hurt, too? I should have gone straight to the police.'

'I'm sure Tanya would know if something had happened to Angel,' he says calmly. 'Have you spoken to her?'

'Yes, but she's in denial it's Angel I saw with the men. I just tried calling her, but her phone is turned off.' I'm suddenly aware that the playground has fallen silent. Everyone has gone back to class. 'Listen, I have to go.'

'Janey, you sound really stressed out. Try to calm down a bit. I think you're getting yourself involved in things here that you're going to regret. Can't you just—'

'We'll talk later.'

I end the call, gather myself and go back inside. I didn't expect that attitude from Isaac. I thought he'd want me to do the right thing and go to the police. It's not a case of 'getting involved', as he puts it; I *am* involved because I saw it all play out in front of me. I can no more ignore it than I can ignore the fact that overnight, my son seems to have turned into a bully.

I have to get through this next hour in class, that's all. Then I can collect Rowan at the end of school and speak to Tanya about

Angel. This mess has got to be sorted out once and for all. In the meantime, I can only pray that Angel is safe and well.

I rush back down the corridor, panicking when I see I'm already late and lessons have resumed in all the classrooms. I burst into Elder class.

'Sorry,' I call, closing the door behind me. 'I got delayed on a phone call and…'

I freeze in the silence of the room.

Ben is staring at me, and the children are all staring at Jasper. I follow their gaze.

The contents of my handbag are strewn across the table. I take a breath to keep calm and walk towards my seat. Without saying a word I gather up my stuff with both hands and dump it back into my bag. Tampons, tatty used tissues, a lipstick mashed up on the table… and then I see it.

One continuous, poker-straight line of precisely torn up little squares sit in front of Jasper, covering one side of the table to the other. The pieces are tiny but something about the colours printed on them looks familiar.

'No,' I whisper. 'Please… no.'

My stomach lurches as I snatch up my purse and open it to find that the only two photographs that exist of me as a child with Aunt Pat, photos I've cherished and always kept close since she died, are no longer tucked inside the plastic pocket.

56

'What have you done?' I screech at Jasper. 'How could you?'

Ben moves quickly, covering the space between us in a few strides.

'Janey, calm down. It's OK.'

'It's not OK!' I snarl, and jab a finger at Jasper. 'You nasty, spiteful boy! Why would you do that? How could you rip up my precious photographs?'

Jasper slinks off his chair and shrinks back against the wall, pushing hard like he's trying to disappear into it. The other kids are perfectly silent, as if they're holding their collective breath.

'Take a step back, Janey.' Ben's voice is firm now. 'Take a breath, go and get a glass of water. We can deal with this.'

More gently, I gather all the squares into a heap.

'Here.' Ben hands me a big envelope. 'It'll help keep them all together.'

As I start to transfer the pieces, salty rivulets run down my cheeks and splash onto the table. There seem to be hundreds of torn shreds. Family photographs that can never be put back together again. Never.

Hot fury whooshes up from my solar plexus straight into my head.

'Why?' I shout at Jasper. 'Why would you do this?'

He puts both arms over his face and buries his face in his knees.

'He didn't mean to upset you, Janey.' I turn and see Cherry is speaking up. 'He just doesn't understand that he shouldn't do that.'

My fury collapses in on itself like a burst paper bag. Such kindness and understanding from a seven-year-old child to an adult who should know better… I hang my head, feeling sick and disorientated. I'm no better than my son, verbally abusing Jasper like that, using the sort of language we won't tolerate amongst the children. I am ashamed.

'I'm sorry I was unkind, Jasper.' I turn around. 'Thank you, Cherry. What Jasper did made me very sad and I got upset. But I shouldn't have said what I did.'

She nods. 'Me and Jun were very sad when our daddy died. Mum keeps his photos in a special album and she lets us keep it in our bedroom to look at whenever we want. I'd be upset if something happened to our pictures, too.'

They don't see their dad. That's what Ky had told me in the café… as if he was still alive and well.

'You're not supposed to tell anyone that,' Jun hisses behind her and Cherry sits down, alarmed.

Ben raises an eyebrow and I'm shocked into silence for a moment. Kyoko has told everyone the twins' father left her for a younger woman. Now Cherry and Jun are saying he's dead!

I leave the remaining scraps of my photos and grab my handbag, my mind swirling with a whole bunch of stuff that makes no sense.

'Janey?'

Ben steps back to let me pass and starts to say something else, reaches out to touch my arm. But there's a high-pitched drone in my ears and I feel my feet propelling me forwards until I'm at the classroom door. Then I'm out in the corridor, and before I can stop myself, I'm running out of the building.

57

I head for Tanya's house on foot. If I get back in that car I feel like I'll suffocate. I don't text or call her first.

'Janey!' My head jerks up to see Edie calling and waving from across the road.

I cross over, pasting as normal a look on my face as I can muster, but it's all I can do not to simply carry on walking. I just need to speak to Tanya and sort this whole mess out.

'Are you OK? After the party, I mean? Kyoko says you two are good again.'

'I wouldn't say that exactly,' I huff. 'We're being civil to each other which is a start.'

She nods. 'Did you see the WhatsApp messages? It's so unnerving to think that this stuff is happening just around the corner. Alistair said it could even affect the value of our houses.'

'I'm more concerned about the safety of our kids,' I say a little curtly, irritated by her ridiculous priorities.

'Of course, and we feel exactly the same.' Edie nods in full agreement, seemingly oblivious to my annoyance. 'But I bumped into Tanya at the deli earlier and apparently the police are going to be putting out a call for any witnesses to come forward. She's already talking about forming some kind of pressure group and getting our local MP involved. She's fantastic at getting things done like that.'

At the deli? What the hell was Tanya doing there when her daughter is in danger? Could it be that Angel is home now?

The irony that Tanya is spearheading some kind of campaign speaks volumes. Whatever it is she suspects or thinks she knows that Angel's up to, it's not the assault. She'd never humiliate herself or her daughter by doing this if she did.

I wince at the thought of the backlash, the shame it will bring to her door and the damage to Angel's reputation whether she was present at the time of the attack or not. This sort of thing sticks.

'How long have you and Tanya been friends?' I ask Edie, as we walk.

'Oh, we've known each other forever,' Edie says, pushing hair out of her eyes. 'We used to work weekends together in a financial services call centre when we were still at college.'

'Really? Wow, that's a friendship that's stood the test of time.' Even if they do have the odd argument, as Angel said.

'Hmm, I guess,' Edie says non-committally. 'That's not to say we haven't had our ups and downs, like most friends.'

'Of course, that's to be expected.' Is it my imagination, or is there a bit of an edge to Edie's tone? It feels as though she's trying hard not to say too much.

I really like Edie, but I don't feel I know her as well as Tanya and I couldn't trust her not to repeat what I say. But maybe I could bring the conversation around to the subject of Angel, at least…

We're turning the corner into Buckingham Crescent now, and that means it's only a few minutes until we go our separate ways. I cut straight to the chase.

'I called at Tanya's house a few days ago and Angel came home from school ill, poor thing. Do you happen to know if she's better? I forgot to ask Tanya.'

One side of Edie's mouth curls up. 'Don't be fooled by our darling Angel. She's extremely good at wrapping everyone around her little finger, especially her mother.'

'You don't think she was ill?'

'I can't say for sure because I wasn't there, but put it this way.' Her voice drops lower. 'I heard she's got one of the worst absence records at that school. Stomach aches, headaches, raging sore throats… they seem to be on a rotation. I've tried to point this out to Tanya, but you might as well talk to a wall when it comes to Angel.'

'Kids, eh?' I keep my tone light. 'Still, Tanya must've been young when she had her. Maybe that's why she feels so protective of her, with her dad not playing a role and all.'

'Maybe so. But it doesn't do Angel any good for Tanya to give in to her demands all the time, or to turn a blind eye to her skiving off school for that matter. If that girl gets into trouble she's only got herself to blame.'

That's a strange thing to say. 'Sounds like Tanya doesn't tolerate any criticism or advice when it comes to Angel,' I remark.

'You bet!' Edie shakes her head. 'Angel by name and Angel by nature… according to her mother, at least. But she's not a little girl any more, she's a young woman.'

'She might look like a young woman but she's still only fifteen,' I say.

Edie doesn't comment on that, she just gives a cynical smile. We walk a little further before she says, 'There's a lot of stuff happening behind the scenes you're not aware of, Janey. People aren't always what they seem, you know.'

'What do you mean by that?' There's just something about the way she says it that pulls me up short.

'A conversation for another time, I think.' She laughs. 'You'll no doubt find out soon enough.'

58

She was never going to get out of here. She knew that now.

But it had become easier to accept somehow, and it occurred to her that that was because hope was now dead. When the hope was still there, it had built her up and up just to send her crashing to the floor as the days passed and nobody came.

She could now completely circle her wrist between her thumb and index finger, with room to spare. Before they took her, she'd been trying to lose a few pounds and had had to swap the silver bracelet her mother had bought her for her birthday for a bigger size.

She thought the girl was starting to get cold feet about coming down here. She'd started looking at her in disgust, wrinkling her pretty nose against the bad smell. Maybe soon she'd convince the man to finish it. He'd strangle Susan or maybe suffocate her, and then perhaps it would be some other poor girl's turn.

She knew there had been more before her because she'd heard them whispering. They never used her name; they only referred to her as 'nine'.

'When will we move on to ten?' the girl had whispered to him last time. 'Nine stinks now, I don't know how you can touch her.'

He'd turned and stroked her pretty long hair. 'Patience, my love. We'll move to ten soon enough.'

And instead of crying out in panic and alarm and begging for her life, Susan had closed her eyes and prayed that they would move to ten very soon and she'd finally be free of the pain he inflicted on her once and for all.

59

I press my finger to the doorbell and leave it there. Thirty seconds later, the door is pulled open.

'For God's sake, what's the...' Tanya folds her arms. 'Oh. It's you.' Her tone is stone cold, her eyes dull.

'I need to speak to you,' I say. 'Can I come in?'

She seems to consider this for a moment, then stands wordlessly aside and I step into the hallway. She's changed into baggy sweatpants and a grey T-shirt. Her eyes look red and her mascara is smeared.

'Have you heard from Angel... is she back home?' I ask.

When I mention her daughter's name, the cold front seems to thaw a little. All of a sudden she looks like she has the weight of the world on her shoulders.

'Look, Janey, you've said your piece and I'd rather you didn't mention Angel again. So if that's why you've come here, then save your breath. She's not your responsibility.'

'But you're not making the connection.' I falter. 'The assault near the National Water Sports Centre...'

'What about it? What's that got to do with Angel?'

'The photo posted online... That's the man Angel was with and that's the car she got into.'

Tanya grabs my arm and looks at me pleadingly.

'Janey! Why are you saying this stuff?'

'Because it's the truth… it's what happened!' I cry out. 'I came to you first as a matter of courtesy. Also, the fact that you're planning on calling a meeting about the attack. I want to save you the embarrassment before I go to the police.'

'The police?' she repeats faintly.

'They'll soon be appealing for witnesses to the incident,' I explain. 'Surely you understand I'm obliged to tell them what I saw? If Angel doesn't know anything about the attack, then she's got nothing to worry about. Have you spoken to her yet?'

Tanya's face screws up into a tight knot as she lunges at me, stopping just a few centimetres from my face.

'You keep my daughter out of it. Don't you dare mention her name to the police. I know for a fact she had nothing to do with this.' She prods a finger, just stopping short of impacting my cheek, but I keep a stoical expression, even though inside I'm quivering. 'You're getting involved in stuff you know nothing about.'

'What kind of stuff?' I say faintly. 'Are you saying you know she's involved in this?'

'No!' She runs fingers through her lank hair. 'Not in the way you're trying to frame it, anyway. I can't go into it. It's… it's nothing at all to do with you so just forget it.'

'I can't forget it, Tanya. I know what I saw and I've got the photos to prove it this time.'

She draws herself up to her full height, her eyes sparking. 'Have you ever done anything wrong, Janey? Have you got something in your past you'd rather people never knew about you?'

I take a sharp breath in. She knows I have.

'I wonder what people will say if your own grubby secret somehow got out?' Her face is alight with malice. 'I wonder if they'd judge you unfairly?'

'Th-that's different,' I stammer, my legs feeling weak. 'I had nothing to do with what happened. Do you know where the box is?'

'You've more to worry about than a missing box. Think about it, Janey. Someone like you working in a school with all those innocent children. It's shocking!'

'Now just wait a minute. If Angel has taken—'

'No. *You* wait a minute. You're desperate to tell the truth about my daughter but has your integrity not been compromised by keeping shtum about your own past? You didn't feel a burning need to air the truth about that, now did you?'

'I… That's something else entirely. It's—'

'Oh yes, I thought it might be. How very convenient. I wonder if people would agree with you. Mrs Harlow, who gave you the job, the parents of the children who place their trust in you to care for their kids. I wonder if they'd think of it as *something else entirely.*'

The look on Jasper's face earlier flashes into my mind. I handled the incident so badly and I haven't even told Tanya about it yet. Thanks to Rowan and Dexter, he'd already had a horrible experience in the playground but I was upset and reacted unkindly. But I'm a good person. I am. Whatever has gone before, however much Tanya taunts me, I know deep down there is no blackness in my heart. And yet I know people might look at that incident and see something else completely.

For the hundredth time, I curse my drunken stupidity in confiding in Tanya that day. Even though I'm falling apart inside, I won't let her see she's getting to me.

'Angel was there, Tanya, and a man has been assaulted. The point is, like it or not, I *am* a witness,' I say levelly. Inside I'm quaking but I force myself to look calm. 'I can't withhold information about the assault from the police, you know that. And I'm really worried she could be in some sort of danger herself, mixing with these people. Surely you're concerned about that too? I know how much you adore her.'

She looks at me in the strangest way. For a moment I think she's going to confide in me about something, but she blinks away the emotion and addresses me pleadingly.

'Look, you can tell them *almost* everything. Tell them you saw the man, describe his car, what he looked like… that's fine.' Just for a second, I catch a glimpse of the pure fear and desperation that lies beneath the hostility. She *is* desperately worried about her daughter, I see that now, but something is stopping her admitting it. 'Just don't mention Angel, I beg you.'

I turn my palms up, try and appeal to her. 'Tanya, I—'

'You can't do this to me, Janey. You can't do this to Angel. She's just a kid, she's not sixteen yet! I don't know why she wasn't at school or why she was in the company of those men. I'm having problems accepting it might be true, despite your photographs.' She grabs one of my hands and encases it with both of hers, and I feel her fingers quivering against my own. 'If Angel was there when someone was assaulted, if she knows these men, there's one thing I would bet my life on: she can't possibly have had anything to do with that assault. She must've found herself in the wrong place at the wrong time. I think deep down you know that too.'

My hand lies limply in hers and I look into her face. She knows something, something she's not saying. She has to. She adores Angel and I'd have put money on her turning hysterical if she thought her daughter was in the slightest danger. This… this ambivalence isn't normal for a mother, especially one like Tanya who constantly tries to exert control over how her daughter spends her time.

'There's something happening with Angel that you already know about, isn't there?' I say quietly. 'You know she's involved in something and yet you're not prepared to do anything about it even though she might be in danger. Why is that? How has she got involved with men twice her age?'

Her eyes dart away from my own.

Out of the French doors I can see the hot tub with its cover on. Vivid memories of the first time I came here flood my mind. I remember the first impression I got of Tanya as the mum of a teenager. It was totally normal.

She'd wanted to check that Angel's friend's parents were home. She fretted if Angel had eaten and she reminded her not to be late back. Yet when I told her the first time about seeing Angel out of school and talking to an older guy in the square, she barely batted an eyelid. And when I witnessed the incident where we now know someone had been attacked, Tanya's only concern seemed to be me telling the police. She didn't show any worry about what Angel had gotten herself into.

None of this is normal behaviour for the mother of a young girl.

Tanya stands and eyes me belligerently, her arms folded.

I say, 'When I first came over here and we talked in the hot tub, you mentioned that Angel had seemed to become secretive. You said she was spending lots of time out of the house.'

She doesn't miss a beat. 'And what's that got to do with you?'

'I'm trying to work out how you go from being a loving, caring mother, to attacking someone who has seen your daughter in danger.'

'All I know is that if you go to the police, you'll regret it.' She knits her arms tightly in front of her. 'I'm telling you for your own good as much as my own, Janey.'

The threat hits me like a slap in the face, but I don't say a word.

Instead, I turn and walk out of Tanya's house. Quite possibly, I think sadly, for the last time.

60

I walk out of Tanya's gate and begin to walk back up the road, looking at my phone.

'Janey!' A croaky voice hisses to my left.

I glance there but don't stop walking. 'Not now, Polly,' I sigh. 'It's not a good time.'

'What's happening? I know something is, Tanya is acting strangely. Calling someone repeatedly out in the garden and shouting into the phone.'

I stop walking and Polly steps out from behind her hedge.

'What is she saying on the phone?'

'Things like *it's got to stop* and *I've had enough of all this*.' Polly shakes her head. 'It's all falling apart. I knew it would.'

Polly's face is flushed, her eyes bright. As she speaks, her hands are animated. She's sensed something different in the air and wants me to tell her what it is.

'Like I said, Polly, it's not a good time.'

Predictably, her manner changes in an instant.

'You're going to regret discounting what I say so easily.' She jabs the air with a finger. 'They've turned you against me like I knew they would but I had high hopes for you. I thought you were different. I thought you'd listen.'

I shake my head and wave her away, striding off towards home before she starts wittering on about the damage to her sweet peas again. Polly doesn't know anything, she's just desperate to get herself involved in some way. I flick through my social media channels as I walks and see that local police have reached out on Twitter and Facebook regarding the assault. They haven't given many details about the incident yet but have asked anyone with any information to get in touch.

When I get back inside, I reach for my phone and press the link on the telephone number for the Nottinghamshire Police information line.

The call is answered after a couple of rings.

'I… I'm calling about the assault near Holme Pierrepont today. I saw the man whose photo has been released online this morning driving that BMW.'

The officer's voice changes and becomes more urgent. He takes my particulars, my name and address. My head is thumping, a constant dull ache and I rub my temple. He asks if the phone I'm calling on is my own mobile phone number.

'Yes.'

Then he says, 'OK, can you tell me what information you have, Mrs Markham?'

I explain about parking on the side street and seeing the altercation outside the Victorian house.

This produces a barrage of questions. What time was it? Where exactly was this? What was the name of the street and the number of the property?

I answer before continuing, 'I saw the man on the CCTV still get out of his car and push another man.'

Another clutch of questions before he asks, 'So you saw the two men having an altercation. Was there anyone else with them?'

My throat seems to close. He's somehow got to the crux of the matter in just a couple of minutes.

'Hello? Mrs Markham? Was there anyone else with the two men?'

'A girl.' My voice sounds strangulated. 'A young girl was there too but she didn't do anything. She just stood and watched and then got into the car.'

He asks me to describe the girl, which I do. There's a pause as I wrestle with my conscience, then I say, 'The thing is, I know who the girl is. I can assure you she would have had nothing to do with the assault, though. It's just that—'

'What's her name?'

'This is really awkward. You see, her mum is my friend and this situation has put me in a terrible position.'

'The girl's name, madam?'

'Angel Conrad. She's only fifteen, she's still at school.'

It's a tortuous exchange that culminates in me giving him Angel's address and her parents' names. I play dumb and say I don't have a telephone number.

'You said her mother is a friend of yours?'

'Yes, sort of… I see her at the school gates. That's all.'

The lies stack up unbidden. My heartbeat seems to be pulsing in my ears and I'm saying the first thing that comes into my head. I just need this conversation to be over.

'Right, well I'll pass the details of your call on and someone will be in touch to take a statement.'

'They'll come here, to the house?'

'Possibly, yes, due to the serious nature of the crime. Is that a problem?'

'No, but… no. That's fine.'

I end the call and sit staring at the phone.

Tanya's face, a mask of burning fury, fills my mind. But I know I've done the right thing. I didn't really have a choice. Surely Tanya must realise that. In the bathroom I splash cold water on my hot cheeks and stare into the mirror. My eyes look unfocused and I think I have a sore throat coming. I need to speak to Isaac. I'll try him again when I've had a drink of water.

I've just reached the bottom of the stairs when my phone rings. I look at the screen; it's an unknown number. I would usually ignore it, let whoever it is leave a message, but in view of what I've just done, I answer it.

'Mrs Markham? My name is Detective Chief Inspector Jed Warner. We've just received details of your call to the police information line regarding the attack at Holme Pierrepont. I'd like to pop over with a colleague to take a statement right away, if that's convenient.'

'You mean *right now*?' My heart hammers. This is far quicker than I expected. 'I have to pick my son up from school in just over an hour.' Thank goodness Rowan has his art after-school club tonight or I would be already running late.

'Time is of the essence, as I'm sure you can appreciate, Mrs Markham. I can guarantee we'll be in and out in good time for you to pick up your son; we're only five miles away from you at Oxclose Lane station.'

'OK,' I hear myself say faintly.

I'm going to tell the police the facts and hopefully that will be the last of it. It will be easier to explain when they're here in person.

Hopefully I can convey how awkward the situation is and how Angel can't possibly be involved in the assault. I mean, given my sightings of her recently, it's clear she's not quite the saint her mother believes her to be, but teenagers can push the boundaries. Everyone knows that. It's still a long jump to being involved in assaulting someone.

Edie seemed to be very cynical about her, but I've seen how Angel is with her brother and with Rowan. Kids are very astute in picking up on personalities, and they both love her.

How bad can she be?

61

The detectives arrive within twenty minutes of DCI Warner's call.

I stand at the front window and feel a wash of relief as I see they're in an unmarked police car, meaning there's nothing obvious to attract the neighbours' attention. Polly in particular.

I open the door before they knock. There's a broad, thickset man together with a younger one who is lean with a face full of sharp angles.

'Mrs Markham? We just spoke on the telephone. I'm DCI Warner,' the older man says. 'This is my colleague, DS Gary Pike.' They flash their badges, too quickly for me to see the detail. 'Thanks for agreeing to speak to us at such short notice.'

I offer them a drink, but thankfully they both decline. I honestly don't think I'm capable of taking the necessary steps to make coffee.

'I realise you've already given a few details when you rang the information line,' DCI Warner says. 'But if you don't mind, we'd like you to tell us everything again. If you could start right at the beginning, that would be a great help.'

DS Pike opens up a notebook and sits watching me thoughtfully, his pencil poised.

'Earlier today I popped into West Bridgford to call at the Post Office. I parked on a side street and used a shortcut to get to Central Avenue.'

Pike asks for the name of the side street, and a rough time.

I give him the details. 'I was about halfway between the car and the avenue when I saw them.'

He pushes his notebook in front of me. He's drawn a simple grid. 'If this is your parked car and this is the middle of Central Avenue' – he taps the point of his pencil to indicate the two places – 'where did you enter the shortcut, roughly?'

I indicate the opposite side to my parked car. 'There's a little snicket here behind the Co-op.'

He asks for the make and model of my car and the registration number.

'So you're using the shortcut. When did you notice something amiss?' Warner asks.

'There was movement to the left of where I was walking when I got about halfway.'

'That would be around here?' Pike taps his notebook diagram again.

'Yes, roughly there. I saw a man and a young woman having some kind of disagreement. They were standing by a car, a black BMW with a silver stripe down the side.'

'What gave you the impression they were having a disagreement?'

'There were raised voices. She was jabbing her finger and going at him, like you do when you're giving someone what for, if you know what I mean. At first I only saw the back of her, but I could see she was giving him hell.'

Warner puts up his hand to indicate I should stop talking. 'So if you could see only the back of the young woman, you must've been able to see the man's face?'

'Yes,' I say. 'I could see him clearly.'

Warner gets out his phone and presses a couple of buttons. 'Was this the man you saw?'

A dark-haired man in his late twenties smiles out from the photograph on the screen. He's clean-shaven, wearing a white shirt and navy tie. It looks like the kind of picture taken for a website like LinkedIn.

'I'd say that's him. He looked unshaven, though, sort of tired, and his clothes were more casual than this.' I pick up my phone to show him the photographs. 'Is he OK? I mean, he's not too badly hurt, is he?'

Pike shrugs off my question and looks at the screen. He asks me to ping them over to his phone.

'So the woman is jabbing her finger at him and having a go,' Warner recaps. 'Then what happened?'

'Then an older man – I'd say in his late thirties – got out of the driver's seat of the BMW and charged around the car to where the others were. He looked really angry.'

Warner swipes his screen and shows me the photo I saw online. 'Is this the man?'

I nod. 'That's him. He stormed around to their side and shoved the guy.'

Warner purses his lips. 'And did the younger man respond? Did he push him back?'

I shake my head. 'He seemed a bit wary of the older man.'

'Then what happened?'

'Well, as soon as I saw the girl and realised who it was, I was completely distracted.'

Pike refers to his notes. 'You realised at that point that you knew the girl, is that right?'

'Yes. I recognised her as Angel, the daughter of my friend, who I know to be fifteen years old.'

Warner stops me again and checks Angel's full name, her school, her parents' names and address.

'What happened next?'

'It's all a bit of a blur after that because I was so shocked to discover it was Angel. But basically, the older man pushed the younger one into the car. Angel got into the passenger side and they drove off quite fast, up towards the main road.'

Warner nods, and I sense it's a good time to clarify my problem.

'I need to explain that reporting the incident has put me in a really difficult position. Angel is the daughter of my friend Tanya, and she refuses to believe it was her I saw even though I had the photos to prove it on my phone.'

'Thanks for your time, Mrs Markham,' Warner says. 'You did the right thing getting in touch. We'll contact you again if we have any more questions.'

'You won't use the photos for public release, will you? They'll remain confidential?' My entire head feels hot, as if it's about to blow off my shoulders.

The detectives glance at each other and stand up without giving me any assurances.

I see them to the door, but I still feel a sense of urgency. I need to make things perfectly clear.

'I hope you'll bear in mind that Angel is just a child. She must've just got caught up in something she couldn't get herself out of.'

Warner's expression is grave, with no trace of compassion on his craggy features. 'We heard about an hour ago that the young man in the photograph has died of his injuries, Mrs Markham. So yes, I'd say she's got herself caught up in something very serious indeed.'

And with that, they step out of the house and walk away down the path.

62

'What do you mean, you'll not be home at all tonight? I really need to speak to you about everything that's been happening, Isaac.'

I can't believe what my husband is saying. I move the phone away from my ear a little. I was counting on talking the whole Angel situation over with him tonight after we put Rowan to bed, to calm my nerves a bit.

'Janey? Are you still there?'

I put the phone back. 'Yes, I'm here. I'm just wondering why you can't come home tonight. Why do you have to stay out *all* night?'

'I'm sorry, I really am.' He gives a heavy sigh. 'Believe me, if I could wriggle out of this, I would, I swear. But you know the client who's cancelling the big order? Well, Bob reckons if we pull out all the stops, take them to dinner at a nice out-of-town hotel…'

His excuses fade out. I don't really care what Bob says. At this precise moment, I'm only worried about our marriage.

'There's a slim chance I might be back, but I can't promise. Sorry.'

'Isaac, I'm not stupid. I know there's something wrong.' My voice breaks and I quickly swallow it down and clear my throat. 'I'm not stupid. That's all I'm saying.'

'What? I never said you were…'

'You're treating me as if I'm the dumbest woman on earth,' I say, my voice steely. 'I won't stand for it. If you don't want to be married any more, then get the hell out of our home. Understand?'

Silence on the end of the phone.

I'm in danger of saying things in haste, things I might regret, but my face is burning, my chest feels tight as a drum, and I just can't seem to stop.

'Janey.' His voice sounds beaten. Exhausted. 'Listen, you're barking up the wrong tree here. There's nobody else in my life, I swear it.'

'Something's not right. I've known it for ages, but… Well, I've just looked the other way and hoped it would somehow all be all right.' My throat is choking up with tears again.

'We'll talk. I promise.' He hesitates. 'I can't do anything about tonight now; I only wish I could. But tomorrow we'll talk properly. We will.'

I feel the fight drain out of me. 'I'm not happy, Isaac, but I guess I have no choice.' I glance at the clock. 'I have to leave in the next couple of minutes to pick Rowan up. But we have a lot to talk about tomorrow.'

Isaac apologises yet again and I end the call, then slip on my shoes and denim jacket and leave the house. He hasn't even remembered I was supposed to be working in school this afternoon. How did he become so disconnected?

I thought I'd feel better after challenging him, but I don't feel better at all. My guts are churning and my head is pounding.

If anything, I feel worse than ever.

63

I get back to school ten minutes before the end of lesson time. I walk around the back of the building towards the glass doors of Elder class.

It's highly irregular, I know, but it's the fastest way I can put things right with Ben. He'll quite rightly be furious with the way I dealt with Jasper and then walked out of class, leaving him to cope with the fallout. I hope I can salvage the situation before it spirals out of control.

When they see me outside the doors, the kids all spin around in their seats and I can see them pointing, their mouths wide. I see the tall figure of Ben begin to stride across the classroom. Jasper is sitting in his corner, staring at me. He's with Nadine, the TA from the class next door, but there are no other children sitting at his table.

Ben unlocks the doors and sticks his head out.

'Janey! What the hell?'

'I know. Sorry. About earlier, I mean. I have a big personal problem I should've told you about.'

Ben steps outside, pulling the door to behind him.

'The way you handled Jasper's behaviour was unacceptable.'

'I was completely out of order. I know that and I'm sorry.' I sigh. 'Listen, I'm not supposed to work tomorrow, but I could come in for a couple of—'

'Hasn't Jennifer been in touch?' He frowns. 'You can't come in again until you've sorted things out with her.'

'You've reported me to the head?' I dealt badly with the situation but somehow I thought Ben would discuss it with me first before going to the top.

'Of course I didn't report you,' he hisses, glancing behind him to make sure the kids can't hear. 'But someone did. Someone's shafted you really badly, Janey.'

'Is everything OK, Ben?' Nadine appears behind him, opening the door wider and stepping forward. 'Can we help you with anything, Janey?'

'I just… I came to speak to Ben.'

'I think it's Mrs Harlow you need to be speaking to,' she says frostily before turning to Ben. 'The children are ready for their read-aloud before the bell now.'

'Yes, of course. Thanks, Nadine,' Ben says. She stalks away and he steps back into the classroom.

'Ben?' I say hoarsely as he reaches for the door handle. 'Do you know what's been said… to the head teacher, I mean?'

'Sorry,' he says non-committally.

'Are you sorry you don't know or sorry you can't tell me?' I ask him.

'I hope you get it all sorted out, Janey. I really do,' he says before closing the door.

When I turn around, I see there are lots of parents on the playground now. They all seem to be watching me with interest, and it's eerily quiet compared to the usual background chatter at pick-up time.

I head for the Buckingham mums' group, immediately noticing that Tanya isn't among them. I nod to a couple of other parents I recognise on my way over, but I can't fail to notice there's a definite chill in the air, despite the warmth of the sunshine.

I stop in my tracks as I see someone walking towards me. Small and thin, Jasper's mum's face is twisted and pale.

'The other parents told me! I know all about you… who you are,' she says breathlessly. 'You had no right to be near my son. Don't you think he has enough problems?'

'Charlie,' I say calmly, ignoring the rush of heat in my face. 'I owe you and Jasper an apology. Shall we take this inside?'

I'm desperate to avoid putting on a show for everyone here.

'Is it true?' she says, her voice cold. 'What they're saying about you?'

Other parents approach, emboldened by Charlie's question.

My shoes feel like lead, rooting my feet to the spot. She isn't talking about my outburst in class, she's talking about…

'You've no right to keep that to yourself when you're working with our kids,' calls a parent I recognise but who I've never spoken to. 'We trusted you. We have the right to know our kids are safe!'

'I… I haven't got anything to do with—'

Their voices merge together and I feel myself swaying. My forehead is damp, and when the light breeze touches it, the effect is cooling.

'Stay away from our kids!' Something soft hits me on the back of the head. A rolled-up kid's football shirt falls to the floor.

I spin around, but there are so many of them now, eyes wide, mouths open, faces twisted with hate.

I feel my knees go first, and then I'm falling. The playground asphalt is suddenly next to my face, and someone's shoe is so close I can see the scuffed grain of the leather.

They're all still shouting when I close my eyes.

I don't know how long I'm down there but when I come round, Ben is kneeling by my side and Edie is standing there holding Rowan and Aisha's hands.

'You're behaving like animals.' She glares around at the few parents still close by. 'Back off!'

'She's the animal,' a voice calls out gruffly.

'She hasn't done anything wrong,' Edie shouts back. 'She can't change her past, any more than the rest of us can.'

Silence. I look at her and press my lips together in gratitude.

'Mum?' Rowan says in a small voice. 'Are you OK?'

'Of course, I'm fine,' I say, forcing myself to sit up. Ben holds out a hand to help me. 'I just felt a bit faint, but I'm much better now.'

'Take a few minutes,' Ben says. 'Deep breaths. That's it.'

'I feel like an idiot,' I say, shaking my head. 'It was just the shock. You know, when Charlie started saying stuff about…'

'I know,' he says quietly, and nods. 'However she feels, this shouldn't have happened. The other parents had no right to treat you like that.'

'This is Tanya's doing,' I say to Edie. 'It has to be.'

Edie bends forwards and squeezes my arm. 'Listen, Janey. I'm going to take Rowan back to ours, OK? He'll be fine with Aisha and there's no rush for you to pick him up. Take as much time as you need. Did you want me to call Isaac?'

'Thanks, Edie, but no,' I croak. 'But thanks for taking Rowan.'

Rowan steps forward to give me a kiss.

'Are you going to be OK, sweetie?' I ask him.

He nods, averting his eyes before he says, 'It's not true, is it, Mum? It's not true what they're all saying about—'

I cut him off before he can finish and because I can't stand to see the shock and disappointment on his face when he looks at me, I tell him an outright lie.

'No, Rowan, none of it is true at all.'

64

Ben helps me to my feet and we walk slowly back into the building.

'I've heard of the school grapevine, but this gossip has been supercharged,' I say as we make our way to Mrs Harlow's office. 'How did it get round so fast?'

Ben shrugs. 'I guess your friend made sure it did.'

That figures. Tanya is very well connected with everyone who's anyone in the area. Lots of the parents are on Facebook; there's even a Lady Bridge parents' page, a forum for parents to air their complaints about the school. I'll no doubt be star of the show on that, but I've no intention of looking and inflicting the certain vitriol on myself until I feel a bit sturdier.

But I can't get out of speaking to Jennifer, the head. She sent Ben out into the playground with instructions to bring me to her office when I'm feeling a little better.

When he's satisfied I'm OK, he leaves me sitting on a comfy chair in Jennifer's outer office where visitors check in. I think about trying to reach Isaac again and decide against it until I've got the meeting with Jennifer over with. Things are fraught between us, but still, I really wish he were here with me right now.

Mrs Harlow's secretary, Sandy, offers me coffee, which I decline. I notice that for the duration of my wait she keeps her eyes diplomatically lowered to her keyboard until the head comes out and calls me through to her small, functional office with its single desk and unadorned walls.

She leads me to a small grouping of comfy seats around a low coffee table over in the corner. She's a tall, slim woman with a brisk but kind manner. We both sit down and she pours me a small glass of water without asking if I want it, checking I'm comfortable before she starts to speak.

'Did you get everything sorted out with Rowan?' she asks.

I nod. 'Aisha's mum, Edie, has taken him to her house. She was a godsend in the playground while I was still feeling a bit shaky.'

'That's good. But I was referring to the confusion earlier, when your husband came to collect Rowan from class.'

I look at her blankly. 'I'm sorry, I don't know what you mean.'

Mrs Harlow gives me a knowing smile, like I'm pulling her leg.

'Mr Markham came to collect him just after you left school, for his hospital appointment?' She phrases it as a question, as if she's reminding me of something that's obviously slipped my mind. But her smile fades as she takes in my puzzled expression. 'The children were rehearsing for the whole-school play, so he decided to leave without him.'

Hospital appointment?

The first thing that occurs to me is that Rowan might be ill and Isaac has kept it from me. But no, that's ridiculous. Rowan is clearly a healthy child, and as I have dealt exclusively with his doctor's and dental appointments from his birth, I'm their first contact. It would be virtually impossible for Isaac to keep such a problem from me.

I spoke to Isaac earlier and he never mentioned he'd been here, at the school, a five-minute drive from the house? It doesn't make sense.

'Were you unaware that Rowan's father was collecting him?' Mrs Harlow is concerned now. 'Apparently he telephoned this morning and left a message with the office. We have Mr Markham down as a parental contact, along with yourself. Is that correct?'

I snap to my senses before the situation gets out of hand.

'Yes, of course. I'm so sorry, the appointment must've slipped my mind.' I let out a nervous laugh. 'With all the upset this afternoon, my head is completely scrambled.'

'Don't worry,' she says, looking relieved. 'I can assure you there are some days I'd forget my own head if it were loose! I hope you were able to make another appointment. Do let me know if there's anything we should know about in relation to Rowan's health, or anything else we can help with.'

'Yes, thank you,' I say faintly, reaching for my water again. 'I will.'

'I'm sorry I had to call you into the office under these circumstances,' Jennifer says. 'And what just happened in the playground out there… The parents who verbally attacked you were totally out of order and I'll be writing to them about their behaviour. There's no place for that sort of thing here at Lady Bridge.'

There are no judgemental words, and for that, I'm grateful. My chest feels a little less tight and I take a tiny sip of water, pushing the confusion about the mystery hospital appointment out of my head for now.

'Having said that, I do wish you'd confided in me when you accepted the job,' she says softly, picking up a pen and putting it back down again. 'I could have been better prepared, protected you more.'

I hang my head. She's right, but I wouldn't have known where to start. I'm still getting to grips with Mum's deathbed confession.

'I'm sorry,' I whisper.

'You don't have to apologise,' Jennifer says firmly. 'From what I gather, this… situation from your past is a burden that has been thrust upon you with very little warning. How that must feel, I really can't imagine.'

I nod. The air in the office feels thick and stifling. I can't stop wondering what Isaac was doing, coming to school like that and why he hadn't mentioned anything to me. I'm desperate to call him, have it out with him but my phone is turned to silent and buried in my handbag, so it'll just have to wait. Rowan is safe, and that's all that matters for now.

'What I'd like you to do, if you're willing, is tell me, confidentially, in your own words what happened back then, in your past,' Jennifer says gently. 'The unadorned truth, Janey, that's what I'm asking for, so I can best support you as a valued member of staff.'

And so I do. I tell her everything.

65

After leaving Mrs Harlow's office, the first thing I do is try to call Isaac. After the fifth attempt, I leave a voicemail and send him a text. I don't bother going back into the house; I just jump into the car and put my foot down.

I feel raw from confiding my deeply personal business to the head. She remained calm and kind, but I saw shadows flit across her face when she realised the seriousness of the situation. Her eyes bored into mine as she made up her mind about who I really was. I swear I could *feel* it.

When I'd finished, she gently suggested I take a few days off while she speaks to the governing body and puts in place certain procedures that will make life easier for both me and the rest of the staff.

At the first set of traffic lights, I pull Isaac's business card from my purse, tap the postcode of his office into Google Maps and hook my phone up to the car's media screen. The satnav instantly calculates it's a twenty-two-minute drive at this time of day.

I'm not expecting Isaac to be there at the office, but someone might still be around who knows what his plans were for today, even if they're not answering the phone. I get a vision of us sitting with a drink later tomorrow night when Rowan is in bed, and Isaac shaking his head.

I got hopelessly delayed and my phone died on me. I had no way of contacting you. I can't believe you thought I'd just taken off.

It comforts me slightly to imagine what he might say, but I know that so much of what's happened makes no sense. Why did Isaac try and pick Rowan up early? Why did he lie about the hospital appointment to the school? And the biggest *why* of all… why did he do all this without mentioning it to me?

Mercifully, traffic is light and I make good time. As I turn the final corner, I see the large office block up ahead of me. I park up on a side street, open the parking app on my phone and pay for an hour. A large neon sign hangs above the main doors. It reads: *Carlton House*.

I pull the card out of my pocket and double-check the address. This is definitely the correct building. It's Hall Street, and there's a big plaque bearing the number 441.

Swallowing down a sickly taste, I walk up the steps to the main doors to find a middle-aged man in overalls there. His badge identifies him as the janitor and he's trying and failing to hold onto a large parcel and get into the building at the same time. I hold the door for him.

'You're a star.' He blows out a breath. 'I reckon I'm getting too old for this game.'

'May I help you?' A professional young woman in a navy suit and white blouse looks up at me from the curved reception desk.

'I'm here to see Isaac Markham, please.' I decide on the confident approach rather than start dithering about whether he might be in the office or not.

'Isaac Markham,' she murmurs, reaching for a notepad and writing down the name. 'And what company is that?'

'Abacus.' I frown. I'm standing right here in the fancy company headquarters, so I would think it should be obvious!

'Of course. Let me check. Is he expecting you?'

'No. Well, not exactly. I'm Janey Markham, his wife.'

I pick up a leaflet from the counter top and waft my face with it. I just can't seem to cool down.

She nods and taps an extension into the phone. After a few seconds, she looks regretful. 'Sorry, he's not answering.' She glances at something on another sheet of paper. 'Oh, it seems he's leaving us.'

'What?'

'There's a note here to say I need to process a receipt as he's paid up the outstanding lease.'

Nothing is making any sense.

'I'd like a word with someone else then, please,' I say firmly. 'From Abacus.'

'I'm afraid there *is* no one else,' she says without attempting to try any other extension numbers. 'If your husband isn't here, then the office will be locked.'

'I just wanted to ask if he'd left a forwarding contact number with one of his colleagues at all?' She stares at me as if I'm just not getting it.

Just then the phone rings. She stares for a moment at a flashing button, checks a list in front of her and then answers. 'Good afternoon, Royd Logistics, can I help you?'

Royd Logistics… not Abacus?

She scribbles a message on her notepad, and when she ends the call, I ask, 'How many businesses are in this building?'

'Nearly thirty now,' she says confidently. 'We only have two spare offices up for rent at the moment. Your husband's will make three, but theoretically he can still use it now the lease payments have been satisfied.'

'Are the offices all fully serviced?'

She nods. 'All bills and a reception service included. I can give you a leaflet if you like?'

My heart thumps in my chest as finally the penny begins to drop.

The receptionist hands me a brightly coloured brochure. It's a rather stereotypical, dated approach, the cover featuring an attractive receptionist handing a letter to a confident and successful-looking businessman as he walks past her desk.

Present a professional corporate image to the world, screams the tag line.

'Could I pop up to my husband's office, please?' I feel like I'm watching myself from the other side of the room. 'I'm sure one of his colleagues would be able to tell me where—'

'As I said, there's nobody up there and his office will be locked,' she repeats patiently.

'But what about the other people who work at Abacus?'

She shakes her head and looks at me sympathetically. 'Your husband *is* Abacus, Mrs Markham. He's one of our sole traders.'

I stand and stare at her as I desperately try to place the jagged pieces of this distorted picture together in my mind without coming up with something truly awful. But it is becoming painfully clear that Isaac has lied to me. He's told me a really, *really* big lie. There was never a new job, a dynamic young company, and I'd bet my bottom dollar there's no boss called Bob who's been keeping him out at meetings or driving around the country either.

I stagger slightly and hold onto the edge of the reception desk.

'Mrs Markham, are you OK?' She looks alarmed about what she might be called on to do, rather than displaying any genuine concern.

I can't answer her. All I can do is run through all the opportunities for more of Isaac's lies when I've given him the benefit of the doubt or accepted his lame excuses.

The mystery caller when we first moved in. Who was that at the door? All the late-home-from-work excuses, his sudden illness at the restaurant...

'Mrs Markham?'

'Thanks,' I say faintly. 'I'm fine.' I manage to put one foot in front of the other and walk slowly towards the exit. With each step my head feels lighter and I feel more and more naïve.

Isaac's words echo in my head: *Listen, you're barking up the wrong tree here. There's nobody else in my life, I swear it.*

All this time I've been suspecting my husband of completely the wrong thing. Isaac isn't having an affair; it's nothing as straightforward as that! He's been living some kind of elaborate lie, a different life. Staying away from home more and more to try and cover up the cracks in his story. But what exactly has he been trying to keep hidden from me?

He must've planned all this for months. Sold me the whole elaborate fantasy of moving away for a fresh start, bagging a fantastic new job at nearly twice the salary, and I played into his hands like a dream. The only thing I fretted about was whether he was having an affair, and he told me the truth about that.

There's nobody else in my life, I swear it.

I stop walking. Just stand there in the middle of the floor space. A thought flutters up and stings me right between the eyes.

'Is everything OK, Mrs Markham?' I hear the receptionist call across the lobby, but I don't respond.

If Isaac's fancy new company hasn't paid our relocation expenses or provided the sizeable starting bonus that gave us a healthy bank balance for the first time in years, then who the hell has?

I turn around to the receptionist, pasting a smile on my face. 'Could you direct me to the bathroom before I leave?' I ask.

'Of course!' She looks relieved that's all I'm asking for. 'Just down there, to the left.'

Following her directions, I walk briskly towards the back of the large entrance area, then, with a cursory backward glance to satisfy myself she's busy, I dart through some double doors marked *Stairs*.

66

After slipping out of the reception area, I find myself on the first floor of the office block, I walk down the corridor reading aloud the company signs on the doors: *Swift Insurance*, *Dottie's Design Studio* and *Martian Media Services*. I reach the end of the carpeted corridor and take the next set of double doors to ascend to the second floor.

There, the third door on the right bears a plain white sign with a black border and the plain Arial font that Isaac prefers to use in all his Word documents.

Abacus.

I try the door and discover that, predictably, it's locked.

I jump as the stairwell doors clunk behind me and someone emerges, whistling.

'Can I help… Oh, hello, again!' It's the janitor I helped at the main doors when I arrived. He glances at Isaac's office door and back at me. 'Everything OK?'

I hear myself start to talk before I even know exactly what I'm going to say. 'I'm such an idiot. I've driven for half an hour to bring this mail in and do a bit of admin, and I've forgotten my keys. I'll have to go back down to reception and ask if they'll let me in.'

'No need to go to that trouble.' He pulls out a clanking tangle of keys from his pocket. 'I've got a master key here that'll solve your problem.' He gives me a cheeky wink. 'I won't tell anyone if you don't.'

'Oh, that'll save my legs. Thank you!'

I watch with bated breath as he turns the key in the lock and pushes the door open a sliver.

'How long will you be, do you reckon?'

'No more than thirty minutes tops.' My voice comes out a bit strangulated, but the janitor doesn't seem to notice.

'No worries. I'll have a wander by in half an hour and lock up again if you've gone, but no rush.'

I thank him again and watch as he ambles back down the corridor before disappearing into an office further down.

I step inside the room and stand there in the doorway for a few moments, letting out the breath I've been holding. I look around, take in the stark reality of all Isaac's false claims and promises. Here it is, the mighty Abacus. The tiny office cast-iron proof of my husband's momentous lies.

A pedestal desk sits in front of a small window with a drawn blind. Apart from an office chair, there is no other furniture. Just half a dozen hard plastic boxes dotted around the floor, all of them filled to the brim with paperwork.

He may have paid up the lease, but he's obviously intending to come back here at some point.

I step inside and close the door behind me. The room is dim with the blind closed, and I snap on a harsh overhead fluorescent tube light. Then I walk around the desk and sit in the chair, leaning back and closing my eyes for a few moments while I wait for my pounding heart to settle down.

How has Isaac lived with himself, lying through his teeth all this time? It must have been exhausting. And for what? Why leave his job and weave this elaborate web of deceit? What has he gained? The obvious answer is: all the extra money this new job is supposedly bringing in.

I look at the mess on the desk in front of me. I can barely see the surface for piles of paperwork – none of it neatly organised, which is unlike Isaac. He's always kept his home office immaculate. I scan half a dozen random pages. They look like copies of balance sheets and other complicated numerical information, headed by the names of various companies.

I push the paperwork aside and see that underneath is one of those desk mats that also includes a big sheet of notepaper on which to make notes whilst taking telephone calls. It's covered with squiggles, doodles and short messages, some with telephone numbers in Isaac's distinctive sloping handwriting. There are so many notes and references I could sit here all day and struggle to decipher them. I haven't got that luxury, so instead, I grab my phone and take a photo of the entire sheet. I can expand it in sections on my iPad when I get home.

I sift randomly through the papers both on the desk and in the plastic box nearest to me. None of it means anything to me and I don't recognise any of the company names on the balance sheets and other spreadsheets. Making sense of what Isaac is actually up to feels like an insurmountable problem.

I look at the scattered papers on the desk again. They're the ones Isaac has obviously been interested in enough in to pull out and study at his desk. Surely there must be something here that will give me a clue and help me to understand his motivation.

I pick up my phone again, ready to snap each piece of paper, and then shake my head in frustration and push it into my bag. I gather up all the loose papers on the desk into one neat pile, then find a large envelope and stuff them inside.

It's too late to hide from Isaac the fact that I now know he's been lying. I don't *want* to hide it from him. I want everything out in the open once and for all, even though it's going to cost us a great deal of pain and finish our relationship completely.

As I lean down to close the deep pedestal drawer, something catches my eye. It's an unopened envelope addressed to Isaac, marked *Private and Confidential*. It has the look of a bank statement, and when I turn it over, I see it has a return address for First Direct, which I know to be the online bank Isaac had his personal account with when we first got married.

Feeling increasingly nervous that the janitor will return and start asking awkward questions, I add the bank letter to the stack of papers I've already stuffed into the large envelope.

A great weight settles on my chest when I wonder what I'll find among all this information. Part of me desperately wants to know the truth; the other part dreads finding out, because I love my husband and I don't want a divorce. The thought of Rowan having to deal with that at such a young age breaks my heart. But living this lie will damage us all in the end.

I shake the thoughts off. First I just need to find out the truth of what my husband has been up to.

67

I get back in the car and sit there for ten minutes straight. I don't look at my phone, don't call Isaac. I know Rowan is safe with Edie and she's made it clear I don't have to rush back to pick him up.

I just sit there and think through the past few months – before we left our old house, before Isaac left his old company. I think about how, almost overnight, he changed from a depressed, increasingly isolated man with money problems into someone who suddenly saw his opportunity to prosper and improve our lives.

I remember these two versions of him clearly, but what I can't recall, despite racking my brains, is exactly what happened to bridge the gap. I'm not even sure anything did. He just came home one day and told me he was going for the interview at Abacus. He said, 'If there is no risk, there is no reward.' And the rest is history.

We found the house within a day of him accepting the job. Anyone might think the whole thing was a done deal before he even asked my opinion.

I realise now that I've been woefully naïve. The timing of Mum's revelation couldn't have come at a worse time. I've been so blinded by it, confused by the tangle of feelings, ranging from guilt to despair to fury.

My fingernails burrow into the soft flesh of my hand. I must be the dumbest wife ever, to just swallow everything he told me without question. I'm old enough to know that people don't change overnight. Change is a process and often a very lengthy one.

I pick up my phone. There are no text or voicemail notifications, no sign Isaac has tried to get in touch. I call his number and go straight through to voicemail. I leave a message.

'Call me.' My voice in previous messages has gone through the whole range: demanding, threatening, pleading. Now it sounds completely flat and devoid of hope.

I send a text.

Call me urgently. I've been to your office.

When I can no longer think clearly, I start the engine and drive home. If he's not with 'Bob' and clients – if they even exist – then where the hell is my husband?

Inside the house, I kick off my shoes, dump my handbag and the envelope containing the papers and run upstairs to the bedroom that doubles as Isaac's office when he's working from home.

We decided the room was big enough to house a double bed for the rare occasion we might have guests, and also Isaac's small desk with a two-drawer filing cabinet, pushed up against the other wall.

I rifle through the papers on the desk and find nothing of interest. In fact I see that some of these letters – official quotes and correspondence confirming the start of various projects – pertain to Isaac's old company and are about a year out of date.

A thought flits through my mind: why has Isaac been looking at these papers? It doesn't make any sense.

I tug at the top filing cabinet drawer and find it locked. A quick search doesn't turn up a key, so I grab a metal rod that Isaac uses to open the skylight and wedge it into the crack, forcing the drawer open.

My throat tightens when I see that, apart from a few pens and some blank sheets of paper, the drawer is completely empty. I use the rod again on the bottom drawer, and this time get a little luckier. There are some pages of notes written in Isaac's hand,

and also a small stack of unopened letters, bound together with an elastic band, some of which look identical to the bank one.

I gather up the notes and letters and head downstairs again.

An hour later, I get up from my position on the floor, legs outstretched and my back leaning against the sofa. Papers and letters fall from my lap like dead leaves as I stand, grimacing at the stiffness in my joints.

I sit on the edge of the sofa and bury my face in my hands.

The unopened envelopes revealed statements from a bank account in Isaac's name dating back three months. An account containing thirty-five thousand pounds I knew nothing about. It looks like the balance of the account was originally fifty thousand pounds, but a few weeks ago, Isaac withdrew a ten-thousand-pound lump sum – presumably his 'signing on' bonus from the new company – and then a little later another five thousand.

The copious notes in his handwriting seemed to be lengthy observations of the profitability of several companies. He's always preferred making notes with a paper and pen rather than on his laptop. However, a closer inspection of his scrawl reveals nothing of any meaning to me.

Now I look up and catch sight of Isaac's cordless office phone, which I brought down from upstairs.

On impulse, I pick up the handset and dial 1471. An automated voice reads out the last number called from the phone. It doesn't mean anything to me. Why should it? I can barely remember my own number.

I press 3 to redial the number. The call connects and begins to ring.

'Hello?' says a slightly accented voice on the other end. A moment of silence, and then, 'Isaac, is that you?'

I know that voice well. It's Kyoko.

68

They hadn't been down for days now. It was a blessing, even though Susan was in so much pain.

She thought perhaps she had internal bleeding. Every time she moved just an inch, the pain sliced through her like a cheese wire.

Perhaps they'd moved on to number ten. Or maybe not. Maybe other girls were smart enough not to fall for their tricks. Maybe they'd be suspicious of his fancy car and the pretty girl so much younger than him in the passenger seat.

It wouldn't be long. Susan could feel it.

She hadn't eaten in days, and she'd sipped the last of the water hours and hours ago… possibly yesterday.

She thought of wildflowers in the meadow she used to play in at the back of her nan's house, the breeze cooling the back of her neck on a stifling hot day. She thought about Bosley, her dog, a Heinz 57 who exploded with love for her every time he saw her, whether she'd popped out of the house for five minutes or was away for five days.

She thought about her loving parents and the way her mother had warned her to be careful and stay safe every time she left the house.

Susan had been so lucky to be loved by all of them. She felt thankful to God and knew he would take her in his loving arms very soon. She was not afraid.

She closed her eyes and drifted to a place of calm, away from the damp, dark basement.

It was nearly time now.

She could feel it.

69

With so much drama in one afternoon, I feel utterly exhausted. When I heard Kyoko's voice, I just ended the call, unable to say anything at all. Finally, it looks like I have the truth about those two.

I've taken a couple of paracetamol to try and stave off the mother of all headaches but the thudding pain in my skull shows no signs of abating. I send Edie a text asking if she'd mind keeping Rowan for another hour or so just to give me some time to rest. Her reply is swift.

Course not. Hope everything is OK.

I lie down on our bed, and when the alarm on my phone wakes me up thirty minutes later, my eyelids are crusty, stuck together. I prise them apart and stagger into the en suite, where I study my face in the mirror. An angry swollen sty is blossoming on one eyelid, and both eyes are red-rimmed and a little oozy. It looks as if I've managed to acquire an infection.

I scrabble about in the medicine drawer and find some medicated eye cream that Rowan was prescribed once when a football grazed his cornea. Isaac and I were both watching the friendly match and panicked terribly when the ball hit him in the face and he rolled over on the pitch. His eye bled and looked a mess, and we rushed him to A&E. In the event, thank goodness, it wasn't at all serious, but you do what you need to do to keep your kids safe, don't you? That's why Tanya's reaction just doesn't stack up.

I pull the tiny tube of cream out of the packet and squeeze a blob on to a clean finger. It's probably out of date, but it will have to do until I can get to see a doctor. I smear some over both lids and then splash water on my cheeks to try and wake myself up.

I feel drugged, but I didn't drink last night and I'm not taking any medication apart from the paracetamol. It's not just my head but my entire body that feels weighted down, as if every movement is a tremendous effort. I feel as though I'm battling through a sedative effect. What I really want to do is close my eyes, pull the covers over my head and sleep.

Everyone I can talk to has either walked out of my life, is ignoring me or I've offended in some way.

I've never felt so alone. Not even after Mum died. I'm hollow inside, drained of hope or any idea what I can possibly do next. I feel utterly hopeless, paralysed with dread, thinking of the terrible news that every minute could bring about what Isaac is up to… about Angel and the assault.

I'd managed to convince myself that Isaac's strange behaviour over the past few weeks was just an attack of nerves linked to the new job. The fake company, the hidden bank account… He's gone to such trouble to deceive me. But *why*? It just doesn't make sense. Even if he'd found he'd simply fallen out of love with me, or he'd met another woman – probably Kyoko – and wanted to be with her, wouldn't separation and ultimately divorce be so much easier and less involved than doing all *this*?

I take the facts and turn them this way and that in my mind like a jigsaw puzzle. None of the pieces fit, because something is missing. There's something – possibly right in front of my nose – that I'm just not seeing.

I'm turning off the taps at the bathroom sink when I nearly jump out of my skin. Someone is ringing the doorbell repeatedly. The shrill call of it cuts like a knife through the silence of the house, seeming to exaggerate its emptiness and Isaac's absence.

I rush over to the window and whip the curtain to one side so I can look down on the area directly in front of the door. Whoever it is is standing too close to the house for me to see. Surely if it's the police, something to do with my witness statement, there'd be two of them again? It would be difficult for two bodies to huddle so close to the door. Then I get a flash of denim fabric as the person takes a step back. It looks like a woman. On her own.

Forgetting the fact that my hair is sticking out at angles and I have cream smeared all around my eyes, I rush downstairs just as the doorbell sounds again.

I hastily put the chain on, opening the door the few inches it will allow.

'Kyoko?' I whisper, shocked. Then I come to my senses. 'What do you want?'

I get ready for her barbed reply but her face is soft and open, the attitude gone. She looks pale, with sunken eyes that seem to swallow the light rather than reflect it. The corners of her mouth are downturned and there are dark circles under her eyes. She looks like she hasn't slept in a while.

'What is it? Have you come to tell me I'm imagining it all again?' My voice emerges lower and croakier than usual.

'No. I'm sorry to disturb you and sorry to just turn up like this, but' – she looks over her shoulder as if she's checking there's nobody else around – 'is there any chance I can come inside, just for a few minutes? I can't really explain everything out here.' Her eyes dart up to next-door's bedroom window.

'Have you come here to gloat? Because I'm not interested in hearing it.' I squint at her painfully through the pounding behind my eyes.

'No! No, it's not that.' She glances around again and her voice drops lower. 'It's just… I want to tell you what happened to me. That's all. In case it might help… Isaac.'

'Help Isaac?' I'm feeling increasingly nervous. My husband is lying to me about virtually everything, and my life is spinning on its axis.

'And help you too, Janey. It's time you knew everything.'

70

I unlatch the chain, and wordlessly Kyoko steps inside.

Today, she's dressed in ripped jeans and a faded denim jacket. Today, she wears minimal make-up, her hair casually pulled back into a messy ponytail.

I poke my head out of the door and glance left and right, but there's nobody around in the crescent. When I close the door and turn back, Kyoko is looking all around her. At the walls, the stairs, down the hallway through to the kitchen.

'What's happening?' I say, my mouth dry.

'I've come to tell you the truth,' Ky says.

Does she mean the truth I asked her for before? Is this about how she and my husband have been having an affair all along? About how they've decided they want to be together?

Fear crawls up from the bottom of my spine like a cold wet slug, blindly aiming for my heart.

I walk through to the kitchen and, without invitation, Kyoko follows me.

'Sit down,' I offer when we reach the kitchen just because I can't bear her to stand anywhere near me. I flick the kettle on and look at Ky. 'I have to pick Rowan up from Edie's house soon, so I don't have long.'

'Edie has Rowan?'

She pinches the top of her nose and squeezes her eyes shut and I wonder why that even matters to her. Maybe she has instructions from Isaac to try and snatch him… he's already tried to pick him up from school early without my knowledge.

Kyoko slips onto a bar stool and I notice that the sleeves of her long cotton top are poking out of her denim jacket. She pushes them back, revealing painfully thin wrists.

For something to do, I spoon ground coffee into the cafetière and fill it with boiling water from the kettle. I know I'm subconsciously trying to delay the information I'm dreading she's going to tell me about her and Isaac. I swear I can feel Ky's dark eyes boring into my back as I prepare the drinks, but when I turn round, she's staring at one of Rowan's paintings pinned to the wall next to the fridge.

I leave the coffee to brew and lean back against the sink, watching her watching me. I remember the things about Ky that don't quite add up. The change of name, the lie about where she and the twins lived, and Cherry's sad revelation about her father in class.

For a few seconds we regard each other without speaking. I'm too tired to ask her why she's here, and she looks like she's struggling to find the best way to confess that she and my husband love each other. All I can think is that when she tells me, I'm going to keep a poker face if it kills me. I will *not* give her the satisfaction of seeing me fall apart. Ridiculous that in the end, that's what matters. But somehow it does.

After a few moments of silence I can sense an air of sadness emanating from her like an invisible fog. I should know; I can feel my own dense emotions seeping from my pores like some kind of infected sweat.

My fear about what Isaac is up to, whether he's taken the first step of leaving us… it crackles through the air around Kyoko and I. I'm unsure of her motives and I fear what's about to come out of her mouth. But I don't feel afraid of *her*.

'I don't know you very well, Ky, but I do know some things *about* you that don't quite add up.'

She looks up sharply and I turn away to check on the coffee again. My heart is pummelling away at my chest but I keep my head held high. I won't give her the satisfaction of feeling superior to me in my own home.

'The first thing you should know,' Kyoko says with a heavy sigh, 'is that I'm not the person you think I am.'

'Really?' I say, not prepared to tell her exactly what I already know.

'My name was Yuno Harris and I've never lived in York. I moved up to Nottingham from Kent, not York, like I told the others.' She pauses as if steeling herself to say the next words. 'My husband… We're apart not because he had an affair with his secretary but because he died. Rupert took his own life two years ago.'

Does she think she can just take my husband because hers is dead? That might sound callous but I'm beginning to think that's what she's come here to admit.

'All this time you've thought I was a nasty piece of work, jealous that you'd gotten so close to Tanya.'

'Well, I—'

'You were partly right, Janey. I've been trying my level best to drive a wedge between the two of you since you came on the scene, but obviously it hasn't worked.'

'But why? Why would you do that?'

'Two reasons. The first was that before you became part of the friendship circle, I was making great progress. I was the closest person to Tanya, and that served my purpose perfectly. Secondly, believe it or not, I was trying to protect you.'

I forget about making the coffee.

'OK, back up a little. What exactly were you trying to protect me from?'

'From going through everything I've had to endure. I wouldn't wish that on my worst enemy,' Kyoko says softly.

This isn't adding up. As far as I'm aware, Kyoko can't stand my guts. I really don't know why I've let her into my home so willingly.

'Look, I have to pick Rowan up very soon, so can we just get to the point?'

'Fair enough. My husband, Rupert, got himself caught up in some dodgy business deals. He wasn't a bad person, far from it. But these people, who I never got to meet, he initially met at a networking event. They were very persuasive and offered him what sounded like a fantastic opportunity for a one-off commission of his services,' Kyoko says.

'What did he do for a living?'

'He was an I.T. developer and programmer by trade,' she says quietly. 'Like Isaac.'

I hate her even saying his name but I keep my lips sealed for now, and wait.

'After he'd done the job and realised the implications of his actions, Rupert was racked with guilt. He tried to distance himself from the people involved, tried to pull out of their web but found he couldn't... they pursued him, threatened him, you see.' Kyoko lets out a long sigh that seems filled with a thousand regrets. 'He didn't confide in me because he wanted to protect me and I suspect he thought I'd leave him when I found out where all the money came from.' She swallows, her eyes glistening. She doesn't notice me blanch at what she just said as I think about the bank statement I just found upstairs. 'Instead of letting me in on the nightmare, Rupert tried to deal with it himself. In the end, it got so bad, he felt the only way out was to... hang himself in the garage.'

My hand flies to my mouth. There I was, telling her to just get on with it and then she comes out with the most terrible thing imaginable.

'I was comatose with grief at his death; it just didn't make any sense to me that he'd leave me and the kids and that was torturing me almost as much as losing him. But then two days after he died, I got a package through the post. It was from Rupert himself, posted before he killed himself.' She steels herself. 'Over time, he'd compiled detailed evidence, basically kept a paperwork trail of what had happened to explain it all to me: how he got involved with these people, how they'd threatened to hurt me and the children if he didn't do as they wanted. In the package, there was also a bank card and statement for a very healthy savings account I knew nothing about.'

I'm speechless at the similarities. 'Why didn't he take the evidence to the police instead of taking his own life?'

'Because he knew he'd broken the law himself by becoming involved and working for them. He knew they would make him pay in ways too terrible to comprehend.' She closes her eyes, shakes her head. 'I know he sounds ruthless but that's so far from the truth. He made a mistake and tried to get back on the right track again. He'd gotten himself in this place mentally where he thought he'd never see the light again. He thought he was a burden to us and that we'd be better off without him.'

'What exactly did he do for them?' I ask faintly, not sure if I want to know the answer.

'He'd done a couple of jobs hacking young successful companies on their way up and about to float on the stock market. He'd stolen their intellectual property – trade secrets like of identical client lists and details of design and manufacturing processes – making them vulnerable to ruthless competitors. The people who controlled the operation, Palace Securities, would then offer to to sell their secrets back to them or, if they refused, they'd post them on the dark web. Rupert told me several companies had been ruined by refusing to play their game. This only made the others pay up quicker.'

'Surely one of the companies who refused to pay up could have traced who'd stolen their information and alert the police. They had nothing to lose at that stage.'

Kyoko shakes her head. 'It's not easy for a small company to get justice in these matters. The biggest companies can launch powerful lawsuits and have the financial clout to follow up prosecutions. But smaller companies have fewer resources and can't foot the legal fees and costs up front. Plus its really difficult to trace a good hacker because they hide behind sophisticated virtual private networks.'

It all sounds like technological gobbledegook to me. I don't see how this has got anything to do with her having an affair with Isaac but I don't interrupt. I might not fully understand the stuff she's telling me but some of it sounds uncomfortably close to what Isaac might have been involved in himself.

'In his letter to me, Rupert admitted he'd been horribly naïve. Palace Securities told him they just wanted to *look* at the stolen information, use it to help their own business interests. They never said it would be used to blackmail or ruin anyone. After a couple of jobs, and when he realised they were ruining people who had worked hard to build up their businesses, Rupert told them he wanted out.'

'Let me guess,' I say. 'They didn't take kindly to that?'

'At first they were fine, said they were grateful for what he'd done and if ever he wanted to change his mind, they'd gladly give him more jobs. And they offered him a bonus payment so he could set up his own business and pay them back when he got it up and running.'

I swallow hard, thinking about Isaac's job at Abacus. This is starting to feel uncomfortable.

'Foolishly, he took them at face value and accepted their offer. The head honcho, a woman, was so nice, apparently. He wrote, and I quote, "She seemed so supportive and, like an idiot, I believed she genuinely wanted to help me."'

Kyoko continues, her voice softening as she gets to the worst details.

'He started his business and it seemed to be doing well but in the information he sent me, he wrote that Palace Securities got back in touch, started slowly but surely to apply pressure again. When it became obvious he wasn't going to play ball, the blackmail started.'

'But surely, if they went to the police about what Rupert had done, they'd be giving themselves up too,' I say.

'They weren't threatening to tell the police. They said they'd blacken his name in business circles so nobody would touch him and then, finally, they began threatening harm might come to me and the kids in a road traffic accident or a home robbery gone wrong…

'In the end, he could see no way out but to kill himself to free me and the kids. He said, in his letter, that as long as he was alive, they'd never stop. That there had been others before him. He instructed me to destroy the information once I'd read and understood what happened and then not tell another soul about it. He wanted me to use the money in the secret bank account to make a fresh start and forget all about Palace Securities and what they did.'

'And did you… destroy it?

She stares out of the patio doors into the garden. 'I did make a fresh start with the kids like Rupert wanted us to. But I also changed my name and moved here to Nottingham. As it turns out, Rupert didn't know me half as well as he thought he did. I made my mind up that these people wouldn't get away with causing my husband's death. No way. I resolved there and then that somehow, I would bring them to justice and stop this happening to other families.'

'They're here… in Nottingham?' My eyes widen as Kyoko nods. She glances around the room again and settles on the window and the moody sky beyond the glass.

'I didn't know anyone here, and although I tried to reach out to new people at the local playgroup and suchlike, I felt quite lonely and isolated. I knew it was important I portrayed myself as just another single mum, no threat, nothing to draw attention to myself. I rented a small house right on the edge of the crescent and just waited, took my time. Then one day I got to the school gates with the twins and a woman pulled up alongside us in a big fancy car, asked if we were the new people on Buckingham Crescent.'

I know without her saying that it was Tanya.

'She changed my life, introduced me to her friends and invited me to lots of events. Before I knew what was happening, I was pulled into a culture I didn't belong in and couldn't really keep up with.'

I'm too crushed to comment, but she doesn't seem surprised by my silence.

'I knew I was being drawn into a toxic friendship group but that's exactly what I came here for, to infiltrate their world. She had no clue I was Rupert's wife, didn't get her hands dirty at that end of the business.'

'So... you haven't come here today to tell me you're having an affair with my husband?'

She looks at me. 'We both told you there was nothing in it and that's the truth. I'd seen the signs Isaac was getting in over his head and I knew they were getting to him just like they got to Rupert. When you came upstairs at the party, I was telling Isaac my story. Telling him to be careful.'

I cover my face with my hands. 'You're not the only one who's fallen under Tanya's spell, Ky. I swallowed everything she told me too. I'd got no clue she was involved in any dodgy business dealings.'

'Tanya?' Ky looks at me and frowns. 'It's Edie we're talking about. Tanya's just as much a victim as the rest of us, in her own way. When you moved here, I was on the cusp of getting her to tell me everything, and that's why I tried to warn you off so hard.'

My son is with Edie. I stand up and my head spins. 'I have to get Rowan back.'

Kyoko lays her hand on my arm. 'Sit for a few more moments, Janey. You look like you're going to keel over.'

I feel as if I might faint. I sit down to gather my senses so I can go get my son. 'How is Tanya involved in this?'

'Edie and her husband, Alistair, are the masterminds behind Palace Securities. They force other people to take the risks and do their dirty work. My husband, Tanya's husband, Tristan, and now Isaac too. Not to mention some of the other women they hang around with being involved to some extent or another… they've all succumbed to the chance of a big payday by taking on jobs from Edie, not realising they can never opt out again.'

I think about Isaac and Tristan, deep in conversation at the party. The same stressed behaviour from Tristan as I'm accustomed to from my husband.

'Tanya was instructed to befriend you to find out your secrets, to get information on you that Edie can use if Isaac steps out of line,' Kyoko goes on. 'Edie's holding stuff over Tanya, too. She pays Angel and some of the other Buckingham women to befriend businessmen so she can get compromising pictures of them. There's no sex involved, but the photos are enough for their wives to believe they're having affairs. She then uses these to blackmail the men. Tanya knows something's happening, but Edie has her in a tight grip. She's driving a wedge between Angel and her mother and Tanya is fragile underneath the bluster. I'm not sure she's going to cope.'

I cover my face with my hands. Angel with those men… I was right it's something Tanya knew about. The man who was assaulted and died, it must have all got out of hand.

'This house used to be owned by Palace Securities. You're not the only family to live here that's involved with Edie. She likes to keep her people close.'

So the day after we moved on to the crescent and met Edie at her garden gate, Isaac knew. He knew from the outset – probably right from the day he showed me this house on Rightmove – that we would be living amongst jackals and he never said a word.

'Are you in touch with Isaac? I've been trying to contact him… he tried to pick Rowan up from school this afternoon without me knowing.'

'I haven't heard from him but at the party he told me he wants to get you and Rowan away from the area. He said Edie knew about some kind of secret of yours and was holding it over his head so he'd taken the evidence, he said.' Ky shrugged, obviously not understanding he'd been referring to the box. Isaac must've taken Mum's box after all to protect me!

I snap out of my thoughts.

'Edie has Rowan,' I gasp. 'I have to get him back.'

'Whatever you do, don't tell her you know.' Kyoko grabs my arm tightly. 'Act normal. Together, we can beat her, Janey. I'll wait here, if you like, until you get back. In case Isaac comes home.'

71

I tear up the street towards Edie's house. When I reach the gate, I take a deep breath and ring the bell on the keypad on the entrance pillar.

'Yes?'

A tiny red light comes on and the video screen flickers although there's no picture yet.

'It's Janey, Edie. I've come to collect Rowan.' It takes tremendous effort to remain calm. I just need to get my son back safely. That's all that matters right now.

'Come through, darling.'

There's a loud click and the gate begins to swing smoothly open, revealing the beautiful landscaped gardens. Then the wide white front door opens and Edie stands framed in the doorway, a vision in a floaty kaftan elegantly embroidered with tiny shells. I feel sick.

'Sweetie,' she declares as I reach her. She air-kisses either side of my face. 'I'm so pleased you dropped by. We're the only ones here, so your timing is perfect.'

She's seems so genuine and caring…

'Where's Rowan?' I ask, panic nibbling at the edges of my words. I can't hear laughter or the noise of two children in the house.

'They're around somewhere, maybe in the garden. Leave them while they're quiet; more time for us to chat.'

She leads me through to the lounge. The carpet covered in diamond-shaped hoover lines that someone – I assume the housekeeper – has gone to great lengths to print onto the pile as you would on a lawn. Everything for show. Nothing is real here.

'Please, Janey, let's talk. What a terrible shock for you in the playground. I hope you and I know each other well enough now that you'd have faith in my friendship.'

I force a smile and then stare out of the wall of glass that overlooks the landscaped back garden and consider this point. Kyoko has never been overly friendly, whereas Edie has always been helpful and kind. What if, in panic, I've misplaced my trust? What if Ky is lying through her perfect teeth?

Edie sidles up to me and lays a comforting hand on my shoulder. 'How's Isaac?'

'He's OK.' I look down at my hands, feeling hollow. But I should move the conversation away from Isaac. 'Tanya is furious because I went to the police about Angel, and as you know, somehow the whole school knows my business. Knows about my past.'

She places a pink gin and tonic on the table in front of me, the ice clinking.

'It's quite a mystery,' I say carefully, staring at the beautiful cut glass tumbler. 'The way everything is going wrong. It's almost as if someone's behind it… but why?'

'I suppose it's easy to think that might be the case,' she says, sipping her own gin but never taking her eyes off me.

My efforts to remain calm evaporate in a second. Despite Ky's instructions, I just can't keep this up.

'I'd like to take Rowan home now.' I stand up. 'I don't feel well. I'm sure you understand, after the day I've had; I need to get home for when Isaac gets back.'

But she doesn't move, doesn't say anything.

'Can you get Rowan for me, please, Edie?'

'All in good time,' she says. 'He's quite safe, don't worry.'

I walk over to the glass doors and open them. 'Rowan?' I call into the vast garden. 'Time to go home.'

'My, my, we *are* in a rush.' Edie stretches out languidly on the sofa. 'Calm down, Janey. You can relax here.'

Heat fills my chest and head. 'Where's Rowan?' There's a full feeling in my throat, like I might be sick. I'm panicking and there's nothing I can do to stop it. 'Please, Edie. I have to go. I need to take Rowan home now.'

'We have stuff we need to talk about,' she says curtly. 'Sit down.'

I run to the bottom of the stairs. 'Rowan!' I yell. 'Are you up there?'

No answer.

There's a door to my right and I fling it open. The garage. It's dark in there and I snap on the light. 'Row—'

My voice dies as I take in the car in front of me. A black BMW with silver trim along the side. The back panels have been stripped and the seats removed.

I yelp and jump back. A tall man is walking towards me. I squint into the dim light of the garage and then I realise. It's the man I saw watching us in the restaurant.

'Meet my husband and Isaac's boss, "Bob",' Edie laughs. 'Alistair.'

I back away as he fills the doorway. His black hair casts a shadow over his face, his eyes dark and hooded.

'Now perhaps you can see why Tanya was so reluctant for you to go to the police about Angel,' Edie says. 'There's a lot happening behind the scenes here you're totally unaware of. But given your pedigree, your past, you shouldn't be too astounded at what people will do to cover up their shame. It was only a matter of time before your secret got out, Janey.'

'You! You were the one who spread the gossip.'

She looks unruffled. 'People have a right to know who you are. You were working with our children; you can't be allowed to keep your past hidden like that.'

One rule for one…

'Tanya told you?'

She nods. 'I knew Tanya was getting too close to you. For some unknown reason she seems quite fond of you. She told me about the box of evidence eventually but we were too late. You'd already got rid of that.'

The BMW on our road… 'Did he come to the house?' I glare at Alistair and he laughs.

'Not me, one of my security employees. I was at the restaurant the same time as you, remember? Sorry to wreck your romantic evening but I was with a client and saw you arrive. I texted Isaac as you were walking to your table, asked him if he'd like me to enlighten his lovely wife about who she was really married to. Oddly, he didn't seem too keen.'

Edie laughs as I remember Isaac bumping into me, distracted by his phone as we were shown to our table.

'I'd had to threaten Tanya with Angel's safety but you managed to scupper my plans too, with your witness statement to the police. I could hardly teach her a lesson with them watching. But I was able to repay you by letting everyone know you're rotten to the core.'

'I've done nothing wrong, I have no police record,' I say calmly. 'Unlike you, who are responsible for suicides, ruining businesses and the misery of innocent families.'

Isaac is the one who took Mum's box of evidence so Edie hasn't got the full story, thank goodness.

'You've done your homework,' she says lightly but she's ruffled, I can see it. 'Who have you been talking to?'

'Someone much smarter than you,' I retort. 'You're a liar and a cheat and all this' – I sweep my arm around the room – 'is paid for with other people's misery!'

Her placid face contorts into a mask of fury.

'You have a murderer's blood running through your veins!' she screeches, lunging across the room towards me. Her fingers clamp the sides of my face, squashing my features. 'The Basement Murders… that was your aunt. God, you even look like the bitch!'

She's right, I do look like Patricia Knott, my mother's sister, who together with the father of her childhood friend, Samuel Bennett, murdered eight girls between the ages of fourteen and twenty-two. Mum told me on her deathbed.

But Edie hasn't got the full picture, because my mother also told me that the infamous murderer I'd been raised to call Aunt Pat, wasn't my aunt at all.

She was my biological mother. And Samuel Bennett… he was my father.

72

'Put your phone on the table,' Edie says.

'What?'

'Prove you're not recording this conversation and I'll gladly tell you the truth. Maybe you'll see what we can offer your family and get your stupid husband to toe the line again.'

There's a noise out in the garage and a voice I know so well says, 'You won't tell her anything. I'll tell her. All of it.'

'Isaac!'

He stands in the garage doorway, Alistair looming behind him.

'Thank God! Where have you been?' I rush to him, bury my face in his shoulder before standing back and looking at him. He's dishevelled and bleary-eyed.

'We'll talk later, Janey.' He sounds so weak. 'Let's get Rowan and go home. I've given them what they want.'

He's given her Mum's box?

'He signed the paperwork… with a bit of encouragement,' Alistair tells Edie in a gruff voice.

'Why don't you tell Janey everything *now*?' Edie laughs before addressing me again. 'You thought I was a stranger, someone you met when you moved here, right?'

I don't answer her. I've already worked out that Isaac must've known Edie when we first met her on the crescent that day. I look at him, but he stares straight ahead.

'I've known Isaac for nearly eight months now. How do you think you even got to move so quickly to Buckingham Crescent in the first place?'

Only yesterday I'd have replied that it was Isaac's new job opportunity that hastened our good fortune, but now I know that never existed.

'I won't keep you in suspense, Janey. You moved into your house in Buckingham Crescent because of *us*. Alistair told Isaac about the house – which Palace Securities owned, by the way – and I knew he could afford it because I'd paid him very well for a little job he'd done for me earlier in the year.'

'Isaac?' I whisper.

'I was stupid, Janey,' he says in a hoarse voice. 'I did one dodgy job for a big payout. It sounded straightforward. Acquiring some small business accounts online. Edie promised me it was just a one-off and offered to get me set up with my own business, make a fresh start with the new house and so on. But all she really wanted to do was entrap me.'

Edie smiles, takes another sip of her gin before speaking.

'Don't look so shocked. Did you not know your husband is a very talented man?' Her tone is patronising, and I have the urge to grab her glass and tip the contents over her glossy red locks. Instead I stay still and keep my mouth shut. If she stops talking, I'll be none the wiser, and I have been in the dark for far, far too long. 'When Isaac met me at the IT professionals' networking event at a hotel in Nottingham, he'd already wasted his considerable gifts for years, trying to earn a decent crust in the corporate world, working above board. He did one job for me and your life was suddenly elevated beyond your wildest expectations. If only he hadn't turned into a coward overnight. His prospects were so promising.'

I look at Isaac, but it's Edie who speaks.

'Let me tell you something about your husband you don't know. He's an excellent thief.'

'Isaac has never stolen anything,' I say before I can stop myself. 'He's the most honest person I know.'

'If that's what you really think, then you're in big trouble, missy.' She laughs. 'I'm not talking about a thief who dons a mask and breaks into houses for a few paltry bits of silver. He's an intelligent thief of the highest order, can steal virtual millions in minutes.'

I stare at Isaac. *Acquiring some small business accounts*, he'd just called it.

'I'm a hacker, Janey. At least I have been, just the once, for her.'

'That's right. He breaks through the most sophisticated security and steals corporate secrets, don't you, Isaac?' Edie crows. 'It's amazing how much those desperate men and women will pay to get their secrets back. It's a skill that bought you your house, Janey, a skill I could use again and again, if he'd come to his senses. Remember I told you once that you'd be buying a bigger house on the crescent in no time at all? That could still happen. It's not too late.'

'But why?' I ask her. 'Why do this? You've got everything you could need here, so much money and power. Why keep going?'

Edie looks at me with disdain. 'There speaks someone with little drive. Do you think this lifestyle funds itself? The more you have, the more it takes to keep it. I would've stopped eventually, but for now, my aim is to get some serious money in the bank, and no one, least of all *him*' – she turns a furious look on Isaac – 'will stop me. I had the perfect formula in choosing my IT experts: people who were in debt, who needed the cash. Most people want to carry on earning those sorts of amounts; it's just your husband who had to buck the trend.'

'It wasn't just Isaac, though, was it?' I keep my voice level and stare her out. 'There have been others. Rupert Harris, for instance. Tanya and Tristan and Angel… a lovely young girl you've pulled into your utterly rotten world.'

Edie literally takes a step back, the colour draining from her face. 'How did you…'

'I told her, Edie.' Kyoko appears in the doorway. 'You're getting sloppy. Left the gates open.'

Edie doesn't answer. Just looks from Ky to Isaac and I can almost feel her mind whirring, trying to make sense of the connection.

'Alistair told me I had a choice,' Isaac says. 'To carry on with our business agreement and lead a great life with my family, or have it all taken away from me.'

'We thought that was fair.' Edie's eyes gleam in the starkness of the daylight, giving her a manic quality.

'Whatever he's done, it's not in your power to take us away from him.' I glare at her. 'You don't own him, Edie, or us.'

She gives me a sickly smile. 'That's a matter of opinion. I can get him a lengthy prison sentence and you too.' She clicks her fingers in the air.

I actually laugh. 'I think you'll find the authorities won't put me away for the crimes of an aunt who died when I was fourteen years old.'

'But you *were* part of the fraud and the hacking. You're as guilty as he is,' she says calmly. 'Cast your mind back… Do you remember signing papers for the house, and before that, contracts for credit cards and a lower-rate mortgage to help with your debt?' She falls silent and waits.

'Ignore her, Janey,' Isaac stammers. 'You and I will talk about this later.'

'No, wait,' I say faintly, thinking back.

Before we moved, there always seemed to be paperwork Isaac needed me to sign – the sorts of things Edie's mentioned – and always, it seemed, at the busiest times. When he was about to leave for work and I was half asleep; in the middle of packing Rowan's rucksack for a school trip. Once, when I was rushing out of the door, late for a dental appointment, there was an important document that *had* to be signed in order to cut a reasonable chunk from our mortgage payment.

'I see you *do* remember,' Edie says slowly. 'You remember very well. And I, at least, believe you didn't know what your husband was up to, but the authorities? Well, you may find they take a dim view of all those false companies you set up as sole director to channel his ill-gotten gains.'

She's lost me now and she knows it. She opens a laptop on the table and sets about tapping the keyboard. After a few moments, she swings it around to show me a list of company names, Carrington, TechMidlands IT and Abacus among them.

She then clicks into each one and shows me my own name as director.

'He appointed you so as not to raise suspicion when he channelled funds. The new company seemed to have no connection to him at all at first glance. They're all set up in your maiden name.' She closes the laptop. 'Lucky he had such a dumb wife who'd sign anything he put in front of her nose.'

She's right and I feel sick. How could Isaac do this to me? To *us*?

Momentarily, I can't speak. But I won't give her the satisfaction of turning on my husband while she enjoys the show.

'Isaac, I want to leave. Can you find Rowan?' I manage to utter after a few seconds.

He nods, slinking away like a dog who knows it's done wrong. I hear him calling Rowan's name up the stairs.

There's something I want to know from Edie, so I start by lulling her into a false sense of security.

'We're going to move away from here, whether you like it or not,' I say. 'But first, tell me something. Why involve Angel in dangerous activities? She's still a child, just fifteen years old. Why do that to Tanya, who's been a loyal friend?'

'Tanya is wrapped so tightly in my web, she'll never escape,' Edie says proudly. 'And as for spoilt princess Angel, I had to find better ways to keep my people under control.'

I can't help shaking my head at her choice of words. She talks about people like commodities, like mere *things* she controls.

'Alistair was in charge of the honey traps with a few of his henchmen to enforce certain measures. Angel was the perfect lure: young but could look much older, beautiful… and willing to do the odd job for me for a nice fat cash payment.'

The horror of it hits me. Angel with those men.

'It's not as bad as you think,' she says, laughing at my expression. 'It's surprising how easily you can frame a photo to look more than it is. A beautiful girl bending close to a man, an attractive young man with his arm around a middle-aged businesswoman.'

'What about the assault… Angel was involved in that.'

'Ahh, that was a little tussle that went wrong. But Angel wasn't in the car when that happened, Alistair had already dropped her off. Fortunately one of his henchmen is happy to take the rap – manslaughter – for the death of the young man. For a price, of course.'

'We tried a honey trap for Isaac too,' says Edie, as if she's read my mind. 'But seems he's loyal to you after all.'

Bizarrely, relief and guilt equally flood my body as I realise that although Isaac may have committed fraud and lied to me about serious matters, he was telling the truth about one thing at least; he loves me. I cling to that.

Edie falls quiet, tips her head to one side and listens.

Then I hear it. The wonderful sound of children laughing… my son's laughter amongst it. Feet hammer downstairs and my face lights up with relief as Rowan and Aisha enter the room followed by Isaac and Alistair.

'Did you honestly think I'd hurt Rowan?' Edie says, almost offended. 'Unlike your family, I'd never hurt children. I'm doing all this for Aisha, so she can have the life I didn't have as a child. Losing my mum only crystallised my ambitions.'

'I wouldn't put anything past you,' I hiss. 'You're the lowest of the low. All these years, controlling people. Even Angel and Tanya. You say you don't hurt children… what about Ky's twins? They've lost their father because of you.'

There's an almighty banging at the door.

'Police! Open up!' a male voice yells gruffly.

'What? How have they… how do they know…' Edie grabs Aisha and dashes past me towards the rear patio doors.

'Ow, Mummy, you're hurting my arm!' Aisha squeals.

Isaac moves fast, lurching forward and grabbing Edie. Holding Rowan tightly, I indicate for Aisha to come to me, and she does so, shaking and crying.

There's an almighty crash in the hall as the police enter the house. Alistair bolts for the garage door and both children shout out in alarm. 'It's OK,' I try to reassure them, with little success. 'It's going to be all right.'

'Mummy!' Aisha cries as police officers grab a struggling, yelling Alistair and two more officers rush over and pull Edie from Isaac's grasp.

'Edie McCaid, I'm arresting you on charges of perverting the course of justice, contributing to the delinquency of a minor…'

The officer's voice is drowned out by the sound of rushing in my ears.

'It's all lies,' Edie screeches. 'These two are liars!' She glares at me and Isaac, her eyes wild. 'I had nothing to do with it, you've got no proof of—'

'I'm a witness.' The calm, measured voice of Kyoko cuts through the confusion.

'What are you talking about?' Edie says, incredulous.

Ky turns to the police officers. 'I have evidence from my late husband, details of their business dealings, passwords, strategic plans… everything. I think you'll find whatever you need to convict them in there.'

Edie is pale and still. Kyoko's input seems to have shaken her above anything else.

'My parting gift to you, Edie,' Kyoko tells her sweetly. 'I hope you rot in hell for what you did to my family.' She closes her eyes. 'Rest in peace, Rupert my love, I miss you.'

The police lead an unresisting Edie out to the car with Alistair already detained and handcuffed in another police vehicle.

Isaac puts his arms around me and Rowan, holds us both close.

'What's happened, Dad?' Rowan's eyes are wide. 'Where are the police taking Aisha's mum?'

'We'll talk about it when we get home, son,' Isaac says, ruffling Rowan's springy hair. He looks at me. 'It's a lot for him to take in.'

I wave to Ky as she stands talking to a police officer, her arm around Edie's daughter. She knows Aisha well and has offered to care for her but the police have insisted social services must decide what needs to happen.

We've agreed we'll make ourselves available for police interviews tomorrow. Isaac has resolved to tell the truth about his business dealings with Edie and his part in the company scam that she and Alistair made vast amounts of money from.

'I'm ready to face what I've done,' he says sadly. 'There's no other way.'

We turn out of the gates and bump into Polly.

'I sent them,' she says proudly. 'The police. I knew it wasn't right, you see. I've lived on the crescent a long time and I've long suspected they're a load of crooks. "All fur coat and no knickers", my old mum used to say about that sort.'

'Thank you, Polly, for ringing the police.' Isaac says. 'I dread to think what might have happened if you hadn't.'

'I've seen how they treat people, how folks have come to live in that house before and been ruined, or left, never to be seen again. I knew something wasn't right and I tried to tell you in my own way, Janey.'

'I'm sorry I didn't listen, Polly,' I say, shamed.

'I could see you were going the same way. Saw that little ragamuffin Angel letting strange men in the house when you went out… it was never going to end well.'

We walk back down the road with Polly and thank her again for her help before she goes back home.

Then the three of us sit together and eat hastily made sandwiches. We talk to Rowan in general terms about what has happened, reassuring him that he and his friends are safe.

When he goes to bed, Isaac and I finally talk.

'Janey, I'm so, so sorry for all the lies. I was foolish and naïve to get involved with Edie and Alistair,' he confesses. 'I didn't know how she planned to use the information I stole from the websites, but that's no excuse. I shouldn't have done it and I'll have to take the rap.'

I push thoughts of a lengthy prison sentence from my mind.

'Tell me everything,' I say. 'From the beginning.'

He starts to explain, in layman's terms, about a process called spear phishing.

'We've all received an email or an instant message that includes an attachment or a link to a website, right?'

I nod. 'I got one yesterday purporting to be from HMRC yesterday with details of a refund. I deleted it without opening the attachment.'

'That's exactly what I'm talking about. See, I would send one to the business owner and when they opened it a vulnerability in the system browser would be exploited.'

I put a hand up to digest what he just said. 'So when they opened the attachment it would basically infect their computer?'

'You've got it.'

I frown. 'But if I've got the sense not to open a suspicious email, surely a business owner who knows the security risks regarding company information wouldn't just open it without a thought?'

'Correct. Which is why the email has to be believable. With a bit of research, I'd send it from a potential customer, mentioning one of the company's specific product lines in the subject of the email. If there's something personal in there, people will often blindly trust the sender.'

I look at him then. This kind, supportive man who I've been married to for over ten years.

'Please don't look at me like that, Janey.' He grimaces and rubs his chin. 'I'm aware I sound like an absolute lowlife and I admit I've done a very bad thing. I've tried so hard to put that behind me but they just wouldn't let me go.'

He goes on to tell me how Edie appeared to be very supportive of his decision not to continue working for them, said she'd help him set up his own business when he made it clear he no longer wanted to be involved in fraudulent activities.

'I honestly thought I could make a go of it. So I set up Abacus, a company that would help entrepreneurs to get a strong start in the early days when most new start-ups fail.'

'You missed a bit out, Isaac. You told lie after lie to me… the headhunting, signing-on bonus, double salary. You really put some thought into it, thought it all through to the last tiny detail and I swallowed it all, like the idiot I am.'

'You're no idiot, Janey. That's why I had to make it sound like the real deal. I always intended to tell you the truth but not until I'd sorted out our life. I couldn't stand the thought of you and Rowan suffering. But Edie blacklisted me amongst the business community so nobody wanted to work with me. All the hours I was out of the house, I was trying to make new contacts and meet with existing clients. I was desperately trying to repair the damage Alistair was doing to my reputation.'

Then a thought occurs to me. 'You told me Alistair, aka Bob, put you on to this house… why on earth would you want to live on the same street as them if you were hoping to make a fresh start?'

'I didn't realise they lived here!' His jaw flexes as he bites down on his back teeth. 'I took Alistair at his word when he told me about the house, I thought he'd just spotted a real bargain. Remember when the estate agent said they were dealing with a management company?'

I nod, frowning.

'Well, that management company was Alistair and Edie. They owned this house. They'd rented it out up to us moving in. Getting us to buy this house was just another way they could try and control me because they knew I'd be in close proximity and would have access to my family.'

Now Isaac's rudeness to Edie, on the day he first 'met' her, made perfect sense.

He hangs his head. 'At first Alistair was so supportive, claimed he wanted to help but then he just brought me information on potential jobs, trying to get me to do "one more for the road", as he put it.

'When Angel came to babysit that night, I couldn't believe my eyes. She'd come on to me in a hotel restaurant a few weeks ago. That's why I stared at her; I was trying to place her because she looked like a woman in her early twenties that night, all dressed up with heavy make-up. Likewise, she was shocked when she recognised me. I tried to warn you away from Tanya but you were having none of it. So when we went out for our date night meal, I was on tenterhooks from the off and then I saw Alistair there. As it happened, he was with a client but I didn't know that, I thought he'd come to tell you everything. That's what he'd threatened he'd do if I didn't play ball.'

'And yet you willingly let Angel look after Rowan?'

Isaac threw his hands up. 'If I'd told you, it would've blown open everything that had been happening at work… that you knew nothing about.'

I feel revulsion that he put our son in danger rather than come clean.

'I'd told her you had a secret in your past one night when we got drunk at a business dinner. I took your mum's box and put it into a storage facility after you told me you'd confessed your secret to Tanya. I knew Edie would use any information she found in it ruthlessly. Even though I've no idea what's in the box, I had to protect you from that.'

'You knew how worried I was about the missing box and yet you didn't tell me you had it!'

'Again, I couldn't, Janey! I would've had to reveal everything if I told you why I'd taken the box.' He blows out with frustration. 'I'd tried to warn you off making friends or discussing my job with the neighbours when I realised the extent of Edie's influence around here. Then her threats suddenly escalated. She told me she was going to leak your secret at school. I tried to pick Rowan up to protect him from the fallout, and I came to the house for you too, to tell you everything. But you weren't there.'

'You seem to have forgotten I was working at school for most of the afternoon until I had a meltdown at Jasper in class, that is. I stormed out and when I eventually went back in again, parents started coming up to me in the playground, being abusive. That's when Edie offered to take Rowan to her house.'

'Always one to capitalise on a situation,' Isaac said grimly. His face softens then and he reaches for my hand. 'It was a moment of folly, getting involved with Palace Securities, Janey. I was a fool, thought I could pick up the chance they offered me to change our lives and then put it back down again. But they trapped me.' His eyes glisten as he squeezes my fingers and looks into my eyes earnestly. 'More than anything, I love you and I love Rowan. I'm so sorry for what I've done… can you ever forgive me?'

'I don't know,' I say, pulling my hand away gently as his face falls. 'I'm sorry, Isaac, but I just don't know.'

The Post, 22 December 2002
FINAL VICTIM OF BASEMENT KILLERS FOUND ALIVE
Knott and Bennett foiled by tip-off

The family of eighteen-year-old Susan Marsh were celebrating a Christmas miracle last night after their daughter was discovered just hours from death in a concealed basement prison in rural Nottinghamshire.

Police conducted a massive search, the biggest in UK history, to sweep the area after an anonymous tip-off.

'We never gave up hope,' DCI Keith Bainbridge told *The Post*. 'But we knew the chances of finding Susan alive were fading with every hour that passed. Thanks to brave, determined locals who refused to take no for an answer, we were able to locate and save her.'

Patricia Knott, 28, and Samuel Bennett, 48, were being hunted by police in connection with Susan's disappearance and with eight other murders. But the killers went on the run despite police putting out a plea for them to contact them to give details of where Susan was being held. They did not do this, in the full knowledge that they were condemning her to certain death.

Later, the pair were involved in a head-on collision with both dying instantly at the scene.

Susan went missing on her way to a friend's 18th birthday party.

'It's the best Christmas present in the world,' Carol Marsh, Susan's mother, told *The Post*. 'We thank the community, God and most of all the brave person who called the police anonymously to give details of our daughter's whereabouts.'

73

One month later

When Mum told me the awful truth about my real parents the day before she died, I tried to hate Aunt Pat. But I simply couldn't connect the aunt I knew and loved with the woman who did those terrible, terrible things. My aunt was the only light in a dreary, boring existence growing up. I believed she loved me. I still believe she loved me, in her own way.

So for a time, I tried to hate the girls… was it something they did? Could they have in some way hurt my aunt? I couldn't hate Samuel Bennett, my aunt's boyfriend, because I didn't know him, had never spoken to him. Even now, I cannot comprehend he is my biological father. I'm not interested in the fact I have other family out there somewhere, linked to him. I can't even think about it.

But what I could do, what came easier, was to resent my mother. She was easy to hate. It made sense to detest her because she kept the horror from me.

That was how I felt at first.

The fact that Kyoko and I have ended up as good friends is probably the strangest thing to come out of all of this.

Edie and Alistair, Tanya and Tristan… and lots of other minor players in the area, they're all the subject of a police investigation. All are on bail currently but Rowan and I have moved back to

Mansfield and rented a small house, in a tiny village, away from it all. He's delighted to be going back to his old school after admitting Dexter had begun controlling his every move. Kyoko has also moved to a rented house in a street near us and we are all supporting each other. Polly has gone to stay with her family down south – turns out she does have family who care about her after all, despite the lies Tanya and Edie told about her. Polly even had CCTV footage of Tanya ripping up her plants, all to try and drive her out because she was taking too much interest in their lives. Trying to warn off new people like myself. We're in touch via email.

With the help of Ben Sykes and Mrs Harlow, the Headteacher of Lady Bridge, Rowan and I met up with Jasper and his mum. I'd talked to Rowan prior to this about the bullying incident and he'd immediately become upset.

'I don't know why I did it, Mum. I don't hate Jasper,' he sobbed. 'I just… I felt like you liked him better than me. Dexter said if we upset him enough, he might leave Lady Bridge.'

I'd never stopped to think about how Rowan felt in the face of such big changes, I'd just assumed he was happy with his life. But it seems he'd become more than a little insecure.

Rowan apologised to Jasper and then I apologised to both Charlie and Jasper for my own behaviour. The meeting was a little stilted, as I'd expected, but I think they both understood we regretted our actions. By the end of the meeting, whilst Mrs Harlow, me and Charlie were still chatting, Rowan was admiring Jasper's Hedwig he'd made from Lego.

It was the best news to hear that Samina would be taking over as Jasper's classroom support worker.

Mrs Harlow mentioned that she was working with a number of agencies and the children of all the people affected by the Palace Securities scandal. DCI Warner had already told us that Tanya and Edie's extended families were rallying to look after Angel,

Dexter and Aisha. I really do hope everything works out the best for all the kids.

But for the adults, police are confident that with Kyoko's rock solid evidence from Rupert, they'll secure hefty convictions all round.

Isaac's own fate is still up in the air but he's helping police with their enquiries and we hope he may get a lighter punishment because of this. He's in his own bedsit but sees Rowan regularly and we are talking. And that's all I can say about it for now.

Kyoko sits with me as I open the wooden box. We look at each newspaper clipping in turn and I ask her to read out the descriptions of the missing girls.

'"When she was last seen, Nancy was dressed in jeans and a denim jacket with white trainers and a pink top. She wore dangly earrings and a gold and ruby necklace",' she says, her voice respectfully quiet.

I close my eyes and consider her words as she rustles through the cuttings.

'Here's another,' she says gently. '"Susan left home to attend a party wearing beige slacks and a cream silk blouse with high-heeled beige court shoes. She also wore a distinctive white-gold and diamond bracelet on her left wrist."'

I unroll the faux-suede jewellery case I found in the bottom of the box, smoothing out the soft folds and patting the storage pockets within it. First I gently lift out a gold and ruby necklace, the precious gems sparking like fire in the lamplight. Ky gasps as I then slide out a white-gold and diamond-studded bangle, its dull sheen glistening with renewed life like an elderly person waking from a long, long sleep.

Together, we look at the pieces sadly.

'Aunt Pat – my mother – gave me these as gifts,' I whisper. 'I thought they were gifts of love, but they were the vilest trophies you could ever imagine giving to a young girl. There would have been so many more of them if my mum – my real mum, who raised, protected and loved me – hadn't intervened.'

'Oh, Janey.' Ky's face is ashen. 'I don't know what to say. Those poor girls.'

I set the jewellery aside. 'It's time for these pieces to go home.'

Two months later

The detective leads Kyoko and I through to a quiet room with soft chairs. A diminutive figure sits alone, stooped slightly forward staring at the floor. When the door opens, she visibly jumps and looks up at us. For a moment, her soft brown eyes are filled with fear and then with a flash of something else.

'Susan, this is Janey Markham and her friend Kyoko,' DS Pike says quietly.

'You look like her,' she whispers and knots her shaking fingers together.

I freeze and stare at this frail woman who I know to be thirty-six years old but who looks twenty years older. The awful connection between us buzzes like a living thing.

I don't know where to look or what to say.

I feel Ky's hand on mine as she moves forward, towards Susan. I take a stumbling step to follow her and stop again as Susan stands up. She has a discreet stick to aid her and she tucks it slightly behind her leg and holds out a small, shaking hand.

'I'm not her, Susan,' I say gently. 'She was a family member but I'm nothing like her. I was brought up by a loving, good mother. I'm sickened by what happened to you and to the other girls.'

I think about my birth certificate, how my mother is Irene and not Patricia on there. In terms of my personal paperwork, Aunt Pat remains Aunt Pat. Samuel Bennett has no connection to me on paper.

'Hello, Janey,' she says in a soft voice. 'I'm Susan.'

Her hand is cool, her fingers small and bony as they press into my palm. I can't breathe; my throat is swelling as if something is—

'She's going to fall,' I hear Ky call out, and the detective grasps my shoulders from behind and steadies me. 'Breathe, Janey. Breathe,' Kyoko says soothingly.

I drag in some air and give a little nod. 'I'm OK.' I reach for Susan's hand again.

'Let's sit down,' Susan says, and I sink with relief into the seat next to her.

'What happened to you… I'm so, so sorry. I can't imagine what you went through back then. I—'

Susan covers my hand with hers. 'It wasn't your fault. We're both here now and that's what matters.'

'But… but you suffered then, and now…' I indicate the stick. 'You're still suffering.'

She nods. 'I was diagnosed with multiple sclerosis eight years ago. My health isn't the best now, but I have a wonderful partner, Ricky, and every day still feels like a bonus to me.'

'I want you to know I was only fourteen, when they… when they took you. Me and Mum, we thought she was away working, you see. We thought—'

'Janey, I would never blame you.' Susan's hands feel warm now as she presses them firmly on mine. 'You were just a child and your mum… she sounds like she was a good woman. You two did nothing wrong.'

My wet cheeks burn as if my tears are on fire as they spill down my face, bathing our joined hands in sadness and regret. Our bowed heads touch, and then we're holding each other, both crying, the terrible events of the past are like a spear that pins the two of us together.

This is what my mum was trying to save from, all those years. She must have tortured herself every day about doing the right thing by me. If she didn't tell me then there was a possibility someone else would do it in years to come. Someone with an axe to grind or someone who wanted to hurt me with the information. Would I have blamed her for keeping it from me? Probably.

Now I understand my mother hadn't lied because she didn't think enough of me; she'd kept me from the horror because she loved me with all her heart. She kept it all inside, rotting and paining her, every minute of every day. The twisted logic she lived by, that I believed was her reaction to me not being good enough, was a symptom of the effort it took to keep what was happening from contaminating my innocence. She tried to keep me away from people because she herself simply could never trust others again.

She told me, on her deathbed, she hadn't an inkling what Aunt Pat was up to during her long absences from home.

'I didn't know what she'd done until the day the police came to the door, Janey, and it nearly killed me.'

'But you'd always disapproved of her even before that, Mum. Why was that?'

'Her lifestyle. I suspected she was messing about with Bennett, a married man, even before she fell pregnant with you. She was just a child! I threatened to report him to the police and tell his wife but she denied everything and said that if I did, she'd denounce me as a liar. Your father told me I must be imagining it and to back off. She loved partying and living for today. It just didn't sit well with me. When she told me she was pregnant, I was afraid what would happen to you, and me and your father had tried for years to have a child so… we made an agreement that suited everyone that you would be ours on paper as in life.' Mum was weak and there were long pauses between her words. 'Pat hid the pregnancy well, stayed away from home for most of it. In the meantime, I faked pregnancy and somehow, it all worked out. Folks didn't ask as many questions in those days.'

When the truth about their murder spree came out, Mum found cuttings from newspapers that Aunt Pat had kept. 'I couldn't just throw them away, it would have felt like I was trying to erase the memory of all those poor girls.' She'd confiscated the inappropriate jewellery I'd been given and kept it in her box for when I was older, not realising where it came from.

We all want a good life for our children: my mum, me, Tanya and, I believe, even Edie in her own twisted way. But how far should we go in our quest? What should we put up with, or hide, to stop our kids from hurting or facing the truth?

I don't know the answer to these questions yet. But I have an eight-year-old son whose grandparents are arguably amongst the most prolific serial killers in the UK in the last fifty years. Soon, I will understand my mother's dilemma more.

'My biggest regret is losing both my parents within two years of me being found,' Susan says. 'They had me in later life and the toll my abduction took on them was just… They thought I was dead, you see. They were victims of what happened too, but their deaths are not counted in history's reckoning.'

'Janey?' Kyoko holds the jewellery case out and I wipe my eyes and take it.

'This is a long time coming home, but I think it belongs to you, Susan. DS Pike is ensuring the other piece I have goes to Nancy's family.' I unroll the soft case and cradle the silver bracelet in the palm of my hand.

'It was my eighteenth birthday gift from my parents,' she gasps, holding her hand up to her mouth. 'I'd only had it a week when…'

She slips the bangle on and holds it there, her eyes closed.

'I feel like a piece of Mum and Dad are here with me again,' she whispers. 'Like I've recaptured a lost piece of them.'

She rotates her thin wrist in the rays of weak sunlight coming through the window.

We all watch in silence as the precious metal lights up before our eyes. It's sparkling now, full of life and finally out of the gloom.

A LETTER FROM
K.L. SLATER

I do hope you have enjoyed reading *Little Whispers*, my eleventh psychological thriller. If you did enjoy it, and want to keep up to date with all my latest releases, just sign up at the following link. Your email address will never be shared and you can unsubscribe at any time.

www.bookouture.com/kl-slater

I've always been quite interested in identity and the way we see ourselves. But what if we saw ourselves as one thing for most of our life and then that image was shattered when someone suddenly revealed something about our past we were totally unaware of? Are we still the same person? Or does that knowledge turn us into someone else?

When I started writing *Little Whispers*, I found myself pairing this idea with another key thought: can we ever be responsible for someone else's mistakes? This is the core of what I set out to explore in the book.

As a writer, we get to place our characters in some pretty uncomfortable situations and watch how they work themselves out of them. Janey, my protagonist, feels ashamed about her past, even though she could do nothing about what happened. It led me to ask the question, how does our past impact on our today? What insecurities and hang-ups does it place on our shoulders… and can we ever leave the past behind and start afresh with a new confidence?

When Janey's mother reveals a life-changing secret, Janey starts to ask questions of herself and her mother. Is Janey a good person? Did her mother have a right to keep such an enormous secret to herself for so many years? The new knowledge Janey has soon becomes a burden that begins to affect what she thinks about herself and also how she sees her late mother.

If you would like more information about or help with any of the issues covered in the book, there are many excellent resources that can be accessed by searching online.

Little Whispers is set in Nottinghamshire, the place I was born and have lived all my life. Local readers should be aware I sometimes take the liberty of changing street names or geographical details to suit the story.

Reviews are so massively important to authors. If you've enjoyed *Little Whispers* and could spare just a few minutes to write a short review to say so, I would so appreciate that.

Until Book 12, then…

Warmest wishes,
Kim x

KimLSlaterAuthor

@KimLSlater

KLSlaterAuthor

www.KLSlaterAuthor.com

ACKNOWLEDGEMENTS

Enormous thanks to my editor, Lydia Vassar-Smith, who is a massive support every step of the way for each new book; *Little Whispers* is no different.

Thanks to my agent, Camilla Bolton, for her constant support and advice in every aspect of my writing career.

Thanks also to the rest of the hard-working team at Darley Anderson Literary, TV and Film Agency, especially Roya Sarrafi-Gohar and Rosanna Bellingham.

Thanks to *all* the Bookouture team for everything they do, especially to Alexandra Holmes and Kim Nash. Thanks to copy editor Jane Selley and to proofreader Becca Allen.

Thanks as always to my good friend, Angela Marsons. We've shared many ups and downs over the years and she is my go-to for advice, support and (mostly) a good old chuckle!

Massive thanks must go to my husband, Mac, for his love and support, and to my daughter, Francesca, my mum and my family.

Special thanks must also go to Henry Steadman, who has yet again designed a thrilling and striking cover.

Thank you to the bloggers and reviewers who do so much to help make my books a success. Thank you to everyone who has taken the time to post a positive review online or has taken part in my blog tour. It is always noticed and very much appreciated.

Last but not least, thank you *so* much to my wonderful readers. I love receiving all the wonderful comments and messages and I am truly grateful for each and every reader's support.

Printed in Poland
by Amazon Fulfillment
Poland Sp. z o.o., Wrocław

60403013R00204